AN IRRESISTIBLE TEMPTATION

"Kiss me again," she purred. She lifted her chin to look up at him, and he peered down at her through his lashes. Her eyes were full of wonder, mischief, and something else, something that stunned him and made him want to throw caution aside, to hold her and kiss her again, long and hard.

Adoration. She looked at him with adoration.

No one had ever looked at him like that before. His sisters looked at him with fondness. A few of the young women of his village looked at him with hunger. But what he saw in this white woman's eyes was beyond tenderness, beyond lust, and completely without fear. She adored him.

"Kiss me again," she breathed.

He shook his head.

"Please?"

"No good can come of it," he choked out.

"I don't care."

NATIVE WOLF

Copyright © 2015 by Glynnis Campbell

Cover design by Tanya Straley & Richard Campbell
Formatting by Author E.M.S.

Glynnis Campbell – Publisher
P.O. Box 341144
Arleta, California 91331

ISBN-13: 978-1-634800-89-1
Contact: glynnis@glynnis.net

Published in the United States of America

NATIVE WOLF

CALIFORNIA LEGENDS BOOK 2

GLYNNIS CAMPBELL

DEDICATION

In homage to the real Yoema*—
the last surviving member of her family
after California's Trail of Tears—
with honor and respect

And for those who remember
and seek to mend the broken past

* This story is purely a work of fiction and not based in any way upon Yoema's life. For a real account of her life, read "Yoyema (Little Flower)," written by her great-granddaughter, Rose Waugh.

OTHER BOOKS BY GLYNNIS CAMPBELL

Acknowledgments

Thanks to
Claire Danes and David Boreanaz,
Betty and Earl Talken for the field trips,
William Clark and Dale Josephson for their family history,
Mike Gilman for his blacksmith expertise,
The helpful docents at the Colman Centerville Museum,
My friends at The Gold Nugget Museum—
Denver Williams, Janeece Webb, Becky Dresser,
Hoopa Tribal Education Association—
Leandra Billings and Marcellene Norton
for their gift of The Hupa Language Dictionary,
The Hupa Nation,
The Round Valley Indian Tribes,
Roger Ekins for hiking "The Flumes and Trails of Paradise,"
and the too-numerous-to-mention Paradisians
who share my love of history and are always
so generous with their time and information!

CHAPTER 1

PARADISE, CALIFORNIA, 1875

Claire crammed her collection of dime novels into the carpetbag, on top of her spare set of clothes. But her most beloved book—a dog-eared copy of *THE TRAIL HUNTERS OR MONOWANO THE SHAWNEE SPY*—she tucked inside the top of her cotton camisole.

Then she caught her lip under her teeth. Was she doing the right thing—running away? She gazed out her second-story window at the midnight sky above the Parker Ranch, the only home she'd ever known. Her eyes moistened, and the stars blurred.

But it was too late for regrets. There was just one more thing to do before she finished dressing and headed out into the night, toward an uncertain future.

She glanced at the letter on the bed. It was brief. But there was really nothing more to say.

Dear Father,
By the time you read this, I will be gone. I am sorry to have been such a disappointment to you. I hope my leaving will not

bring undue shame to the Parker name. Please give my apologies to Frank. I am certain he will find a more suitable bride. I have had to take the dappled mare, but will send compensation for her when I find employment.

    Kindest regards,

    Claire

Beside the letter were the things she planned to wear on the journey—her plain brown dress and matching bonnet, calfskin gloves, wool stockings, and sturdy low-heeled boots. Next to them was a pair of scissors. These she picked up, stroking the cold blades with trembling fingers.

Her father might disapprove of her tears over the death of Yoema, the native woman who'd raised her, but he couldn't stop Claire from showing her grief in the way of Yoema's people.

Claire held her breath as the scissors sliced through the first lock of her waist-length hair with surprising ease. She let the pale tress fall from her fingers onto the bed, where it glistened in the candlelight. Then, with tears filling her eyes, she cut another...and another. The scissors snicked with cruel efficiency in the silent night as strand after strand slid down over her camisole and dropped onto the quilt, severed from her as quickly and irreversibly as Yoema had been.

She'd lost *two* mothers now.

Her real mother she only vaguely remembered. Claire had been a little girl when she died.

It was Yoema who'd brought her up. Though Claire's father had refused to let Claire address the native woman as Mother, Yoema had been the one who bathed and dressed her, told her stories, sang her songs, and comforted her when she was hurt. Yoema even sneaked copies of Claire's cherished dime novels to her, though the woman clearly disapproved of them. Yoema had given Claire the affection that her father was incapable of expressing, affection that had died years before, along with Claire's real mother.

Even at the tender age of six, Claire had tried to fill her mother's shoes and become the woman of the house. But her father had made it clear in his tight-lipped grief that nobody would ever be as pretty, as talented, or as good as his dearly departed wife.

It wasn't her father's fault. Claire was old enough to know that now. He'd simply adored his wife. No one could live up to her memory...not even his own daughter.

A tear escaped down Claire's cheek. Out of habit, she brusquely wiped it away. She'd learned very young that weeping was something her father couldn't abide.

Fortunately, Yoema had always given her a shoulder to cry on.

But now, Claire had no one.

A fresh surge of tears threatened to spill over. She squeezed her eyes shut against it, continuing to snip blindly at her hair, leaving it in jagged jaw-length spikes.

When the last lock fell, she opened her eyes, dropped the scissors, and gazed at the remnants of hair strewn across the bed. They were a painful reminder of the finality of death. But they also symbolized acceptance. Now there could be no wishing for Yoema's return, any more than she could reattach the hair to her head. What was done was done. *Akina,* as Yoema said. That was all.

Chase Wolf slugged back the shot of whiskey. He grimaced as the rotgut burned the back of his throat. It was potent, but not strong enough to ease the guilt gnawing at his insides. He slammed the glass down on the low table in front of him, startling the woman who was pouring drinks.

"Easy, Chase." His brother Drew laid a hand on his arm.

Chase shook off Drew's hand. He was in no mood to take it easy. But he supposed they didn't want to draw attention to themselves either. That was why they'd come to the Parlor, a discreet bordello, rather than one of the regular saloons.

Drew looked right at home in the overstuffed red velvet chair, but Chase felt as out of place as a trout in a tree. More velvet draped the walls, vases of fresh flowers decorated the room, and a chandelier dripped crystals from the middle of the ceiling. A balcony opened onto the sitting room where Chase imagined scantily-clad ladies paraded at a safe distance before prospective clients.

Fortunately, at this late hour, there were only the two of them and the madam, who had probably seen everything under the sun. So when a pair of half-breed twins strolled into her establishment after midnight, she didn't even bat an eye.

Sitting beside Drew in another plush chair, Chase glanced at their reflection in the enormous mahogany-framed mirror filling one wall. He supposed they looked even more similar now, since he'd chopped off his long hair in mourning and put on a shirt.

He raked his hand through the short black waves and scowled. His ebony eyes narrowed back at him. He didn't see the resemblance. To his way of thinking, he looked nothing like his twin.

His brother Drew Hawk took after Trickster Coyote. No matter how much trouble the rascal stirred up, Drew managed to steal away with a grin, unscathed. He was a quick draw and lucky at cards, what the whites called a man's man. But he could charm the ladies with words that would put a blush on a peach. Already Drew had the madam pouring him drinks from her dusty-shouldered reserve bottle stashed in the back.

Drew loved the limelight.

Chase preferred the shadows.

Drew embraced the white world of their mother, Mattie.

But Chase clung to the old ways, the native ways of Sakote, their Konkow father, and the Hupa village where they'd been raised, ways threatened more each day with the intrusion of the whites.

His brother followed the whim of the wind, but Chase walked the path of the Great Spirit. That path had brought him two hundred miles from the reservation to this parlor house in Paradise, California—once the land of his ancestors, the Konkow people.

Drew nodded toward Chase's empty glass. "You want another one?"

The madam stared at Chase in expectation—her bottle of whiskey uncorked and a knowing smile pasted on her brightly painted face. He declined with a shake of his head. He'd already had way too much to drink. She pouted, shrugging at Drew and re-corking the bottle.

Drew took a slow sip from his own glass, then swirled the golden brown liquid lazily around. "You want my advice?" he said. "Let it go."

"Nope," Chase said.

That was the one thing he couldn't do. He'd had a vision from the Great Spirit. And a man didn't take such things lightly. In that vision, Chase had seen his Konkow grandmother—not dead, as everyone had long believed, but alive and dwelling here in the white man's town. Chase had been given a sacred message. The Great Spirit had told him that it was time for him to find her, to close the circle and heal the past.

So Chase had planned to make the long journey to the place of his birth. But that trip had been delayed. He'd missed seeing his grandmother alive by a matter of a few weeks. He'd failed the Great Spirit. Now he had to do everything he could to make amends.

"Listen, Chase." Drew set down his drink and clapped him on the shoulder. "She's gone now. There's nothin' you can do to change that."

Remorse weighed heavily on Chase's spirit. He scowled at his empty glass, working the muscles of his jaw. All those years, their grandmother must have believed she'd been forgotten by her people. He shrugged off Drew's hand. "I should have come sooner."

"You couldn't. You know that. If you hadn't put off the trip to mend Joe's wagon, he would have been out of work this winter."

He knew Drew was right. But the week of blacksmithing to repair Joe's broken axle and shattered wheels had cost him everything. "I should have come."

"Ah, hell, Chase. It's not like we knew her. We were still in cradleboards when we left. Grandmother Yoema was..."

Chase stiffened, his nostrils flaring. His sharp glare silenced his brother. It was unwise to speak the name of one who'd gone from this world. He glanced into the corners of the parlor reflected in the mirror, half expecting his grandmother's summoned spirit to materialize.

"Look, Chase, even Father didn't come," Drew argued. "He knew it wouldn't do any good." He shook his head. "He said his goodbye a long time ago. For him, she died on the march."

Chase's jaw clenched at the painful reminder. Maybe he'd take that refill after all. He raised his empty glass toward the madam, who was happy to oblige him, then downed the three fingers of whiskey in one searing gulp.

The march. He knew the story well. A dozen years ago in this place, tensions between the land-hungry whites and the vanishing tribes had grown into rampant violence. Whites were slaughtered, natives massacred. Finally, the white soldiers—at a loss over what to do with the Indians they'd reduced to starvation—decided to relocate them. Rounded up like cattle, they were driven nearly a hundred miles to Nome Cult Reservation.

Only half of the natives survived the grueling march over rocky terrain. Chase figured that was still a good deal more than the army intended. Though Chase's grandfather, the proud headman of the Konkow tribe, searched for his wife Yoema, he was unable to find her and assumed the soldiers had killed her. Grief-stricken, he starved himself to death on the journey.

But Chase's recent vision had told him that Yoema had not been killed. Indeed, the letter that his Uncle Hintsuli had forwarded to the family from the reservation at Nome Cult several days ago confirmed that fact. Chase's grandmother *was* alive...or at least she *had* been. She'd been kept all these years by a rancher near the old Konkow village. According to the letter, she'd succumbed only recently to a fever.

At the news, Chase's parents, Sakote and Mattie, had mourned quietly. After all, like Drew said, they'd made peace with her passing long ago.

But Chase couldn't let it go. The Great Spirit had called him to his grandmother's side while she lay dying, and he'd failed her. Now, according to his vision, it was his obligation to help her finish her spirit's journey, to complete the circle, to heal the past.

"Hey, tell me something," he mumbled to the madam, who was rearranging the flowers on their table. When she didn't realize he was addressing her, he got her attention by reaching out and grabbing her wrist.

She gave a little gasp, and Drew frowned at him in clear disapproval. With a wince of apology, Chase released her. Sometimes a blacksmith forgot his own strength.

She swallowed visibly. "More whiskey, mister?" she asked.

He didn't bother to answer. "Where's the Parker Ranch?"

"Now wait a minute, Chase," Drew protested. "You can't just go waltzin' up and—"

"Where is it?" Chase locked gazes with the madam.

"Shit." Drew rolled his eyes and threw up his hands. "What are you gonna do, Chase?"

Chase ignored him, staring at the woman, willing her to tell him what he wanted to know.

She did. "It's west of here, a couple of miles along the main road."

"Chase," Drew warned.

He nodded thanks to the woman.

"Chase!"

He turned to go, but Drew caught his arm. "You're not goin' there. Not now. Not in the middle of the night. Look, we're both pretty liquored up. Wait till mornin', and I'll come with you. You can't go off half-co—" His glance caught on something over Chase's shoulder, and he suddenly stopped with his mouth agape.

Not much could leave Drew speechless. Chase frowned, glancing up at the reflection of the room in the mirror, just in time to glimpse the swish of blue skirts as one of the shady ladies upstairs entered a room and closed the door.

Chase could see by the look on Drew's face that he'd get no more interference from his brother tonight. He shook his head in disgust.

"Enjoy yourself," he muttered, snapping up Drew's whiskey and downing the rest of it. He plunked a silver dollar on the table, sure that by the time he hit the brothel door, his brother would be halfway up the stairs.

Once outside, the chill night air smacked Chase in the face, taking the edge off the dizzying effects of the whiskey. Still, he stopped on the boardwalk in front of the Parlor to get his bearings.

He shouldn't have taken that last shot of whiskey. Hell, he

probably shouldn't have taken the last *three*. He'd never had Drew's constitution. But he needed the whiskey's fortification for the task ahead of him.

Overhead, a sky full of stars kept a close vigil on the earth. Their patterns circled the star in the north, showing him the way. He stepped off the boardwalk and trudged along the main street of Paradise. He passed a dry goods store, a schoolhouse, a hotel, a church, and four saloons, where the muffled music and flickering lamplight seeping through the doors signaled that—in the saloons at least—the night was young.

A full acorn-white moon helped him navigate the curving road. He descended the ridge, his boots soundless in the soft powder of the well-worn path. Eventually the fragrant pines thinned, yielding to stands of oak. Hills thick with spring growth rolled gently on either side of the road.

One of those new barbed wire fences sprang up, dividing the lush grass from the grazed. It served as a bitter reminder of how the ranchers' distorted sense of entitlement had destroyed the beautiful land. Land that had once sustained hundreds of Konkows was now browsed to the dirt by the voracious beasts the white men brought with them. And to protect their cattle, the ranchers shot any creatures that threatened the land they claimed for their own, whether they were coyotes, wildcats, or Indians.

Chase's mouth twisted as he looked into the distance at the endless stretch of fence. Such an expanse had once supported several Konkow villages. Now it belonged to one greedy man.

He gave his head a sobering snap, but it didn't help much. He still weaved as he walked along the row of posts, following them until the moon had climbed two fingers higher into the heavens. Finally, an ostentatious sign across a gated side road announced THE PARKER RANCH in letters burned into the wood. At the corner of the sign, the letter P within a circle formed the ranch's brand.

Chase spat his disgust into the dirt. Branding irons were the one thing he refused to forge in his blacksmith's shop. The domineering whites thought they could own beasts. They felt justified in burning animal flesh with hot iron, trapping cattle behind fences of metal thorns, killing them with no blessing, no honor. He'd even heard that some of the whites believed the Konkows were animals, that ranchers herded and slaughtered them like livestock.

Chase was feeling the full effects of that last drink now. Anger flared in him as quickly as brush fire. He stared hard at the brand on the sign as rage shuddered through him. Had Parker believed that? The rancher had torn his grandmother Yoema from her husband's side, made her his property, his slave. Had he branded *her* with his mark, too?

The idea sickened Chase. He staggered, clutching the barbed wire in his fist to regain his balance. He hardly felt the star-shaped barb piercing his palm.

Vengeance. The feeling rose so powerfully in him that he could taste it at the back of his throat. Here was his answer, he thought. This was why the Great Spirit had chosen him. He was suddenly sure of it. As blood of her blood, it was Chase's obligation to exact revenge for the rancher's atrocities upon his grandmother. That was the way to heal the past and close the circle.

Sweat beaded his upper lip as he let his gaze travel past the gate, down the winding road, along several outbuildings and a barn, finally fixing on a whitewashed house of shamefully lavish proportions. The opulence of it sharpened his wrath.

The stars overhead doubled in his vision. Chase shook his head to dispel the annoying blur. He clenched his fist tighter around the barbed wire, ignoring the trickle of blood that dripped through his fingers. If he was going to take vengeance, he had to have a clear head. It was a dangerous thing he attempted. He needed his wits about him.

With one hand on the knife sheathed at his hip, he stole through the gate. The long driveway allowed time for his anger to smolder, time to mull over his mode of revenge. What was fitting, he considered, for a monster who ripped apart families, who degraded natives like they were cattle, who kept old women enslaved until they died, never again to see their kin?

Chase ground his teeth, pulverizing any shred of mercy he possessed, the way tribal women ground acorns between rock. He had a sudden primitive urge to follow the old ways of his father's people—beating the man with a club until his body broke or shooting him full of arrows until he screamed for death. But he couldn't afford such luxuries, not now, not here on the man's property.

Perhaps he'd steal the rancher away then, sever him from his family as Chase's grandmother had been severed from the Konkows.

A horse whickered in the barn, startling Chase. He melted into the shadow of the golden oak that stood guard over the massive house.

Eventually, the air grew silent again, except for the distant baying of a lone coyote. Chase lifted his eyes to the grand mansion shining in the moonlight, and the corners of his mouth turned down.

Natives had probably built this princely manor for a white man who'd never soiled his hands in the Great Spirit's earth. While revered Konkow headmen and gifted shamans like his grandmother blistered their palms and bent their backs to serve the rancher, Parker and his family lived like spoiled children, untouched by harsh winds or scorching sun or the indignity of hard labor. He wondered how Parker would fare as a slave, sweating and toiling for the profit of another.

Then a dark inspiration took hold. His lips slowly curved into a grim smile.

The march to Nome Cult.

He would force Parker to endure the march, as his people had. He'd prod the rancher across a hundred miles of rugged land, without water, without food, without shelter, until there was nothing left of him. An eye for an eye, a tooth for a tooth, as his white mother's Bible preached. That was how his grandmother would be avenged. That was how her spirit would find peace.

Resolve and liquor made him bold. He silently climbed the steps and circled the porch until he found a window left open to capture the night breeze. He brushed aside the sheer curtain. Moonlight spilled like pale acorn soup, over the sill and into the darkened house.

A sudden swell of vertigo tipped him off-balance as he climbed through the window. He made a grab for the curtain, tearing the frail fabric. Luckily, he had enough presence of mind to silence an angry curse, and his feet finally found purchase on the polished wood floor.

He swayed, then straightened, swallowing hard as he perused the costly furnishings, which were as sumptuous as those at the Parlor.

A pair of sofas so plump they looked pregnant squatted on stubby legs carved with figures of leaves. Four rush-seat chairs stenciled with twining flowers sat against one wall. Delicate tables perched here and there on legs no thicker than a fawn's. A massive marble fireplace with an iron grate dominated the room, and an ornate clock ticked softly on the mantel. An unlit chandelier hung from the ceiling like a giant crystal spider, and a dense, patterned carpet stretched in an oval pool over the floor. Sweeping down one side of the room was a mahogany staircase, and the walls were adorned with paper printed in pale vertical stripes.

His gaze settled on the enormous gilt-framed oil portrait hung above the mantel.

Letting the torn curtain fall closed, Chase ventured into the room to take a closer look. The title at the bottom read, SAMUEL AND CLAIRE PARKER. Hatred began to boil his blood as he let his eyes slide up to study the face of his enemy, the evil rancher who'd enslaved his grandmother.

Samuel Parker had a stern, wrinkled face, a balding head, dark eyes, and a trailing gray mustache that made him look even sterner. He was easy to hate. Chase's lip curled as he savored the thought of dragging the villain out of bed.

Then his gaze lit on Claire Parker. A wave of lightheadedness washed over him. It was only the whiskey, he told himself. Yet he couldn't take his eyes off of the face in the painting. The woman seemed half her husband's age, as innocent and fair as Parker was darkly corrupt. She had long fair hair, partially swept up into a knot. Her features were delicate, and her eyes were serene and sweet. He'd never seen anyone so beautiful.

After a good minute of gawking, he finally squeezed his eyes shut against the image. The woman's looks didn't matter. Her heart was doubtless as evil as her husband's.

A flicker suddenly danced across the landing above, and Chase faded back into the wallpaper. The glow of a candle lit the top steps, making shadows flutter about the walls. And then, at the top of the stairs, the portrait of the woman appeared to come to life.

Claire Parker.

The flame illuminated her face, giving her creamy skin an ethereal glow. Her long hair had been cut since the painting. Short, blunt strands now caressed her chin. But the blonde locks shone in the candlelight like the halos of the angels in his mother's Bible. She wore a white lace-trimmed camisole, an ankle-length petticoat...and nothing else. Timidly she descended the steps in bare feet.

He stood frozen while the woman—unaware he lurked in the shadows—crept slowly closer. He didn't dare breathe as she brushed past him.

She hesitated, close enough for him to tell the portrait didn't do her justice. Claire Parker was breathtaking—delicate, innocent, fair. Yet there were dark hollows beneath her eyes that made her look sad. For a brief moment, he felt sorry for her.

Then, just as quickly, he remembered who she was, what she was, and the reason he'd come. He couldn't let a pretty face distract him from his vengeance.

But how would he steal past the lady to get to her husband? He couldn't afford to wait for her to go back to bed. The longer he remained in the house, the greater his chances of getting caught.

Hell. He had to do something. And soon.

Instinct took over. It must have been instinct. Or the whiskey. Because if he'd thought about what he was doing for one minute, he never would have taken that first step.

Sliding his knife silently from its sheath, he slipped out of the shadows and came up behind her. Before she could wheel around in surprise, he clamped a hand over Claire Parker's mouth and set the sharp blade against her slim throat.

CHAPTER 2

It happened in a heartbeat.

Only moments before, Claire, hearing the soft sound from downstairs and sensing a shadowy presence in the room below, had foolishly believed it might be the spirit of her beloved Yoema. Hope filling her heart, she'd crept down the stairs.

But in an instant, those hopes were dashed. A huge hand closed over her mouth, choking off her gasp of shock. And a sharp edge of cold steel pressed against her neck.

She dropped the candle on the carpet, extinguishing its light. Her heart jammed up against her ribs, fluttering like a singed moth. Her throat clogged with panic. Air whistled through her flared nostrils. Her fingers splayed ineffectually as the blade threatened her with a menacing chill. She stared ahead with blind terror, sure the knife would end her gulping any moment.

She felt utterly helpless, not at all like the heroes of the dime novels she kept under her bed. She had no revolver. She had no Bowie knife. And she had no idea what her attacker intended.

For a long, drawn-out moment, the man did nothing, which was almost worse than killing her outright, for it gave her time to think, to dread.

Who was he? What did he want? Was he going to hurt her? Kidnap her? Murder her? The panicked whimper born in her throat was cut short by his tightening grip. Who *was* he?

The pungent smell of strong whiskey and wood smoke rose off of him, stinging her nose. The palm crushing her mouth tasted faintly of blood. His fingers, pressed into her cheek, were rough and callused. One thick-muscled arm, slung heavily across her bosom, trapped her. And where he secured her against his broad chest, he was as hard as a tree trunk.

She didn't dare resist, scarcely dared to breathe while the knife rested so close to her madly pulsing vein. If only she hadn't left her scissors in her bedroom...

The man moved his arm to struggle awkwardly with something behind her. She squeezed her eyes tight, praying he wasn't unfastening his trousers.

Then, for one moment, the cool blade disappeared from her throat. She stiffened like a clock spring, poised to bolt free. His hand fell away, and she sucked in a great gulp of air to scream.

But he was too quick for her. He jammed a wad of dusty cloth into her open mouth. She fought to keep from gagging, wincing as he knotted it tightly at the back of her head. Then he brandished the shiny silver blade in front of her eyes, flashing a silent threat in the moonlight.

This time, instead of cowering in fright, she let his gesture fuel her courage. Mustering her strength and calling to mind all the Buckskin Bill adventures she'd read, she swung her clasped hands across his forearm and brought her heel down hard on the top of his foot.

His forearm didn't budge, and she felt the bone-jarring

impact of her bare heel upon his stiff boot all the way up her leg. She winced in pain. If only she'd had her Sunday church heels on, she might have heard much more out of him than just an annoyed grunt.

Instead of thwarting him, her struggles seemed to increase his determination. He hugged her closer against him, so close she could feel his hot whiskey breath riffling her hair. He raised the knife in his huge fist till it glinted with menace before her. Then he began dragging her backward across the room.

In desperation, she tried to wrench out of his iron grasp, twisting enough to catch a glimpse of his shadowed face before he jerked her back against him.

What she'd seen surprised her. Even in the dim light, she could tell he was a native. His eyes, narrowed with intent, were as dark as the night, and his short, unruly hair shone like ebony silk. His features were evenly chiseled and rather handsome, from the bold bridge of his nose and his square jaw to the lean cords of his neck and his strong brow.

Why would an Indian attack her? The Indians who worked her father's ranch were friendly and harmless.

Still, there had been tales of scalpings years ago, perpetrated by savages who'd learned such violence from vicious white settlers. Dear God, did he mean to take her scalp?

Suddenly she could draw no air into her lungs, and a hysterical thought kept circling her brain—she'd surely cheated the man of his prize if he meant to scalp her, for only moments ago, she'd cut off her hair in mourning.

Stunned and breathless, she hardly resisted as he continued to lug her toward the open window. But when he climbed out and began to haul her over the sill, pushing her head down with one massive hand so she wouldn't bang it on the sashes, she awoke from her stupor.

23

Heavens, the man was abducting her!

They were halfway out of the house when panic made her fight in earnest. She grabbed hold of the window, refusing to let go. She twisted and flailed against him until he fired a guttural grunt at her, probably an epithet in his native tongue.

In a matter of seconds, of course, his strength won out. He unlatched her hands with a sweep of his arm and pulled her out onto the porch into the stark night.

Maybe she could still make noise, she thought in desperation. Her screams might not be heard through the gag, but if she stomped on the planks and made a huge fuss, surely her father or one of the ranch hands would come to investigate.

The man must have read her thoughts. Before she could make a single sound, he picked her up, tucked her between his arm and his hip like a sack of feed, and stole off the porch with the silent step that was a hallmark of the local tribes.

Suspended on his hip, with her arms trapped against her sides, she couldn't do much more than squirm against him, which didn't hamper him in the least.

She peered between the blunt strands of her newly cropped hair. Though he weaved a bit, he seemed to be heading for the barn.

A slender slice of moonlight spilled in when he eased the door open, but the horses in the front stalls were unperturbed by the presence of an intruder. Hoping to startle them into a frenzy of neighing, Claire thrashed wildly in her captor's grip. He grunted and squeezed her tightly about the waist, cutting off her struggles and her air. Then he took a coil of rope from a nail in the wall and started forward.

He quickly found what he wanted—Thunder, her father's five-year-old prize stallion. Stroking the horse's chest, he managed to nudge Thunder out of the stall. Then, using one hand and his teeth, he fashioned a loop to slip over the horse's head.

She expected he'd make a break for it. He'd swing up bareback and throw her across his lap, slap Thunder's flank, let out a war whoop, and race into the night. As soon as he did, of course, a posse of her father's men would mount up and ride after him like the devil. They'd put a bullet in the villain before the moon rose even halfway across the sky.

But he did no such thing. He led Thunder out of the barn as stealthily as he'd come in. To her amazement, the normally headstrong stallion followed willingly, as if the two of them were partners in crime.

Still clamped firmly under the brute's huge arm and against his lean hip, Claire tried to calm her racing heart and make sense of things. Surely this couldn't be happening. Surely a stranger couldn't march up to the front door of the formidable Parker house in the middle of the night, snatch her from her own parlor, and make off with her by the light of the full moon.

Yet no one had heard him come. No one had roused when he left. It would be morning before anyone missed Claire. And, heaven help her, she'd left a note saying she was running away. Her father probably wouldn't even bother to come after her.

What were the man's intentions?

Obviously, he didn't mean to kill her. She'd be dead already if that were the case. Maybe he meant to hold her for ransom. Samuel Parker's prosperity was well known. This savage wouldn't be the first scoundrel to go after her father's wealth.

But he was by far the boldest.

They'd left the drive now, gone out the gate, onto the main road. The land on the other side was wild, uncultivated and overgrown, and the Indian led Thunder straight into the weeds. Tall grasses brushed the horse's flanks and whipped at Claire's petticoat as she sagged in the man's grip.

Once they'd descended the rolling hill, out of sight of the

Parker house, he stopped to remove the noose from Thunder's neck. Seizing the opportunity, Claire thrust out with her feet, kicking one of the beast's hocks, hoping to spook the horse into galloping back to the ranch.

But the Indian calmed the animal with a few murmurs and a pat to Thunder's flank, turning on Claire with a withering glare, as if she'd kicked the horse just for spite.

He righted her then, planting her atop the weed-choked ground. Before she could catch her balance, he dropped the noose about her, cinching it tightly around her waist.

When he casually swept up the hem of her petticoat, exposing her knees, Claire's eyes widened, and her heart skittered along her ribs. Perhaps she'd been mistaken about the man's intent after all.

But, drawing his knife, he slashed a long strip from the hem and let the garment fall. Then he put away the blade and seized one of her hands.

Instinctively she pulled away, but was caught fast in his great fist. He looped the cloth around her wrist, pulled it behind her, and crossed it over the other hand, knotting the cotton strips together.

Satisfied with his handiwork, he stepped back, his thumbs hooked insolently into the waistband of his trousers. She stared at him, wondering how drunk he must be to take pride in subduing a woman her size.

He must have read her mind. A scowl darkened his features, and for a moment, Claire thought she detected a hint of shame marring his drunken arrogance. Then he growled and turned his back on her, destroying all notions of civility.

In a movement surprisingly fluid for such a large man, he swung up atop Thunder. Coiling the loose end of the rope around his fist, he nudged the horse forward. The rope pulled taut around her waist, and Claire was forced to follow.

Caught off guard, she staggered and almost fell. What kind

of abduction was this? Surely the man would want to flee as swiftly as possible to avoid capture. Why wasn't he sweeping her up and tearing off across the countryside?

He rode slowly, but keeping up was difficult. Claire was no longer accustomed to walking barefoot. Her father had cured her of that uncivilized habit years ago. The ground was rocky and uneven. Every few steps, she winced as star thistles bristled against her ankles and sharp pebbles poked her heels. Burrs caught in what was left of her lace hem, and her petticoat grew sodden with its harvest of dew.

She twisted her ankle on a stone and nearly went down again. The pain as she hobbled forward made her eyes water, but she didn't dare stop. She feared if she hesitated, he'd ride on anyway, dragging her through the thistles.

But despite her best efforts to be stoic, her eyes filled with tears. A trickle wound its way down her cheek and was swallowed up by the cotton binding her mouth.

It wasn't the pain that triggered her crying. And it wasn't fear, not really. It was grief.

From the day that Yoema fell ill, Samuel Parker had insisted that Claire hide her sorrow. After all, no one knew the truth about Yoema's relationship to Claire. They assumed the native woman was a servant, no more. So for the sake of propriety and obedience to her father, Claire had kept a stiff upper lip and denied herself the relief of tears. Yoema had been buried quietly, and Claire was expected to carry on as if nothing had happened.

But now she was removed from the eyes of society, stripped of everything that had kept her sailing on a shaky but even keel. Her emotions felt as raw as the soles of her feet. And her father wasn't around to witness her weeping, to be disappointed in her. So all the pain she'd bottled up inside, all the bittersweet memories she'd repressed, all the tears she'd been unable to shed, gushed forth in a torrent so powerful that before long, her chest heaved with wrenching sobs and the gag grew wet with her weeping.

She no longer cared about the stones cutting her feet, no longer wondered about her captor. All she could think about was the woman who'd cared for her since she was a little motherless girl, who'd taught her the names of the animals, who'd held her when she was sad and lonely, who'd told her stories and sang her songs, and whose voice was now silent. Forever.

This time, when Claire tripped on the edge of a rock, she landed hard on her knees. She expected to be dragged through the weeds, and frankly she didn't care if he hauled her that way for ten miles. Now that the egg of her sorrow had been cracked, she realized that nothing could hurt her as much as the loss of the woman she'd called Mother.

The moment she struck the dirt, however, her captor halted, turning to see what delayed her.

Overcome with woe, she sank forward over her knees and buried her head. She didn't care if he watched her. He was nobody. She didn't have to keep a brave face for him like she did for her father. Her breath came in loud, wheezing gasps, filtered by the smothering cloth. Her throat ached with an agony of grief, and the sobs that racked her body felt as if they tore her soul asunder. Overwhelmed by heartache, she didn't notice at first that the Indian had dismounted and now loomed over her.

His fingers suddenly grazed the top of her head, startling her, and she almost choked on her tears as she glanced up at him. Though his face swam in her watery vision, he seemed shaken.

Of course he was shaken. Men never understood women's weeping. But she didn't care. She stared up at the frowning savage, openly defiant, tears streaming down her cheeks, silently daring him to ridicule her.

His scowl deepened, and he jutted out his chin. His mouth worked as if he were trying to decide whether to swallow or spit. Then, with a whispered expletive, he released her. Winding one arm around her waist, he hauled her to her feet and nodded sharply as if to tell her there would be no more falling down.

She wiped her wet cheek on her shoulder, staring coldly at him, but he refused to meet her eyes. He wrapped his end of the rope one more time around his hand, turned away, and remounted. His back expanded and released once with a deep breath before he clucked to the horse, urging it forward one step.

Claire stood her ground, refusing to move. Her grief was turning rapidly to anger. What kind of a brute abducted a woman by night, forced her barefoot across rock-riddled hills, and ignored her tears of distress? In her dime novels, even the most dastardly villain possessed at least a shred of common decency.

Damn his coal-black eyes! If he wanted her to move from this spot, he'd just have to drag her.

When he turned to peer at her, the corners of his mouth were drawn down. He tugged once more on the rope.

Raising her chin, she took a step backward.

His eyes widened. He tugged again, pulling her forward a step.

Incensed, she marshaled her strength and hauled back on the rope as hard as she could.

To her satisfaction, she managed to alter his look of annoyance to one of surprise, though for all her efforts, he didn't budge more than a few inches.

His amazement was short-lived. He simply let go of the rope, and she sank with a plop onto her bottom. Before she could scramble upright, he slipped from Thunder, stalking toward her, muttering under his breath all the way.

Leaning forward, he upended her, slinging her over one ox-like shoulder. The air whooshed out of her, and she closed her eyes against the dizzying sensation of her precarious perch. Then he tossed her sidesaddle across the horse and swiftly mounted up behind her.

Flinging a possessive arm around her waist, he nudged Thunder forward, mumbling what sounded suspiciously like "damn fool Indian," and rode stonily into the deepening night.

At first she sat upright, stiff, unwilling to even think about letting her body come into contact with his. But as they rode on, mile after mile, her strength flagged. The sleep that had evaded her for days finally caught up with her, lulling her muscles into complacency and urging her eyes closed.

She stirred once along the gently rocking ride, fluttering her eyes open long enough to note that the sky had taken on the purple cast of the far side of midnight. Then she settled back in surrender against the stranger's chest. Her grief spent, she found curious comfort in dozing against the warm cotton shirt, safe from sorrow, safe from memories, safe from judgment.

Hours later, the sound of soft snoring woke her. Claire opened her eyes to a morning filled with apricot-colored light. Before her, the rolling hills lay silvered with dew and dotted with dark oaks, and the rising sun stretched fingers of gold across the emerald knolls. For one brief moment, she forgot where she was and simply enjoyed the glorious view.

Then the man—who was pressed far too intimately against her—snorted awake, and she remembered everything. Her captor had apparently slept for some time, for the horse had stopped to graze upon a patch of clover, and it looked like they were miles from anywhere.

"Shit!"

Claire flinched. So the savage *did* speak English...or at least knew one useful word. He shifted on Thunder's back, and she realized, much to her chagrin, that unless the man wore a Colt down his trousers, her hands, bound behind her, had just brushed the most private part of his anatomy. She curled her fingers in horror, relieved when he finally dismounted.

The stallion neighed, and then returned to chomping at the sweet grass. Her captor circled into her view, hitching up his trousers and scrubbing the sleep from his eyes. Then he lowered his hands from his face, and Claire saw him by the light of day for the first time.

He was truly massive, larger than any man she'd ever seen, broad of shoulder and chest. The muscles of his arms strained the blue flannel of his shirt, and his hands looked big enough to hide a whole poker deck.

But it wasn't his size that made her throat go suddenly dry.

The man was devilishly handsome. She could see now that he wasn't a full-blooded native. His short black hair had a slight curl to it, and his chin was dark with stubble. His skin was as golden as wild honey, and his teeth were snowy white where his lips parted. Deep, brooding eyes, shadowed by fatigue, shone like marbles of obsidian as he scrutinized her. And something about him looked curiously familiar.

"Ah, hell."

She blinked, impressed by his command of English, if not his vocabulary.

But the third word she pretended she didn't hear. He turned his back to her and kicked hard at the dirt, raking his hair back with both hands.

She wondered why he was upset. He had no reason to blacken the air with his cussing. *He* wasn't the one trussed up like a steer for branding. *He* wasn't the one stolen from a snug home and dragged across the hills half the night in his unmentionables. *His* throat wasn't as dry as gunpowder, and his legs weren't bloody with thistle scratches.

He spun back around, glaring at her as if she were somehow to blame. She tried to glare back at him. But Thunder chose that inopportune moment to amble forward, stretching his neck down for a choice bunch of clover. Claire's eyes widened as she began to slide inexorably, helplessly from her perch toward the hard-packed earth.

CHAPTER 3

The instant Chase saw the panic in those big, beautiful green eyes, he instinctively lunged forward and caught the woman before she could slide off. Unfortunately, his efforts trapped her awkwardly between the horse's shoulder and his own chest. Her eyes widened even more, and he cursed, realizing that with her hands tied behind her, she could lend him no assistance whatsoever.

She slipped down his body, inch by delicious inch. Her soft breasts were crushed against his hard ribs, and her flimsy petticoat rode halfway up her legs before he could disentangle himself from her. At last he managed to get her feet on the ground.

Now if he could only regain his *own* balance.

What the hell had he been thinking last night, stealing a white woman? Whatever was in that whiskey, it must have robbed him of his last bit of sense, making him believe he had a hunger for vengeance and the stomach for violence.

Chase wasn't a killer. Or a kidnapper. Hell, he wouldn't even step on a spider. Cruelty didn't come naturally to him.

Neither did embracing a beautiful woman. Women didn't come close to Chase much. His size usually scared them off. And if that didn't do it, his scowl would.

Not this one. The lady might be a tiny thing, as pale as a flower, as delicate as a fawn. But there was strength in her spirit, fire in her heart. Damn, even in his sleep, his body had gotten riled up over her.

A moment passed before Chase realized his arms were still wrapped around the woman. Outrage sparked in her eyes, and he released her like a white-hot poker.

She probably figured he meant to ravage her. He was sure white men did such things. But Chase would no sooner take a woman against her will than he'd brand an animal.

He stepped away, shaken. He managed to keep enough wits about him to gather the end of the rope in his fist so she wouldn't run off and get herself into worse trouble. Then he sank down onto the trunk of a fallen tree to consider his predicament.

Shit! Why hadn't he listened to Drew? Chase had obviously had more whiskey than sense last night. And today, unlike the sweet flavor of revenge he'd imagined, the reality of holding a helpless woman captive left a bitter taste in his mouth.

He rubbed the back of his neck, glancing sideways at his hostage, who looked like some beautiful snow-white angel dropped out of heaven into the dirt. What the hell had he done?

A half-breed couldn't kidnap a white woman, particularly the wife of a rich rancher, and not expect half the population to come after him with guns blazing.

Worse, the horse he'd borrowed was a fine-looking animal, probably breeding stock. Hell, Parker might mourn the loss of his stallion more than his wife. Chase didn't know what they did to a man who took another man's woman, but they hanged you for horse thieving.

He scratched uneasily at his throat.

Vengeance had seemed like such a good idea last night. Now it felt like the biggest mistake of his life.

He squinted into the dawning day. Unlike his brother, he measured the hour not with a pocket watch, but by the position of the sun. By now the old rancher would be missing his young wife. He'd probably already assembled a search party.

Chase winced as his gaze followed the meandering path of bent grass they'd left in the meadow. A *child* could track them along a trail like that.

He peered again at the woman tethered to him. She stood straight and proud, for all her crying last night, and there was something alluring about her sleep-mussed hair and dirt-smudged face.

He should probably just let her go, her and the horse. He could untie her, put her on the stallion, give the horse's flank a slap, and send the rancher's precious wife safely home, none the worse for wear, before she could burn his ears with a spate of well-deserved cussing. Then Chase could clear out, go back to Hupa, and forget he'd ever passed this way.

It sounded like a perfect plan. There was just one problem.

His brother Drew was still in town, and the town wasn't all that big. Sooner or later, Drew was bound to cross paths with Mrs. Claire Parker. And of course, the instant she laid eyes on Chase's twin, she'd tattle to her husband that *that* was the no-good half-breed who'd made off with her.

Chase couldn't put his brother in harm's way like that. The twins had a habit of looking out for each other. Drew might be clever, but he'd never slip through the noose of a powerful husband bent on vengeance.

No, Chase couldn't let the woman go until his brother was safely out of town. He wouldn't allow Drew to pay for his stupid mistake, especially since Drew had tried to talk him out of it. This was *his* problem, *his* destiny. The Great Spirit had set him on this journey. And no matter how impulsive Chase's actions had been last night or how much danger he now faced, he had to confront that destiny alone.

Whatever he did, he'd have to do it soon if he didn't want Parker's men breathing down his neck.

He supposed he should say something to the woman. He should put her fears to rest, let her know he meant her no harm, explain that it had all been a mistake.

But, damn it all, he didn't have Drew's slick way with words. Every time he opened his mouth, trying to find a reasonable way to explain what he'd done or to justify what he was about to do, he had to close it again.

It wasn't like she was going to forgive him for kidnapping her. And she sure as hell wasn't going to understand why he meant to hang onto her a little while longer.

So he dealt with the problem in his usual way—with silence. He didn't untie her for fear she'd try to escape and hurt herself. He didn't meet her eyes, knowing the innocent confusion he'd see there would only frustrate him. And he gave up trying to talk to her. He needed to focus instead on figuring out just where they were going.

He supposed he was lucky the horse hadn't moseyed back to the Parker Ranch while he dozed. The beast probably would have gone by the main road, whinnying at the gate to announce their arrival.

There was no question in his mind that he had to return Mrs. Parker to Paradise as soon as possible, then hightail it back to Hupa with his brother, even if he had to drag Drew from between some woman's thighs. What he needed was a discreet back entrance to the town that would allow him to slip in and out without attracting attention. But since he was in unfamiliar territory, he'd have to rely on his native instincts to help him read the land and find that back door.

In the distance to the southwest, a small range of buttes

rose up in distinctive humps from the flat grasslands. The Konkow called the buttes Histum Yani, the Creator's sweathouse. Drew and he had kept them on their right shoulder on the journey here.

He squinted toward the foothills where the sun was rising. According to his father, just below the ridge upon which the town perched, a deep canyon cut through the earth, creating a valley. Long ago, his father's sister Towani had lived in that valley, before her husband Noa had taken her away to his home on the island of Hawaii. Chase remembered his father saying that a forked creek wound through the canyon, and caves pitted the steep stone walls.

If he followed the creek upstream, it had to eventually rise to its source, somewhere above Paradise. On horseback, the journey shouldn't take more than a day or two, and once there, he could make his way back down and enter the town from the uphill side. No one would expect him to circle back into the mountains and come from that direction, especially since his tracks so far had led in the opposite direction, toward the wide, fertile grasslands and civilization.

To elude his trackers, he'd have to move quickly. He was in open prairie at the moment, completely vulnerable. He needed to get out of sight, and he needed a place to hole up for the night. He wondered how far the caves were. Maybe if he rode swiftly, he could make it there by nightfall.

First, however, he needed to relieve himself of the excess whiskey he'd had last night.

He was halfway to his feet when he felt the woman's wide-eyed gaze on him.

Hell.

He couldn't just drop his drawers in front of her. He obviously hadn't worked out the details of this brilliant kidnapping plan. But then he hadn't imagined his victim would be a lady.

And now that he had her, he was troubled by the fact that she was so...real. Things would be a hell of a lot easier if she were flat and lifeless, like the portrait hanging in Parker's mansion. Instead, her big green eyes were clear and perceptive, filled with wariness and intelligence and courage. It was unnerving.

He silently cursed his quandary. He'd do his best to take Mrs. Parker's sensibilities into consideration, but he wasn't about to leave her unguarded to go find a tree.

So he compromised. Tugging her along on the rope, he found a waist-high clump of buckbrush to use as a screen between them, turned his back, and used his free hand to unbutton his trousers.

Claire felt her cheeks go hot with embarrassment. Lord, had the savage no decency? How could he do...that...right in front of her? It was uncivilized. Thoroughly disgusting. Utterly vile.

And yet a darker thought taunted her, nibbling at her brain like a mean little mouse gnawing at the underside of a horse trough. What was she going to do when she faced the same urges? Fortunately, she was too edgy to relieve herself just now, and when the half-breed whipped toward her, buttoning up belatedly enough to give her an unexpected glimpse of bronze flesh and black curls, all such urges fled.

She squeezed her offended eyes shut, trying to erase the image that now seemed branded upon her brain, and didn't move until she felt a tug on the rope circling her waist. She took one blind step, stubbing her toe on a rock, and sniffed sharply against the pain.

She shot her captor a glare full of blame. His mouth worked, as if he were simultaneously displeased and disgraced. Then he spoke his first civil words to her. "We've got a ways to go. I'm going to put you on the horse."

She swallowed hard, caught off-guard by the quality of his

voice—soft, deep, and full of breath, like the rare autumn breezes that rustled the pines. The fact that he spoke flawless English gave her hope.

Perhaps she could reason with the half-breed after all. He must know he couldn't ransom damaged goods. If she could get him to remove her gag, maybe she could strike a bargain with him.

But he wouldn't even meet her eyes. Frowning as he towered over her, he spanned her waist with his huge hands, lifted her onto Thunder's back as effortlessly as if she were made of feathers, and then mounted up behind her.

She kept her fists primly closed, painfully aware that the particular part of his anatomy she'd just glimpsed was only inches from her bound hands.

Claire wondered if the man realized where he was headed. She knew from the position of the Sutter Buttes that they were traveling roughly north. They couldn't be more than ten or twelve miles from the Parker Ranch.

The morning wore on, and they crossed the sparsely-treed plain toward a low ridge of hills. Claire's impending need began to make itself known as the dilemma she'd anticipated earlier slowly blossomed into a full-bloomed necessity. Her struggles didn't go unnoticed. Her captor grunted at her in disapproval when she squirmed against him. A second twitch elicited a "hold still" from him. When she twisted for the third time, he dismounted, perplexed, to scowl up at her.

Her trouble must have been written on her face. He quickly snatched her from Thunder's back, deposited her on the ground, and nudged her toward a stand of buckbrush.

He never let go of the tether, but he at least had the decency to turn his back. Silently cursing her inconvenient anatomy and the fact that her hands were bound, Claire did the best she could under the circumstances.

Afterward, physically relieved and emotionally mortified,

Claire refused to look into the man's face. As he lifted her back onto the horse, she stared fixedly at the shirt button in the middle of his chest.

"Next time," he mumbled, "say something."

She glared down at him from atop the horse with all the rage she could muster. How in blazes did he expect her to say anything when she was gagged?

The man let his guard drop momentarily to mount, and for one mad instant, Claire imagined she might ride off without her abductor and escape across the countryside. Impulsively, she punched her bare heels hard into the horse's flanks.

Thunder reared, but didn't budge from the spot. By the time the stallion's hooves hit the ground, the man had swung up and steadied the startled beast.

"And don't kick the horse," he growled.

Claire was incensed. How dared this stranger tell her what she could and couldn't do? Thunder was her father's horse. Besides, she hadn't kicked him. She'd only...nudged him. She suddenly wished the half-breed were in swinging range of her foot. She'd show him what a kick was.

But she didn't have time to even turn and glower at him. He reached across, making a swift and startling adjustment to her seat, drawing one of her knees over Thunder's neck to let it dangle down the other flank, leaving her straddling the stallion in a most unladylike fashion and bringing a stunned flush to her cheeks.

All at once, at the half-breed's urging, Thunder plunged forward. As they began barreling along at a reckless pace that left the wind whistling past her ears, Claire was suddenly grateful to have her knees free to grasp on for dear life.

The steed coursed wildly across the sod, his dull hoofbeats matching the rapid pumping of her heart. Though tempted to squeeze her eyes shut in terror, she dared not even blink for fear of tumbling to the ground. The man bent over her, folding her forward with his brutish chest until she saw the grasslands before them only in intermittent glimpses between the eager bobs of the stallion's head.

The man's enormous arms enclosed her while he snagged Thunder's mane, and she felt the tension in his thighs as they gripped the horse's flexing muscles behind her. Horse and man breathed as one, sucking in gulps of air and huffing them out with each long stride. Her captor's warm breath blew like a stirring wind across her ear, exciting her in ways that were almost as terrifying as the ride.

When they slowed to breach a grove of oaks, Thunder whinnied and shivered, apparently delighted to have stretched his legs in a headlong run. Claire, too, felt a secret thrill, as if she'd done something forbidden.

Of course it was forbidden. Her father wouldn't have allowed her to sit astride like a man. He was always after her to behave more like a lady. And he would have tanned the half-breed's hide if he knew his prize stallion had been ridden so hard.

Where was he taking her anyway? She wished she could ask him. Not that he'd give her an answer. He seemed to be a man of few words, most of them vile.

They rode on in silence, weaving through the oaks, galloping across open country, while the sun climbed higher and higher in the sky.

By midday, they'd passed through a half-dozen of the rolling knolls that swelled the plains below Paradise. Claire was hungry and thirsty, and with each mile, her dread increased. What did the man want with her? The farther they traveled, the less chance she had of being found.

As the sun began its westward descent, she came to a decision. There was little hope of reasoning with the savage. She couldn't rely on her father's rescue. And dime novel hero Daniel Boone was nowhere in sight.

Soon she was going to have to take matters into her own hands.

Chase glanced up at the sun's position and then studied the terrain ahead. In another hour, they'd reach the foothills, where the land began to surge up from the valley floor—a herald of the steep, majestic ridges to come. Then he would head northeast, toward the mountains.

So far he'd been lucky. He'd managed to stay clear of the main road, sailing hastily across open seas of grass and finding temporary harbor in the concealing oak groves.

Still he left a trail. There was no doubt about that. He was moving too fast to cover his passage. A good tracker would know by now which way he was headed. But half a day's advantage and Chase's estimation of what lay ahead might give him an edge.

And then what? Chase wiped the back of his hand across his damp forehead and tried not to think about it. When they were safe, when they reached the cliffs, then he'd decide exactly what to do about his unwilling captive with the pretty green eyes.

His stomach gurgled, reminding him he hadn't eaten since the night before. He wondered when *she'd* last eaten. A woman that scrawny probably had to eat pretty often just to keep from blowing away.

By the time another hour passed, the weary sun had tucked itself beneath a blanket of storm clouds forming in the west, and his blacksmith's appetite had grown to enormous proportions.

Chase had never truly gone hungry before. He'd grown up in plenty. The hunting skills of his Konkow father, the profits his white mother earned from her paintings, and the simple abundance of the land had provided him with all he could ever want. Now his stomach grumbled like an old bear.

He supposed he should gather what food he could before sunset. Fortunately, it was the time of *dunghit*, spring, when shoots and roots and bulbs were ample. They might not be the tinned oysters the white lady was accustomed to, but they'd nourish her well enough.

He guided the horse toward a shady spot afforded by a dozen sycamores, where a tiny spring fed the marshy ground. He hadn't realized how thirsty he was until he heard the sound of the taunting trickle. With the gag in her mouth, poor Mrs. Parker was probably drier than powdered pinesap.

He should have stopped to let her drink a long while back...just like he should have foreseen she'd have to answer nature's call. But damn it all, he was used to taking care of horses, not women.

He hardly knew what to do with women. He wasn't like his brother Drew, who, with only a wink and a smile, could have the most formidable lady eating out of his hand. Around females, Chase felt like a big, clumsy wolf.

He dismounted, and she stiffened suddenly. The clever lady wasn't as weak and subdued as she pretended to be. He could see some rash, desperate plan brewing in her eyes. Her body quivered like a doe's, ready to bolt, and her nostrils flared with rapid breath. He snagged the rope circling her waist before she could do anything foolish and pierced her wild eyes with his own in warning.

The sun had painted the top of her nose pink, and her lips were wind-chapped, but he'd be damned if she wasn't still the most beautiful woman he'd ever laid eyes on.

Guilt made him frown, which was the wrong thing to do. Her gaze grew even more reckless and determined. If it weren't for the gag, she'd probably be screaming like a wildcat.

Hell. How was he going to ease her fears? He meant her no

harm. Well, actually, he did. Or had. But not any more. Not enough harm to make her eyes go all panicky like that.

He carefully tightened his hand around the rope. She was apt to spook at the slightest movement, and he didn't feel like chasing her halfway across the hills. He supposed he'd better try to talk to her.

"I'm going to take off the gag now." She still sat as stiff as a buck catching the scent of a hunter. "But I expect you to stay nice and quiet."

She only stared at him. He supposed he'd just have to trust her. She was probably too scared to scream anyway. Grasping her carefully around the waist, he helped her to the ground. Damn, the woman was as light as thistledown. Had hunger made her even more insubstantial?

She stood still as he worked on the knot at the back of her head, and he gazed curiously at her shorn hair. It was the soft, pale yellow of foxtail stalks in *xonsil*, summer, but it was uneven, as if it had been hacked off in anger. He wondered if someone had punished her by cutting it. It must have been pretty, the way it had looked in the painting, pouring like a shimmering sheet of molten brass past her shoulders. Still, there was something about the ragged strands falling over her face that was just as pretty, sort of innocent and vulnerable.

After he untangled the knot, he spun her around and carefully tugged the bandanna from her mouth, wincing as he saw the red marks the cloth had left along her cheeks.

Damn. *He'd* done that. *He'd* made those marks.

He scowled. Was he no better than the white soldiers who'd taken his people? He'd let liquor get the best of him. What he'd done was shameful. And cruel. And he deserved every...

Before he could finish the thought, the woman sucked in a great gulp of air, opened her mouth wide, and let out a scream so piercing it would have frozen the blood of a Hupa warrior.

CHAPTER 4

The old man growled from the doorway, taking aim with his rifle. "You son of a bitch, I'll shoot you where you stand."

Drew Hawk sincerely hoped not. First of all, he didn't want to die in a brothel. And second of all, he didn't want anyone putting a bullet in him without knowing what the hell he was being shot for.

The gunman's obsequious young associate tried to smooth his ruffled feathers. "Now, Mr. Parker," he said, "you just let me take care of this." He rested his palm over the old man's trembling gun hand, lowering the rifle.

Drew breathed an invisible sigh of relief. It wasn't that he couldn't have dived across the bed, snatched his Colt from the night table, and fired off all six rounds before the man had a chance to blink. He just didn't want to.

The young man gave him a greasy smile. "I'm sure the Injun doesn't want any trouble, do you?"

Drew narrowed his eyes. Despite the young man's dapper plaid suit, a head of well-oiled blond curls, and a square, freshly shaved chin, his smile looked as out of place on his face as a preacher at a faro table.

"Oh, I'm not lookin' for trouble," Drew said pointedly. "But I sure as hell won't turn my back if it comes lookin' for me."

The young man gave him a patronizing grin. "Then you won't mind telling Mr. Parker here where you were last night."

"I think that's pretty obvious." This pair of sniffing bloodhounds had come barging into his room before he'd even had a chance to wake up. He didn't know what had happened to the beautiful angel who'd shared her bed with him. But for the whopping twenty dollars he'd paid her, he certainly hadn't intended on spending the night anywhere else.

The young man snaked out a hand and twisted it in the front of Drew's undershirt. "Don't get cocky," he sneered.

If Drew hadn't felt so hung over, he would have punched the man's dainty nose halfway into his skull.

"Frank," the old man said, dotting sweat from his furrowed brow with a handkerchief, "we're losing precious time."

Frank hesitated, then released him, smoothing the wrinkles out of Drew's cotton shirt with exaggerated care before Drew batted his hand away.

Parker stepped forward, his rifle tucked harmlessly beneath his arm now, and peered carefully into Drew's eyes.

"My little girl disappeared last night." The old man's mouth trembled. He clamped it firmly shut. "Someone...took her."

Drew smirked. "And you figure, me bein' a half-breed and all, I must be the one who stole the little filly?"

Frank exploded from his stance. But Drew was ready for him this time. He shot out an arm and slammed the astonished fop up against the wall.

"Frank!" Parker bellowed. "Please."

Frank squirmed beneath the pressure of Drew's arm. Drew could see the dandy was itching for an excuse to beat the daylights out of him. But he wouldn't do that while Parker was watching. So Drew let him go, straightening Frank's fancy vest with false courtesy just for spite.

Parker continued. "Mister, I'm not accusing you, but I've been ranching in Paradise for years. I know who belongs here and who doesn't. Now it looks to me like you're the only stranger in town."

The gears turning in Drew's head ground to a sudden halt. Ranching in Paradise. Parker. Hell, the old man must be Samuel Parker of the Parker Ranch. Wasn't that where Chase had been headed last night?

Years of playing poker allowed Drew to keep a straight face. But this news was like a fifth ace turning up in his hand all of a sudden, and he knew he'd better bluff his way out of this game fast.

"Well now, that's a fact," he said congenially. "I *am* a stranger in this town. But I just arrived yesterday. I've hardly had time to wet my whistle, let alone perpetrate any mischief."

Drew's mind whirled. Parker must have questioned the madam. That's how he'd found out Drew was upstairs. But she hadn't volunteered the fact that Drew had a twin brother. God love the savvy madam, she knew when to keep her mouth shut.

Meanwhile, the old rancher seemed lost in his thoughts. "The kidnapper cut off her..." His voice broke as his fretful gaze wandered restlessly over the planks of the floor. "Cut off her hair."

Drew's eyes flattened. Chase wouldn't have done something like that to a little girl.

"We figure it was an Injun," Frank sneered.

"Truth is," Parker amended, "I don't know what to figure."

He fixed Drew with eyes as cold and hard as his rifle barrel. "But if you know anything…"

Drew slowly shook his head. "I was up here all night, entertainin'. The madam can vouch for me."

It was a gamble, counting on the madam. She might have covered for Drew, him being a paying customer and all, but her loyalty concerning his brother could probably be bartered for a couple of gold coins.

Parker nodded, brushing back his gray mustache with solemn dignity. "Sorry about the rifle."

"Understandable. If it were *my* little girl, well…" Drew left the thought unfinished.

The old man nudged Frank out the door. "If you hear anything…"

"I'll be sure to let you know."

No sooner did the door clap shut than Drew snagged his shirt and trousers from the bedpost, eager to find out what had happened to Chase.

The woman scared the hell out of him.

How she'd managed to hide so quietly under the covers, he didn't know. But when she suddenly threw back the bedclothes, his heart jumped into his throat, and he went for his gun.

Fortunately, her gasp brought him to his senses before he could fire off a round. But it was a shaky hand he ran through his hair as he placed the Colt back down on the night table.

"Sorry, ma'am," he wheezed, sinking weakly down onto the edge of the mattress.

Damn, he'd forgotten how breathtaking she was. Or maybe now that he was sober, he saw her more clearly. Loose black ringlets trailed recklessly over her shoulders, which were deliciously bare except for the thin ribbons of lace holding up her camisole. Her skin glowed the shade of pressed olives, smooth and rich, as if someone had poured oil in just the right amount over her delicate bones. Her white cotton camisole was laced up over her bosom now, but he remembered glimpsing the sweet upper curve of her breasts. Fine, dark brows arched over deep whiskey-colored eyes, and her chin possessed the most flirtatious cleft. But that full, expressive, ruby mouth of hers and that tiny, seductive mole situated right beside it—that was what strained his drawers to bursting.

In fact, seeing her all breathless and fretful, her lips parted and sleep-swollen, Drew could easily talk himself out of chasing after that fool brother of his. Hell, Chase probably didn't have anything to do with the little girl that had gone missing anyway. His brother generally steered clear of children and other small creatures, always afraid he'd hurt them.

Chase had had way too much to drink last night was all. He'd likely just passed out in a field somewhere. He sure as hell didn't need Drew's help. Chase always landed on his feet. He was the sensible twin. If anyone was going to get into trouble, it was Drew. Besides, Chase had said it himself—this was *his* journey. Drew had only come along for the adventure.

As he lay back on his elbows and let his eyes drink their fill of the lovely lady before him, he thought the woman tucked delectably into his bed looked like the adventure of a lifetime.

CHAPTER 5

At the woman's earsplitting scream, Chase's heart vaulted into his throat like a spooked jackrabbit. Dropping the bandanna, he lunged forward and clapped a hand over her mouth, instantly cutting off her cries. He cast his glance wildly through the trees. If the woman had alerted anyone...

She wriggled free and took another swig of air. This time he caught her before she could make a sound, trapping her between his hands, one over her open mouth, the other behind her head.

But like a squirrel that's fought its way out of a basket trap more than once, she wasn't giving up. She bared her teeth and chomped down hard on his palm.

It hurt like hell. His blacksmith's calluses protected the meat of his hand from too much real damage. But her sharp teeth still managed to break open the skin where the barbed wire had already cut him. He released her like a hot poker, glancing in shock at his bleeding hand.

She spat on the ground, apparently averse to the taste of his blood.

Annoyed at his inability to control such a small creature, he snatched her by the front of her camisole and dragged her toward him until she dangled on her toes. Shards of gold shot through the serpentine green of her eyes, and her gaze still glimmered in rebellion.

He lowered his eyes. At the spot where he clenched her camisole, something peeped out above the lacy top—the yellowed pages of a book. He narrowed his gaze. What the hell was that?

Her eyes widened in panic. "No!"

Too irritated with her to consider the wisdom of his actions, he set her back on her feet, and then seized the corner of the book and withdrew it.

She gasped in disbelief, turning bright scarlet.

He scowled at the orange cover. *THE TRAIL HUNTERS OR MONOWANO THE SHAWNEE SPY*, it read. Under the title was a drawing of a native man holding hands with a white woman in the middle of a forest. The coincidence was unnerving.

With a disconcerted blink, he curled the soft-covered book and smacked the roll against his palm. "I only meant to let you get a drink of water." He sniffed. "But maybe I should just gag you again." He hoped she couldn't guess that his threat was as full of holes as a maiden's first basket. "What do you think? Do you think you can be silent?"

She swallowed hard. She might be stubborn, but her thirst apparently outweighed her desire to disobey him, so she gave him a nod of consent.

He waved her off and waited as she knelt beside the spring to get a drink. When she finished, her face and hair were wet, and droplets trickled down the front of her camisole.

"I'm going to drink now," he said. "You stay quiet."

She only stared at him, her face faintly mutinous. He

tucked her book inside his shirt, wound the end of the rope around his good hand to keep her on a short leash, and crouched beside the spring.

He was so thirsty and the water so sweet and cool that, for a moment, he almost forgot about the woman...until she spoke.

"They're coming for you, you know," she said, making him freeze mid-swallow. Her voice surprised him. It was soft and yet somehow far more powerful than her scream. It tickled his ears the way a rabbit fur blanket did, making his head buzz, warming his flesh. He realized instantly—and too late—that he should have kept her muzzled.

"They're coming for you, and when they find you," she gently reasoned, her voice a deceptively calm eddy over a current swirling with tension, "they'll kill you."

He let the rest of the water fall from his hand back into the spring. She wasn't telling him anything he didn't already know. But it was the last thing he wanted to hear. He glowered, hoping to silence her.

Still she rattled on, desperate to get words out before he shut her up. "If it's money you want, you won't get much if I'm—"

"Hush!" He narrowed his eyes in clear warning, to no avail.

She kept talking. "And if you hurt me, he'll pay you nothing."

This time he growled at her, using the snarl that sent his little sisters fleeing in terror.

She recoiled, but it seemed nothing would keep her quiet. "My father is not a patient man. The longer you keep me, the worse it'll be for you."

The only word Chase heard was "father."

"What?" He felt the hairs prickle at the back of his neck. "What did you say?"

"I said, my father is not a patient—"

"Your...father?"

"Yes. My father. Samuel Parker."

Chase suddenly felt numb.

Her brow creased into a puzzled frown. Then understanding slowly blossomed in her face. "You didn't know I was...? You didn't take me for the ransom? Then why..."

Suddenly the whole course of events struck Chase as a grand jest, like one *Xontehl-taw*, Trickster Coyote, might play upon a hapless hunter.

"Shit," he said, throwing his head back to stare askance at the treetops. He chuckled grimly, then blew out a long resigned sigh.

This was great. This was just great. The woman—no, *girl*—wasn't Parker's wife. She was his damned flesh and blood. And she figured he'd taken her for the ransom. He shook his head. The Great Spirit must truly wish for his death.

"You don't mean to..." she said softly, blanching, "to kill me, do you?"

He furrowed his brow. Of course he didn't mean to kill her. Then again, that *had* sort of been his intention when he'd carried her off in a drunken haze.

He shook his head. He must have been out of his mind to think he could somehow fix everything by taking a life for a life. Chase wasn't a killer. Hell, he couldn't even let his enemy's daughter go *thirsty*.

Confounded by conflicting emotions, he turned away, burrowing his hand into the spring, scooping water up over his face as if he could wash the uncomfortable truth from his eyes.

"Let me go," the girl suggested. "I'll say I...I took the horse and got lost. If you don't let me go, my father will chase you to the ends of—"

He stood up. He'd heard enough chatter. Besides, her words were only echoing his own uneasy thoughts. He took the few steps to snatch up the discarded gag and hunkered down beside her.

She scrambled backward. "Please. No. I'll be quiet. I won't say a word. I promise."

He shouldn't trust her. He knew that. In his experience, a promise meant nothing to white people.

Still, he was burdened by guilt. The girl's fear made him feel like a beast. He supposed he should have been accustomed to that. People always expected him to be dangerous. It was partly because of his blacksmith's build and partly because everyone compared him to his brother. Where Drew was a charmer, Chase always scared women. No matter how kind his intentions were, every frown, every growl, each too-rough gesture reinforced the misconception that he was a brutal man. It was his unfortunate curse.

And it was too late to fix that now. The girl had already decided he was a savage. He might as well act like one.

He twisted the bandanna in his hands and started toward her again.

Unfortunately, he made the mistake of looking into her eyes. In a matter of moments, the deed could have been accomplished, and they could have ridden on in silence. But when she gazed at him—her big eyes all dewy and helpless—he melted like an iron billet over the fire.

Counter to all common sense and his better judgment, he withdrew. He knotted the bandanna around his own throat instead, which was probably a fitting gesture, considering the noose he'd soon wear if he didn't start using his wits.

"No more talking," he warned as he lifted her to her feet, fully knowing she'd be unable to comply. In his experience, no woman could remain silent for more than two breaths.

But to his amazement, as they rode on, she made not a peep. They traveled across increasingly wet ground, following the trickling spring until it disappeared underground and emerged again as a tiny stream. He tied the girl's leash to a tree so he could pick creek lettuce, bracken fern, and wild onions. It was too dangerous to build a fire. He didn't know for sure, but it was likely there were miners on the main creek who'd be able to spot their smoke. They'd just have to make do with what they could eat raw.

The girl didn't like the food much. She wrinkled her nose as he hunkered down and tucked bites of fern and lettuce into her mouth. But true to her word, she didn't complain. She even choked down a few wild onions, though they made her eyes water. It was a shame the blackberries weren't ripe yet. She'd probably like those.

Damn. What was he thinking? He wasn't supposed to be making her happy. He was only supposed to be keeping her alive.

With a self-derisive snort, he scanned the sky. The sunlight was fading fast. What remained was obscured by a steel-gray blanket of ominous rain clouds. They'd have to wind their way through the gorge before the spring storm began and the trail turned into a muddy mire.

The girl shivered. The air didn't seem that cold to him, but he came from a cooler clime. He also wasn't a pampered white woman accustomed to living indoors. He supposed that thin wisp of a garment didn't do much to keep her warm. She probably wasn't even wearing anything under it.

The thought made his throat close.

He must have been staring at her, for the girl drew her knees in defensively. He cursed under his breath. They had to go now...before the squall struck...before darkness fell...and before he started thinking too much about all that delicate white skin.

Claire shuddered again, but it wasn't from the cold. She'd seen something in the half-breed's gaze, something perilous, like the flicker of a spark inside a black coal.

Not speaking was unbearable. Not knowing his thoughts, not understanding his intentions was sheer torture.

What did he want with her? He hadn't even known she was Samuel Parker's daughter, for heaven's sake, so he must not have taken her for the ransom money. He'd seen to her hunger thus far, so he didn't mean for her to die…at least not yet.

In her dime novels, the Red-Skins sometimes stole white women and children for the sport of it. But Claire had never thought that was very believable. Yoema had argued that the native people were too busy trying to keep food in their bellies to go riling up white men just for fun.

Perhaps he'd stolen her to be his servant. She'd read that Indians did such things, raiding neighbor tribes for slaves. If that was the case, he was in for a disappointment. She'd had maids all her life, and a cook prepared meals for the whole ranch. She knew nothing about keeping a house.

The strange glimmer in the man's eyes, however, sent her thoughts coursing along an altogether different path. Maybe he'd abducted her to be his…wife. She gulped, trying not to think about that terrifying prospect.

Regardless of what she'd let him believe, she didn't really expect her father to come riding to her rescue. After all, she'd left behind that confounded letter. Her father would assume she'd run away. He'd never guess she'd been kidnapped.

Gagging down the last wad of half-chewed fern, she tried to gather enough spit to wash away the nasty taste of the onion. She sure hoped the half-breed knew the difference between provender and poison. This couldn't be his usual fare. No man could grow shoulders that wide…arms that thick…a back that broad…feeding on weeds and roots.

Claire had assumed they were stopping here for the night, but her captor apparently wished to ride on. As he lifted her once more onto the horse, she bit back a groan. The flesh of her inner thighs, protected by only a single layer of cotton, was chafed and sore.

How much farther did he intend to ride? A storm was headed their way. If they didn't find shelter soon, they'd be drenched.

She frowned, puzzled, as he began to ride northeast, straight into the canyon. He clearly wasn't familiar with the territory or he'd realize that the deep gorges below Paradise were crawling with miners. Maybe she wouldn't need to be rescued by her father after all.

But the man was clever enough to ride under cover of the thick broadleaf trees that carpeted the valley and at a safe distance from the creek, where the dredging operations were. He also chose to follow the more westerly fork, which was less populated. The canyon walls rose higher and higher as they rode on. When the last of the sun's glow faded from the silvery cloudbank and the first tenuous drops of rain spattered the rocky path, Claire spotted their destination. High up on the cliff wall was a row of niches like giant black spider eyes looking down upon them. Caves.

With a cluck of his tongue, the half-breed urged the horse tentatively forward across the uneven rubble until the rocks grew too large to navigate. He dismounted and lifted Claire down, then led the stallion slowly and carefully up the side of the steep mountain along passes no wider than the horse's belly. So terrified was Claire along the perilous trail—with her hands bound behind her, her only lifeline a rope between her waist and the man's fist, and the rain softening the ground to slick mud—that she noticed neither the cold nor the cuts on her feet.

Somehow they made it. Somehow, by the time the rain began to fall in earnest, bombarding the earth with punishing force, they reached a deep, dry cave, tall enough to shelter even the horse.

Heaving a sigh of exhaustion, Claire tossed her head, splattering raindrops everywhere. Her short hair was tiresome. It constantly fell in her eyes. It also afforded her no modesty, she realized, blushing as she realized the downpour had left her camisole completely transparent. Lord, she might as well be naked.

Desperately embarrassed, she tried to hide behind the horse. But the half-breed, annoyed by her incessant tugging on the rope, pulled her forward again.

His nostrils flared once, and though his gaze traveled over her swiftly, he missed nothing. That strange fire blazed in his eyes again, and she bit back an angry sob.

As quickly as it had bloomed, however, the menacing flame in his gaze was extinguished. The man looked away and, raking a hand roughly through his drenched locks, stomped the water from his boots. He pulled her waterlogged dime novel out from inside his shirt and tossed it onto the cave floor.

She closed her eyes, trying not to think about her utter helplessness. Somehow she had to get away from her captor. His strength, his savagery, and that dangerous light in his eyes spelled nothing but trouble for her.

She shuddered once, drawing his gaze again. This time he cursed, dropping his end of the rope. He spun her around and used his knife to cut her hands free.

She rubbed her numb wrists and turned to face him, shielding herself from his view as best she could with her arms.

The man's mouth twisted. Muttering something unintelligible, he quickly unfastened the buttons on his damp shirt, wrenching it from his shoulders. He stepped forward, averting his eyes, and snapped the garment in front of her.

It took Claire a moment to understand what he was offering, partly because the last thing she expected from him was kindness and partly because she was reeling from the sight of his suddenly bare chest.

Thick ridges of muscle crossed his ribs and swelled his shoulders. No hair marred the sleek perfection of his form, and though the outside light grew pale, his skin seemed to glow golden. His arms appeared as if sculpted of dense clay, and the powerful breadth of his chest accentuated the narrowness of his hips, where his trousers hung low, revealing his navel.

A strange and sudden heat—not quite anxiety, not quite shame—suffused her. The breath caught in her throat, and her heart staggered a beat.

He impatiently snapped the shirt again, growling, "Turn around."

She did. He dropped the heavy shirt over her shoulders. It was wet, too, but at least it afforded her some modesty. She slipped her arms through the sleeves, which hung far past her fingertips, and attempted to button the front, but her fingers were too stiff with cold to perform the task. Instead, she awkwardly tucked the shirt into the rope around her waist.

When she turned back, the half-breed was seeing to the horse, lifting the animal's hooves to check for rocks. She swallowed hard. The muscles of the man's back were as lean and solid as those of the prize stallion.

He glanced at her once, then again, and finally a third time. With a huff of exasperation, he let Thunder's hoof down, sheathed his knife, and strode toward her. Undoing her sloppy handiwork, he removed the noose from around her waist, and then proceeded to fasten the shirt buttons from the bottom up.

She bit the inside of her cheek as his naked torso filled her vision and his fingers brushed far too close to her person. It was incredibly bold of him to bare his chest in front of her. Not even her father's ranch hands would do such a thing. It was improper. Indecent.

Claire held her breath. Despite the chill of the twilight,

heat seemed to emanate from the man before her. She felt a flush rise in her cheeks. Finally, unable to abide staring at his chest any longer, she stole a glance up at his face. His chin was shadowed with stubble, and though his mouth curved downwards, it appeared softer somehow, less cruel. His cheekbones were high, his jaw was square, and his dark brows furrowed over deep-set eyes. In fact, except for his bristled jaw and the telling curl of his jet-black hair, he possessed all the features of native blood.

While she studied his face, his eyes lifted to hers. Suddenly, she stared into depths so fathomless and enveloping that she felt momentarily lost. Time halted as her soul was drawn into the circle of his eyes like a pail lowered into a deep well.

Then the horse whickered, and the moment vanished. The half-breed stepped away from her, collecting his rope. She wrapped her arms defensively about her waist, swiftly dropping her gaze.

The man guided Thunder away from the mouth of the cave, using the rope to tether the stallion to a sharp outcropping of rock.

The rain made soft music as it continued to pelt the ground, and its pewter curtain faded in the dying light. Soon it would grow dark. Claire scanned the jagged walls. She wondered if she was better off knowing or *not* knowing what else lived in the cave.

"Try to get some sleep."

She whipped around, startled again by the man's unabashed half-nakedness. In her agitated state, the last thing she was prepared to do was sleep.

"May I speak?" she inquired.

After quick consideration, he dropped his gaze. "Nope."

"I won't shout," she reasoned. "No one can hear us up here anyway."

"No," he bit out.

Muttering an angry curse, she flounced off toward the entrance of the cave.

He came up behind her, catching her elbow with such speed and stealth that she cried out in surprise. Then he hauled her toward the back of the cave.

Of course, she thought. He didn't want her signaling anyone below.

Where did he expect her to sleep then? If he'd let her speak, she might ask him. Instead, she cast her glance about the cave, wondering where she was supposed to bed down.

"Here," he said to her unasked question, pointing to a reasonably flat stretch of dry rock.

She didn't bother arguing with him that she'd more likely fall asleep on a bed of nails than in a cave with a half-naked half-breed. Instead, she lowered herself to the cave floor and curled into a ball on her side, facing the wall and closing her eyes to shut out the image of masculine muscles imprinted on her brain.

She stiffened and clenched her eyes all the tighter when she felt the man stretch out beside her, far closer than decency allowed.

She wasn't about to fall asleep, not while he lay so near and not while lurid stories of Red-Skin abductions and enslavement kept circling in her head.

She was going to have to make a break for it. That was all there was to it. She had to get out of the savage's grasp. She didn't know for certain whether rescue was on the way. But no self-respecting dime novel hero ever waited for someone else to save the day.

Eventually, the man's breathing slowed as he sank into a deep sleep. Outside, the rain ceased and the clouds dissipated.

Blessed starlight flooded the mouth of the cave, as if showing Claire the way out.

Her knee popped as she pressed herself up. She was sure she'd awaken him, but his breath continued, slow and steady.

He'd left her dime novel at her feet. She tucked the precious book into her camisole. Then, edging forward with painstaking stealth, she skirted past the dozing man and across the cave floor. Finally she untied Thunder, leading him quietly to the entrance of the cave.

The way down the mountain appeared less treacherous now. The rough edges of rock and crevice seemed muted, softened by the moon's glow. Distance was difficult to measure in the deceptive light. What had taken an hour to climb looked like a short jaunt to the valley floor. On the ascent, she'd been far too fearful to pay attention to the route the man chose. She'd have to rely upon her own judgment for the path down.

She took the first few paces out of the cave. The mire was slick under her feet. She experienced a pang of doubt as her heel slipped sideways, knocking a smattering of pebbles over the edge. Regaining her footing, she took a breath to steady her nerves and continued forward, guiding the horse along the narrow trail.

The ripped ruffle of her petticoat trailed through the mud. The soles of her feet were bruised by sharp rocks. Strings of her chopped hair hung in her eyes. But she didn't care. Soon she'd be out of her hulking captor's clutches.

A wisp of cloud left behind by the storm veiled the moon's round face for a moment, obscuring the landscape, delaying her. When it cleared, she clucked softly to urge the horse forward, wincing as his heavy hooves seemed to pound upon the wet sod.

She'd just reached the first switchback down the hill when she skidded on a mossy patch of ground and lost her balance.

Cartwheeling her arms, she came down hard on her bottom and slid. Only Thunder's rope, clasped tightly in her fist, kept her from slipping down the hillside onto the sharp granite rocks below. For an awful instant, she hung by the white-knuckled fingers of one hand, biting back cries of panic. Her rushing pulse filled her ears as gravel trickled down beside her like a vicious taunt.

For once, Claire appreciated Thunder's stubbornness, for if he hadn't fought the lead, she would have pulled him down with her, and they both would have skidded down the slope. Instead, clinging to the rope with sheer determination, she managed to gather her feet under her and scramble back onto the trail.

She flopped onto her back in relief, lying there for a full minute, all the while wondering if she'd made a mistake attempting such a daring escape. But what other choice did she have? She couldn't overpower the muscled giant, who could carry her in one arm without even breathing heavily. So she had to rely on outwitting him.

Wiping dots of sweat from her brow, she rose on trembling legs and stroked Thunder's muzzle to calm him. Then she stepped carefully forward, checking each patch of ground like a skater testing thin ice. It might take longer this way, but at least they'd have a better chance of making it safely to the valley floor.

The downpour had done more damage to the path than Claire noticed at first. Great ruts were gouged into the vertical wall by rivulets of rain. What footprints they'd left on the way up were obliterated in the clay. Silt blanketed the bases of the sparse brush that clung to the hillside. And whole sections of the already constricted trail were undermined and washed away.

It seemed like it took an eternity, but by some miracle she managed to coax Thunder along the storm-damaged path, almost all the way to the base of the mountain. Unfortunately, with less than a dozen feet more to descend, the trail dwindled away to nothing.

Claire cursed under her breath. She couldn't stop now. She could almost taste freedom. One way or another, she had to get to the bottom.

Pressing her back against the muddy wall, she managed to sidle along a spare stretch of eroded ground to a rocky landing. But when she coaxed the stallion to follow, he danced backward, reluctant to cross the too narrow passage.

"Come on," she whispered, tugging lightly on the rope, "you can do it."

He tossed his head, refusing.

"Come on, Thunder," she begged. "Just a little farther." She whistled very softly and clucked to him.

He pranced tentatively forward, then back.

"That's a good boy. Come on."

He tested the surface with his front hooves, crowding them onto the path. Satisfied the ground was solid, he bounded forward. But the stance of his back legs was too wide. His right leg crumbled the loose soil, the earth fell away, and he stepped into empty air.

Thunder gave a startled snort, and as Claire watched helplessly, the steed tried to gain a purchase on the slick mud, to no avail. While she looked on with mouth agape, the great stallion slid on his side down the rest of the slope.

It happened so quickly, there was nothing Claire could do. If she hadn't let go of the rope, she would have followed him down.

To her relief, somehow Thunder managed to get his legs under him. But no sooner did his hooves touch the ground than he scrambled up, shivered once—none the worse for his slippery slide—and shot off like a jail-breaker back through the canyon pass.

"What the...?" Claire watched in frustration and fury, her mouth agape. She didn't dare raise her voice to yell at the despicable deserter. But she couldn't sputter out enough vile names under her breath for the disloyal beast who'd abandoned her without a backward glance.

Now she'd be forced to escape on foot. And there was no time to waste. She gathered her muddy skirts in one hand and prepared to slide down by the same route Thunder had taken. She never saw the man's shadow slipping down the mountain. By the time she noticed, he was already charging toward her like a wild buffalo.

CHAPTER 6

hase had no time for the wide-eyed woman. He had to retrieve the horse. Hell, without the horse...

He scowled and scaled down the mountain as fast as he could, half sprinting, half sliding. When he reached Claire, who hunkered down into a defensive ball, he leaped over her and clambered to the bottom, chasing after the runaway stallion.

But the barn-sour beast was long gone. And there was nothing he could do. There wasn't a man alive who could run as fast as a homesick horse.

"Ling-miwhxiy!" He kicked hard at the dirt, spitting epithets after the beast, and then finally turned back in defeat, raking his hands through his hair and pacing off his fury.

Trickster Coyote must be rolling with laughter now. The woman had just put a huge wrinkle in Chase's plans to return her in a timely fashion.

Damn it all! He needed to get her home. The longer he kept her, the worse it would get.

The woman was frightened.

He was racked by guilt.

Her father was probably half crazy with worry.

And now that she'd made a rash escape attempt and lost the horse, putting things to rights was going to take even longer.

He shook his head. He guessed he should have let the woman in on his plans. Maybe then she wouldn't have interfered with them. And he supposed he should have realized she'd try to flee. But he hadn't expected her to have so much fight left in her. She'd looked so frail and helpless last night, shivering like a wet colt in his oversized shirt. It hadn't occurred to him that beneath that soft exterior hid the spirit of a warrior.

He dropped his shoulders in resignation and narrowed his eyes at the mountain. He'd be damned if the woman wasn't still trying to run off, scrambling down the muddy hill in the opposite direction.

He had to admire her initiative and her moxie, but she was headed for trouble. Without the horse, he doubted she could find her way home. White women weren't used to surviving in the wilderness. If she didn't die of hunger, she'd probably get herself killed by a mountain lion or a rattlesnake.

He couldn't leave her to her own devices. It was his fault she was in the middle of nowhere. It was his obligation to get her safely home.

Fortunately, it wouldn't be hard to catch her. She was a tiny thing. He could easily outrun and overpower her. So he crossed his arms over his chest, in no hurry, and waited for her to tucker herself out.

She flashed him a few fretful glances, continuing her descent until she'd almost reached the bottom of the hill.

Then he sighed and walked patiently toward her.

Claire knew she was doomed. Without Thunder, she didn't stand a chance against the half-breed. He was bigger, stronger, and faster than she was. But she refused to surrender. After all, Kit Carson wouldn't surrender. Davy Crockett wouldn't surrender. Buckskin Bill...

Her eyes widened as she saw he was coming for her, walking as if he had all the time in the world, which was more unnerving than if he'd come at a run. Giving a little squeak of panic, she redoubled her efforts, resorting to scrambling away on her hands and knees when she took a tumble in the mud.

She'd just reached the valley floor when she was suddenly hauled up by the scruff of her neck like a stray kitten. She gasped, flailing against her captor, hoping to twist free. But all her squirming didn't seem to affect his grip in the least.

Forgetting her promise, she sucked in a breath to yell for help, in case some stray miner was in hearing distance. But he must have anticipated that, for he quickly shifted her in his arms and buried her face against his chest, muffling her cry.

To her alarm, she got a mouthful of bare flesh. She sputtered and beat at his restraining arms, horrified to be in such a shocking position. But it did no good. Smothered against his body, her shrieks of outrage came out as barely audible squeals. And the louder she tried to scream, the tighter he clutched her.

Realizing he wouldn't let her go until she stopped screaming, she forced herself to cease. But that made her even more aware of their impropriety.

Never had she been in such intimate contact with a man. Where her mouth pressed against his taut muscle, his skin was distressingly warm and real. As he continued to confine her there, she found to her horror that she could feel his chest rising and falling with each deep breath. Her own rapid breathing moistened his skin, and she could smell...and taste...the faint salt of his sweat. It was...mortifying.

Just about the time she was sure she could endure no

more, he finally spoke. His voice resonated in his chest and sounded almost as ragged as she felt. "Are you going to be quiet now?"

She nodded, eager to be out of his embrace.

"You promise?"

She nodded once more.

Slowly, tentatively, he loosened his grip on her, though he kept one hand bunched in the shirt at the back of her neck. She pulled back, and her lips released from his chest—almost, to her humiliation, like a kiss.

"You're lucky you didn't get yourself killed," he scolded in a harsh whisper. "Don't run off again."

She might have promised not to make noise, but she hadn't promised not to fight him. She renewed her struggles, pounding at his chest and kicking at his legs. She might as well have been battling a bull. The half-breed only grunted and hoisted her up again, leaving her swinging at empty air.

He muttered something in his own tongue and then hefted her across his shoulder, holding her there by gripping her backside in a most indecent manner. She would have fought her way free, but just then he began trudging back up the steep rise, and she didn't dare upset his balance for fear of sending them both down the mountain.

By the time they finally reached the cave, she wasn't sure if she was more blanched white with fright or flushed red with shame at his cavalier handling.

The minute he set her on her feet, she fled to the back of the cave. She was furious...with him, with the horse, with herself. This had been her big chance to escape, and she'd failed. Worse, she'd been subjected to unspeakable humiliation at her captor's hands.

Seething with anger, she wrenched his shirt from her shoulders, spitting a curse under her breath with each button she unfastened. She was completely flustered and disgusted by the brazen savage, and she didn't want anything to do with him. She didn't care if she froze half to death—she never wanted to see...or, God forbid, touch...the half-naked half-breed again.

She wadded up the shirt and tossed it at him. He caught it in one hand. Then she crouched in the dark, watching his massive silhouette as he crossed the passageway, and waited for him to put the shirt on. To her consternation, he didn't.

She wondered what he'd do to her. Would he punish her for losing the horse? Would he tie her up so she couldn't flee? Would he subject her to some new degradation?

In the end, he did nothing. He didn't even give her a tongue-lashing. All he did was tuck the wadded shirt beneath his head and stretch out at the mouth of the cave, where she'd have to climb over him to escape.

She rocked back onto her bottom and hugged her knees, thoroughly miserable. Curse it all, she couldn't even escape properly. She withdrew the soggy dime novel from her camisole again and plopped it down beside her, glaring at the heroine on the cover. Claire was no intrepid Maude Burland—that was certain. Her books made it sound so easy to outwit villains. Indeed, Claire was beginning to question the accuracy of the stories.

To add insult to injury, within moments she heard her abductor drawing in the deep, untroubled breaths of slumber, as comfortable on the hard stone as she was in her feather bed at home and as sure of her captivity as a cat with a mouse trapped under its paw.

She dropped her chin onto her knees and scowled at the cave floor. Gradually, as the minutes ticked by, her anger began to diminish. But soon other feelings crept in to replace the anger—all-too-familiar feelings of defeat and disappointment.

Could she do nothing right? Sometimes she felt like a

complete failure. She'd never been able to please her father, and now even *she* was disappointed in herself.

Why wasn't she as brave and capable as the characters in her books? Why wasn't she fearless, flawless, and tough as beef jerky? Dime novel heroes never lost their horses. They didn't bungle their escapes. They didn't cry when their mothers fell ill and...

Her throat tightened. Yoema had been the one person Claire could please. Her Indian mother had loved her for who she was. A tear formed in the corner of her eye as painful memories of Yoema surfaced, memories Claire could share with no one—memories of Yoema's cheerful black eyes and healing hands, of her intriguing stories, her love of animals, her deep respect for nature. And, as on so many nights of late, the memories kept Claire awake.

Her chin began to quiver. Yoema had always sung her to sleep. Without that familiar song, without those nurturing arms and that gentle voice, sleep lost all its comfort.

She closed her eyes and tried to imagine the Indian woman beside her, brushing her hair, the long hair that Claire had cut off as abruptly as the old woman had been cut from her life. She heard the melody winding around her ears in the darkness.

The tune started softly in Claire's throat, almost of its own accord, thin and fragile against the heavy night. She mouthed the simple words around the lump of sorrow thickening her voice.

"Unno winno, unno winno, unno winno."

Though the song saddened her and a single hot tear made its way down her cheek, she continued to sing...unaware that the half-breed had awakened.

Chase felt a prickling sensation, like a spider creeping across his flesh, as the faint song pierced the black night and his memory. It was a Konkow song, one his father had sung to him when he was a boy. The voice was weak, broken by soft sobs, but he still recognized the tune and the murmur of the words.

As the melody continued, echoing eerily against the cave walls, the breath caught suddenly in his chest. What if it came from a *chindin*, a ghost, using the white woman's voice to speak to him in a tongue he understood? Could his grandmother's spirit be calling to him through the woman?

With nerves stretched as taut as a curing hide, he twisted toward the girl and snarled, "Hush!"

She gasped. He'd startled her. But at least the haunting music faded from the cave.

"Why do you sing that song?" he hissed, his voice harsh with alarm.

She sniffled. "Leave me alone."

He jumped to his feet and stalked toward her. He heard her scuttle back, but there was only rock wall behind her. He lunged forward in the darkness, grabbing for whatever he could reach. She shrieked, but his own fear made him insensitive to hers. He wadded the front of her camisole in his fist, yanking her toward him.

"How do you know that song?" he demanded. Unlike his flippant brother, Chase believed in the spirits. He'd received visions all his life, and he knew their power. The white woman couldn't possibly know the song she sang. It must have come through her from the world beyond.

The girl shivered in his grasp, like a captured fledgling. "M-my mother sang it."

He ground his teeth. "You're lying."

"No." He felt her fluttering breath upon his face.

"That's not the song of a white woman."

"No. My...my Konkow mother sang it."

He tightened his fist in the fabric, drawing her nose to nose with him. Konkow mother? What kind of fool did she think he was? Claire Parker was no half-breed. Chase should know. Native blood was impossible to hide. This woman had wide green eyes and sun-bright hair, delicate bones and skin the color of a white deer.

He whispered the words into her face. "Konkow mother? You have no Konkow mother."

To his amazement, she didn't argue with him. Instead, her chin trembled at his accusation, and she began to weep.

Her soft sobs caught at his heart, and his superstitious dread quickly dissolved. Whatever spirits might have lurked in the cave had probably fled at the sound of the woman's weeping. He should release her and leave her to her tears.

Yet he couldn't bring himself to let go of her. She might completely collapse if he did. He wondered what troubled her so much. Then he smirked in self-mockery. *Aside* from the fact that she'd been abducted from her home, dragged through the hills, and forced to sleep in a cave with a stranger.

"Why are you crying?" he demanded, wincing as his voice came out harsher than he intended.

His words only inspired a new flood of tears, and he cursed that gift he had for frightening ladies and babies. He loosened his fist in her camisole. But to his amazement, before he could retreat to a safe distance, she seized his hand between her two, clinging to him as if he were a bark canoe in a raging river.

"I did have a mother," she insisted with a sob. "I did. I had a Konkow mother. She taught me that song." She held fast to his hand now, squeezing it, her words rushing out like a babbling spring that must hurry over the rocks before it's swallowed up. "She sang the song to me every night. It was a song of her tribe. She—"

He snatched his hand back with a curse. He saw clearly now. The woman was trying to trick him. She hoped to gain his confidence, to convince him that she wasn't a white woman, not the enemy, not the daughter of Samuel Parker, but a daughter of his father's people, the Konkow.

He shook his head. "You're as white as your *kilwe* father." She may not know the Hupa word for evil, but she couldn't mistake the tone of his voice.

"She wasn't my real mother," she admitted breathlessly. "My real mother died when I was a little girl."

He attempted to ignore her chatter, but she clutched his arms and continued hammering at his thoughts like a woodpecker at an oak trunk.

"But she cared for me like a daughter. She told me stories and sang songs for me. She healed me when I was sick. Yoema was the only—"

He sucked the breath hard between his teeth and knocked her hands free.

Her voice sounded deceptively innocent. "What is it? What's wrong?"

His heart pounded, and his breath rattled in the deathly still of the cave. She knew his grandmother by name. Was it possible? Had his grandmother been the woman's personal slave?

"Don't speak that name," he muttered.

"Yoema? But she—"

He lunged forward, grabbing what he found of her person to shake her. "Do not speak my grandmother's name!"

She gasped. After a moment of breathless silence, she murmured, "Your grandmother?"

Chase could feel the woman's rapid pulse under his fingers, for he'd caught her by the throat.

"But how can that..." Her unfinished sentence hung between them as tight and deadly as a drawn bow. Then he felt her swallow beneath his thumb. "Oh. *Oh.* If she's your..." She let out her breath. "Then you're... You must be... You're one of the...the Two-Sons."

She said it just like that, Two-Sons, as if it were one word, under her breath, an unutterable curse, just the way his Konkow grandmother would have spoken it.

To the Konkow people, it *was* a curse. It was the reason his parents had left their village to journey north to Hupa. Twins were an anomaly among the Konkows, unnatural and dangerous. Though his parents never spoke of it, Drew and he knew what they were. They also knew they had cheated death. If they hadn't been carried away to Hupa as infants, either one or both of them would have been killed. Such was the Konkow way.

And because the boys were essentially dead to her, their grandmother would never have learned their names.

But apparently she hadn't forgotten them. She'd spoken of the Two-Sons to this white woman. Despite their exile, she'd held her grandsons in her memory. The thought touched his heart, even as it widened the crack of sorrow there.

"It's true, isn't it?" the woman murmured. "You *are* one of the Two-Sons."

He didn't answer.

"The twins who had a Konkow father and a white mother," she said.

He didn't answer.

"Who traveled far away to the north."

She obviously knew all about him. There was no point in denying it.

He grunted in confirmation.

She nodded. "Then there's something I've waited a long while to ask you." She pried his hand from her neck. "Where the *hell* have you been?"

CHAPTER 7

Chase flinched. Like an expert hunter, the woman had found the gap in his defenses and shot an arrow straight into his heart.

"She said you would return," she bit out. "She believed you and your brother were coming home." She punctuated her angry words by poking him in the chest. "But you never did. I began to think there were no Two-Sons at all, that she'd made them up."

He seized her hand to stop her poking, then lowered his brows in a defensive scowl as he growled, "We were never told our grandmother was alive."

Her voice was bitter. "It never occurred to you to try to find out? For years she waited for you," she choked out. "She died, waiting for you."

"Now wait just a damned minute," Chase argued. "It was *your* world that destroyed my grandmother. You and your father killed her."

"What!"

He cursed at her in the Hupa tongue, then bit out, "You

don't think I know what your father did?" A confusion of emotions—fear and anger and despair and regret—swirled together, melting like ore in a crucible, and poured out in an unstoppable stream. "Taking my grandmother from her people, from her family, keeping her as his slave." His ragged whisper broke under the weight of his pain. "The rest of her people, *my* people—her husband, her sisters, her son—he discarded like waste."

"That's a lie!"

"*Qutxut!* It's true! While my grandmother was forced to slave for you," he said, spitting derisively at the ground beside her, unable to temper his bitterness or silence his tongue, "her *own* young son, her *real* son, was left motherless."

"You don't know what you're talking about."

"*Nida-nonuntse!*" He didn't want to hear her denials. What had happened to young Hintsuli, to his people, was an atrocity. Someone had to answer for it. "My grandmother's spirit is uneasy. She demands *lenulya*. You know this word. It's written in your Bible. *Lenulya,* vengeance." Still clutching her hand, he moved close and seared her face with his whisper. "*Lenulya* is mine."

The half-breed's harsh words burned Claire's skin like a brand, marking her with deadly promise. But she wasn't afraid. Despite his massive paw swallowing up her hand and his hot breath upon her cheek, now that she knew who he was, how could she be afraid of him?

"No," she said. "You're wrong. She loved me. She told me you would come, and she said it would be a *good* thing. She said you would fix the past and—"

He released her abruptly, and his loud exhale filled the cave like the steam from a locomotive. Without a word, he walked back to the mouth of the cave.

Claire remained in the shadows, not moving, not speaking, for a long while. Where on earth the half-breed had heard such horrid things about her father, she didn't know. But he seemed to believe them with all his heart.

Claire knew otherwise. Samuel Parker wouldn't enslave anyone. He might be stern and unsentimental, but he was a decent man, a fair man. He may not have loved Yoema like Claire did, but he was always kind to her. He would never have separated the dear woman from her family. The man was mistaken. There was nothing to avenge.

"My father is a good man," she called out to him as he bedded down again at the cave entrance. "We all cared for Yoe-, your grandmother. If you take me home, you'll see—" She stopped, suddenly remembering that, for all intents and purposes, she no longer had a home. She'd run away. There was nothing left for her at the Parker Ranch.

In fact, now that she thought about it, she realized that returning home was out of the question. If she went back, she'd have to face her father's disappointment. And she'd have to deal with her hot-tempered fiancé, Frank. He wouldn't take kindly to Claire's breaking off their engagement.

As odd as it was, she might be better off casting her lot with this stranger. He wasn't exactly a stranger, after all. He was the flesh and blood of her beloved Yoema. Indeed, he even looked a bit like his grandmother. A tiny smile touched her lips. He had the same high cheekbones, dark scowl, and sparkling eyes.

If only he weren't so full of hatred and vengeance, Claire thought as she lay down on the hard cave floor, she might actually welcome his companionship. After all, she had no one else in the world.

By the time Chase awoke, the sun was just beginning to run its golden fingers over the leafy tresses of the trees on the far ridge. He pushed up onto one elbow and glanced at the back of the cave to make sure his captive was still captive.

She was asleep, huddled into a ball in her mud-caked white camisole. Her hair stuck out at odd angles. Her face was smudged with dirt. But he'd be damned if she still wasn't as pretty and delicate as a pale butterfly. Looking at her sweet face, he regretted his harsh words of last night. He'd let anger get the best of him. He'd been upset about the lost stallion, riled up about the march, and jittery about his grandmother's ghost. The woman had hit a nerve when she'd asked where he'd been all these years.

She was right to wonder. It was a mystery, and Chase didn't much like mysteries. Word had been sent from Samuel Parker to Nome Cult the day that his grandmother died. But what about before? Why had his Uncle Hintsuli known nothing about her captivity at the Parker Ranch? Why had the family believed for so many years that she was dead?

It was too late for those questions, he supposed. It had all happened long ago. Even Claire couldn't really be blamed. She'd been a young child when her father enslaved his grandmother. She may have never even heard of the march. It wasn't the sort of story a father would tell to his little girl, especially when he was the villain of the story.

Chase only hoped he could keep a better rein on his temper today than Claire had had on the horse last night.

The truth was the troublesome little lady had put Chase in real danger now, letting the horse go free. No longer able to rely on outrunning their pursuers, Chase had to try to outsmart them. The sooner they lit out, the better.

He called out softly. "Woman."

She slept.

"Miss Parker."

Still she slept.

He rose on his haunches. "Claire."

She stirred, then yawned, then stretched. He caught a glimpse of one long, lovely leg before she tucked it quickly back under her skirts.

"Time to go," he grunted, tying his shirt sleeves around his waist.

She sat up with a sleepy frown. "Go where? Where are you taking me?"

He didn't know how to answer her, so he didn't bother. He just waved her forward. "Come on."

She crossed her arms. "Why?"

He scowled. She'd certainly woken up in a mulish mood. And now that she knew who he was, she didn't seem quite so afraid of him. He wasn't sure that was a good thing. "Because I said so."

She thrust out her stubborn chin. "And what if I won't come, grandson of Yoema?"

He growled. Now she was baiting him. And she was being ridiculous. The woman was half his size, and she was cornered in the cave. She must know he wouldn't hesitate to toss her over his shoulder again.

He hopped up to his feet and took two steps forward.

Her eyes widened, and her arms fell out of their fold. "All right, I'll come." She snatched up her precious water-warped book, shot to her feet, and almost bumped her head on the roof of the cave. "But I want you to know I'm not coming willingly."

He arched a brow at her. That much was obvious. "We have far to go. I can carry you, or you can—"

"I'll walk on my own, thank you," she primly announced, tucking the book into her camisole and picking her way toward him.

He extended his hand, which she ignored. But he wasn't about to lose his valuable hostage in a landslide, so he insisted on taking hold of her elbow as they descended.

Once they reached the bottom, he grabbed her by the

wrist and pulled her hastily along the pass. There was no time to waste. Samuel Parker's posse had probably picked up their scent by now.

Claire refused to be intimidated. This Two-Son might be as big and surly as a grizzly, bristling and growling and snapping at her, but he didn't frighten her anymore. Yoema had spoken often to Claire about her vision, the one in which the lost twins returned to Paradise, healing the past and making the circle whole again. And if Yoema believed that was a good thing, it must be so.

Still, as he began hauling her at breakneck speed past stands of toyon and redbud, through nettles, star thistle, and what she was sure was poison oak, her mood soured. She wondered if Yoema had misinterpreted her vision and the heroic role of the Two-Sons in it.

For one thing, Yoema's grandson didn't seem very gallant. He was nothing like the heroes in her books. Those heroes didn't have smoldering black gazes. They didn't travel in stony silence. They didn't wrap their hands possessively around the heroines' arms. And they wouldn't dream of venturing out of doors without a proper shirt.

Dime novel heroes were kind and sweet. Their noble deeds often moved Claire to sigh in adoration. This man with his fierce, wild, unpredictable, savage, reckless ways made her cheeks burn and her heart race.

Fortunately, at the moment, she was too busy keeping an eye on the path to spare more than an occasional glance at his half-naked body. But his shocking immodesty was never far from her thoughts.

As they trudged higher into the mountains, the oaks gave way to scrub pines. Buckbrush slapped at her ankles. Manzanita scraped her arms. Her eyes filled with grit. Her feet grew numb.

By midday, she was exhausted. She gasped at the stitch in

her side. The only thing that kept her from falling into a dead stupor were the man's grip on her and their unrelenting gait.

When they came to a grassy break in the wood, they stopped at last. The instant he released her, a small voice inside her told her to run—run like the wind. But she was too tired to even answer it. She collapsed onto the moist ground, careless of her already filthy clothes. There she remained, as docile as a kitten, and then watched with mild interest as he began to creep stealthily across the sun-speckled meadow.

His knife was unsheathed. His gaze was focused. His movements were slow and graceful, like the tomcat that stalked mice in her father's barn. He was a natural hunter, she realized, watching the muscles of his lean torso tense as he stole through the grass. Then, before she could blink, he raised his arm and, with a flick of his wrist, sent the knife sailing forward.

Whatever creature he'd chosen for a target gave a short yip, and she winced. He returned moments later with something dead slung over his bare shoulder. She looked away. She hoped he didn't expect her to eat a raw wood rat or possum or whatever horrid rodent he'd slain.

It turned out to be a rabbit, and he apparently *didn't* plan to eat it, at least not yet. He tied its legs with plant fiber and hung it from a twisted reed that he slung around his hips like a gun belt.

With the game secure, he began poking at the wet ground with a stick, digging at the base of some plant. He uncovered the bulb beneath, mumbled a few foreign words, cut the leaves away, and brushed the dirt off on his trousers. Then he cut the bulb in two and extended a piece to her.

She looked away. She was hungry, but not *that* hungry. She might make a feast of wild greens, but she wasn't about to eat a strange bulb he'd dug out of the ground. It might make her sick...or worse.

"Take it," he grunted.

"I'm not hungry."

"You have to eat."

She shook her head. The heroes in her books could go for days without food.

He grumbled something, crunching into his half of the bulb. His grimace told her it was about as appetizing as she'd expected.

She closed her eyes with a sigh and imagined the meal she'd be eating at the Parker Ranch—a plate piled high with roast beef, potatoes, and two, no, *three* baking powder biscuits with butter and peach jam, followed by a big, scrumptious slab of apple pie.

Stubborn woman, Chase thought as he finished off the beargrass bulb. Sooner or later she had to eat something. He'd been lucky spying the rabbit, but he didn't feel safe stopping to build a fire until nightfall. By then, she should be hungry enough to eat dirt.

He glanced at her, sitting there on the ground, her petticoat puffed around her like a spent dogwood blossom. She had skin like his mother's, delicate and as white as the spots on a fawn, and already her shoulders and the bridge of her nose glowed pink.

He untied his shirtsleeves from around his hips and handed the shirt to her. "Your skin is burning."

"I'm fine."

"You're not fine. You're all...pink."

She blushed, turning pinker. "Don't worry about me."

"Put the shirt on...unless you want me to hold you down and wrestle you into it."

Her eyes widened. His narrowed. Finally, deciding his threat was genuine, she donned the shirt.

Chase knew she was tired, but they had to keep moving. He pulled her to her feet, tugging her after him like a dawdling child.

As they hiked into the mountains, the pines thickened, and cedars scented the woods. Though they traveled parallel to the main deer trail, the foliage was dense now. And so far, there were no visible signs of pursuit.

They drank from the springs and tiny streams threading through the rocks. Once he saw her catch her reflection in a small pool, and she fingered her snarled and ragged locks in useless vanity. By afternoon, she dragged along at a snail's crawl, every step looking like her last. At this pace, they would never outdistance their pursuers.

Finally she sank down onto the ground, unable to go any farther. He hunkered down beside her and rubbed the back of his neck, considering his options.

Long ago, Chase's mother had told him the story of how she'd met his father. Mattie had injured herself in a fall, and Sakote had carried her for miles on his back, seeing her safely home. Under the current circumstances, Chase thought it seemed like a practical way to travel.

He reached out toward Claire, seized the front of the shirt he'd loaned her only a few hours ago and began unbuttoning it.

She instinctively grabbed his hands to stop him. "What are you doing?"

"I need the shirt back."

She cast him a puzzled glance.

Then her face fell, and she blanched. "I'm slowing you down. You're leaving me here, aren't you?"

Before he could reply, she slapped his hands away and began unfastening the shirt herself.

Fine," she said, her voice crackling with anger. "Go. But Yoema would be very disappointed in you. Very," she said, tearing the shirt from her body, "disappointed." She hurled the shirt at his chest.

He scowled. He supposed it was natural enough for her to assume he'd abandon her in the wilderness. But she was wrong.

"I'm not leaving you."

He whipped out the shirt by its sleeves, swirling it over her head and enveloping her in the flannel. Ignoring her stammers of confusion, he pulled the sleeves forward beneath her arms. Then, before he could change his mind, he turned around and hefted her quickly onto his back, tying the sleeves of the shirt around his neck.

The woman sputtered in surprised outrage as he caught her hindquarters in the bottom half of the shirt, securing the sling around his waist in a knot. He boosted her up once to settle her into place with her arms clinging to his shoulders and her knees resting on the bones of his hips. Then, hooking his thumbs under the makeshift straps to keep the sling from choking him, he stood up and started down the path again.

She was lighter than his first *xonsat*, the young buck he'd shot with bow and arrow and packed home on his back when he was eleven winters old. But she was a hell of a lot more trouble than the deer he'd killed. She struggled against him, making noises of indignation, and her body—warm and soft next to his—stirred and distracted him.

He trained his eyes on the path ahead and tried not to think about that part of him that liked this new position all too well. He focused instead on how much deeper into danger he traveled with each step.

CHAPTER 8

Claire was so mortified she could scarcely draw breath, clinging to the savage's back like some overgrown papoose. When she finally managed to gasp in a lungful of air, she could find no words equal to her humiliation. So she simply spluttered like an over-boiling teakettle.

The way she was bound, she had no choice but to embrace him for fear of falling. Her legs were draped around his hips as brazenly as a saloon girl's. And she was pressed so tightly against his bare flesh that they shared sweat.

The half-breed didn't seem bothered by any of it. He proceeded down the trail, smoothly and effortlessly, as if carrying a woman splayed across his naked back was something he did every day of his life.

Of course, she mustn't let him continue, no matter what a relief it was to her stinging feet. It was completely indecent, and she couldn't let him compromise her in such a fashion. She'd never allowed any man such liberties, not even Frank.

Heavens, she hadn't let her fiancé so much as kiss her on

the cheek. Frank was always the perfect gentleman, politely distant, never overstepping his bounds despite his status as her husband-to-be. He never threatened her or offended her in any way. In Frank's company, she always felt absolutely safe.

This savage, on the other hand, was rash, rude, and completely uncivilized.

Finally she gathered enough wits about her to speak. "Put me down, sir." Her voice cracked as she felt the sleek skin of his back slide across her inner thighs.

He plodded on, ignoring her.

"I said, put me down."

He only jounced her again into a more comfortable angle, bringing new heat to her face, and continued on.

Her jaw dropped. "I insist you put me down this insta—"

"Insist?" he said with a bark of laughter.

Her ruffled feathers made her brave. "I can and I do insist," she proclaimed. "This is improper and untoward, and I won't endure it. When Frank hears what you've—"

He stopped abruptly. "Frank?"

"My fiancé," she announced smugly, even though that was technically no longer true, now that she'd broken things off. In case he didn't recognize the French word, she added, "My intended husband."

He didn't respond with the shocked gasp she expected, nor did he apologize and set her down. Instead, he shook his head, made a rueful sound reminiscent of a chuckle, and pressed onward.

"Stop!" she cried, incensed. "Stop it this instant! I have my reputation to consider."

"Your reputation," he growled, "is the least of my troubles."

"Oh!" she groaned in frustration. But she supposed he was right. A half-breed stealing a white woman would be hanged before he could utter a syllable in his defense. His neck was of far more concern to him than her propriety.

Still, his familiarity chafed at her, figuratively and literally. His lean hips rubbed at the insides of her knees with every stride, and her petticoat bunched higher and higher, threatening to expose her unmentionable parts to the curve of his spine.

It stretched the limits of her endurance. Her body began to respond to the ill treatment, stiffening and flushing in places it should not. It took all her will to draw her mind away from the sensation of his damp flesh upon her. She must think of something, anything, to keep her sanity about her.

Perhaps she could force him to reason. For the moment at least, she was alive and relatively unharmed. Perhaps he'd listen to her if she spoke calmly and rationally. Maybe she could make a fresh start with Yoema's grandson and convince him he was making a huge mistake.

She cleared her throat, steeled her nerve, and, despite the ludicrousness of her present position, donned her best sitting room manners.

"If we're going to be...traveling companions," she said evenly, "I think we should at least be properly introduced. My name is Claire Parker."

"I know."

She waited for an appropriate response. None was forthcoming.

"And you?" she prompted. "What's *your* name?"

He didn't answer.

"You know," she informed him patiently, stifling her temper, "it's considered common courtesy to exchange names."

"To *your* people," he told her. "*My* people consider it bad manners."

She forced a polite chuckle, as if he'd made a clever joke.

"Don't be silly. Your people. My people. If you're one of the Two-Sons, you're half white, for heaven's sake."

The man released an irritated sigh and tromped along even more heavily than before.

She tried again. "If you don't tell me your name, how will I know how to address you?"

"Who *else* would you be talking to?"

She compressed her lips, striving to be civil. "I suppose I could call you Mr. Half-Breed," she murmured. "Or One-Son. Or Yoema's Grand—"

"Kisan-yiman-dilwawh," he grumbled over his shoulder.

"Is that...your name?"

He grunted.

"Ah." Now she was getting somewhere. "Pleased to make your acquaintance, Mr....Kisan...yiman..."

"Dilwawh."

"Dilwawh." What a long and difficult name. She wondered what it meant. She'd learned from Yoema, whose name meant Little Flower, that most Indian names came from nature. "How do you do?"

He didn't reply. She couldn't blame him. After all, "how do you do" *was* a rather inane expression, difficult to translate and hard to answer.

"Claire is a French name. It means bright," she offered. "What does your name mean?"

"Kisan-yiman-dilwawh?" He sniffed. "He Who Beats Chattering White Woman."

The hopeful smile she'd pasted on her face fell flat, and on impulse, she smacked the back of his head with the flat of her hand.

"Ow!"

"I am *not* chattering. That is an ungentlemanly thing to say. Yoema would be very disappointed—"

He stopped in his tracks. "Will you stop saying her name?"

Claire would be damned if she'd let the savage dictate to her what she could and could not say. The words tumbled from her lips in a rush of childish passion. "Yoema! Yoema! Yoema!"

She regretted her impetuousness almost at once, for he spat out a long string of words she was sure were epithets.

"Stop it!" he threatened, "Or maybe I *will* beat you."

Claire acquiesced, not because she believed him—he was proving to be all bark and no bite—but because she could see he was as stubborn and strong-willed as his grandmother when it came to getting his way.

Still, his insistence on silencing Yoema's memory disturbed her. How could he forbid Claire to speak the name of her Konkow mother? How could he deny his own kin's existence? How could he allow Yoema to fade from the world unnamed and unremembered?

Chase wondered if Xontehltaw, Coyote, was laughing at his empty promise. He might make Claire ride on his back. He might compel her to eat food not to her liking. He might make her wear his shirt and force her to sleep on the hard ground. But he'd never raise his hand against a woman.

Turning back to the path, he grimaced in self-scorn. Some avenging savage he was. The woman was right. He *was* half white. And at the moment, he felt every civilized drop of that white blood.

Hearing his grandmother's name sent a superstitious shiver along his spine. But that wasn't the only reason he'd scared the woman into silence.

Each soft word she uttered chipped away at his honor and made him regret his mistake in kidnapping her even more. Her beautiful wide eyes reminded him that she was a virtuous young woman and made him feel like a poor excuse for a man.

Honestly, he didn't want her to know his name. He didn't

want her to acknowledge him at all. He'd just as soon she forgot all about him. A proper young lady like Claire had no business carrying on with a savage like him. He wished he'd never made the mistake of stealing her. He wanted things to go back to the way they were before he'd met Claire Parker.

Which made him all the more angry when his body, responding to the seductive sensation of warm feminine flesh on his back, started behaving as if it would like to get to know her better.

By the time the sun had crossed the sky and hovered on the crest of the western hills, Chase was dead tired. It wasn't his burden that made him that way. A blacksmith's back was as solid as a tree trunk, and the woman was no heavier than a down quilt. No, it was his mind that was exhausted. His thoughts had run in circles all day.

For the sake of his grandmother, he should loathe Claire Parker. In deference to his tribe, he should despise the whites, who had stolen everything from the Konkows. But feeling the woman's smooth, long limbs wrapped around his hips filled him with emotions completely unlike loathing.

Here he was, in the midst of mortal peril, hunted like an animal, walking a thin path between life and death. Yet his body still responded to its natural cravings, undaunted by the danger. And at the moment, more than food, more than water, more than shelter, he craved the woman.

He let out a ragged sigh, hoping and yet dreading that her heel would slip a little lower.

Such thoughts were wrong. He knew they were wrong. Still...

He clenched his jaw and trained his eyes on the trail ahead. It was far too pleasurable, all her silky warmth upon his skin. And it wasn't hard to imagine tossing up her skirts and seeking relief in her lovely body. He nearly groaned aloud at the idea.

But Chase was no savage, no matter what she believed. So he decided he'd better stop for the day while he could still heed the voice of reason.

A posse was unlikely to travel in the dark through the mountains. Chase figured he could risk building a fire to cook the rabbit, now that the sun was going down. A crevice in the rock wall ahead formed a hidden half-cave, a good spot to lodge for the night.

Eager to unburden his soul as well as his back, as soon as they reached the recess, he loosened the shirt sleeves and let the woman slip to the ground. She gasped in pain as her tender feet contacted sharp stones, and he winced at his own carelessness.

"Sit," he ordered, then amended, "if you want."

She lowered herself onto a flat rock.

He slipped the shirt on, leaving it unbuttoned. The flannel was warm from her body. It smelled like her—soft and sweet and womanly—and he had to fight to keep his mind on the most important task at hand, starting a fire and getting them fed.

But as he stacked the kindling, his eyes wandered again and again to the ragged soles of Claire's bare feet. The sorry sight made him feel like a monster. He wished he'd noticed before. He would have offered to carry her sooner. He might have even given her his boots, except that they were several sizes too big.

He settled for dragging a broken chunk of log in front of her, patting the top of it and mumbling, "For your feet."

Claire didn't dare meet his eyes. She'd had the most troubling thoughts for the past several hours, and she feared they might be written all over her face.

She quietly propped her heels on the log and pulled her petticoat down over her knees and shins. Not that it mattered. She'd been riding with her legs wrapped around the half-breed's bare waist for the past several hours. Her modesty was beyond repair.

So were her nerves.

She'd had a long time to think as he packed her through the canyon, and she was shocked by the direction of her thoughts. She should have been frightened by his threats of vengeance, concerned about his dishonorable intentions, and worried about what was to become of her. Instead, all she could do was think about was how much he reminded her of Monowano, the handsome Indian hero of her favorite dime novel.

This Two-Son wasn't quite as uncivilized as the Red-skins in her books, of course. He wore denim trousers instead of buckskins. He had no feather headband or bear claw necklace. And rather than a flintstone, he carried sulfur matches, which made starting a campfire much easier.

Once it was going, she stole a glance at him across the flames. He really was magnificent. Firelight haloed his head and flickered in his black eyes, transforming him into a dark angel, dangerous and intriguing. It illuminated the angular planes of his face and the muscular contours of his chest. And to her morbid fascination, his unbuttoned shirt kept gaping open, exposing his delicious golden skin and reminding her of how warm his body had felt against her thighs.

A delicious shiver went through her bones.

Heavens, what was wrong with her?

He turned the spit, and a whiff of roasting rabbit made her mouth water.

Maybe she was only delirious from hunger.

No, he was definitely doing something to her insides that had nothing to do with her appetite...and it felt curiously pleasant.

It was absurd, of course. He'd kidnapped her. How could she possibly find him attractive? It went against everything she'd ever read. In her novels, heroes were heroes, and villains were villains. Things were always black and white.

The half-breed was distorting her perceptions of good and evil. He spoke of revenge, yet his compassion betrayed him. He seemed obliged to punish her for her imagined crimes, but he grappled with guilt over doing her harm. He was big and brooding and brutal in appearance, yet there was a gentleness about him that belied his stormy countenance. And more than any fictional character she'd ever encountered in a book, he was utterly fascinating.

Was he friend or foe? She wasn't sure anymore. Perhaps he wasn't sure himself. All she knew was when he looked at her...like that...she felt it all the way down to her toes.

Chase grimaced. For a woman who had good reason to wish she'd never laid eyes on him, she sure was staring at him a lot. Maybe she was just half-starved. She did have kind of a hungry look in her eyes. And now and then, when she caught the appetizing aroma of the roasting meat, her tongue slipped out to lick her parched lips.

It was hard watching her suffer, knowing he was to blame. She reminded him of the story of his grandfather on the march, wasting away in the name of grief.

Chase wasn't used to being watched like that, and under her scrutiny, he almost dropped the skewered rabbit onto the coals. Thankfully, he snatched it from the fire, and his callused fingertips scarcely felt the heat. He pulled off a hunk of seared meat, blew gently on the morsel to cool it, then extended it to Claire, relieved to discover that she seemed to like rabbit.

He tore off his own portion with his teeth. The meat was succulent and smoky. He thought he'd never tasted anything so delicious. But then he'd never been so hungry.

They ate in silence. The only sounds were the smacking of their lips, the gently crackling fire, and the tentative chirps of crickets. He offered her another piece when she was done, and then another. Truthfully, he could have eaten the entire rabbit himself. He regularly polished off three whole rabbits at one sitting. But every time he looked up at her and saw the shadows under her eyes and her sunburned cheeks, guilt spoiled his appetite.

So he gave her the rest of the rabbit, pleased when she stripped every last morsel of meat from the tiny bones.

Meanwhile, he gazed into the fire, absently breaking the empty skewer into smaller and smaller pieces.

His mind was bothered.

All his life, he'd trusted the Great Spirit to lead him down the true path. The vision Chase had been given was strong. He'd clearly been led to Paradise. He'd been led to the Parker Ranch. He'd even been led to Parker's daughter. Why else would she have come downstairs at that exact moment?

Yet he couldn't help but feel that the Great Spirit was wrong in leading him to seek vengeance. It wasn't right to hold Claire accountable for her father's sins, especially when she'd been too young to understand them.

As much as Chase was obligated to grant his grandmother the peace she deserved, he didn't have the heart to hurt an innocent woman. How the white soldiers on the march could have closed their eyes to the Konkows' torment—watched women and children starve, grow sick, and die—and do nothing, he didn't understand. Even he, Chase Wolf, son of the wronged Konkow, couldn't perpetrate such cruelty in the name of revenge.

But how else could he bring closure to his grandmother's soul? How could he break free of this hopelessly tangled web without getting himself hanged by Parker, angering the Great Spirit, and bringing the wrath of his grandmother's *chindin*, her spirit, down upon him?

He tossed the last of the broken stick into the fire and rubbed the crease from his forehead. Right or wrong, his mind was made up. Until he got Claire taken care of and safely home, he would trust his own instincts and save the Great Spirit's demand for *lenulya*, vengeance, for another day.

He rose, and then hunkered down beside Claire, nodding as he eyed the bottoms of her feet, illuminated now by the fire.

"Let me see," he said, holding out one palm.

She gulped, giving him an unsure glance.

"Come," he repeated, beckoning with his hand.

"I'm fine," she breathed. Her tone said she was not fine.

He frowned. "I want to look at your cuts."

She stiffened. "I...don't think that's a good idea."

"You're afraid."

"No."

"You think I'll hurt you."

"No."

Chase's mouth worked impatiently. Even the mules he shod were not so headstrong. His calm demeanor was starting to slip. What was it about the stubborn woman that rankled at him so? "Woman. Let me see."

"My name is not Woman," she declared, her spirits remarkably renewed by virtue of a full belly. "My name is Claire."

He reined in a growl of frustration. "Claire. Let me see," he said with as much calm as he could muster, adding for good measure, "please."

"I really don't think that's nec—"

Impatient, he seized her ankle to inspect the damage, ignoring her halfhearted protests and feeble slaps. The top of her foot was scratched from thistles, and scrapes and thin cuts crisscrossed her sole. The taste of shame grew heavy in his mouth. *He* was the cause of those cuts. *He* was the source of her pain.

Carefully, he lowered her foot. Then he retrieved the

scraped rabbit skin he'd left hanging in the brush, sat cross-legged by the fire, and drew his knife.

Claire could feel her ankle tingling where the half-breed's fingers had wrapped around it. The sensation wound its way up her leg and settled brazenly between her thighs. It was a heady feeling—forbidden and dangerous—and yet it filled her with shocking warmth and pleasure.

She watched him through half-lidded eyes as he cut two long, narrow strips from the rabbit skin and split the rest of the hide evenly down the middle, wondering how he could maintain such a calm demeanor while her emotions were whirling like a cyclone through her brain.

She caught her breath as his hand trapped her ankle again, sending that strange tremor up her thigh. He stretched his free arm toward a vine of wild grape that had grown up a nearby scrub oak, clutching a bunch of its leaves in his fist. Murmuring something in his own tongue, he tore the leaves free.

Grasping her injured foot, he carefully pressed the cool, soft leaves over her broken flesh. The gesture brought a flood of memories washing over her. Yoema had done the same thing for her when she'd skinned her knee jumping rope. She'd said the grape leaves helped to heal sores.

He then wrapped the rabbit pelt up around the leaves and over the top of her foot, fur side in, securing the makeshift boot around her ankle with the hide strip. While she sat in numb wonder, he repeated the process for her other foot. Then he sniffed in approval and sheathed his knife, settling back on his haunches to stare off toward the rising moon.

The fur felt marvelously soothing upon her feet. But why, after speaking so vehemently of vengeance last night, would he do her such a kindness?

What an enigma he was. She studied his beautiful face as he frowned into the distance. He was fiercer and bolder than

Monowano. He didn't possess the reserved, gentle, sweet nature of her dime novel hero. But there was something primitive and powerful about his presence, something that made her heart beat fast and drew her to him like lightning to a lightning rod.

"Chase." He said the word softly, out of the blue.

She blinked. Maybe she'd only imagined he'd spoken, for he was staring blankly at the ground.

"Pardon?"

He picked up a trio of pine needles and drew them lazily through the silt at his feet. "Chase Wolf."

She drew her brows together, baffled.

He trained his eyes directly upon her then. Reflections of the fire flickered like golden butterflies in their ebony depths, entrancing her. "My name," he explained. "I'm called Chase Wolf."

CHAPTER 9

Claire held her breath, too astonished to speak.

"How do you do?" she finally managed, speaking purely out of habit. She extended her hand nervously, withdrawing it again when she realized the inanity of the gesture. "I'm..."

His eyes narrowed at her discomfiture. Was there a glimmer of amusement in his gaze, or was it a trick of the moonlight?

"Claire Parker," he supplied.

She blushed. Of all times for her to become tongue-tied...

"The daughter of Samuel Parker," he confirmed.

She nodded. His voice was breathy, deep, and warm.

His gaze dropped casually down the front of her camisole, sending an uncomfortable shiver through her.

"And woman of Frank," he added.

She gathered the neckline of her camisole together in one hand. "Fiancée."

His stare thankfully returned to her face. "Mm. So Frank is not yet shackled to the *yiman-dilwawh*?" When she furrowed her brow in confusion, he translated. "The chattering white woman?"

She opened her mouth to protest, and then decided it was a waste of breath. She didn't want to have to explain Frank. She also suspected she'd have to choose her words wisely, since she wasn't sure how long Chase Wolf would put up with actual conversation. There was a long silence. Finally she mustered up enough courage to ask what she most longed to know. "Pardon my bluntness, Mr. Wolf, but exactly what are your intentions?"

He looked off toward the west, where the last of the sun's lingering glow faintly burnished the indigo drapery of the night sky.

"I wish to speak of the past," he said at last.

"The past?"

"The march to Nome Cult."

She furrowed her brows.

"You've never heard of it?" he asked.

She shook her head.

He nodded. "Your father hid it from you."

"Hid what?"

"What did my grandmother tell you about her people—her husband, her brothers, her children?"

Claire frowned. "She said they were gone."

His face grew suddenly sad. "Gone." The word sounded melancholy on his lips. "But she didn't say where?"

"I assumed she meant they were...dead."

"Not dead. Not all of them. But they might as well have been. She never saw them again." He stared into the flames, his mouth grim, his thoughts far away. "I'll tell you the secret your father has been keeping from you, the story of my grandmother's people."

Claire clasped her hands and waited patiently as he tossed the trio of pine needles into the fire and watched them curl and burn.

Then he began his story. "For generations, the Konkow people lived here in peace. Even when the white men came...with their diseases...with their beasts that ate the food of the people...the Konkow were silent." Atop his thigh, his fist clenched once, then released. "But the whites became greedy. First they wanted all the gold...then all the food...then all the land. And when Konkow lived on the land they wanted, they took it from them."

Claire sat transfixed. Up till now, Chase Wolf had been a man of few words. What he was telling her must be important to make him open up to her and speak at such length.

"Soon the people began to starve. They had no choice but to take the white men's animals for food." His eyes took on an even darker cast. "And when they would steal a rancher's steer, they would be shot."

Her brow creased. Surely he wasn't talking about her father. Her father would never shoot a native. Samuel Parker got along fine with the local tribes. He said they were trustworthy, hard-working, and loyal.

"One day, the whites got tired of shooting the Konkows and decided to send them away forever. The army rounded them all up—scores of men, women, and children—and drove them like cattle, west to a place called Nome Cult."

Claire didn't see how that could possibly be true. There were a few Konkows who worked at the Parker Ranch. But she remained silent to hear him out.

A taut thread of tension underlined his words. "It was a march of a hundred miles. Those who refused to go were killed. Those who went and could not keep up were killed. Those who became ill were killed."

Claire paled. It was a horrifying story. But surely that was all it was—a story. Yoema had never told her about any march. Neither had her father.

Though his voice was quiet, he bit out the next words

between his teeth. "Samuel Parker took my grandmother from her family to keep her for a slave and sent the rest on the march. My grandfather, believing his wife had been killed, refused to eat. He starved to death on the journey."

She gasped. "Where did you hear such a horrible thing? My father never kept a slave in his life. Yoema *chose* to live with us. And except for the Two-Sons, she never spoke of family or—"

"She would not have. She didn't know if they were alive or dead."

Claire shook her head. "No, it's just not possible. My father is a good man. And Yoe-...your grandmother..." She hesitated. Now that she thought about it, it was curious that Yoema had never talked much about her husband or her children, only her grandsons. What *had* happened to the rest of her tribe?

She bit the inside of her cheek and looked up at him again. He believed what he was saying with all his heart. She could see sincerity in his eyes. She could also see pain.

Without thinking, she reached out and covered his hand with hers. "I think there's been some terrible misunderstanding. I'll get to the bottom of this, I promise you. When my father..."

At the same instant, they both glanced down sharply at their joined hands.

But when Claire would have pulled away, he caught her wrist, startling the breath from her.

"What I'm trying to say is..." he began. "It's not right to hold you accountable for what your father did. I know that now." She doubted that he was even aware of it, but he began idly running his thumb back and forth across the back of her wrist as he spoke. "But I need to make things right for my grandmother. I need to send her on her journey. I need to give her spirit peace."

She gulped. His rhythmic stroking was doing strange

things to her, soothing and exciting her at the same time.

He shook his head. "But taking revenge on the daughter of my enemy isn't the way to do it."

He let go of her then, and she could breathe again. Her skin still burned where he'd touched her, however, and she was having trouble thinking straight.

She creased her brow. "Do you mean to...take me home then? Back to my father? Back to my fiancé?"

He nodded.

"I see," she said.

It was the way the stories always ended—with the villain vanquished and the heroine living happily ever after. And yet a strange emotion followed that thought, an emotion she could neither explain nor excuse.

Disappointment.

She frowned. She didn't want to go home.

"When?" she asked.

"Soon."

"But not right away?"

"I can't just yet." He grimaced and tossed a pine cone onto the fire. "It's...complicated."

She actually breathed a sigh of relief.

"Meanwhile," he said, "we have to keep moving. Your father probably has a whole posse tracking us. And now that we have no horse..."

Claire bit her lip. Her father might be out looking for his prize stallion, but she doubted he was looking for her. Still, she didn't think it wise to let Chase know *all* the sordid details. "I don't think you have to worry about my father."

He gave her a doubtful smirk. "If you were *my* daughter, I'd carve your kidnapper to bits." He bent his head forward, furrowing his hands through his thick hair. His long sigh fluttered the flames.

"But if I tell him you're the grandson of Yoema—"

As soon as she spoke the name, an eerie, dolorous moan floated past, shattering the peace of the evening and chilling Claire to the bone.

Before she could ask what the devil that was, Chase sprang from his haunches, dragging her up against him to protect her with one brawny arm, and faced the shadowy wood with his knife drawn.

Chase felt a cold shiver. like a rattlesnake's warning. slither along his back. His pulse pounding, he scanned the bushes. Had the white woman summoned his grandmother's *chindin* to the world of the living?

Several tense moments passed, measured by the rapid beating of his heart. Nothing but firelight skittered over the manzanita leaves, and the only sounds Chase heard were the soft pop of flame and the shallow, quick breathing of his captive.

Finally the low cry came again. With a shaky sigh of relief, he lowered his blade and shoved it back into its sheath.

"Owl?" Claire whispered.

"Mm," he grunted. But he didn't let her go. Nor would he until he extracted a promise from her. "Swear to me you'll speak my grandmother's name no more."

She wilted against him.

"Give me your word," he said.

She shook her head. "How can I?" Her next words came out like the sad, soft sigh of the wind. "You don't understand. She was my friend. She was my mother. For heaven's sake, she was your own grandmother. How can you bear to let her die...forgotten?"

Chase swallowed hard. Like the sliver of bone on a fishing line, her despair had caught him by the throat. He fought the strong urge to turn her in his arms so he could hold her.

Of course, he wouldn't do that. Even his sisters knew that Chase was not the brother to run to when they needed comfort. His big arms always crushed them, and the littler girls were smothered by his ferocious hugs.

"She won't be forgotten," he whispered fiercely, his breath ruffling her hair. "She's the reason I've..." He almost said the words "come home," but Paradise had never truly been his home, had it? "The reason I've returned."

"You said you came for revenge."

Her words melted his heart. He lowered his tense shoulders. "I don't know what I came for. I only know I have to make things right for my grandmother."

Holding her like this—her body soft and quivering like a dove's—he found it hard to imagine he'd ever considered torturing her.

"Revenge never makes things right," she murmured.

She was probably right. Hell, he wasn't sure anymore. His purpose had seemed much clearer before he'd crossed paths with Claire Parker.

"Just promise me you won't say my grandmother's name."

"And if I won't promise?"

With a whispered curse of disbelief, he wheeled her about by the shoulders, holding her at arm's length.

"Why do you persist? You're like the bee who keeps buzzing at the grizzly when the bear could smash it with one swipe of his paw."

"I persist, because, unlike you," she said pointedly, "I knew her. I loved her." Her eyes filled suddenly with tears. "And, God help me," she choked out, "I miss her." She buried her face in her hands.

And then he did it—exactly what he should not have. He pulled her toward him and tucked her against his chest, folding his arms around her frail body as carefully as he could.

It was crazy. Her people had subjugated his. Her father had enslaved his grandmother and caused his grandfather's death. He should despise Claire Parker.

But when he held her like this, snuggled against him—her hair tickling his chin, her sniffles wetting his bare chest—she seemed neither murderer nor oppressor. She seemed only a very sad and lonely young woman.

Without thinking, he lifted his hand to cradle her head, marveling at the fine texture of her hair. He suddenly realized why it was cut short. She must have hacked it off herself, just as he had his own, in the Konkow display of grief. Those were not what his white mother called crocodile tears. The woman's sorrow came from her heart. She *had* loved his grandmother.

"Do chweh," he murmured, stroking her hair. "Don't cry."

He continued to speak words in his tongue, words of comfort she might not understand, but words that would soothe her by virtue of the soft whisper of his language. And she began to respond, calming to his voice like a skittish mare.

It had been a while since Chase had held a woman. Yet holding Claire felt right. She fit perfectly in the cradle of his arms despite her small size. Where her soft cheek pressed against his chest, it seemed she warmed his heart. And the way she relaxed against him with such trust made him feel protective and significant.

Part of him wanted to hold her like this all night. But he expected, once she spilled all her tears and her weeping became soft sniffles, she'd squirm out of his embrace.

To his surprise, she didn't. If anything, when she was done crying, she seemed to nestle closer to him. He closed his eyes, savoring the moment, resisting an almost irresistible urge to lower his lips to kiss the top of her head.

Whether it was the feminine warmth of her body, the flattering trust she placed in him, or simply that he'd gone too long without a woman, he began to respond to her closeness. His heart pumped more forcefully, and his blood warmed. He swallowed hard as a powerful wave of desire surged through him. When that surge rose to lodge between his legs, making him swell with blatant lust against her, he squeezed his eyes tight against the divine sensation.

Finally, reluctantly, he forced himself to pull away.

The last thing he expected as they parted was her barely audible sigh of disappointment, which seemed to echo his own regret.

Without her, his arms felt curiously empty. His shirt, wet with her tears, clung to his chest, leaving him even colder. But that was just the sobering slap of reality he needed. He had no business feeling such things for Claire Parker.

"I'm sorry," she said, wiping her eyes. "I didn't mean to...to weep all over you."

His voice came out on a croak. "No need to apologize."

"I just...miss her so much." She tried to put on a brave smile.

He nodded.

"You're very...like her, you know," she ventured, "your grandmother."

He furrowed his brow. This was something he hadn't expected. He'd never met his grandmother. But this woman had been raised by her. *His* grief was a matter of tradition and of moral outrage. *Hers* was personal.

"Tell me about her," he coaxed, beckoning her to join him by the fire. Maybe the flames would keep him warm, since he no longer had a tempting woman to do that. "Tell me about my grandmother." Then he added, "But be careful not to summon her ghost, or she may lose her way to the spirit world."

Claire sat by the fire and tucked her hair behind one ear. "Is that why you don't want me to say her name?"

He nodded. "It's bad luck to speak the names of those who are gone."

Claire bit her lip. She was managing to keep her voice calm and collected. But if Chase Wolf knew what she was thinking at the moment, he'd be far more afraid of *her* than of his grandmother's ghost.

Being in his arms had felt amazing, like finding a key that fit perfectly into the lock of her heart. It seemed like she'd been waiting all her life for his embrace. And now that she'd experienced it, she didn't want to give it up, didn't want to let him go.

It was alarming, how right it felt, how much like coming home. She wanted him to hold her again, wanted to feel those strong arms around her, to feel the warm breath of his words against her ear.

It was madness, like being pulled into a treacherous whirlpool of desire. Yet it seemed equally mad to keep her distance when she yearned so much to be back in his arms.

She couldn't keep her eyes off of him. The firelight made his hair shine like a raven's wing. It flashed off his white teeth, gilded his skin and leaped in his dark eyes. And the thought that he'd instinctively shielded her from harm and lent his shoulder in comfort...such manly, protective gestures made her shiver with desire.

"Are you cold?" Good Lord, the man had his shirt halfway off already.

"No!" she blurted. "Thank you."

The last thing her wildly pulsing heart needed was more tinder for the fire. She should never have exposed her emotions to him, never imposed herself upon him like that, weeping all over him, for heaven's sake. Yoema's blood might flow through his veins, and her spirit might dwell in his heart, but he was definitely not sweet, gentle Yoema. He was a man, and he was...

A savage.

But, dear God, he was a delectable savage. The thought

echoed so loudly in her head that she feared she'd said the words aloud. How could she possibly feel...that way...about a man who'd abducted her?

And yet she did. She wanted him to hold her in his arms again.

"Tell me about her," he urged, squatting on his haunches across the fire from her, his shirt gaping open, his large hands propped idly over his knees.

Claire tore her gaze away to study her tattered fingernails. "Your grandmother?" she managed to choke out. "Well, she used to tell me stories when I was a little girl."

"What stories?" he murmured.

"She told me where fire came from. And why skunks smell so awful. And about the creation of the world by Wonomi and Turtle. You know these stories?"

He nodded.

"She called me her little white dove. She sang me to sleep and took care of me when I was ill. The grape leaves you put on my cuts—she used to do the same thing."

"My grandmother was said to be a great healer," he murmured.

She swallowed, her face still hot, as she gave him a sidelong glance. The way the fire flickered in his eyes and washed over the hollow planes of his face evoked more than just a fond memory of Yoema. His sheer strength, the breadth of his shoulders, the subdued power of his hands, and the stark, wild beauty of his features, took her breath away.

"Yes," she said absently. Then she clasped her hands upon her lap, determined to maintain her composure. "She was also a great healer of the spirit." Claire's voice softened in remembrance. "She comforted me when my favorite old cat died." She smiled at the memory. "We even had a *weda,* a burning ceremony, for the poor thing."

"What else?"

"One time, I baked an apple pie for my father's birthday. I left it on the windowsill to cool, and a crow demolished it. Your grandmother replaced it for me, even though the closest thing she could manage was acorn bread."

"*Mati.*" He used the Konkow word.

"Yes, that's right." She lowered her eyes, lost in thought. "When I complained about my freckles and the fact I was as skinny as a sapling, she would brush my hair and tell me it was prettier than the gold the miners hungered after."

She brought one hand up to her precious tresses, forgetting she'd lopped them off, and her smile wavered. Lowering her hand, she continued. "I remember one day when I was small, we went together to the general store to buy a length of calico for curtains. We were spotted by the Johnson brothers, a pair of dreadful bullies. They sneered and called me a half-breed, which, of course, was untrue, and I..." She gasped, catching her lip under her teeth, and glanced at him, but his expression as he stared into the flames was inscrutable. "Oh, dear. I didn't mean..."

Without looking up, he replied with a snort, "There's no shame in being a half-breed."

Claire stared at him in wonder. "That's exactly what *she* said. That was the first time she told me about you, about the Two-Sons."

He said nothing, only narrowed his eyes. She noticed tension about his mouth, as if a question hovered there, waiting to be asked.

"She said your mother was a beautiful white woman from the gold camps who drew pictures," she continued, "and that your father was a great Konkow hunter. She said that when you and your brother were born, it was the will of the Creator that you be spared. She said you flew away to the north, but that you would return one day to her, that you would bring good luck, that the..." She screwed up her forehead, trying to

110

remember Yoema's exact words. "The broken past would be mended."

Chase was silent for so long, Claire began to wonder if he'd forgotten she was there. The moon climbed higher in the sky, and the owl they'd heard earlier hooted from farther and farther away. The fire dwindled, but he did nothing to revive it, only staring fixedly into the glowing coals as if he read the future there. Finally he spoke.

"What other way is there to mend the broken past of Nome Cult but by retribution, by an eye for an eye?" The calm of his voice chilled her, and though she was certain he meant her no harm, his solemn face appeared strangely menacing in the scarlet glow of the dying fire.

"I don't know," she told him honestly. "All I know is that she loved me. And I loved her." Her voice wavered and cracked, but she continued. "She told me it was her destiny to be a mother to the little white dove. She said Wonomi, the Great Spirit, had told her so in a vision."

A lengthy silence followed while he gathered his thoughts. Finally he trained his forthright gaze upon her again. He exhaled deeply, like a warrior who has just waged and lost a long and grueling battle.

"*Lenulya*, revenge—it's not in my heart." He shook his head. "I could never harm the spirit daughter of my grandmother."

Spirit daughter. Touched by his words, Claire stared into his midnight black eyes. Her throat closed, and rising tears stung her nose. He acknowledged her as Yoema's child then. *Spirit daughter.* It was such a perfect name. Yet no one had called her that, not even her father. As close as Samuel Parker had allowed the native woman to get to her, still he'd never used the word "daughter." The relationship between Claire and Yoema was something they never spoke of, except in terms one might use for a servant or lady's maid.

Yet this man, this stranger who didn't know her, who didn't know his own grandmother, saw what was in her heart. He recognized that their bond had been more than that of friendship, that Yoema had been, for all intents and purposes, Claire's mother.

His simple words soothed her ragged spirit and lifted a heavy weight from her soul. At last, someone understood.

"Thank you," she choked out.

He frowned as if he didn't deserve her gratitude. Then he awkwardly cleared his throat and nudged the coals with the toe of his boot.

Despite his dark scowl, a wave of familiar comfort washed over her as she gazed at him. There was no mistake. Yoema lived in the warm copper of his skin, the obsidian black of his hair, and the soft twinkle of his eyes.

She murmured, "She would have been proud of you."

The furrow between his brows deepened at her words. He clearly didn't believe her. "You should sleep now," he grunted.

She nodded.

But sleep was far from her mind. Though she curled up on her bed of fragrant pine boughs, she lay awake, musing on Yoema's mysterious prophecy about mending the past and wondering what part the woman's handsome grandson played in it. Dozens of questions kept her brain buzzing.

What had happened to the other Two-Son? Were Yoema's other relatives alive? Was Chase's story of Nome Cult true? Why hadn't her father or Yoema ever mentioned the march? Chase had said he wouldn't take revenge on her, but what were his intentions toward her father? Where *was* her father? Where was Frank? Had he found her note? And if so, were they worried about her or just disappointed?

Much later, as the moon sat skewered on the point of a lightning-ravaged cedar, Claire tossed and turned on her makeshift bed, sighing with the effort of quieting her mind.

Suddenly, Chase's voice intruded upon her restless thoughts. It was rough and low, more whisper than song. But the kind gesture moved her and brought a tiny smile to her lips. *"Unno winno, unno winno, unno winno."*

She drifted off to the familiar strains, snuggling more deeply into the soft bed. The lullaby of sweet memories rocked her to sleep, and the fragrance of pine scented her dreams.

CHAPTER 10

The amber light of the rising sun poured through the pines like water through a fishing net, warming Chase's bare chest. Rising to his elbows, he looked down at his sleeping captive, who lay curled on the boughs, wrapped in his shirt. Her delicate lashes rested like soft feathers against her cheek, and her lips parted with each breath.

He wished he didn't have to wake her. She slept so peacefully, her eyelids undisturbed by dreams, her breathing slow and deep. But the past evening they'd spent too much time in what his mother called dawdling, and they needed to go soon. Heading in this unexpected direction, he'd probably lost his trackers. But he couldn't be sure.

He squinted into the dawn and scrubbed at his jaw. His face was rough with whiskers. They itched. Perhaps he'd shave first. Then he'd wake her.

Edging quietly toward the cedars a good distance away, he took a whetstone from his pouch and started to hone his knife. The woman stirred once to the raucous cry of a nearby jay, but fell immediately back to sleep. Chase resumed sharpening, and then proceeded to scrape the stubble from his cheek.

He was troubled by some of the harebrained notions that kept flitting through his mind, ideas like spending more time with the white woman, listening to more of her memories about his grandmother, sharing stories about his life in Hupa.

It was nonsense, of course. He had to take her home. These weren't the days when a warrior stole the woman of a neighboring tribe and kept her for his own.

Besides, he thought, flinching as the blade nicked his jaw, Chase Wolf didn't need a woman to clutter his life, especially not a white woman. He was content to live alone in his village, among his own people, with no burden other than the demands of his work.

And Claire Parker? She belonged with her father in that big white house with servants and feather beds and barbed fences to protect her from the dangers of the natural world. He snorted in self-mockery, imagining her recoiling in horror at the sight of his humble cedar plank home in Hupa.

He studied her again. She looked so damaged and helpless, lying there in her frayed and dirty petticoat. Her skin was chafed, and her hair was tangled like the straw on a stable floor. He wouldn't blame Parker for thinking the worst when he saw his daughter.

He pinched a drop of dried sap from the cedar trunk, crushed it, and pressed the powder against the small nick along his jawbone, stanching the blood.

Then he trudged back to the bed of boughs, hoping the crunch of pine needles beneath his boots would wake the woman. But she slumbered on. He crossed his arms over his chest. He supposed she slept so well because she'd lain awake half the night. It was good he'd finally lulled her to sleep with that Konkow song.

He crouched beside her. Her breath fluttered the collar of

the shirt, *his* shirt, the one he'd tucked around her last night when he felt her shivering beside him.

He reached down and grasped the toe of her rabbit fur moccasin. She didn't awaken.

He gently jiggled her toe. Still she slept.

He took hold of her ankle and jostled her foot firmly. "Claire."

She opened her eyes in panic and rose on her elbows, mumbling, "Late for church?"

He smirked.

"Oh!" she sighed when she'd blinked the fog from her eyes. "Oh. I dreamt it was Sunday, and...never mind. You wouldn't..." She shook her head.

He understood, a little. His mother had spoken of church, of the whites' Creator and how they feared him. He supposed it was that fear that had brought her awake so suddenly.

"You..." She wiped at one sleep-glazed eye with the back of her hand and studied his face. "You shaved."

He grunted self-consciously, wishing he hadn't bothered. The twinkle of approval in her stare made him uncomfortable.

She finally lowered her gaze to scrub vigorously at her face, like a raccoon washing. Her voice was muffled by her hands. "My, I haven't slept so soundly since..." She broke off abruptly, peering at him over her fingers with sudden tenderness. "Thank you," she murmured.

He scowled. What could she possibly have to thank him for?

"For singing me to sleep," she said.

Fondness shone in her eyes now, too much of it. Uneasy, he looked away and flicked a beetle from his boot. "You would have kept me awake all night if I hadn't," he grumbled.

The woman shouldn't be grateful to him. For anything. He'd put her through much misery. He deserved her hatred, not her thanks.

But she smiled at him, not believing his grousing for one moment, then flushed pink when she lowered her gaze and noticed he was bare-chested. Realizing where his shirt had gone, she extended the crumpled garment toward him. "I'm sorry. I...I don't remember—"

"You were cold," he explained, taking the shirt. He slipped his arms into the sleeves. The cotton was still warm from her body.

Shaken by the direction of his thoughts, he quickly buttoned up the front, then gestured toward the bushes. "If you need to..."

She evidently did, for she scurried to enjoy the rare opportunity he allowed her to be alone. He dismantled the bed of boughs and picked wild grape leaves while she took care of her needs. When she returned, he motioned her to sit on the rock near the ashes from last night's fire.

Her limp seemed less pronounced now. Her feet must be healing.

She didn't say a word until he'd un-knotted the moccasins and unwrapped the fur, then carefully peeled the withered leaves from the broken skin. "Do they look better?"

He gave her a curt nod, then bundled the new leaves over the healing sores and replaced the moccasins.

"Thank you," she said softly.

There it was again—gratitude he didn't deserve.

He brushed his hands together brusquely and stood. "If you don't heal, you'll slow our progress," he tried to convince her, his words expressing none of the compassion he felt.

"I see." Again, she wasn't fooled. And her knowing smile only increased his irritation as they started down the slender deer trail that wound along the mountain.

Samuel Parker turned his mount to get a better look at the

lone animal grazing on the far hilltop. "Is that...Thunder?"

Frank, always eager to be in the thick of things, drew his pistol. "You and the men stay here, Mr. Parker. I'll go take a look-see."

Frank rode off while Samuel waited stoically on his horse. Only by virtue of the iron backbone that was a hallmark of the Parker breed did he manage to keep his dread in check. After all, it wouldn't do to let his ranch hands see him unmanned by the fear wrenching at his gut. If that was indeed his stallion, where was Claire?

He hadn't wanted to let anyone in on the details of what he'd found in Claire's room, but there was enough evidence to suspect foul play. If she'd truly meant to run away as her note indicated, she would have taken her packed bag. But there was a fresh set of clothing on her bed. She'd left behind those infernal dime novels she was always reading, the ones she thought he didn't know about. She'd never saddled up the dappled mare like her letter said. And her beautiful golden hair...

Samuel swallowed down the lump in his craw and clenched his hands tightly on the saddle horn.

All he'd told Frank was that Claire had gone missing, that someone must have taken her. There was no need to get the boy riled up over her breaking off their engagement. Besides, it was too soon to know exactly what had happened. There had been no ransom note, but if that was the kidnapper's purpose, Samuel would gladly pay whatever it cost to get his daughter back. And Claire would no doubt be so grateful to be home and under the protection of her fiancé after such an ordeal that she'd forget all about calling off the wedding.

In the distance, Samuel saw Frank dismount and cautiously approach Thunder, while the coy animal kept dancing out of his reach. Finally, the young man lost his temper, hurling his hat to the ground. With a taunting whinny, Thunder then trotted past Frank and headed straight toward Samuel and the search party.

The ranch hands caught the runaway beast, who looked like he'd had enough adventure for one night. Samuel got off his horse to inspect his prize stallion. The horse had no saddle, just a rope around his neck. Whoever had taken Claire had either been in a panicked rush or accustomed to riding bareback. He thought again about the half-breed he'd questioned at the Parlor. The man had had a pretty solid alibi. Still, he seemed the most likely candidate.

Thunder's left side was lightly scraped and coated with dirt, as if he'd been in a mudslide. Could the stallion have lost his footing in the rain? And if so, had Claire been hurt in the fall? Was she lying helpless somewhere with a broken neck?

The idea froze the blood in Samuel's veins. But he couldn't let fear paralyze him. If Claire was in trouble, time was of the essence.

Frank rode up then and slid out of his saddle with a scowl. "Son of a bitch. Look at that flank. What the hell did that bastard do? Thunder's our best stallion. When I get my hands on the sick son of a bitch who did this..." He kicked at the dirt. "Damn!"

The young man's appraisal of the situation didn't sit well with Samuel. Shouldn't Frank be more concerned with Claire's welfare than getting revenge on a horse thief? Then again, he supposed they were all under a good deal of stress. Frank could be forgiven for getting his priorities mixed up.

Still, Samuel didn't think Claire's kidnapper was a "sick son of a bitch" at all. He'd been clever and careful. He'd taken Claire with stealth, not bravado. As for stealing the horse, Frank had been unable to find fresh prints to indicate the man had arrived at Parker Ranch on horseback, so naturally he'd needed transportation. And so far there'd been no evidence of real harm to Claire. He'd cut off her hair, yes, but there was no blood, no sign of a struggle except for a dropped candle and a torn curtain.

In fact, for a time Samuel wondered if maybe his daughter had left willingly with someone—a friend or a lover. She'd been awfully upset over Yoema's death, and she'd meant to run away. Still, to leave her things behind...

Frank took off his hat and swatted it against his trousers. "When I find the two-bit ass-wipe who did this," he snarled, "I swear, Mr. Parker, I'll string him up by his guts."

Samuel frowned. One of the things that had always impressed him about Frank was his devotion, to the ranch and to him. Frank's position as boss had evolved as a matter of course, since the young man had spent two years at the Parker Ranch, tirelessly learning the business, taking part in buying and selling stock, treating the cattle and horses as if they were his own. That the man had earned the affections of his daughter only sealed Samuel's commitment to grooming Frank to take over the ranch upon his demise.

But Frank was also young and impetuous, a little too quick to jump to conclusions. Samuel thought this time he might be wrong.

"The tracks lead this way," Frank announced, already picking up the trail into the mountains. "Keep your guns close at hand, boys. He can't have gotten very far without the horse."

"Wait."

Samuel narrowed his eyes at the mountain pass. It was a curious choice. He would expect the man to hightail it out of the foothills and get as much distance between him and the Parker Ranch as possible. But Claire's abductor seemed to be circling back toward Paradise. It could be the fellow was lost, but Samuel didn't think so. Maybe, just maybe, Claire had convinced him to take her home.

At any rate, the last thing Samuel needed was a half-dozen

ragtag ranch hands who thought they were gunslingers set loose in the canyon. They were used to driving cattle, after all, not hunting criminals. And it was too easy to imagine overeager Frank shooting a hapless miner.

"Put your guns away before you kill each other," Samuel decided.

Frank's lips thinned in frustration, but he complied.

As the men rode on, Samuel held on to the desperate hope that Claire was still alive and safe.

Claire peered at her reflection in the shallow pool. Her hair was longer on one side, and it stuck out at crazy angles. She wished she'd managed to do a better job of cutting it. The uneven locks kept falling into her eyes, annoying her.

Since Chase had shaved off his stubble and emerged even more handsome, she'd grown increasingly self-conscious about her own ragged appearance. She had to admit, however, that her irritation had more to do with vanity than physical discomfort.

They'd stopped for water and to feast on the baby fern, wild lettuce, and grass nuts growing in abundance near the spring. Claire had taken advantage of the break to wash her face, but there wasn't much she could do about her hair.

Chewing morosely on a mint leaf, she looked up to find Chase studying her from his seat on a chunk of granite. He tossed the last tiny grass nut into his mouth and chomped it down. Then he told her, "It's crooked."

She sighed. "I know."

He sniffed. "I can fix it." He drew his knife.

She eyed the sharp blade. Did she want her abductor that close to her with a knife?

He arched a brow, adding, "Unless you're scared."

"No." That she would never admit.

He patted the ground between his feet. "Here."

She questioned her wisdom in obliging him. Even if he didn't mean to stab her, he had no references for the job.

In the end, she decided it was worth the risk. She seated herself before him on the thick cushion of pine needles, drawing up her knees and locking her arms around them. It was an intimate position, tucked there between his thighs, one she didn't dare think about too deeply.

His touch upon her was gentle, far gentler than she would have imagined, given his massive hands. Lacking a comb, he wove his fingers through her hair, tugging carefully when they snagged on tangles. At first, she cringed, all too conscious of the fact that her hair was matted and snarled from rain, sleep, and travel. But as his fingers drifted across her scalp, she closed her eyes and forgot about her drab locks, relishing the sensation like a well-caressed cat.

"I'll take you home soon," he murmured.

She opened her eyes, and that strange mix of relief and regret tugged at her heart again. She bit at her lip, forcing her voice to nonchalance. "When?"

He pulled a section of her hair taut, and she felt the knife slice smoothly through it. "Soon."

She'd never met a man of so few words. She closed her eyes again. "You know, your grandmother used to entertain herself for hours," she remembered, "coiling my hair into fantastical braids. My father often accused her of making Konkow baskets on my head."

He grunted, or maybe it was a chuckle, and then sliced again. A sprinkle of cut hair fell across her shoulder.

"I think you may have done this before," she said, impressed by how skillfully he could trim hair without the benefit of scissors. "Are you a barber?"

This time, she was sure he gave a snort of laughter. "I'm a blacksmith."

Her eyes went wide. She was entrusting her wispy curls to a ham-handed blacksmith? Dear God. Then again, she supposed her hair couldn't possibly look worse than it did now.

A blacksmith, she mused. No wonder he had such a powerful build. She closed her eyes again, picturing him in a long leather smith's apron while he pumped the bellows to make the coals burn scarlet upon his brazier. She imagined the sweat dripping down his bared forearms as he struck a glowing red chunk of iron with his heavy mallet. And her imagination began to make her heart beat faster with a curious excitement.

Somehow this brawny blacksmith had gentled his strength for her. His fingers were feather-light upon her hair. When his knuckles grazed the side of her neck, a delicious warm current sizzled through her body. His touch was rousing her senses in the most peculiar way.

Another clipped lock dropped onto her bent knee, and she lazily brushed it away.

The sun steamed the dewy ground now and warmed the cotton ruffle draping her legs. Sparrows twittered in the deerbrush. From beneath her lowered lids, she watched a trail of black ants traversing a rotting log and a chipmunk searching through the pine needles under it. Above, tattered clouds, strewn across the periwinkle canopy like the batting from a torn quilt, turned from pink to gold to white. The mountains were awakening.

Claire breathed a wistful sigh. Despite the harrowing journey, despite her scrapes and sunburn and fatigue, at this moment she felt strangely content, and she was in no hurry to have her adventures come to an end. This real-life escapade was far more thrilling than a dime novel.

She smiled. Yoema would have shaken her head at that. The old woman had always grumbled over the ferocious pictures of Red-skins in Claire's books and clucked her tongue when Claire recounted the outrageous tales of double-dealing gamblers and dastardly gunslingers.

Of course, in *this* story, Claire was the sweet and virtuous heroine. And Chase Wolf—was he the villain or the hero?

She let her eyes drift shut while she contemplated the question. Certainly he was as fierce as some of the muscular Indian villains painted in such lurid detail on the covers of her books. And he'd abducted a white woman—a recurring theme in many of the stories. But he'd also nursed her injuries, hunted game for her, sung her to sleep, and now he saw to her feminine vanity. Surely those were hallmarks of a hero.

Claire squirmed into a more comfortable position between the blacksmith's sturdy thighs. Whichever he was, hero or villain, Yoema's half-breed grandson wasn't evil. He seemed kind and caring, a decent man with deep convictions who'd simply made an honest mistake. She only prayed that when the final showdown came, whatever it was, just as in her books, justice would prevail and the ending would be a happy one.

CHAPTER 11

Chase clenched his teeth and groaned inwardly as Claire wriggled backward, insinuating her shoulders farther between his legs, closer to that part of him that had begun to harden with mindless lust.

"Hold still," he ground out.

Damn. The last thing he needed was to be aroused by the white woman. He had to keep his mind on preparing for the confrontation with her father. Hell, if Samuel Parker could see what was going through Chase's mind right now, he'd geld him quicker than he did his cattle.

He took a deep breath and blew it out forcefully, trying to banish the visions from his head the way a *kedaay*, doctor, would dispel evil spirits.

But it was useless. His swelling *whedze* didn't know the difference between desire of the body and desire of the mind.

Anxious to finish and to rid himself of the temptation he'd unwittingly placed between his thighs, he leaned forward to quickly complete his work, slicing the sides of her hair even with her chin.

Her jaw was fine-boned, like the face of a deer, and now that her tresses exposed its delicate edge, he realized anew how small and fragile the woman was. In truth, she wasn't much bigger than his little sister Iris. Iris was only thirteen summers old. Claire Parker was a grown woman. He saw her in profile now, and his gaze dropped to her lips, stained red by the wind. Yes, he decided as his nostrils flared unexpectedly, she was most definitely a grown woman.

He absently ran his fingers through her newly-trimmed tresses. Her eyes remained closed, the lashes delicate against her cheek, but as he watched, her lips parted, sweet and succulent, and he swore he glimpsed hunger in that ripe mouth. Fighting a surge of almost painful yearning, Chase tore his gaze away and withdrew his hand.

What was he thinking? What was he doing? His breath quickened in his chest as he tried to convince himself that the longing he'd seen in Claire''s face was an illusion, as insubstantial as a vision in the sweat lodge.

Surely he was mistaken. She couldn't feel desire, not after what he'd done to her. It was only the bright sunlight that had made her close her eyes, sleepiness that had opened her mouth that way.

Still, the memory of her expression left him uneasy. He grew even more keenly aware of their intimate position, of the sheer cotton barely covering her shoulders, the compelling curve of her back, the tiny snips of her golden hair scattered across the tops of his trousers.

"Are you finished?" Her voice was as thick as honey.

He didn't realize he'd stopped, but perhaps it was just as well. Her hair hung evenly now. Jabbing his knife into the log beside him, he brusquely ruffled her tresses with both hands to shake out the excess clippings. There was a slight curl to her hair, and it fell in soft waves about her face.

She lifted her fingers tentatively to examine his

handiwork. He tightened his jaw at the sight. Her fingernails were dirty and broken, yet another reminder of the damage he'd done.

"Maybe I'll start a new fashion," she breathed, turning her head to give him a tenuous smile. "Do I look better now?"

He couldn't bring himself to return her expression. Not while she sat between his legs, so close to...close to where a sleeping wolf, potent and dangerous, stirred. He stared at her, not daring to move, hardly daring to breathe.

"You look beautiful." He hadn't meant to blurt that out. Chase *never* blurted.

She blushed, lowering her eyes. "Oh, surely not. My gown is filthy. My hair is matted. My skin is—"

"These things don't matter."

What was he saying? Why did he continue to talk? He should silence his tongue, put away his knife, and start along the trail. But he couldn't stop the words from coming out. He spoke like the elders of his tribe, doling out portions of wisdom as if he had all the time in the world.

"What matters is the spirit within," he said.

As soon as she captured his gaze again, he knew he'd made a perilous mistake, like a rabbit setting foot in a fox's den, for her face beamed with the most wondrous expression, a mixture of awe and gratitude, things he absolutely didn't merit. The shame of it made him retreat as quickly as the rabbit. He snorted, yanking his knife from the stump.

"Or so say my people," he added gruffly.

He suddenly longed to flee, to run from that serpentine-colored gaze that imbued him with a kindness he didn't possess.

But Chase Wolf never ran from anyone. He was a blacksmith, after all, with the size and muscle that went with the job. The woman was no bigger than a fawn. Hell, he'd carried her on his hip with one arm. So why did he want to run from her now? Why did she inspire such fear in him?

His heart pumped erratically, and until she finally moved from between his legs, he couldn't even draw a clean breath.

"It was kind of you to do this for me," she purred, her face perfectly framed now with gentle waves of gold.

Damn, what was wrong with the woman's voice? She sounded like a kitten with a belly full of cream. And the fact that her throaty murmuring teased and caressed his ears only roused his anger all the more.

Why *had* he trimmed her hair and treated her cuts and blisters? He told himself it was for that hour when he would return her to her father. After all, if there was any hope of escaping with his life, Chase had to deliver the man's daughter with as little damage as possible. Maybe if the rancher saw she was unharmed, he'd be inspired to mercy.

But there was more to it than that. When Chase looked at Claire, he didn't see an object he must return to its owner in satisfactory condition. He saw a woman—a woman who lived and breathed, a woman who had feelings and dreams and fears. Every time he looked at the scrapes on her legs or her wind-chapped lips or the jagged strands of her hair, he felt overwhelmed with remorse. Somehow he had to make up for the wrong he'd done her.

Of course, he wouldn't tell her that. There was no reason to explain himself, not to a woman he'd never see again.

The truth of that disgruntled him, though he didn't know why. They didn't belong together, after all. He'd take her back to her grand ranch house, and, if the Great Spirit willed, he'd escape with his life and return to his village. *Heyung,* that was how it was. There was no other possible ending.

She gave him a gentle smile. "Well, anyway, Mr. Wolf, thank you for the barbering."

Her expression weakened his resolve like flame softening an iron billet. But he couldn't afford to let his heart get in the way of his head. For both their sakes, he must maintain his distance from the tempting white woman.

"Don't thank me." Briskly sheathing his knife, he kicked apart the nest of pine needles. "Maybe I was just getting tired of seeing it like that." Then he started down the mountain along a deer trail.

Claire's smile faded. She'd just begun to feel like there was a connection between them, a bond of body and spirit, like the completion of a circuit as powerful as lightning. Then he had to go and say something awful like that, something he obviously didn't mean.

In a fit of childish temper, she picked up a pine cone from the ground and hurled it after him. To her shock, it struck him smack in the middle of his back.

He froze, and she covered her mouth with both hands.

He slowly turned around and fixed her with a look of puzzlement. "Did you just throw a rock at me?"

She lowered her hands to her chin. "Not a rock. A pine cone."

He furrowed his brow. "Why?"

She opened her mouth, but she couldn't think of words to adequately describe just what he'd done to make her so angry.

"Don't do it again." He shook his head, then turned around, calling over his shoulder, "Come."

Something about his indifference and his bossy tone made her even more irate. She scooped up another pine cone and threw it. This one whizzed past his shoulder. To her satisfaction, he dodged in surprise.

"Ha!" she said.

This time when he wheeled around, his eyes were wide in disbelief.

When he took a step toward her, she reacted instinctively, reaching down to seize another pine cone and another, firing them off in rapid succession. He ducked one of them and batted the second away, but he kept coming.

Suddenly struck by the absurdity of the situation, she let out a nervous giggle and beat a hasty retreat while continuing to catapult as many pine cones as she could get her hands on.

"Why, you little..." he muttered, and he began advancing on her with more purpose.

She squeaked in panic and turned to flee. But she managed only two steps before he caught her from behind, grabbing her by the waist.

"Nooooo!" she squealed, breaking into peals of uncontrollable laughter as she fought to get free.

"Hold still," he bit out between his teeth.

She giggled, twisting in his arms.

"Hold *still*."

She squirmed around until she was facing him.

"Hold..."

His eyes went smoky, and the laughter died on her lips as she realized she'd just placed herself in a most compromising position. Her breasts were crushed against his chest, and she was trapped between his thighs.

Her gaze fell to his mouth. His lips were parted, and she could feel his warm breath upon her face. She could feel his fingers clutching her lower back. And then she felt something else, something pressing hard against her belly.

She suppressed a gasp and forced her gaze back to his eyes. They had softened to the color of a deep pool, calm and translucent. Dear God, he was so handsome and virile and alluring...

"No," he whispered in warning.

She pretended she didn't hear him as she slid into the soothing waters of his dark orbs, lost in the sensual waves closing over her head.

"No," he repeated, his voice ragged. "I have to get you home."

She gulped. Had he guessed what she was thinking?

He was gazing at her mouth now, and she self-consciously licked her lips.

"You know," she began on a breathless murmur, "we're not headed in the right direction." Lord, his brazen stare was scattering her thoughts. "Paradise is..." As her gaze dropped again to his slightly parted mouth, her voice trailed off, and her head was suddenly filled with the irrelevant, irreverent thought that Chase Wolf was probably the most breathtaking man she'd ever seen in her life.

It was dangerous, thinking such things, dangerous and irresponsible.

She saw his mouth tighten, as if he struggled with some life-altering decision. And then, without asking permission, she made a dangerous decision for both of them. She leaned forward to steal a kiss.

He stiffened when her lips contacted his, but she didn't let that stop her. She pressed against him once, twice, and he quickly became receptive. His lips softened until they were warm and supple against hers.

She tilted her head slightly to deepen the kiss, and slowly he began to return her advances.

When he reached up to cradle her head, she relaxed in his tender embrace. And when he gently opened her jaw with his thumb, parting her lips to taste her more thoroughly, she felt hot lightning coursing through her body and electrifying her senses.

It seemed like every nerve awakened inside her, brought to attention by the delicate brush of his tongue. Her skin tingled with heat, and her heart raced with a secret thrill.

She lost count of their kisses as one melded into the next. Soon she tangled her hands in his shirt, clutching at him with sensual desperation, trying to pull him closer. He obliged her, wrapping one arm around the small of her back and pressing her forward against him.

How many times had she closed her eyes and imagined her first kiss from a dime novel hero? How many times had she dreamed of this—of a man's lips on hers, melting her inhibitions and leaving her breathless with desire?

Their mouths parted for an instant, and she sighed, murmuring faintly, "Oh, Monowano..."

He suddenly went rigid.

She froze, realizing what she'd said. Her eyes flew open.

He pulled away.

"Shit," she blurted, instantly covering her mouth.

He was frowning again. Behind her hand, she silently repeated her curse, wishing she could recall her foolish outburst. But the spell was already broken. The magical moment was gone forever.

He set her firmly away from him then, and his voice cracked when he said, "We should go."

"I didn't mean to call you... It was an accident. I'm sorry."

He turned his back and started off. "It never happened," he called back over his shoulder.

"No, *that* wasn't an accident," she gushed. "*That* was...was wonderful."

He stopped mid-stride. But almost immediately, he reconsidered and continued walking away.

"I mean... That is..." She could feel her face flushing with embarrassment. "Don't go!"

He stopped again and took a deep breath. "It never happened," he repeated. "We have to go now. I have to get you back home."

She didn't want to go back home. She *really* didn't want to go back home, not now—now that she'd tasted...heaven. How could she make him stay?

"There's something you should know," she blurted out, biting her lip when he turned slowly to face her. "My father isn't looking for me."

"What?"

"He doesn't know I've been..." Kidnapped? Abducted? Stolen by a man with eyes the color of the night sky and a kiss to die for? She gulped. "He doesn't know the truth."

His scowl deepened.

And then, out of desperation and desire, Claire did a selfish and unforgivable thing. She lied to him. "He thinks I've gone to...Chico, the next town...to visit my aunt."

His eyes narrowed, then swept her quickly from head to toe. "In your petticoat?"

She gulped and inserted one truth. "I was in the middle of getting dressed when you..." Then she licked her lips and tried not to blush as she continued to lie with all the conviction of a snake oil seller. "Anyway, I left a letter for him. I told him I'd be gone for a few days. So..." She lowered her eyes, unable to meet his suspicious stare. "He won't be looking for me."

Chase wanted to believe her. Whether it was the possibility of not actually having a posse after him or the prospect of kissing her delicious mouth a while longer, he wanted to believe that Samuel Parker was napping in an armchair at his ranch, completely oblivious to his daughter's abduction.

But he knew better. She wasn't looking him in the eye. He also knew that if he and Claire continued along the path they were headed, they'd both get themselves into a heap of trouble. Letting lust have its way was like giving a horse its head. Sooner or later, they'd end up in territory where they didn't belong.

"What about his missing stallion?" he asked.

She shrugged. "Thunder gets out all the time."

"Really?" He didn't believe that either. "Then what about your aunt? Won't she notice when you don't show up?"

She opened her mouth, then closed it. Just as he suspected, she was up to something.

"Your father *is* looking for you," he decided.

"Maybe," she admitted. Then she brightened. "But he'll never think to look for me here. He'll go to Chico."

Chase furrowed his brow. If he didn't know any better, he'd suspect Miss Parker was trying to convince him not to take her home.

"So you see?" she said with far too much enthusiasm. "We're perfectly safe."

Chase scowled. She *was* trying to convince him not to take her home.

That was a hell of a thing.

"Don't worry, sir," Frank Sullivan announced, his eyes gleaming at his discovery of the buried ashes from a fire. "I'm onto him now."

Samuel was only half listening. He was more interested in the faint tracks leading to and from the campfire. They didn't quite match.

Samuel's insides had twisted every time he discovered an imprint of his daughter's bare toes in the mud. But the tracks leading away from the campfire revealed that the smaller of the two travelers now wore shoes, or at least something resembling shoes. How was that possible?

He glanced again at the charred bones atop the smothered fire. They belonged to something small. Probably a rabbit. The man must have killed a rabbit for supper.

"We should be heading out now, sir," Frank said. "We don't want the quarry to slip the net."

Samuel stared at Frank, who stood beside his mount, tapping his quirt impatiently against his thigh. But Samuel's mind was elsewhere.

If the man had killed a rabbit... The rabbit skin. Claire's shoes might be made out of rabbit skin. He strode forward, eager to prove his theory.

"I want to see the clearest tracks," he told Frank.

"But, sir..." There was that false forbearance again. It was beginning to annoy Samuel. "I've already determined that—"

"Never mind that. Just show me the tracks."

He could almost see waves of indignation rise off of Frank, but the young man held his tongue. He walked off a few paces and squatted in front of a bare patch of mud. "Here."

Samuel crouched beside him and peered closely at the tracks, running his fingers around the edge of the smaller print. "She's wearing shoes now."

Frank spit into the bushes. "Probably just rags from her gown or something, wrapped around her feet."

Samuel didn't think so. Whoever had his daughter was seeing to her welfare. He was convinced of it. Which could mean only one thing.

"Let's go," he told Frank.

There was hope. The kidnapper wasn't going to hurt Claire. He wanted to ransom her.

CHAPTER 12

"**K**id-witch," Claire repeated solemnly.

"*Kidiwische, -wische,*" he corrected.

Claire knitted her brows. His language was difficult, beautiful but difficult. She gazed out again across the sun-kissed lea, where newly-hatched white butterflies filled the air like snowflakes.

"And it means?" she prompted. She had been pestering Chase Wolf all morning about the Hupa language, much as she'd done with Yoema when she was learning the Konkow tongue.

He frowned, but she could tell he wasn't as irritated as he let on. "You're more curious than a raccoon."

"Raccoon. You mean, *minawe?*" she asked coyly.

A reluctant smile bloomed on his face. "*Minaxwe.*" It sounded so much better on his lips, husky and exotic. It made her ears shiver.

"Mm." She watched the butterflies disperse slowly into the woods.

"Thing that blows on the wind."

She looked askance.

"Kidiwische," he explained. "Butterfly. Thing that blows on the wind."

Claire nodded. His language was so poetic. "And how do you say—"

"No more, little *loqchwo,"* he groused. "That's enough for today."

"Loq- loq-," she attempted.

"Loqchwo, mockingbird."

He plunged onward out of the trees. He didn't seem quite as worried about her father tracking them, but that didn't mean he wasn't still intent on taking her back to Paradise.

She wished she could change his mind. It was so beautiful here above the canyon. She was enjoying his company. And she didn't want the adventure to end.

They passed through the meadow, careful not to disturb the few remaining butterflies that flitted and dipped through the air. The sun felt good on her face. The woods were thick at this elevation, and clearings like this were few and far between. The air was cool and clear, scented with pungent evergreen and, in meadows like the one they now crossed, the barely discernible fragrance of spring's first wild flowers.

For a long time, neither of them spoke. Yet the world was far from silent. In the distance, blue jays argued in screeches. Hummingbirds buzzed past in their search for nectar. At least once a minute, Claire heard a chipmunk rearranging pine needles with scrabbling paws.

High overhead, a hawk announced its presence with reedy cries. Claire squinted up at the circling bird.

"Kitsay," she whispered.

Hawk. Chase had told her the hawk was his brother's spirit animal, just as the wolf, *kilnadil,* was his. She watched it wheel lazily across the cloudless, lupin-blue sky, at last disappearing behind the tufted spears of towering pines that swayed almost imperceptibly in the slight breeze.

Claire took a deep breath of fresh mountain air. The day was glorious. In Paradise, it was the kind of day that a gentleman might take his sweetheart on a picnic. He'd stop to pick her a bouquet of lupins and poppies. She'd unpack a basket of fried chicken, fluffy rolls, and apple pie. He'd pour the cider, and they'd lunch on a quilt beside the creek.

She stared at the man hiking in front of her and smiled ruefully. He wasn't exactly a gentleman, and he didn't have flowers. They *had* eaten by the creek—an awful meal of those tasteless bulbs that seemed to grow everywhere and a handful of pine nuts he'd stolen from a squirrel's cache.

Still, her heart and her step were light, and her mood was happy. Maybe it was the thin air, or maybe it was only that up here on the mountain, she was so much closer to heaven. Whatever the reason, she felt deliriously joyful. As wrong and ridiculous and fanciful as it was, a part of her wished they could wander like this forever.

She liked Yoema's grandson. Now that she was confident he wasn't going to kill her or hurt her or steal her for a slave, she could appreciate his finer qualities.

Despite his mass and his menace, his dark scowl and his fierce growl, he wasn't the brute he pretended to be. Like the natives she knew, he had an affinity for nature, and he was sensitive to his surroundings. He detected the presence of animals long before she did, and he always knew just where to dig for food.

There was an inherent kindness in him, too, that belied all his grumbling. He'd carried her when she couldn't walk. He'd made shoes for her, sung her to sleep, trimmed her hair.

And he'd given her her first kiss.

That was never far from her mind. Though he'd chosen to

claim "it never happened," she could still vividly recall the lovely sensation of his arms holding her close, his chest crushing her breasts, his lips coaxing hers with sweet abandon. She wanted him to kiss her again.

Then her thoughts would slip back to Paradise, and she'd be struck by a pang of disappointment. If he returned her, all of this would be over—the adventure of sleeping by the sun's clock and traveling where the path led, living among the trees and the animals like a creature of nature. It wasn't always comfortable, and it wasn't always easy, but it made her feel alive. Or perhaps, she reconsidered, it was her companion who did that.

What would become of her when he said goodbye?

She didn't want to think about it. The future was too uncertain. She wanted to live in the present, wild and beautiful and free.

She shuffled along, kicking ideas about in her head the way she kicked at tiny fir cones on the path.

What if he didn't have to say goodbye? Claire's father was a reasonable man. Surely he'd see at once what a fine person Chase Wolf was, how kind and decent and honest and...

What if she invited him to stay? Paradise was the place of his birth, after all. Chase was a blacksmith. Maybe her father had a use for him. She wondered if she could convince him to let Chase work at the ranch. Certainly he could shoe horses and forge tack, repair scythes and mend broken wagon wheels. Her heart thumped excitedly at the prospect.

She could talk her father into it. She knew she could. After all, hadn't she convinced him to let her keep Yoema?

Then a doubtful scowl burrowed into her forehead. She'd been much younger when Yoema came to stay with her, and she'd just lost her mother. Samuel Parker would have given his little girl the moon if she'd asked for it.

But having a half-breed pay court to her? Her father would

never stand for that. What would people say? Such a thing might sully the Parker name.

Besides, it sounded too much like she wanted to keep Chase Wolf for a pet. She imagined Chase fetching supplies for her father, standing by obediently while Samuel inspected his work, bedding down in the barn with the cattle.

She sullenly kicked a stray pebble from the trail. Chase was like a woodland beast—unbroken and unbound. He could be neither leashed nor tamed. He no more belonged within the barbed wire of her father's ranch than she belonged in the open forest of his people.

It saddened her, and she let out a long, weary sigh.

"Sisil-ninyay?"

"Hmm?"

"Are you tired?"

"No."

"Hungry?"

"No. Well, maybe."

He pointed ahead to a patch of slender-bladed leaves poking up through the exposed roots of a dead pine. *"Qus."*

"No," she groaned in protest. "No more bulbs. Isn't there something else we could..."

She regretted her complaint the instant he turned around. His troubled frown revealed his thoughts. He'd done the best he could to provide sustenance for them, and here she was, acting the ungrateful wretch.

"I didn't mean..." But she could see it was too late for apologies. Her words had already hit their mark.

"I'll see what else I can find," he muttered.

She felt awful, trailing after him in silence as he plodded forward, scanning their surroundings, looking for something more palatable for his spoiled companion. Curse her quick tongue, she'd hurt his pride, and she wasn't sure how to repair the damage.

She hung her head, staring at the path. "You know, honestly, Mr. Wolf, I'd be perfectly happy with—"

He stopped so suddenly that she plowed into the back of him. Of course, his great bulk didn't budge a bit, so she bore the brunt of the impact, earning herself a face full of cotton shirt. His hand immediately reached behind to steady her.

"Tsisnah," he said under his breath.

She pressed her cheek against his back, listening carefully, but heard nothing. *"Tsisnah?"* she whispered.

"A bee."

She screwed up her forehead, still mashed against his damp shirt, content enough there for the moment, particularly if there was a bee on the loose. She wondered why he was so interested in a bee. Perhaps it was sacred to his tribe.

"And where there are bees…" he murmured.

Her brows shot up. Of course. "There is honey." She licked her lips, already imagining the sweet-tasting syrup. "Can you find the hive?"

He didn't answer her. Instead, he grabbed her hand and pulled her forward, his gaze pinned to the insect flitting from bloom to bloom in the clearing ahead. It seemed an impossible task, tracking such a madcap creature on its impetuous flight, but Chase was determined.

The bee hovered at first, gliding leisurely from the vivid orange poppies to the deep violet lupins, and they crept along after, watching its legs grow furry with pollen. Then it streaked abruptly away, flying low over the grass. With an oath, Chase tugged her forward till they were jogging after the bee, hand in hand, like children.

The bee made several abrupt changes in direction, once even diving toward them. Before long Claire was dodging and giggling and zigzagging through the meadow on Chase's lead until she was giddy and breathless. The bee finally lit on a cluster of white sweetpeas, and she stopped a moment to catch her breath, bending forward at the waist.

When she cocked her head to peer up at Chase, she nearly knocked herself off balance. Her normally brooding companion was gone. In his place was a beguiling stranger. A bright grin split his swarthy face, and his black eyes sparkled like jewels. Sunlight danced off his tousled hair and glistened in the sweat at his throat, where a carefree laugh was born.

It rolled out rich and deep, like a church hymn that, before long, demanded she join in. Their laughter intertwined. Then it cascaded. Then it grew to silly proportions over nothing at all, and Claire began to think she'd never laughed so thoroughly in her life.

When at last she managed to regain control, Chase's gaze had fallen to her hand, where his fingers still clasped her wrist. His smile faded naturally, but he didn't release her, and she grew aware of the warmth of his touch where his strong hand enclosed hers. Her heart already raced with the exertion of running and laughter, but when his thumb absently traced an arc over the inside of her wrist, it seemed to stroke the pulse there to a faster pace.

Their eyes caught and held, as if some secret passed between them. Claire's mouth parted in wonder, though she had no words for the feeling his gaze inspired.

At that moment, the bee buzzed past, severing that mysterious connection like scissors snipping string. They both blinked. Then Chase tore off again after the bee, dragging Claire with him. They ran until Claire could run no more.

"I...can't...have to...stop!" she gasped, clutching her side and grinning despite the sharp ache there.

She thought he would be disappointed, but as they came to a halt, he nodded toward the trees. "There."

Perhaps a dozen bees swarmed around the dark bole of a sugar pine. It had to be their hive.

"You found it!" she wheezed, doubling in half.

"You wait here," he told her. "I'll get the honey."

Claire was more than happy with that arrangement, though she missed his hand as soon as he let go. She leaned against a big boulder to watch him.

Using the same techniques Yoema had taught her, he plucked a dead pine branch from the ground and lit the dry needles with a match, blowing out the flame until it smoldered.

He approached the hive cautiously, all the time murmuring something—probably a prayer that he wouldn't be stung. He propped the smoking branch beside the hive, and the bees, mellowed by the smoke, took little notice of him as he drew his knife and slowly, carefully cut loose a small section of the comb.

In a matter of minutes, Chase was heading back toward her, his face triumphant, the golden treasure in hand.

She applauded as he neared. "Bravo!"

He held the comb aloft and beckoned her near with a grin. She tipped her head back and opened her mouth, and he squeezed the comb above her, drizzling the rich ambrosia onto her tongue.

After a few swallows, she licked her lips and pulled him down beside her to take over lapping up the stream of honey.

He cocked back his head, diverting the sweet syrup into his own mouth. The sight of his snowy teeth against his golden skin and his tongue slipping out to lick a drop of honey from his lip did something to her, making her feel as if the butterflies she'd seen in the meadow were fluttering in her stomach.

Maybe it was the glorious sunshine and the shared laughter. Or maybe it was just the seductive sweetness on her tongue. But she suddenly had the reckless urge to taste the honey from his lips.

Before she could reconsider, she opened her mouth beside his, intercepting the sticky stream, and then turned her head to kiss him. To her amazement, he didn't resist. The honey dripped between their joined mouths and glazed their tongues as they waged a sensual war over the precious nectar. Claire had never tasted anything so heavenly, and she licked up every precious drop.

Chase discarded the empty comb and tangled his hand in her hair, drawing her close to deepen the kiss. His mouth was delicious, sweeter than any honey. She felt like she could drink his kisses all day and never be satisfied.

Chase might have been able to pretend that first kiss—the one where Claire had called him by that dime novel hero's name—hadn't happened. But this was completely different.

Kissing Claire in the sunlight—with the hum of bees in the distance and the scent of wildflowers on the air, with the taste of honey on her lips and her sigh of contentment filling his mouth—was amazing.

Her lips were soft and sweet, and the heat of her quickening breath moved him to drink more deeply.

He loved how she fit perfectly into the circle of his arms, how she trusted his protection and didn't fear his strength, how she so willingly let him enjoy her essence. As wrong as it was, as dangerous as it was, he liked her body against him. And he wanted the feeling to last forever.

Soon he felt the stirrings of desire, not only in his head and in his heart, but between his legs. He hardened against her and began craving more than just kisses.

And so, as much as it pained him, he knew he had to stop. This wasn't right. Kissing her could only lead to caressing her, and caressing her...

Hell.

With a grimace of regret, he withdrew.

But the stubborn minx wouldn't let him go. She followed

him, grabbing the front of his shirt and leaning forward to capture his lips once more.

He kissed her lightly, once, twice, and then pulled away, squeezing his eyes closed with the effort.

"Kiss me again," she purred. She lifted her chin to look up at him, and he peered down at her through his lashes. Her eyes were full of wonder, mischief, and something else, something that stunned him and made him want to throw caution aside, to hold her and kiss her again, long and hard.

Adoration. She looked at him with adoration.

No one had ever looked at him like that before. His sisters looked at him with fondness. A few of the young women of his village looked at him with hunger. But what he saw in this white woman's eyes was beyond tenderness, beyond lust, and completely without fear. She adored him.

"Kiss me again," she breathed.

He shook his head.

"Please?"

"No good can come of it," he choked out.

"I don't care."

"You belong to another."

She swallowed hard, as if considering his words, then whispered, "No one will know."

He might have resisted the urge if her gaze hadn't fallen upon his mouth just then, if she hadn't parted her soft pink lips in yearning. But once she did, he was helpless to refuse. He cupped her face, inclined his head, and covered her mouth with his own.

Her eager compliance flooded his veins with liquid fire as he slanted his mouth across hers. His chest heaved, and his heart hammered against his ribs. Flame surged in his loins, melting his inhibitions and hardening him like tempered steel. He fought to keep from crushing her with the growing power of his need.

Then she made a soft moan, an almost imperceptible sound that nonetheless startled him.

He must have hurt her.

The breath caught in his chest. Curse his clumsy strength, he'd hurt her.

He should have known better. He was a damned blacksmith, after all, too rough for a proper lady.

Ashamed by his lack of restraint and his unintentional brutality, he ended the kiss and let her go.

What remained of Claire's thoughts whirled in a tumultuous storm of emotions—desire, fear, joy, panic—making her dizzy.

The moan escaped her before she knew it was uttered. If she'd known what it would do—that it would cause him to abandon the kiss—she would have bit it back till her lips bled.

When he abruptly let her go, she staggered backward as if from a punch. Hurt and bewilderment left her mute. Why had he stopped? Why was he pushing her away? Did he find her somehow distasteful?

"I'm sorry," she whispered.

"You? No." He scowled at the ground. "*I'm* sorry. It's *my* fault," he murmured. "I didn't mean to hurt you."

"Hurt me?" She blinked in surprise. "But you didn't."

"I'm always hurting people."

"You didn't hurt me, not at—"

"I'm just a big oaf," he said, rubbing the back of his neck.

"No, you're not."

He obviously wasn't listening, because he hung his head and sighed. "Anyway, I'm sorry I ever—"

"Sorry?"

"Sorry I pushed myself on you like that. It was crazy and rude and...and unforgivable. And I promise I'll never—"

There was only one way to convince him. Shaking her head, she seized the front of his shirt, and tugged him forcefully forward. She pressed her lips to his—hard—to make sure there was no mistaking her intentions.

Persuading him didn't take long. Kissing might have been new for Claire, but she was learning fast.

What she didn't anticipate was the fever that rose in her as she continued to kiss him with eager abandon. Her blood grew hot, and a keen yearning that started deep within her seemed to take over her limbs, giving them permission to do things she'd never dared before. She ran her palms across his broad shoulders, up his corded neck, and along his strong jaw and threaded her fingers through his thick hair.

She crushed her breasts against him, hoping to soothe the strange tingling there. She pressed her body against his thigh, trying to ease the ache between her legs. She knew it wasn't proper. Only saloon girls did such things. But she couldn't seem to stop herself.

Her breath came faster and faster. Her fingers grasped at him more desperately with each passing moment. She moaned against his lips, and this time, instead of letting him pull away, she clung to him, dipping her tongue inside his mouth with more ravenous hunger than before.

He caught the back of her head, returning her forays with deep but gentle thrusts of his tongue that made her head buzz with pleasure and threatened to rob her of her senses.

But what made her gasp in wonder was when he clasped her buttock and drew her close, pressing the rock-hard bulge in his trousers against her belly. For an instant, she froze in shock. In the next moment, a surge of overwhelming desire rose in her, weakening her knees and making her want to surrender herself completely to him.

Then he growled out an oath and pulled away again.

Chase tried to ignore the bewildered dismay in Claire's eyes.

What in the hell was the matter with him? He'd promised

her he wouldn't kiss her again. So much was wrong with what he'd just done, he didn't know where to begin.

Claire belonged to someone else. No good could come from leading her into temptation—or from tormenting himself with what he couldn't have. Why had he let her entice him into kissing her again? His brain must be going soft.

Unfortunately, that was all that was going soft. Elsewhere he was as hard as granite.

There were two things he could do about that. The first and most desirable option was unthinkable, though that didn't keep him from giving it a hell of a lot of thought.

"What is it?" Claire whispered. "Did *I* do something wrong?"

Yes, she'd done something wrong. She'd played with fire. She'd poked a grizzly. She'd set herself smack in the path of a runaway stage.

But then he made the mistake of glancing down at her wide green eyes and her sad little mouth, and he didn't have the heart to let her believe that.

He sighed. "Nope," he told her. "You didn't do anything wrong."

He was the one who'd done something wrong. Their embrace had shaken him, body and soul. It was as if their spirits had intertwined at the joining of their lips, as if the ores of their two divergent metals had become one under the molten heat of their tongues.

In fact, he'd done so much wrong that it would take more than his ten fingers to count the reasons.

First, she was a white woman.

Second, she belonged to another man.

Third, she was the woman he'd stolen for revenge.

Fourth, it would anger his grandmother's *chindin*.

Fifth...

"Don't you like kissing?"

His voice was half chuckle, half choke. "Oh, I like kissing all right." He liked kissing more than he liked...air.

"Then what is it?" She lowered her eyes. Her whisper was colored with pain. "Am I somehow...repulsive to you?"

A dull blow, like the halfhearted kick of a lazy horse, knocked him in the chest, filling him with remorse. Did she honestly think that? How could she think that?

Claire Parker was as lovely as a spring lily. And desire had made her even more lovely. Her hair was tousled where he'd swept it between his fingers, and her trembling lips were rosy from kissing. When she lifted her gaze, her eyes shone dark with hurt and unspent passion. His heart longed to reach for her, and within his trousers, his *whedze* longed for something even more forbidden. Hell, he wanted her in his arms, in his mouth, in his soul again.

"No," he croaked. "You're beautiful." He clenched his fists, fully aware he should say nothing more, and just as fully aware he was going to anyway. "I shouldn't kiss you...Claire..." She glanced up, clearly startled that he called her by name. "...because it makes me want to do more."

She looked at him then with so much relief, pleasure, and yearning that he had to yank his gaze away before he did something he'd regret.

He studied his boots. "This just isn't the right time or place," he said, though he knew that was a lie. There wasn't ever going to be a right time or place. He'd make sure of that.

As far as now, it was useless to prolong the pain. He needed to seek that second form of relief before he thought any more about the one he craved. So taking hold of Claire's hand, he tugged her forward.

"Let's go find the creek," he said. "I could use a bath."

"A bath?" She blinked. "But it's spring. The water's awfully cold."

"Yep."

Chapter 13

The cold water did the trick.

Chase, freshly bathed and dressed in his trousers, lay on his belly across a flat rock overhanging the stream. He concentrated hard on the shimmering water below, careful not to let his shadow fall across the *loyawh,* trout, gliding in lazy loops beneath the surface. The fish circled the fine milkweed fiber Chase dangled in the creek, then danced close, brushing it with its fin, even nibbling at one of the worms on the slivers of bone tied along the line. But though Chase had dabbled the bait there for what seemed like time enough to grow a full beard, the trout wasn't interested.

He hadn't fished this way since he was a boy. In Hupa, they built an *ehs,* a dam, across the river to trap salmon, or they caught trout with a net. But his father had also shown him the Konkow way of fishing, which was useful in smaller creeks and when traveling. At least, it was *supposed* to be useful. At this rate, Chase was sure that, years from now, someone would find his bleached bones still lying atop this rock and that damned fish still circling around and around the line.

Of one thing he was certain. He didn't have his father's patience. Sakote was renowned in Hupa for his hunting, which required an enormous amount of patience. But Chase didn't like waiting for things to happen. He liked to *make* them happen. Maybe that was why he'd become a blacksmith. There was satisfaction in taking a shapeless lump of hard iron and, using nothing but fire and the strength of his own arm, hammering it, bending it, forging it into something useful.

If only he could forge something to eat. His stomach growled, reminding him of how little he liked this fugitive diet of roots and bulbs and ferns. They'd had that bit of honey earlier, and he'd found a cache of shelf fungus growing on a pine to serve as their noon meal. But Claire had been reluctant to eat the ugly, spongy stuff, and even *he* found it less than appetizing.

He wiggled the line, careful not to jar loose the stone anchoring the line to the creek bed. The trout sidled near, nudging the second bone sliver. Chase held his breath, praying silently to all the gods he knew. The fish hovered in the current, and Chase gently shimmied the line again.

Come, he thought fervently, *come, Brother Loyawh, give yourself to me.* The trout swam to the other side of the line, investigating the bait from another angle. *Yes, yes,* Chase thought, *take it.* But this time, when he jiggled the line, the anchoring rock popped up, startling the fish, and the trout wriggled away with a swish of its tail fin.

"Xongqot!" Chase banged his fist on the rock and watched the current carry his fishing line into an underwater nest of tangled reeds.

"Is something wrong?"

Still on his belly, Chase twisted his head to look behind him. Claire stood in the bright glade, her face washed clean, her hair still damp from the creek, and her rabbit fur boots clutched in one hand. Her sheer white garment shifted in the subtle breeze, alternately clinging to her body, then blowing out to reveal her curves in the strong sunlight. He was so astonished by the change in her, so aroused by her beauty in spite of his own sobering dip in the icy creek, that he almost forgot his discomfiture at being caught in this humiliating situation.

It *was* humiliating. He was half-Konkow, after all, and the son of a great hunter. But so far, all he had to show for an hour of fishing was a sun-baked back and a fiber line snarled in the bracken.

"I took a dip, too, downstream," she admitted with a sheepish shrug.

He nearly choked as an image of her frolicking in the creek without a stitch of clothing on flitted through his mind.

Concerned furrowed her brow. "Did you hurt your hand?" She set down her slippers and stepped forward, giving him a glimpse of the rounded contours of her breasts as the cotton flattened against her. His breath stuck in his throat, and suddenly he couldn't recall what she'd just asked him.

"On the rock," she clarified.

"The rock," he blankly echoed. Then he scowled, as annoyed by the apparent disappearance of his wits as he was at being caught in a childish display of temper. He shook his head. "No."

Hell, he hadn't been able to think straight since morning. The memory of Claire's passionate kiss wouldn't fade from his mind.

Now that she stood before him in the light of day, as dazzling and glorious as an angel, he felt his body again begin to betray him. His heart quickened, and his *whedze,* hidden beneath him at the moment, hardened uncomfortably.

He needed to move. Hoping to conceal the evidence of her effect upon him, he sulkily pushed himself up off the boulder and turned carefully to sit facing diagonally to her, draping his elbow over his raised knees.

Her gaze dipped to his bare torso at once. She gulped, running a self-conscious hand through her hair.

The corner of his mouth drifted upward. At least he wasn't alone in his discomfort. It amused him, this curious fascination she had with his bare chest. White men always wore shirts. Perhaps his was the first chest she'd ever seen. He didn't know why, but the idea pleased him.

She licked quickly at her lower lip, pleasing him more. "Have you caught a fish yet?"

His pleasure dimmed a bit at her question. "Nope." He lowered his gaze, picking a piece of lichen from the rock and tossing it into the creek. "Fishing isn't easy, you know. It requires time and patience."

She wiped her hands on her skirts and ventured timidly toward him. "Are you sure there are fish here?"

"Yep." He resisted adding that it had been years since he'd fished in this manner and that a whole creek full of trout did not ensure he'd catch one.

Claire peered past him, searching the clear water for herself, and Chase watched her at his leisure. He'd spoken the truth when he'd told her she was beautiful, even if he was more accustomed to the looks of Hupa women with their straight black hair and shining black eyes, skin the color of summer deerhide and bellies round with health. There was something about Claire—her glistening white-gold tresses, her liquid green eyes, the sweet mouth he remembered all too vividly, the captivating combination of outer frailty and inner strength she possessed—that bewitched him and lent her a loveliness all her own.

"Is that your fishing line?" she asked.

He followed her gaze. Just below the swirling water, the fiber line waved with the current, taunting him. "It was."

She scrutinized it more closely. "Mind if I try?"

He raised a brow. "You? What does a white woman know about fishing?"

She shrugged. "I've been a time or two."

He grinned, sweeping his arm toward the creek in welcome. He'd seen the way the white men fished, with a coarse line and a steel hook. Claire possessed neither. He wondered what she would do. He rested his chin on the heel of his hand, content to watch.

He didn't believe his fishing line could be salvaged, but somehow, after a couple of tries, using a long stick with a twin fork at the end, Claire managed to pull it free of the reeds. It had surprisingly few tangles after all, though the bait had disappeared. Within moments, she had the wet line stretched out along the bank, inspecting the bone sliver to make certain it was secure.

Satisfied, she set about searching for bait amongst the grass growing by the stream. Using the forked stick, she prodded the soil in several places, digging at the damp ground.

She found an earthworm, but the way she held it between her thumb and one finger, as far away from herself as possible, it didn't seem like something she wanted to do. Grimacing in disgust as it squirmed around her finger, she plucked up the fishing line with her other hand. Chase winced along with her as she pierced one end of the worm's body with a bone sliver. Clamping her lips and working with shuddering haste, she wrapped the worm twice around the bone and attached it in the same fashion to the other end of the sliver.

Blowing out a relieved breath—the worst was over—she picked up the line and started toward him. "May I?"

Fascinated with her determination, he hopped up at once, surrendering his place on the rock. Crossing his arms over his chest, he watched her stretch out along the rock on her belly. Her gown slipped up, revealing the tender hollow at the back of her knee, and Chase fought a sudden overwhelming urge to touch her there. Then she tugged the fabric down with her free hand, and he forced his eyes and his thoughts to the fishing line dropping into the water.

As she silently fished and the sun moved across the top of the sky, he observed her with growing satisfaction. It seemed she was no better at the task than he. Perhaps she had more patience, but patience couldn't force a reluctant fish to sacrifice itself for a man's supper.

When he tired of watching her dangle the line, he let his gaze roam lazily over her backside. The cotton clung to her, outlining the sleek length of her legs and the gentle curve of her buttocks. Her petticoat revealed ankles that appeared too delicate for walking, and the sight of her bare toes, twitching contentedly in the sunlight, coaxed a smile from him.

A curious peace settled over his bones. The warm spring sunlight made him drowsy. The quiet lapping and gurgling of the creek played like a sleeping song in his ears. Soon he found himself leaning back against the trunk of an old sycamore, then sinking onto his haunches to slouch against it, then lowering his head till it rested upon his chest, and finally letting his eyes drift shut.

Her scream sent him bolting to his feet, his heart pounding like a mallet on an anvil.

"I got him!" She squatted like a child on the rock. A fat trout flipped on the line she suspended over the water. There was a huge grin on her face.

The most he could manage while his stomach was still lodged somewhere in his throat from that scream was a weak smile and a nod. He started forward on shaky legs. He would have to disengage the fish for her before she accidentally dropped it back into the water. But just as he got to her, she managed to work the bone free. As if she'd done it a hundred times before, she tossed the flopping trout onto a soft patch of grass.

He furrowed his brow. How had she managed to land a fish? She was supposed to be a spoiled white woman who ate food out of tins. Fishing was part of *his* people's heritage. Brief envy clouded his sunny mood.

But once he beheld the utter joy on Claire's face, the happy sparkle of her eyes, he couldn't help but celebrate with her. He couldn't help but feel a part of her triumph.

"You *have* fished before," he chided, softening his words with a smile.

"I have," she admitted, grinning coyly. "Your grandmother took me fishing many times along the creek that runs through Paradise."

Claire looked so pretty when she smiled. He twinkled his eyes in return. "She taught you well."

"She taught me a lot." Her smile grew wistful as she straightened out the fishing line. "How to make manzanita cider, how to find yellow jacket nests, how to summon deer." She demonstrated, clicking two fingernails together. "She tried to teach me to make baskets, but I'm afraid my fingers are all thumbs when it comes to weaving."

He chuckled at her curious comment, and she stopped what she was doing to stare at him.

"What?" he asked.

"Your laugh," she marveled. "It sounds so much like..." Then she gave her head a shake. "It's very nice."

Claire forced her attention back to the fishing line. His laugh *was* nice. She hadn't noticed before, but his cheerful chuckles sounded remarkably similar to his grandmother's. Of course, it made sense. They were from the same family after all. Claire had just never expected to hear that sound again.

She wanted to hear more of it. And that wasn't all she wanted more of. Chase might have told her it wasn't the right time or place for kissing, but there *would* be a right time and place...very soon, if she had her way.

Until then, she'd have to pursue him the same way she caught fish—with patience and determination.

"Would you like to try again?" she asked, offering the line to him. She knew how competitive men could be. Frank hated it when she bested him in anything—fishing, riding, chess. She imagined it pricked Chase's pride that she'd caught the first trout.

But he shook his head. "The *loyawh* gave himself to *you*. It must be your day to fish."

It was difficult to hide her enthusiasm. In the long weeks since Yoema had fallen ill, Claire had spent very little time outdoors. She'd stayed by the old woman's bedside, leaving only to gather the herbs, roots, and bark Yoema requested to make her medicines. Claire hadn't watched a sparrow hatch or bathed in a creek or fished since last year.

She examined the line. The earthworm was gone. She'd have to dig up another. It was the one part of fishing that repulsed her.

As she turned to find a digging stick, Chase came up beside her, a wriggling worm between his fingers. Before she could say how-do-you-do, he reached for the fishing line and swiftly skewered the worm onto the bone sliver.

One side of his mouth quirked up. "You don't like this part of fishing."

"No." She flashed him a grateful grin. "Thank you."

"I suppose I'll have to clean the fish for you as well," he grumbled in mock disgust.

"Would you?" She playfully batted her eyelashes.

He grunted, but amusement crinkled his eyes. With a sigh, he returned to his spot beneath the sycamore to watch her.

She settled back down onto her stomach atop the boulder, this time tossing the line into the deepest part of the creek. There was a grandfather trout there, she sensed, an ancient fish that had spent many seasons growing to a grand size, a wise fish that lived far beneath the waves, thus far eluding all attempts at capture. But Chase had said it himself—it was her day to fish. Today she'd catch that old grandfather trout.

After a while, with the sun dazzling the water and the creek gurgling a lullaby, insects hovering lazily by the muddy banks and birds twittering in the brush, Claire almost drifted off as the line floated in the current. Her eyes half closed, she scarcely noticed the first tiny tug on the fiber. The second tug widened her eyes. The third slipped the line through her fingers, and she closed her fist with a gasp.

Whatever had locked onto the line was strong, bigger than anything she'd ever caught. It yanked against her grip.

"Oh! Oh!" she exclaimed, holding on with both hands now. Peering into the water, where the line jerked along the surface, she saw a flash of silver curve past. "Oh, my goodness!"

Because both hands were occupied, she couldn't get up from her belly to her knees to get a better angle on the line.

Chase came up behind her and let out a toneless whistle. "That's a big fish."

"It's a *huge* fish."

"Have you got it?"

"I don't know."

"Hold on."

"I *am*."

"It's a *very* big fish."

"I know." She tried to reel the fiber in, but it was impossible to get any leverage with her elbows jammed into the boulder.

"Do you need…do you want help?"

"No!" Her heart might be beating against her ribs like a galloping colt, but she had her pride. She wound the line around her hand—once, twice. The fiber seemed so fine, so frail. Then the fish wriggled violently beneath the waves. "No!"

"Are you sure?" He crouched beside her now, and from the corner of her eye, she saw him rub an anxious hand over his jaw.

"I'm posi—" The trout wrestled with the line again, and in desperation, Claire began to haul in the fiber, hand over hand.

"Careful!"

"I know, I know." She could see the trout's shimmering body now, battling down and then rising up through the current. The fish was enormous, easily as long as her hand and forearm combined, and powerful. If she had this much trouble controlling it in the water...

"Slowly." His fists were clenched now, as if he held the line himself.

The closer to the surface the fish came, the more violent its struggles.

Chase's voice was tense. "Do you need—"

"I've got him, I've got him!" she insisted, though her forearms strained at the fish's wild thrashing.

And then, almost as if the wise old trout had planned it all along, at her next strong tug, the fish popped up through the water, high into the air, wrenched its body sideways, and broke the fiber line.

"No!" she cried.

Chase bounded from the rock before she finished the word. With a wild, crazed leap, he caught the airborne trout between his hands, hugged it to his chest, and dropped into the creek, fish and all, with a huge splash.

CHAPTER 14

laire's mouth was still hanging open when Chase surfaced with the slippery fish flapping against his body and his swarthy face split by a magnificent grin.

"Got him!" he crowed.

Victorious laughter spilled out of her like champagne. Chase tossed his head, sending droplets of water scattering from his drenched locks. The sight of his snowy teeth and the dimple in one cheek made her pulse leap like a frisky lamb.

Then the trout wriggled in a last desperate attempt at freedom, and Chase almost lost him.

"Throw it on the bank!" she cried, giggling. "Hurry!"

He heaved the fish through the air, and it landed beside its now silent brother in the grass, where it flopped in exhaustion, surrendering the battle.

Chase ran both hands through his wet curls and laughed again, that laugh so like his grandmother's. "I think the Great Spirit amuses himself at my expense."

Breathless with delight, Claire stacked her fists and rested her chin atop them. "I think you deserve to eat that entire fish yourself."

"No," he countered. "Grandfather Trout came to you."

"But you sacrificed far more for him. Your comfort..." She bit back a smile. "Your dignity..."

He swatted playfully across the water, splashing her. She squealed and scampered back from the creek's edge.

He emerged from the stream then, and all the cockiness went out of Claire's grin. Something about the way his wet trousers clung to him, the slow drip of water from his fingertips, and his sensual, lazy stride chased all reason from her mind.

He stood before her, brushing the water from his thighs for several moments before she realized she was staring at him.

"I look like a half-drowned wildcat," he said.

"No," she protested, her voice ragged, her heart pounding. "You look..." She swallowed. He looked breathtakingly handsome.

He peered up at her through a wayward lock of hair. "Like a *completely* drowned wildcat?" he guessed.

"No."

She watched as he stomped the water from his leather boots, then knelt to loosen his bootlaces.

"My sisters say I look like my spirit animal, *kilnadil*, an ugly old wolf."

She knitted her brows. Surely nobody said that.

"Sullen," he grunted, tugging off his boot. "And savage."

She caught her lip between her teeth. Two days ago, she might have agreed, but not now. "No. I was going to say you look..." Her pulse rushed, just as it did when she was about to do something scandalous, like cracking open a new dime novel or cursing out loud. "Lovely."

She didn't know why she'd blurted that out. It was brazen and careless, and completely inappropriate. He'd stiffened and now sat staring at the toe of his boot. What a ninny she was, spilling her innermost thoughts that way. *Lovely?* Men didn't want to be lovely. Handsome perhaps, or dashing, but not lovely. Daniel Boone and Kit Carson weren't lovely. She lowered her eyes, feeling her cheeks grow hot.

He resumed untying the second boot. "I think maybe you wouldn't say so if I'd dropped your fish," he teased.

She glanced up. The shadow of a grin lurked at the corner of his mouth, inviting her to smile as well. "You may be right," she admitted.

He snorted. The boot came off with a sucking sound, followed shortly by wet gray socks he tossed over the branches of a bush. He flexed his bare toes in the sunlight. Lord, even the man's feet were lovely.

She tore her gaze away and tried to think up some inane tidbit of conversation, lest he discover the unruly direction of her thoughts.

"How many sisters do you have?" she managed.

He unfastened his waterlogged deerskin pouch, then strewed its contents, tools mostly, out to dry in a sunny patch of earth. "Six."

"Six?" She leaned back against the trunk of a golden oak. "I always wanted a sister," she confessed.

"They're bothersome." Despite his words, there was a fond smile on his face as he hung the pouch on the lowest fork of the oak.

"You look after them, of course," she chided.

He shrugged. "Someone has to keep them out of trouble." He drew his knife, setting it on the great boulder before he stretched out on his back to dry in the sun. The menacing glint of steel seemed to underscore his words.

She dug into the leaf mulch with one toe. "I *have* no brother to look out for *me*. I suppose that's why I'm always in such trouble."

He rocked his head toward her and squinted one eye. "Trouble. You?"

"So my father says."

"What trouble?"

"Oh." The list was endless. "Giving cream to stray kittens. Feigning illness to get out of church. Calling Mr. Forester an old buzzard. Forgetting to close the corral gate. Dancing with the Indians."

His brow clouded at that, and she hastened to explain.

"Some of the ranch hands did the Acorn Dance, the *Aki*, in autumn. I used to sneak out at night to dance with them. My father didn't think it was appropriate for a young lady of my station. He forbade me to join them."

"And did you obey him?"

She supposed her sly smile was answer enough.

He chuckled and lay his head back on the rock, closing his eyes. "Trouble."

They talked for a long while then, about Claire's childhood, about his twin brother, who, it turned out, had journeyed to Paradise with him, about fishing, about nothing.

Chase decided that sometime in the midst of their storytelling, the Great Spirit must have dropped a sleeping medicine upon them, for when he awoke later, he saw the sun had already crossed the top of the sky and now began its descent. With a muttered curse, he bolted upright, running his fingers through his hair, which had already dried.

Falling asleep hadn't been his intent. How long had it been? Two hours? A quarter of the day? His trousers were still damp, but then the thick denim probably wouldn't dry till nightfall.

He scowled. He'd been careless. No matter how fine the afternoon or mellow his mood, he still had to be wary. Samuel Parker might be looking for Claire in the wrong place, but it wouldn't be long before he realized that, doubled back, and started searching up the canyon. He could stumble upon them at any time.

Shoving his knife back into its sheath, he glanced about for Claire. She was napping a short distance away, cradled in a nest of fallen oak leaves, her hair caressing her cheek, her chest rising and falling with each calm breath.

He realized with sudden unease that he'd been awfully quick to trust her. She could have walked off and left him while he was sleeping. Hell, she could have stabbed him with his own knife for that matter and left him for dead. Only a few days ago, she'd been desperate to escape.

Now she seemed determined not to return home.

He couldn't complain. Claire was good company. She was clever and kindhearted. She was deceptively strong beneath her delicate woman's body. And Chase liked her laugh. The shine of joy in her eyes when he'd caught that silly fish had made his heart beat like that of a proud warrior in his first battle.

He grinned, remembering. The two fish lay quiet on the grass now. They would make a fine meal. Maybe that was what had kept Claire from leaving—hunger and the promise of trout for supper.

Careful not to disturb her, he crept to the stream to clean the fish, remembering to thank the Great Spirit for the gift of food.

Stringing the trout onto the fiber line to carry them, he narrowed his eyes at the lowering sun. By his reckoning, if they left now, they could make it to the ridge above Paradise by sunset.

Tomorrow, if all went as planned, they'd begin their descent into Paradise. The next day he'd sneak into town and round up Drew. He'd have Claire back in her big white house sooner than she could say "Kisan-yiman-dilwawh."

And if things *didn't* go as planned? Chase glanced over at

the peacefully dozing Claire. For her sake as well as his, he prayed no one would get hurt. If her father showed up, Chase didn't intend to draw the first weapon. He hoped it wouldn't come to that.

Claire stirred in her sleep, and he inclined his head to study the delicate curl of her hand, so innocent, so trusting.

He was going to miss Claire Parker. He liked her. He liked her smile and her shrieks and her stubbornness. He liked the way she looked when she slept, and he liked the sound of her night-soft voice beside the fire. Her tears snagged at his soul, and her laughter lifted his spirit. And the taste of her mouth, the pleasure of her body against his...

He shook his head. It was foolish to dwell on such things. Their paths were not meant to converge, only to cross. It was best they cross quickly. Claire's father would be worried. And Drew must wonder by now what had happened to his hotheaded brother.

Before Chase could change his mind, he slung the pair of trout across one shoulder and slogged through the leaves toward Claire, hoping the noise would wake her.

"It's time to go, *ch'inson*," he said, whispering the endearment.

She stretched like a contented kitten and gave him a sleepy smile that warmed him to his toes.

The twilight sky drew its purple-feathered cape over the deep vale, casting the canyon below in shadow. They had made it to the crest, which rose so high above the valley floor that the emerging stars overhead seemed close enough to seize. The air was cold, the fire searing—extremes, Chase knew, that strengthened steel and man alike.

They huddled together beside the clear-burning fire, too cold and hungry to speak, and cooked. By the time the skin on the trout began to crackle over the flame, Chase had heard Claire's stomach growl a dozen times. Each time it rumbled, she ducked her chin in embarrassment.

"You're like the grizzly," he finally said, jabbing with a stick at the glowing coals, "growling for your supper."

"Chase!" She crossed her arms primly over her belly. "Gentlemen don't mention such things." Despite her haughty tone of voice, gaiety lit her eyes.

"Mm. And ladies don't dance with Indians."

She gave his shoulder a chiding shove, and then looked longingly at the fish. "Isn't it finished cooking yet?"

"Almost," he hedged, his lips twitching.

She sighed, resting her chin upon the heel of her hand.

The fish was ready. But he liked her impatient pout almost as much as her laughter. Like his sisters, she was fun to tease.

Making certain she watched him, he made a great show of studying the trout, frowning intently, angling his head this way and that, poking at the tail with the point of a stick.

Finally, he proclaimed, *"Awilaw!* Now it's done."

She wasn't fooled for an instant. The frosty glare she sent him was tempered by a playful spark of fire. But it was the hard shove she gave him, knocking him off his heels and onto his hindquarters, that made him burst into merry laughter.

"I have a good mind to eat them both myself," she threatened, her eyes flashing.

He sat up cross-legged. "They're your fish by rights," he admitted, his eyes twinkling. "The Great Spirit gave them to *you.*"

Her pretty mouth tightened stubbornly. "I suppose you think my guilty conscience will force me to share my catch."

He shrugged and let out a long-suffering sigh. "I will have to rely on your mercy."

She stared at him in mock severity, her gaze moving from eye to eye, like an enemy gauging his worth.

And then the silence was broken by an exceptionally loud growl from his stomach, which cracked her stern veneer and sent her into helpless giggles.

"Oh, fiddle," she said, wiping her eyes when she'd stopped laughing. "I suppose you did save that second trout."

He grinned, then moved toward the fire. He gingerly loosened the two sticks propped over the flame, careful not to drop the fish onto the coals, and lay them atop several broad blades of wild iris leaves.

The first serving always went to the one who'd caught the fish. Chase tugged a small piece of roasted fillet from the grandfather trout to present to Claire.

Though it didn't burn his fingers, he knew the fish was still hot from the fire. Crouching close to her, he blew a cooling breath across the bite of steaming trout.

She was still smiling when he tucked the tidbit between her lips. Her tongue flicked out to capture the morsel, contacting the underside of his fingers for an instant, and a strange surge like lightning snaked through his body. Before he could withdraw, her mouth closed around the tips of his first two fingers, sucking the fish from them. His heart pounded. It was like a kiss, the way her lips moved, a lover's kiss.

When he dared lift his eyes to hers, she seemed to have swallowed her humor along with the fish. Instead, desire darkened her gaze, and she appeared in no hurry to release his fingers.

He glanced at her mouth once more, and his loins grew taut at the sight of his fingers trapped there, so huge and brutish within her delicate lips. Without warning, her tongue softly brushed his fingertips again. Hot sparks showered through him like iron striking iron, setting him afire with lust, leaving him breathless.

When her lips parted, freeing him, still he didn't withdraw.

They had become two metals melted together, impossible to separate. He lightly grazed her mouth with the backs of his knuckles and felt her moist, ragged breath and the yielding softness of her lips beneath his fingers. He remembered how they felt upon his mouth. He wanted them there again.

Claire held her breath, though her heart pounded forcefully.

She wanted to kiss Chase again—more than anything. But he'd refused her twice now. This time, if he wanted a kiss, he'd have to initiate it.

Meanwhile, she'd do everything in her power to convince him that the right time and place were here and now.

She closed her eyes, relishing the delicate touch of his knuckle across her lips.

But as before, he withdrew. When she looked at him again, his lips were compressed, and his eyes had turned cool and black.

Undaunted, she broke off a piece off a piece of fish and offered it to him from her fingers, the way he had given her the first bite.

He initially refused to take it. But after several heartbeats, she saw his nostrils flare, and he opened his mouth the merest bit to allow her access. She tucked the fish between them, savoring for a moment the suppleness of his lips and the smoothness of his teeth beneath her fingers. It was a dangerous thing she did, like sticking one's head into the jaws of a lion, but longing seemed to take all the common sense from her.

After he swallowed the fish, instead of withdrawing her hand, she timidly brushed the backs of her knuckles across his lower lip, along his stubbled cheek, sampling the textures that made up the man. Breathlessly watching his mouth, she ventured a fingertip between his lips.

Suddenly he bit down, trapping her finger between his

teeth, and her eyes lifted to his in surprise. Despite the punitive gesture, his gaze was inflamed, not by hostility, but by passion. She swallowed hard. More than anything, she wanted to press her lips to the spot where her finger was caught, to kiss him again, to feel the warmth of his breath in her mouth.

She gasped as his hand came up to seize her wrist, forcing it gently but firmly away. He clearly didn't intend to let her yearnings get the best of her. Yet there was no mistaking the sultry heat of his gaze and the raw desire in his voice when he spoke.

"Supper's getting cold." His gaze sank to her mouth, rested a moment, then dragged back up to her eyes.

She knew his mind was not on food. They both knew it. She also knew there were a thousand reasons why she should back away and give up the senseless hope that she might receive another kiss from him. But she couldn't. That hope tethered her there as surely as reins held a horse.

"To hell with supper," she whispered raggedly, a mortified blush suffusing her cheeks, the oath shocking on her tongue. "My lips are getting cold."

His nostrils flared again at her impetuous admission, and his eyes darkened to a dangerous, smoky black, like a coal, appearing cool to the touch, concealing searing fire.

A war was waged in their locked gazes. It was too late to withdraw her rash words, too late to regret her confession. She had bared her desires to him, and now, whether he took up her challenge or cast her aside, there was nothing she could...

Chase surged forward with a growl, half wishing to frighten her away, half wishing to ease his lust upon her mouth again. She gasped, but the fear in her breath was colored by raw desire. Sacred Spirit, he didn't know what he was doing. He caught her hand against his chest, where his heart pounded hard enough to chip iron, and held it there.

Her eyes glinted in the golden light, reflecting the leaping flames of the fire and her smoldering passion, and he yearned to lose himself in their turbulent depths.

Still he resisted her magic. He tightened his grip on her wrist until she flinched, yet she didn't cower from him. Instead, the hunger in her gaze intensified.

He might have triumphed then had he closed his eyes, let go of her, and turned his head away. But at that moment, her lips fell open, pink and moist and inviting, drawing his gaze and sealing his fate.

Desire weighed down his eyes, blinding him to reason, and hardened him like hot steel thrust in icy water. Before common sense could stop him, he spread his fingers to encompass her face, leaned forward, and pressed his hungry lips to hers.

Their mouths meshed as smoothly as gears forged together. Instant lust poured into his body like molten bronze from a crucible. All control was snatched from him as she melted into his embrace.

Gone was his resistance. Gone was his power of reason. He swept his free arm around her back, encompassing her slight shoulders and pulling her close. He laced his fingers through her hair, capturing the back of her delicate ear.

Somehow, despite the fierce lust raging inside him, he managed to be gentle. Somehow he didn't hurt her. Something in the languishing leisure of their kiss forced him to a tenderness he'd never experienced before.

She answered his caresses, slipping her soft arms up toward his shoulders. The forgotten iris leaves with his supper of trout spilled and scattered upon the ground, but he didn't care. Her fingers burned like newly forged steel upon the back of his neck, branding him.

Lost in a vulnerable haze no sane man would ever enter—deaf to the night, blind to the peril around him—he willingly succumbed to the sensuous fog of her embrace. Soon it seemed the two of them were all that existed.

It was like a vision in the sweat lodge, this sensation, something far beyond the simple desire he had felt with lovers who'd come before. Strong magic seemed to enter his lungs like the sacred smoke of the dream pipe, filling him with languid swirls of emotion and powerful spirit messages.

He belonged here.

This was the completed circle.

It came to him as clearly as the stars in the midnight sky.

This was his destiny. This was the will of his grandmother, Yoema.

Startled, he pulled back, tearing free of her, wrenching himself from the astonishing vision. He stared down at Claire Parker, incredulous. How could it be? He had come for revenge, not reconciliation. Hadn't he?

Claire's mouth was swollen from his kissing, and her cheek bore the flush of desire. Her eyes were still glazed with passion as she looked up at him, but distress and frustration were gathering like a brewing storm.

"What?" she asked. "What's wrong?"

He stared down at her a long while, asking himself that very question. The fire snapped softly, and a rare night breeze sighed through the uppermost boughs of the cedars, bringing with it the clean scent of evergreen and riffling the hair of the woman before him.

She was beautiful. Starlight swathed the crown of her head in a silvery veil while firelight burnished her face to the shade of ripe peaches.

She was kind and generous, tender and strong, the kind of woman a man would be proud to claim as his.

And her kiss—her kiss made him forget himself, forget his troubles, and reminded him of what was right and good in the world.

So what was wrong? Other than the fact that she was a white woman whom he hardly knew, a woman who belonged to another man, a woman he'd stolen for revenge?

He knew all this, and yet all the arguments in the world couldn't outweigh the seductive invitation in her eyes and the raging need in his body, too compelling to ignore.

"Nothing," he lied. "Nothing's wrong."

CHAPTER 15

Claire closed her eyes, savoring the taste of him. His mouth, wild and dangerous, seasoned their kiss with forbidden spices that tantalized both her tongue and her thoughts. Scarcely aware of it, she began to answer him, moving her lips over his, sighing against his mouth, gasping as their breath mingled, as their tongues flitted tentatively out and dared to touch.

His fingers pressed lightly into her cheeks as he angled his head to seal his claim upon her. She clutched at the fabric of his shirt, sure she would sink beneath waves of desire if she let go.

It was mad. It was foolish. Utterly reckless. And yet she'd dreamed of nothing else since she'd kissed him that first time. She hoped that this was at last the right time and place, because she didn't want to stop, didn't want to think. Her heart pounded crazily, and a strange, sweet lethargy poured over her like maple syrup over griddlecakes.

Within her, wild fire burned, stealing her breath the way brandy did, spreading outward from her belly, and warming her in untouchable places. She felt curiously alive and tingling, like a long-haired cat in a thunderstorm.

His skin was hot against hers. The stubble of his jaw and his calloused fingertips felt familiar and yet foreign. Still, far from afraid, she was intrigued by the mystery of his maleness. His touch, his taste, his scent were exotic. His size was daunting. But she felt that she belonged here in his arms and that the two of them were somehow meant for this.

His free hand slipped through her hair to clasp the back of her head, pulling her even closer. She slid her arms up around his neck, marveling at the rapid pulse that beat along the sides of his throat. Her own heart raced as he drew her forward, crushing her breasts lightly against his chest.

Then, when she thought she could bear no more, when she thought she might swoon with pleasure, he groaned against her lips, a groan torn from the depths of his throat, an animal sound, and she felt lightning surge through her veins, pricking up the fine hairs in her ears and electrifying the place between her legs.

She answered with her own unconscious moan, unable to speak or move or think. Her voice might have been that of a stranger, for she'd never heard such a sound come from her throat, a moan of longing that seemed to stem from her soul.

Never had she felt so welcome, so complete. She wanted to kiss him forever and ever.

But while she luxuriated in the glorious perfection of their long embrace, with her lips thoroughly wet from kissing and her arms full of him, an even deeper yearning grew within her. She wanted more—more of this, more of him. An ache she couldn't name began low in her belly, seeping into her veins, spreading through her body with a current that left her prickling from the tips of her toes to the hollows of her ears.

It wasn't enough. She wanted, needed...

He released her lips to nuzzle the place beneath her ear,

sending a jolt of pleasure along her neck. Yes, that was what she craved—more of the tiny shocks that took the breath from her in quick gasps.

He slid the camisole from one shoulder. Running the ragged pad of his thumb along the exposed length of skin, he followed that rough touch with soothing kisses. She tipped her head to allow him access, and his fingers drifted lower, across the delicate flesh of her collarbone. His breath came deep and rapid as his fingertips brushed the neck edge of the camisole. One finger slipped tentatively beneath the cotton, as if in question.

She took a deep, affirming breath, and her bosom swelled to meet his light caress. Her breasts tingled, their peaks seeking his touch. She squeezed her eyes shut against the instincts that told her to withdraw, to cover herself, for heaven's sake, to rebuke the brute who trespassed so boldly upon her innocence.

But she wanted this. She longed to feel his palm full upon her flesh, to fill his hand with her aching breast. This time, the groan torn from her throat was rife with sweet frustration.

He went suddenly still at the sound. "I'm hurting you," he murmured.

"No!" she cried, clutching his hand to her bosom for fear he would leave her. "No."

Even with her eyes closed, she knew he was watching her, but she was too drunk with her own desire to face him. What she was about to do was so unladylike, so lascivious, so much like the wicked women in her dime novels—the ones who drank whiskey and played cards and never won the hero—that she couldn't look him in the eye.

What devilry possessed her, she didn't know. She'd never been so brazen, so reckless, so bold. She curved her hand around his, flattening his fingers. Her breath shallow and rapid, she guided his hand down, savoring the rasp of his calluses against the flesh of her bosom. Lower and lower she moved his hand, past the frail boundary of her camisole, along the full curve no man had breached before, until his palm cupped her breast.

Her breath came out in a throaty sigh, and he seemed to suck that sigh from her hard between his teeth. The sound sent a heady thrill of power through her.

His fingers burned her virgin flesh, yet his touch was tender and tenuous. His forehead lowered to rest almost wearily upon her crown, and his trembling breath heated her already flushed face.

She had thought it would be enough, that the touch of his hand on her breast would quench the strange fire filling her body. But it wasn't so. Instead, her desire flared higher. She lifted her face to his, seeking and finding his supple mouth again. This time there was an urgency to his kisses that fanned the flames of her yearning.

His free hand came up to cradle her face, steadying her for his deepening kisses. He tugged her chin down with his thumb, opening her mouth. Her heart raced as he lapped at her in invitation.

He kissed the corner of her mouth, the rim of her jaw, the crazily pulsing vein in the hollow of her neck. And then he moved lower. His lips seared a trail down her bosom. With his teeth, he slipped the strap of the camisole from her other shoulder, baring her breast. A sob caught in her throat as she realized his intent.

She had thought his hand upon her was heaven, but it was nothing compared to the touch of his tongue. Though his jagged breath echoed her own unstable breathing, he managed to govern his desire. His mouth closed over her breast with utmost care, sucking gently and leaving her squirming in delicious torment.

She tangled a hand in his hair, amazed by its softness

between her fingers, and tipped her head back to bask in the starlight. It was scandalous, what he was doing to her, yet it felt amazing.

But even this, even the glorious sensation of his greedy feast, which left her shivering with ecstasy, couldn't satisfy her for long. There was still an empty ache low in her belly, a yearning between her thighs that demanded answer.

As if he sensed her hunger, he shifted upon his knees, dragging her closer, bringing her body flush with his, and she urgently pressed that throbbing place against his thigh. He answered the pressure, knowing what she desired. She reveled in the divine sensation and in the proof of his own yearning—the firm staff that was lodged against her hip. A frisson of intoxicating lust shook her at the evidence of the sheer power of his need.

Far too insatiably fascinated to be discreet, she lowered her hand to boldly explore this new manifestation. He groaned as she stroked him, throwing his head back like a coyote silently baying at the moon. Urged on by the sweet agony in his face, she rubbed her palm against him again and again, until, with a growl, he grabbed her wrist to cease her torture.

"You must...not," he wheezed. She could see it was difficult for him to stop her, and in the haze of her emotions, she wondered why.

"But I...want to. I want you. I want...this," she whispered, the sound like drops of water hitting a skillet of hot oil.

"No," he argued, squeezing her hand. "Now you want this. But later...tomorrow...you'll regret—"

She shook her head. "No." Her breath came quickly, and a sense of panic came over her. She didn't want to lose him, didn't want to lose this moment. "No, I won't. I promise."

She searched his eyes, pleading, but the look he returned was fraught with indecision. The reflection of the fire danced in his dark pupils like a taunt while he let his smoky gaze roam over her face. Finally, his mind made up, he closed his eyes in resignation. His lips thinned to a grim line, and, lifting her about the waist, he turned to gently lay her down on the bed of pine boughs beside the fire.

Kidilqits. Crazy. That was what he was. There were a thousand reasons why he should just tuck Claire into her bed and dive back into the icy creek to cool his lust.

But with his body burning like a summer forge, he couldn't think of a single one. She was so beautiful, so seductive. He wanted her with all his being. He was swollen to bursting with his craving, and when she touched him, when he sensed that her need was as great as his own...

Somehow, despite the erotic blaze raging in his veins, he managed to dredge up enough sense not to do something irreversible, something he'd regret later. She was a white woman, after all, who knew nothing about love play. She'd probably never bedded with a man. So he decided he'd ignore his body's demands, forgo his own needs, and resign himself to simply pleasuring her.

It would kill him, he knew. To watch her writhe and moan under his caress, to witness her rising desire and see the culmination of her ecstasy as she rode the waves of...

He closed his eyes. He wouldn't think about it. He'd kiss her. He'd touch her with his hands. He'd give her the pleasure she desired. And he'd do nothing else.

Claire's short hair fanned out around her face where she lay, catching the light of the fire in a crown as brilliant as the sun's. Her eyelids dipped low, heavy with passion, and her rosy lips parted. Her camisole was bunched about her waist, exposing her creamy breasts, and he yearned to taste her there again.

He reclined beside her, propped up on one elbow. Her eyes widened when he trapped her by slinging his thigh across both of hers. But she made no move to resist, not even when he slipped his hand beneath the hem of her petticoat and up toward the source of her sensuous affliction.

He studied her face to be sure his touch was welcome, though it was sheer torture for him. Her breath came in quick gasps as his fingers brushed the tender flesh of her inner thigh. Abashed, she wouldn't look at him, turning her head aside and resting her open mouth against her knuckles. Yet she didn't ask him to stop. Even while she furrowed her brow in sweet distress, she parted her legs for him. And with an innocence that brought new blood to his loins, she lifted that part of her he desired most, pressing up against his palm for the relief she craved.

Steeling his jaw against a potent surge of yearning, he forced himself to be gentle. She alternately shrank from his touch and welcomed it again, twisting in a fitful battle between propriety and desire. He must take care then not to frighten her, to move slowly, to have patience.

He bit the inside of his cheek. Patience? Hell, all he could think about was delving into her warm, wet, tempting body. If his urges didn't subside, he'd end up soaking in the cold creek all night.

He squeezed his eyes shut, and he let his fingers begin the sensual, playful dance he'd learned long ago from the women of his tribe, a ritual his Konkow father had encouraged him to learn and his white mother had pretended to know nothing about. He had to concentrate—his blacksmith's calluses had numbed him to much—but practice had taught him to, above all, heed a woman's responses.

Claire was responding. All too well. And all too quickly. Soft sobs came from her throat, and she squirmed in joyful anguish. One hand tangled in the sleeve of his shirt, and she rolled her head listlessly from side to side. He sensed her increasing pleasure, yet she wriggled and writhed like a snared fish, as if she might break free of her own emotions the way the grandfather trout had broken free of the line.

He wished he'd watched her more closely. Without warning, she suddenly arched and drove her hips violently upward, impaling herself on his finger.

She stiffened with a stunned cry, and her fist pressed at his forearm in panic. He swore under his breath, cursing himself for a clumsy brute, but thought it best not to withdraw. If he withdrew, she would never know the pleasure of love play and only remember the pain. If he remained, she'd eventually relax. Then he could make amends by showing her the ecstasy of quenched passion.

"It...burns," she gasped.

The hurt and betrayal in her eyes dissolved his lust. All he felt was remorse. He hadn't meant to hurt her, to damage her.

But he should have known. He always hurt people. It was his curse.

"I didn't mean..." he muttered. "This was a mistake. It was all a—"

"Wait," she said, halting him when he would have withdrawn from her after all. She swallowed, lowering her eyes. "It will pass...won't it?"

He studied her face, and indecision clouded his mind. He felt like a wildcat he'd once seen chasing a bluejay into a tree. It had followed the bird onto a thin branch, unable to decide whether to pursue the game farther or climb back down. It chose to follow, and the branch had snapped under its weight. What would happen if Chase continued his pursuit?

"Perhaps..." Claire ventured, blushing profusely, her fingers toying with the buttons on his shirt. "Perhaps if you were to kiss me..."

It was amazing how quickly a man's lust could be revived. And even more amazing how desperately Chase wished to repair the damage he'd caused. If she wanted him to kiss her...

Claire wanted him to kiss her more than anything. After the unexpected sting, she needed to feel the comforting warmth of his embrace again, needed to rekindle the sensual fire that had burned so brightly before.

It had been her fault. She knew that. He'd been touching her tenderly, carefully. Her own urges had undone her. Her impatience had driven her to surge toward him, to fill that empty place inside of her.

Well, she thought, it was truly filled now. In fact, she wondered if she'd ever be able to disengage from him.

Then he kissed her.

It was a slow, lingering kiss, unlike the others. He touched his lips gently to the corners of her mouth, all the while murmuring soft words in his own language. She tried to answer with more passion. But when she did, he withdrew, lightening his touch even more, fueling her to fiercer desires.

He knew very well what he was doing. Within moments, the pain between her legs subsided, and her body hungered for him again. She ascended once more into a world of muzzy contentment.

He moved slowly, his thumb circling over the spot that craved him the most, leaving her breathless. She parted her mouth, begging for the trespass of his tongue, but he only teased her, lapping delicately at her lips.

An odd vibration began in her head, like a swarm of sensual bees buzzing in her ear. The place where his fingers played continued to swell and blossom until her breath caught in shallow gasps and her head thrashed upon the pine boughs.

There was a second of utter still as he clasped her head to his shoulder. Then an explosion of pure joy flashed within her, filling her the way sheet lightning filled the sky. Her cries were muffled in the cotton of his shirt as she rocked through the wild storm in his sheltering embrace.

Then the feeling slowly subsided. He withdrew his hand and smoothed her skirts back down.

Gradually, her harsh breathing softened, giving way to the silence of the mountain. The stoked furnace of her body yielded to the night chill, and then she no longer felt gloriously naked, but awkwardly exposed. She drew her camisole back up over her bosom and burrowed her head against his chest, more afraid to let him see her bare emotions than her bare flesh.

It was wrong, what she'd done. She'd abandoned all sense, all propriety, for a moment's pleasure, just like the bad women in her dime novels. Worse, she couldn't seem to work up any real guilt over it.

But what about Chase? As wickedly seductive as his actions seemed, it was impossible to envision him as a villain.

She gazed down at the dark arm wrapped around her. With his coal-black hair and eyes and his bronzed skin, Chase certainly *looked* like the dangerous Red-skins in her stories. But he was nothing like the savages of Beadle's books. His tongue was soft as it tangled with hers. His kiss was delectable ambrosia. And the way he caressed her...

Her heart fluttered. He'd touched her in ways no man had—not just physically, but in her heart and in her spirit. He'd swept into her life when she'd needed him most, just as Yoema had foretold, to heal the past.

It was meant to be.

They were meant to be.

She knew it. And she knew that while he might not have the polite and genteel qualities of a dime novel hero, Chase Wolf was definitely the hero of *her* story.

Chase held Claire until she fell asleep. Then he carefully lowered her down to the pine bough bed.

She looked so peaceful, so satiated, so content.

He sighed. At least *one* of them was happy.

He rolled onto his back on the hard ground beside her and focused on the stars above. The lust distorting his trousers showed no signs of subsiding, even though his eyes were trained away from the woman who was to blame for it.

He tried to think of something else. Anything else.

His family. He wondered what his sister Rose was doing back at Hupa. Probably snuggling up to that husband of hers, all warm and safe and content, trying to make their first baby.

What about his brother, Drew Hawk? Drew was likely sitting in a saloon, one hand wrapped around a trio of Aces and the other around some supple-hipped saloon girl in lace petticoats.

He grimaced.

How long had it been since Chase had shared his bed with a woman? A long while, apparently, by the direction of his thoughts and the lingering heat of his blood.

He supposed there were too many other things filling his time at the village. He was the only blacksmith in Hupa. His work kept him busy from dawn to dusk, and most nights he was too tired to do more than shovel spoonfuls of salmon stew and peach pie into his mouth before he collapsed into bed.

How long had it been? The last moon? Longer? It didn't matter. He wasn't going to slake his thirst with the beautiful woman sleeping beside him tonight, and the sooner he realized it, the better.

Unfortunately, he couldn't stop thinking about what it would be like to not only make love to Claire right now, but to make love to her over and over, to have a lifetime of lovemaking ahead of them.

What if the notion that had sprung into his mind was true? What if vengeance was not the way to give his grandmother's spirit peace? What if repairing the past meant *loving* his enemy instead, as his mother's Bible preached? Was it possible that a bond between the two of them would complete the circle?

Tempting images of marriage to the beautiful Claire Parker whirled through his mind, settling into an uncomfortable truth.

He didn't want to leave her.

And it wasn't only lust making him feel that way.

It wasn't even that sense of destiny that had come over him.

The truth was he was in love with her.

It was crazy. He'd only known her for a few days. How could he be so certain? And even if he did love her, why did he think there was even a remote possibility of a relationship between them?

They were from completely different worlds. And while that had worked for his parents, Claire was nothing like his mother. His mother had come to the west without a husband, without a penny to her name. She'd been grateful to be welcomed into his father's tribe. But Claire Parker was a privileged young lady with a gentleman she intended to marry and a lavish home she stood to inherit. It was unthinkable that she might willingly throw away the comforts of her white world and go with him to live in his backward native village.

Still, he had to admit it was tempting to think about going ahead with his original plan to kidnap her. Hell, stealing wives from other tribes had been part of his people's tradition for generations.

Of course, he realized, it was also barbaric.

He picked up the dime novel left on the ground beside him, looking at the cover. This wasn't one of Claire's books. No Red-Skin in her stories ran away with a white woman and lived happily ever after.

He put the book back down and frowned up at the stars. Then he closed his eyes to dream of things that would never be.

CHAPTER 16

"Well, sir, with all due respect," Frank announced rather smugly, "it looks like you were wrong." He lifted his oil lamp to illuminate the set of tracks that continued up into the mountains. "He isn't headed back to Paradise after all. I'd say he's on his way to Magalia."

Samuel frowned. It always grated on his ears to hear Dogtown called Magalia. It had been Dogtown for as long as he could recall, until someone had decided that was too unflattering a name and changed it. It had been Dogtown when his wife Margaret was alive, and, damn it, that's how Samuel wanted to remember it.

Frank was muttering to himself again. "Slimy son of a bitch. Just where does he think he's going?"

After three days of tracking, young Frank's veneer of patience was wearing thin, revealing a nasty nature that Samuel didn't much like. All Samuel cared about was finding his little girl. Hotheaded cursing wasn't going to help them.

He stroked his mustache and tried to think. Where could Claire's kidnapper be headed?

"My guess?" Frank said, interrupting his thoughts. "It's one of those infernal Chinamen. Probably got a hideaway in Magalia where he keeps white women." He spat and sneered, "I hear they ship girls back to China. A pretty young white woman like Claire would bring a damn good price."

Samuel clamped his teeth against a retort. Frank was not only insensitive. He was full of shit. The Chinese people in the area were enterprising laborers who worked mostly at growing crops, laundering clothing, and building rail. Most of them had spent a fortune to get to California, with little hope of ever returning.

"I say we cut him off," Frank continued, "head straight for town at dawn and root out his hidey-hole before he can—"

"First thing in the morning, boys," Samuel announced, tired of Frank's pushiness, "you'll take the horses back to the ranch. They won't be any good where we're headed. Frank and I will track the kidnapper on foot from here."

Frank rubbed his chin, trying to decide if he agreed with that tactic. "Are you sure, sir?"

"He's only one man, Frank." Samuel was sure of that. "I think we can handle him."

Frank straightened with pride. "Well, of course, but...leave us your guns, boys. You can never have too many—"

"We don't need more guns, Frank."

Frank looked disappointed, but he nodded. Samuel figured the young man had an extra Deringer in his boot and probably another up his sleeve anyway. And now that Samuel knew their quarry was pretty well cornered against the ridge of Dogtown, he hoped bullets would be necessary only as a last resort.

It was not quite dawn when Chase abruptly opened his eyes. He'd been dreaming of his grandmother. She'd looked exactly like his mother's sketches, and she'd smiled at him and spoken two words in her native tongue—*momi lalami.*

Still shaken by the vivid vision, unsure of the meaning of her words, it took him a moment to realize he'd been awakened, not by the dream, but by an intruder.

The scent alerted him before he heard the scuffling in the brush. He didn't need to see the black-and-white fur to know what it was—*xoljeh,* a skunk.

He raised up on one elbow and scanned the shadowy camp. There it was.

Curse his carelessness, he'd left the half-eaten trout beside the fire. He was damned lucky that nothing more dangerous than a skunk had come for it. There were plenty of wildcats and bears that could have been drawn by the prospect of an easy dinner. Still, a skunk was not to be taken lightly.

And this skunk was edging perilously close to Claire. He watched it as it waddled backward with the trout in its mouth, dragging the fish by the tail.

Chase wasn't about to fight for it. It was his fault it had been left out all night. By rights, it belonged to the skunk now.

But it was scooting back, closer and closer to Claire's head. If it didn't change direction, it was going to run right into her. He had to divert it somehow without waking Claire.

He hissed at it.

It ignored him.

He hissed again, this time waving a threatening arm toward the little beast.

It ignored him.

He picked up a pine cone and lobbed it at the ground in front of the skunk, hoping to scare it away.

It paused for a moment, then continued backing.

The skunk was less than an arm's length from Claire now,

and the sound of the pine cone had roused her. She rolled over onto her side and flailed out her arm, missing the animal by inches.

Chase's eyes widened. "No," he whispered.

She made a soft, sleepy sound as the skunk backed into her outstretched hand.

"Claire," he hissed urgently.

To his horror, Claire, still half asleep, ran her fingers over the skunk's fur as if it were a tame cat.

This clearly upset the skunk. It dropped the trout and hopped halfway around to face this new threat.

Quickly deciding it might be best if Claire didn't wake up after all, Chase found a long stick and waved it at the beast, which was now preparing to defend its meal.

Sure enough, it started hissing.

Claire stirred at the sound and lifted her head.

Chase poked the skunk lightly with the stick, hoping to annoy it enough to get it to leave.

It growled and started stamping its feet.

Claire mumbled something incoherent and pushed up on her arms.

"No, Claire!" he warned.

"What?" she asked sleepily.

"Hold still."

Of course, with a snarling, stomping skunk inches from her head, the last thing Claire was likely to do was to hold still. She rose up with a gasp.

He poked the beast again. *"Tingyahwh!* Go away! *Tingyahwh, xoljeh!"* Chase hopped up on his haunches and poked once more, prepared to move closer if necessary to keep the skunk from attacking Claire.

The skunk turned its back.

"Chase!" Claire exclaimed. "Look out! Don't!"

The skunk's tail quivered.

Chase yelled, "Move away, Claire!" as he tried to push the animal aside with the stick. If it was going to spray, at least he could direct the spray away from Claire, who was now on her hands and knees. "Look out!"

It worked. The skunk, thoroughly annoyed, angled its rear end back around toward Chase and lifted its tail high.

Claire couldn't imagine why Chase was aggravating a skunk. Were there no skunks where he lived? Didn't he realize they were best left alone? Didn't he know what that upraised tail meant?

Now it was probably too late to avoid a spray.

The skunk gave one last warning shiver of its tail.

"No!" Claire shouted. She had to protect Chase. Without considering the consequences of her actions, she squeezed her eyes shut and dove in front of him, right in the line of fire.

She was instantly sorry. The spray hit her squarely in the midsection, and the all-too-familiar stench was horrid at close range. She didn't dare open her eyes. She only hoped the animal was scuttling away after what it considered a successful strike.

"Claire! Are you all right?"

She coughed. "Is it leaving?"

"Yes." She heard him drop the stick. "It's gone. But why did you...?" He came up to crouch behind her, placing his hands on her shoulders. "Are you all right?" he asked, choking on the fumes. "Are you hurt?"

She tried to avoid breathing through her nose. "I'm fine. I'm just—"

"Gah!" he exclaimed as the scent hit him full-force.

"Haven't you ever seen a skunk before?" she asked.

"A *xoljeh*?" he said, gagging. "Of course."

She wrinkled her nose. "Don't you know you're not supposed to poke them?"

"I was just trying to protect you," he said, hacking and wheezing.

"You were?" Her heart softened.

"Yep." He caught her upper arms from behind and helped her up. "But why did you jump in front of it?"

She coughed. "I was trying to protect *you*."

He turned her toward him. "You were?"

She cautiously peeped open one eye and nodded.

His mouth curved up in a half-smile. "That's a real nice thing to... Damn!" He recoiled from the odor wafting off of her, holding her at arm's length to inspect the damage.

She glanced down at her undergarments, grimacing. What would she do now? The disgusting yellow spray stained both her camisole and her petticoat. The pungent scent of skunk was nearly impossible to get rid of, even with strong vinegar.

Chase knew exactly what to do. It seemed to be his answer for everything. He peeled off his shirt.

"Here," he said, handing it to her and nodding at her unmentionables. "You're going to have to get out of those."

It took her a moment to digest what he was saying—his bare chest was terribly distracting—but then she realized he was expecting for her to completely undress.

"Oh, no. I can't do that," she reasoned, blushing. "It's not decent. Besides," she added hopefully, "I'm sure the stench will go away...in time." Actually, she wasn't sure of that at all.

"Maybe in a month or two," he admitted.

She bit her lip. "It's not...that bad." It was horrible.

"Take the shirt."

"I can't possibly—"

"Take it."

"That's very kind of you, but—"

"It's not kindness." He covered his nose with the back of his hand. "I insist."

She blinked in surprise.

"We'll bury your clothes," he added.

"Bury them? But why?"

"So your father won't find them and think you've been carried off by rabid skunks."

He had a point. On the other hand, her father would probably rather she were carried off by rabid skunks than abducted by a handsome half-breed.

Chase busied himself, covering the ashes from last night's fire and turning his back while she slipped out of her clothes and buttoned on his shirt.

As she feared, the shirt wasn't nearly long enough. It barely skimmed the tops of her knees, leaving her calves and ankles exposed, a fact made painfully obvious when Chase turned and gave her an all-too-pleased head-to-toe perusal.

"It's really not decent," she breathed, not altogether disappointed that he was staring.

A spark of mischief lit up his eyes. "I could give you my trousers as well."

"No!" That was unthinkable...though she was thinking about it a lot at the moment. "No, I'll be fine." At least she was wearing more than a Konkow tribeswoman. They wore grass skirts and very little else.

He grinned, and her heart fluttered as she remembered what he'd done to her last night, how he'd pleasured her and made her feel incredible things, how she'd fallen asleep in his arms, and how she'd wished she could fall asleep in his arms every night.

Minutes later, she tightened the ties on her rabbit fur moccasins and watched Chase hunker down to scatter leaves over the top of her buried undergarments. She let her gaze roam over the flexing muscles of his broad, naked back. He had tucked her beloved dime novel into the back waistband of his trousers, and she knew she'd never be able to look at the drawing of Monowano in the same way again.

How much longer did the two of them have? Was it enough time to steal Chase's heart and make him fall in love with her? Could she talk him into running away with her instead of returning her to the Parker Ranch? How could she convince him they were meant to be together?

To her surprise, as they hurried to leave the pungent scene of the crime, it was Chase who gave her the answer.

"My grandmother came to me last night," he murmured.

"She did?" Claire's breath caught, and she clapped a hand to her throat. "What did she say? Was she…was she happy?"

He nodded. "She said something to me, but…" He shook his head in frustration.

"What did she say?"

"I think it was a Konkow word—one I don't know."

"What was it? Do you remember?"

He screwed up his forehead. "It sounded like *momilali*…"

Claire frowned. "*Momi*…" Then her heart skipped. "*Momi lalami?*"

"You speak the language of my grandmother?"

"A little. Was that what she said? *Momi lalami?*" She held her breath.

"Yep. That was it. Any idea what it means?"

Claire smiled gently. A comforting warmth suddenly enveloped her. It felt like Yoema herself had wrapped loving arms around her shoulders. "Tall water."

"Tall water?"

"It's the Konkow word for waterfall."

Chase gave her a quizzical look. "Does that mean something to you?"

"Oh, yes," she said as her smile broadened.

The waterfall was one of her favorite spots, though she hadn't been there since Yoema had taken ill. It was a special place of great beauty, great peace, and—according to Yoema—great power.

Nestled into the hills, the fall was hidden by a thick forest and accessible only by a steep hike over lichen-crusted boulders. Even in summer, the clear stream poured over a stone cliff and tumbled in a single powerful cascade onto a flat rock twenty feet below, spreading into a deep pool that looked like an enormous green bowl. Mist rose from the bottom of the fall, nurturing the moss and ferns that grew in cracks of the cliff face, and delicate black-and-orange salamanders lived at the pool's edge, nestled under giant granite slabs that sparkled in the sun.

There could be no mistake. Chase had had a vision about the waterfall.

Did Yoema intend for Claire to take him there? The waterfall had special significance. Yoema had told her it was the place where the parents of the Two-Sons had fallen in love. Claire could scarcely contain her excitement. With Yoema's blessing and a little luck, maybe the same enchantment would work on Chase.

"Come," she said softly, taking his hand and pulling him along. "I'll take you there."

"Skunk," Frank announced with a sneer of disgust, waving his hand in front of his face as he poked around the abandoned campsite with a long stick.

Samuel Parker held a kerchief over his nose to subdue the awful stench.

"What have we here?" Frank said, kicking aside the leaves that covered a darker patch of ground. "Fresh dirt."

Samuel Parker squinted at the iron-red soil. "The campfire?"

Frank squatted by the disturbed ground a few feet away from the first mound. "The fire was over here." He jabbed at it to prove his point, revealing gray ashes.

"This one is something else," Frank said, digging around a bit, then crouching to inspect it closer.

"See anything?"

"No, but I sure can smell it." Frank dug at the ground with the stick. "Maybe they ate the varmint and buried the stinky parts here."

The next swipe of Frank's stick revealed something that sent Samuel's heart plunging into his gut. It was a scrap of white linen with lace.

For an instant, he couldn't breathe.

Frank kept poking at the ground, poking, poking. Samuel wanted to tell him to stop, just let it alone. But he kept on digging.

Frank frowned. "It looks like a—"

"Claire," Samuel croaked as the blood drained from his face.

It took Frank a minute to understand. When he finally figured it out, he cursed and then fell to his knees, digging like mad with his gloved hands. "That murderin' bastard," he bit out.

Samuel stared, transfixed, even though he knew he should look away. He didn't want to see what lay beneath the dirt. He clamped his jaw tight. He didn't want to see what had happened to his darling daughter, his beloved Claire. He wanted to remember her the way she was. He wanted to preserve her memory, just as he had her mother's.

Frank tugged on the cloth, and it came free of the dirt. "What the—?"

Samuel felt his chin trembling, but he clenched his teeth. It would do no good to break down in front of Frank.

"A camisole," Frank said, tossing it aside. "Wait, there's something else."

Samuel's eyes were so full of unshed tears he could barely see the second garment Frank hefted out of the ground.

"A petticoat, and it reeks," Frank announced. "But where's the body?"

Samuel reeled at his words, and he leaned against a tree trunk for balance.

Frank suddenly realized his indiscretion. "Sorry, sir. It's just that, well... Aw, heck, I'm sure Claire's probably fine." He didn't sound convincing.

Samuel needed to stop and think for a moment. He had to shut off his paralyzing fear and use logic.

He made his way to a boulder by the side of the path and sat down, perusing the campsite. A skunk had been here recently, that much was obvious. He doubted they'd had it for dinner, as Frank suggested, but the smell was strong.

Was Claire...dead?

So far her abductor had been clever. What would be clever about killing Claire?

Nothing. There'd be no ransom, no leverage, no mercy for him if Claire was dead. So Samuel didn't think she was.

But why bury her clothes?

Suddenly inspired, he motioned for her garments. "Let me see those."

Frank handed them over.

What Samuel saw made his heart beat again. Sure enough, there was a telltale yellow stain on the front of both garments. Claire had tangled with a skunk, and the skunk had won.

He couldn't help but chuckle in relief.

Of course, that made Frank stare at him as if he were crazy.

"It's all right, Frank," he said. "She's alive. My baby girl is alive."

CHAPTER 17

If Claire had known how closely they were being pursued, she wouldn't have dilly-dallied on the way to the waterfall. But it was a beautiful spring afternoon, Mother Nature was showing off, and Claire felt delightfully wicked in her scanty attire. The sun felt wonderful on her bare legs. So did Chase's lusty glances.

They stopped to watch a doe with twin fawns. Along the trail, Chase lifted Claire up so she could peer at the pretty blue egg in a robin's nest. Beside a spring, he captured a tree frog for her in his hand. They chased cabbage butterflies, picked lilies, and finally stopped to lunch on fat pine nuts in the heavily wooded forest that surrounded Magalia, the town where the biggest gold nugget in the world had been discovered years ago.

He dusted off a slab of rock for her to sit on. "How much farther to this waterfall?"

"Not far," she said with a shrug. It was more than a few hours' hike, but she wasn't going to let him talk her out of it.

After a while, he pulled her dime novel out of his

waistband to sit beside her, flattening the book on his thigh. "Most white women carry a Bible. Why do you carry *this*?"

Claire blushed, though she should have been used to being teased for her reading choices. "I guess I'm not like most white women."

He quirked up the corner of his lip, amused by her answer.

"Besides," she said defensively, "it's a good story."

He read the subtitle on the cover. "About a Shawnee spy."

"Mm-hmm."

He ran his fingers over the drawing on the cover. "And a white woman."

Was this her chance? Did she dare bring up matters of the heart? "Yes. It's about a white woman..." She paused, and then blurted it out all at once, "Who runs away with a half-breed."

He stiffened for a split-second, but continued to stare at the cover. "Hmm. Sounds...irresponsible."

She gulped. "Does it?"

"Yep."

She traced invisible designs on the rock with her fingertip. "But what if she's...in love...with him?"

He smirked at the picture of Monowano. "Him? How could she love a man like him? She's a proper lady. He's a wild savage."

"That doesn't matter," Claire said. "What's in their hearts—that's what matters. When all the others suspect Monowano is a traitor, she stands up for him. She's willing to sacrifice everything for the man she loves."

He didn't answer at first, and Claire wondered if he understood that she was talking about more than just the heroine Maude and Monowano.

But when he finally replied, it was with a cynical grunt. "Let me guess." He stood and tucked the book into the back of his waistband again. "This savage asks her father for her hand in marriage. He says yes, of course, and they return to his village. He hunts deer, she grinds acorns, and they live happily ever after."

Claire caught her lip under her teeth. That wasn't quite how the story ended. Once Maude's father found out Monowano was half-white, he agreed to let them marry, and they lived in a fine house—a white man's house. But she was sure it *could* have ended with them living in a native village.

Chase shook his head and offered her his hand. "Come on. Let's see this waterfall before you get any more wild ideas in your head about making foolish sacrifices."

Claire frowned. It wasn't a foolish sacrifice to her. But she knew she'd never convince him with words. Chase Wolf was as stubborn as his grandmother. Maybe that was why Yoema wanted Claire to take him to the waterfall, where magic would do what words could not.

Fortunately, it was Sunday, so most of the riverbank mining operations were deserted. Claire knew the best places to travel unseen. They crossed the river at a narrow spot, reaching the opposite bank by clambering over half a dozen closely spaced boulders.

Once they reached the east bank, she quickly found the creek that would lead up the mountain to the waterfall, and they began the steep climb.

Chase let out a silent sigh. He hoped this detour didn't turn out to be a fruitless waste of time. Claire's "not far" was turning out to be a lot farther than he'd expected. He needed to get her back home and out of his life before...well, before he lost his mind.

All morning, he'd been lusting after her. It was hard not to, when his gaze was drawn again and again to the pair of lovely bare legs emerging from that borrowed shirt and tucked into soft rabbit fur boots. And if his thoughts happened to stray to what he'd been doing between those lovely legs last night...

Last night had been a mistake. He knew that now. Claire

may have enjoyed it. But for Chase today, it was pure torture. He desired her more than ever. The tightness of his trousers was proof of that.

He hoped they'd get to the waterfall soon. Mostly he hoped the water would be suitably cold.

He began to hear the tall water long before he saw it. The rush of the creek beside them as they traversed the slippery rocks was now joined by a low rumble farther up the hillside. The way was steep and narrow, littered with last year's leaffall, green with this year's saplings. The air was moist, and the trees formed a dense canopy that drooped across the stream.

Only after they had crested an almost vertical rise—one that Chase couldn't imagine his grandmother scaling—did the waterfall at last come into view.

"*Momi lalami*," Claire announced on a sigh of pleasure.

Chase could only stare, speechless, as they emerged from the shadows and beheld the waterfall in all its sunlit glory. He recognized this place. He'd seen it in his mother's sketches. Against the bright blue sky, a gigantic boulder seemed to hang from the top of the cliff wall. Torrents of water cut a deep groove into the center of the stone and then free-fell in a tumbling cascade as tall as five men, pounding on the flat rock below.

As they climbed up the last few feet and stood on the banks, Chase could see the huge blocks of granite that contained the water in a giant stone bowl. The pool was magnificent—like an enormous, round gem of brilliant emerald—and so deep in the middle that, despite the clarity of the water, the bottom disappeared in inky shadow.

"Isn't it beautiful?" Claire asked breathlessly.

It was more than beautiful. Everything about the place— from the drumming thunder of the fall to the mist that whispered on the air, from the mysterious dark depths of the pool to the tender green of the cliffside ferns, from the plummeting power of the frothy surge to the sunshine sparkling like delicate crystals on the water—seemed almost otherworldly, like elements of a mystical vision.

He shivered once, and he knew it was from more than just the cold spray of the *momi lalami*. This place was special. He could feel it in his blood. He was connected to this place somehow, and in that moment he believed that this was the destination of his spiritual journey.

He took a deep breath, inhaling the moist air as if it were smoke from a sacred pipe. This place had meant something to his grandmother, and he had to discover its significance.

"Come," Claire beckoned. "This is my favorite place to sit."

She led him around the edge of the bowl to a flat slab of rock that was cocked at a slight angle toward the water. Folding the long shirt around her thighs, she sat on the sunlit surface and patted the spot beside her.

He pulled her dime novel from his waistband to sit next to her, cross-legged, and studied his surroundings. The long white veil of water made a graceful drop and crashed with a hiss onto the hard rock below. Feathery green fronds against the wet stone cliff dipped and waved beside the falls. The ripples in the pool caught sparks of sunlight and moved outward to gently lap at the muddy shore. It was a place of great power, but also of great peace.

"Your grandmother liked it here," Claire murmured.

He nodded. It *was* beautiful. But surely his grandmother hadn't summoned him here to look at pretty mist and tumbling water. There had to be something more.

"I must speak to Yimantuwinyai," he decided.

"Yiman-...?" She looked at him uncertainly.

Unable to explain in a few words the complexity of Yimantuwinyai the Creator, he smiled and translated, "I need to pray."

"Ah." She smiled back. "You pray then. I need to enjoy the

sun." She sank back onto her elbows, tipped her face up to the sky, and closed her eyes.

Chase gazed at Claire, thinking she was as breathtaking as the scenery and wishing he could keep her with him forever. But he also realized that holding on to her was as impossible as holding the waterfall in his hands. He sighed and covered his eyes with his palms, blocking the outside world and turning his thoughts inward. He must breathe slowly, let his mind go blank, and become receptive to the word of Yimantuwinyai.

The sound of the water—rumbling, splashing, whispering—became gentle music to soothe his spirit. He cleared all images from his head and let the tension drain away. He took three long, deep, even breaths, exhaling slowly, silently inviting Yimantuwinyai to speak to him.

Halfway through the fourth breath, Chase felt something dragging him out of his dreamy calm, keeping him from entering the vision realm. A tiny frown touched his brow, and he tried again. He inhaled slowly. But again, he felt strangely anchored to the real world. He exhaled. On the next breath, he opened one of his eyes to a slit and peeked out from between his hands.

Claire, the mischievous little minx, was propped up on one elbow and secretly raking his body with her eyes. Slowly. Deliberately. Shamelessly. Worse, as he continued to watch her, she caught her lower lip under her teeth, and the hunger that suddenly smoldered in her eyes practically made him groan aloud.

He must have made some sort of noise, for her eyes flew to his in the next instant. Caught, she lowered her gaze in embarrassment, and then cleared her throat and shifted to face away from him, casually running an idle fingertip over the surface of the rock.

Chase smiled ruefully, both flattered and frustrated by her

attentions. Then he cleared his throat, closed his eyes, took a long breath, and tried again. He needed to understand his grandmother's message. He needed to find out Yimantuwinyai's will.

But now his mind was anything but empty. It was full of visions of Claire's long, luscious legs, her half-bitten lip, and her smoky green eyes.

Claire wasn't sure if the heat coursing through her body was from the sun, humiliation, desire, or all three. She only knew that lying on the sun-kissed rock, in this magical place, gazing on the all-too-delectable Chase Wolf warmed her blood and left her breathless.

She certainly hoped his god and his grandmother would answer his prayers and send him a clear message that they were meant to be together, for Claire couldn't bear for him to go.

Several minutes passed. The water continued to fall. The sun continued to shine. Chase continued to pray. She wondered how long it would take for him to hear from Yiman-whoever-it-was.

She picked up her dime novel and tried reading it, but she found she was re-reading the same passages several times without comprehending them, so she set the book aside.

Several more minutes passed. Claire was starting to get bored.

Sometimes her father's Konkow workers spent hours performing their rituals. She had no idea how long Chase would spend in prayer, but she didn't dare disturb him to ask.

A light breeze stirred, ruffling her borrowed shirt. She wrinkled her nose. It may have been her imagination, but she swore she could still detect the lingering odor of skunk on her skin. She eyed the pool below, wondering if she could steal a quick dip in the pond before Chase finished praying.

Another minute made up her mind. Very quietly, she

moved from her spot, slipped off the rock, and crept down to the water's edge. With one cautious glance back at Chase, who sat motionless in meditation, she shrugged off the shirt and eased into the water.

The cold took her breath away. The pond was definitely more pleasant in the middle of summer. But soon enough she grew accustomed to the chill and began to enjoy the water's cleansing caress. She ducked under the waves and wet her hair. She emerged, then paddled a bit and rolled onto her back. She swam near the base of the waterfall, and then dove back toward the center of the pool.

Occasionally, she cast a glance Chase's way, half-hoping he'd open his eyes. She could imagine what would happen if he did. Once he beheld her in all her naked glory, shining in the sunlight like some ethereal water spirit, his eyes would widen in lusty surprise. She'd pretend she didn't notice him. She'd continue splashing and cavorting to her best advantage. He'd intend to avert his gaze. But he'd be unable to, because she'd prove irresistibly enchanting. Eventually, she'd catch him gawking. She'd gasp, feigning shame, and shyly lower her eyes, all the while giving him ample opportunity to stare. There would be nowhere for her to hide, after all. She'd be completely at his mercy.

She shivered at the deliciously wicked bent of her thoughts. It *could* happen. She only hoped it *would* happen before the cold water turned her into a frigid prune.

She squinted up at the rock again. Chase was still sitting there, cross-legged, his hands covering his eyes, oblivious to her.

She was halfway through a sigh, wondering how she could garner his attention, when, out of the corner of her eye, she glimpsed something atop the waves.

She frowned. At first, it looked like a small black bead skimming back and forth on the surface of the pond. Then she noticed it was drifting closer. Could it be a seed pod caught in a strange current or a water bug zigzagging from left to right over the waves? She treaded water, watching as the curious thing neared.

All at once, she spotted the sinuous curve of the long black tail behind it as it sliced an "S" through the water—"S" for snake.

Her heart vaulted into her throat. In a panic, she shrieked and began flailing in the water.

The beast was admittedly tiny, no bigger around than a pencil, and it had probably mistaken her for a convenient land mass in the middle of the pond. But it seemed so menacing, never altering its course, heading straight for her.

She frantically paddled backward as it continued to advance. When it flicked out its little forked tongue, she shrieked again. And then, forgetting all about her intentions to cavort like a graceful, watery nymph, she began floundering and flapping wildly in the water, squealing in horror.

An instant later, a thunderous splash beside her sent a wall of water over her head and into her nose. When she resurfaced, it was in a fit of gasping and choking.

Something slick slipped past her shoulders and brushed her hip. The snake? She shuddered and recoiled instinctively. As she tried desperately to blink the water from her eyes, she felt something circle her waist, and she thrashed against it in terror.

"Easy! I've got you."

She stiffened. It was Chase. He had his arm wrapped around her, holding her afloat.

"There's a s-snake!" she wheezed.

"A snake?"

She twisted in his grasp, searching the water and finally finding the little beast. To her immense relief, it was headed for the far end of the pool. "There."

"That little thing? I thought you were drowning."

"Drowning? Me?" The thought was preposterous. She'd been swimming all her life. She tossed the hair out of her eyes and looked up at him. Her heart wasn't jabbing quite so hard at her ribs now, but her nose stung, and it was hard to focus on him when he was so close.

He was wet and frowning, like a disgruntled cat in a rainstorm. For an instant, it made her want to smile.

And then she remembered she was naked. He was nearly naked. That was his strong arm circling her bare back and his well-muscled chest pressing against her bare breast. All at once, the last thing she felt like doing was smiling.

The water was not that deep where Chase was now standing, but he suddenly felt like he was in over his head and about to drown.

Despite sitting on that rock for what had seemed like forever—focusing, breathing, clearing his head—he hadn't received a single vision from his god or his grandmother. He'd been about to give up when he heard Claire's cry.

His reaction had been purely instinctive. He'd shot to his feet and dove in to rescue her. The fact that she wasn't in mortal danger made no difference. He felt a sense of protectiveness toward her. Even if she was only squeamish about a tiny water snake, he'd gladly jump in to save her.

But now that he'd made that plunge, he realized he'd made a grave mistake. They were flesh to flesh, their hearts pounding with the thrill of danger, their mouths inches apart.

Like a salmon swimming into a net, he was trapped and there was no way out.

Her eyes, lit by the reflections coming off the water, flickered like green fire. Her lips, parted and trembling, begged to be kissed. And he longed to lap up every drop of water that slipped down her cheek.

Her body was as soft and slippery as wet moss against

him, and she smelled like the creek—fresh, clean, and earthy. She'd stopped squirming in his grasp, and he could see her rapid pulse in her throat.

As if drawn there by force, his gaze lowered. Beneath the clear water, her breasts were pale and beautiful, the tips puckered with cold. Against his will, he moved his hand up to cup one of the lovely orbs, to warm it with his palm.

She sighed, and her eyes drifted close. He lowered his head and grazed her lips with his own, once, twice.

Her mouth was sweet and yielding at first, but rapidly became hungry and demanding. She wrapped her arms around his neck and deepened the kiss, sighing against his cheek.

Lost in lust, he let his other hand drift down her back until he cradled her bottom and lifted her up against him, against that part of him that bulged with longing despite the icy water.

She moaned against his mouth and tangled her fingers in his hair, slipping the tip of her tongue out to taste his lips.

He answered with his own tongue, tilting his head to delve into the tender recesses of her mouth, and moved his hand from her breast down past the curve of her hip, nudging her closer.

Her buttocks felt smooth, ripe, and supple in his palms, and he gave them a slow, gentle squeeze that made her gasp in pleasure.

But it was what she did next that threatened to send him over the edge into an abyss of desire. Weightless in the water, she lifted her legs and wrapped them brazenly around his waist, pressing her core against his belly with wanton, purposeful need.

Claire almost sobbed with rapture at the sensation. Everywhere his skin touched hers, it felt as if rays of sunlight kissed her, a shocking contrast to the cold water lapping at her back. And now that she'd tasted desire, that aching spot between her legs craved what he'd given her before. She squeezed tightly against him, drawing him nearer, seeking an unattainable closeness.

He groaned deep in his throat. Whether it was in pleasure or pain, she wasn't sure, but the sound sent a lusty thrill through her.

Then, all at once, with a growl of frustration, he disengaged from her, dislodged her legs, and hefted her up in one arm, slogging up the muddy bank.

Of course, she realized. It was probably awkward to make love in the water. And that was surely what he intended to do. Once he set her down before him, she could see the obvious evidence of his need straining at his trousers.

With a seductive smile, she leaned toward him and moved her hand down his chest, past his stomach, toward the firm staff that beckoned for her touch.

His lips tightened, and he grunted, but she paid no heed. She brazenly stroked the outside of his wet jeans, shivering as she felt desire as hard as oak under her hand. He wanted her. And she wanted him.

Last night, while she'd reveled in unbridled contentment, he'd reined in his lust. Now he suffered. He hungered. Why should she not grant him the same release, the same rapture he'd given her?

She unfastened the first button of his trousers.

Pulling back with a sharp inhale, he snatched her wrist. "No."

Claire hesitated. "No?"

"Don't do it, Claire." Chase had to force the words from his throat like a canoe through mud, for he sure as hell didn't want to say them. He burned for her, and he needed to cast himself into her crucible.

"Why?" she said softly.

Her question was innocent enough, but it released a torrent of moral arguments in his head, adding to the emotional storm already brewing there.

Why? There were too many reasons to count. Which one would she accept? Which one would she believe? Should he tell her he'd already taken enough from her? Should he explain that he could offer her no future? Should he mention her father? Her fiancé? Should he describe what they would do to him if they found out?

He swept up his shirt from the rocks and covered her with it. It was difficult enough keeping a level head without having to look at all that tantalizing flesh.

"You keep forgetting who I am," he said. "I'm your kidnapper, your father's worst enemy."

"I don't care," she said, clutching his shirt to her bosom. "It feels like we're supposed to be together." She gave him a shaky smile. "Don't you feel that?"

"Our feelings don't matter. And you can't be so certain we belong together. We're almost strangers."

"Strangers?" Claire's brows shot up. "I'd hardly let a stranger...do..." She lowered her eyes and her voice. "What you did to me last night."

His nostrils flared at the memory, and his chest rose and fell with a deep breath.

"Please don't take me back home, Chase," she begged. "Not yet."

"What's the difference if it's tomorrow or the next day?" he asked. "You'll go back."

"I don't want to."

"But you will."

"No," she insisted. She clenched his upper arm in desperation, and his muscle tightened at her touch. "I want to run away with you."

He scowled. "It isn't like in your books," he warned her. "In white men's stories, there is always a 'happily ever after.' That's not so in the real world."

"What about your parents? They ran away together. Aren't they living happily ever after?"

"They ran away because the miners beat up my father and the tribe was going to kill their babies." He sighed. "It wasn't easy for my mother, having no friends, no family."

Claire flashed him an injured frown. "I think you're only saying that because you don't want me."

He stared at her in rapt disbelief. How could she imagine that? Did she not notice the blatant bulge of his trousers?

"Claire," he said, adding the endearment, *"whililyo.* I've never wanted anyone more." He furrowed his hair with his hand. "This is my fault. I never meant to hurt you. But you don't belong to me. You belong to someone else. I can't be...kissing...another man's woman."

"But I'm not—"

"It's bad enough that I kidnapped you," Chase continued, lowering his head in shame. "Worse that I compromised you. I can't return you..." There was no delicate way to say it, "damaged."

She stepped close again and placed a hand on his chest. "But that's just it. Don't you see? I don't want to be returned at all."

He gave her a sad smile. "You have to go home. Your father will worry. Your fiancé will worry. Your aunt in Chico will worry."

"No!" she blurted. "No, they won't."

"Of course they will."

She guiltily averted her eyes. "Not...really."

He crossed his arms over his chest and gave her a dubious scowl.

She caught the corner of her lip under her teeth. "What I said before...about my aunt...I made it up." She gulped. "All of it."

His frown deepened.

"I wasn't visiting an aunt in Chico. I don't even *have* an aunt in Chico," she quietly admitted, adding in a mumble, "or, for that matter, an aunt."

So she'd lied to him? Or maybe she was lying now. He had sisters—he knew what tricksters women could be. Sometimes it was impossible to tell when they were speaking the truth. "Go on."

"The truth is I was running away from home." She glanced up to see how he was taking this news. He kept his expression carefully blank. "That very night I intended to leave. I left my father a note saying I was running away, that I was breaking off my engagement to Frank. So you see? He won't even be looking for me. Nobody will."

Under his crossed arms, his heartbeat quickened hopefully. Was it possible they weren't being pursued? Did no one know she'd been taken against her will? Did Claire *not* belong to another man?

All of this might be true, but he knew better than to listen to his foolish heart. After all, ladies' minds were changeable. Broken engagements could be easily repaired and often were.

"You're a runaway bride," he said.

'Runaway bride' sounded so harsh to Claire's ears, and it wasn't quite true. That wasn't the only reason she'd left. "Not exactly. I mean...I don't love Frank. I guess I never have. But I was running away because...because my father..." What could she say? That her father had never really been capable of loving her after her mother died? That Claire was a source of constant disappointment to him? That, with Yoema gone, there was nothing left for her in Paradise? "My father doesn't approve of me."

"Because you dance with the Indians."

That made a smile tug at her lips. "Maybe. But I don't want to go back there. I can't go back. I won't marry a man I don't love. And I won't be a burden to a father who's ashamed of me." Then she took a shuddering breath and stated the stark truth. "If you don't take me with you, I guess I'll...I'll find somewhere else to go. But I won't go back to Frank, and I won't go back to Paradise. I just won't."

She expected Chase would immediately assure her that of course he would take her with him. After all, he couldn't leave her to fend for herself—not the spirit daughter of his grandmother. It was partly his responsibility that she was in this predicament, and it would be ungentlemanly of him not to offer a hand to help her out of it.

But to her chagrin, he gave her no such assurances at all. Instead, he tried to convince her yet again to go home.

"No one can force you to marry," he said. "Women break off engagements all the time."

That was true. If she *did* break things off with Frank, she might have to suffer the scorn of the townsfolk. But that was nothing new.

"And you're a grown woman," he continued. "You don't need your father's approval."

That was also true. It was foolish to yearn for something she'd never had and never *would* have.

"You're a wealthy and beautiful woman," he said. "There are many white men who can offer you a good life."

"I don't want just any white man," she finally realized. "I don't want anyone but you."

He shook his head, baffled. "You would leave your home, give up that fancy house? You must have trunks full of clothes and great stores of food, servants at your beck and call and suitors falling at your feet. What more could you want? You have everything here."

"Everything?" She clasped his forearm then and looked deep into his eyes, her gaze softening as she spoke to his spirit. "No, I don't have everything. All the pretty dresses in the world wouldn't make me feel as beautiful as I do in this blacksmith's shirt. Sunday roast at the Parker Ranch will never rival the rabbit you cooked for me over the campfire. And I'll never sleep as soundly in my feather bed as I've slept in your arms. Things...are just...things." She placed her hand flat against his chest, against his heart. "This. This is what's important."

How she talked him out of his trousers, he didn't know. How she convinced him that this was the right thing to do, he couldn't say. But suddenly it seemed like they were the only two who existed in this sacred place that so much reminded him of the garden in his mother's Bible.

By the time Claire spread his cotton shirt on the flat rock and reclined in timid invitation—her bare skin gleaming like pearls in the sunlight, her eyes glazed with need—it was too late for him to change his mind. The beast had been unleashed.

"Come to me," she softly asked.

How could he refuse such a sweet request? His body ached for her. His thoughts, however, were centered on one goal. He knew he must temper his lust for fear of hurting her again. She seemed so small and fragile. And he felt so big and clumsy.

He stretched out on his side next to her, and the moment he gazed into her trusting eyes, his concerns vanished. A sense of rightness overcame him. He suddenly felt that this place, this woman, this moment were perfect and always meant to be. By some miracle, despite a star-crossed, crooked, rife-with-peril journey, he'd landed smack in the middle of his life's path, where he was intended to be.

A faint breeze blew past him, taking his cares with it. His spirit was being guided now. There was nothing to fear.

"Kiss me," Claire purred, lowering her eyes to his mouth and licking her lips.

He had neither the will nor the desire to resist her. Weaving his fingers into her wet hair, he turned her head toward his and lowered his mouth.

Their caress was tender and heartfelt. A warm glow enveloped him as their souls seemed to sing together. She sighed into his mouth, and he whispered against her lips.

She raised her hands to cup his jaw, drawing him deeper into the kiss, lightly brushing his cheeks with her thumbs and running the tip of her tongue across his upper lip.

He lifted her head in the cradle of his hands, protecting her from the hard stone as his tongue trespassed gently into her mouth, tasting her desire.

She moaned softly. He drew carefully back, leaving a delicate trail of kisses from the corner of her mouth, across her cheek, to the delicious spot beneath her ear.

She writhed in pleasure and made fists in his hair as he murmured against her ear. *"Medindin'ung?* Do you want this?"

She arched up in response, but he needed to make sure. Freeing one of his hands, he ran a fingertip down the side of her neck, making her shiver, traced her collarbone, and then moved the flat of his palm lightly over her bosom to graze the peak of her breast.

Claire squeezed her eyes shut and sipped in a shuddering breath. The contrast of the cold, clinging droplets and the warm bath of sunlight sent quivers of delight through her. But the shock of his callused hand upon her sensitive skin was earth-shaking.

She knew what she wanted next. She lowered her hands to stroke his broad shoulders, aroused by the firm and supple muscles that flexed there as he moved. She applied pressure there, urging him downward, and he complied, kissing her throat, her shoulder, her collar bone.

He eased her head back down on the rock and threaded his fingers through hers. Then he resumed kissing and licking his way over the curve of her breast until he enclosed one aching peak in his mouth.

She gasped in pleasure and clenched his fingers between hers as he sucked at her, drawing all her lust to a fine point before he released her to make his way to her other breast.

After he slaked his thirst there, he drifted back to her stomach and lower, lifting an inquiring brow above dark, smoky eyes. *"Medindin 'ung?"*

Did she want this? She could read his intent in his smoldering gaze. Oh yes, she wanted it. She blushed and nodded.

The anticipation was sweet agony. He seemed to know it, emitting a soft chuckle as he moved lower, flicking his tongue out in teasing hints of what was to come.

This time she cried out in sheer bliss and squeezed his fingers until she thought she would crack his knuckles. But he continued until her need grew and intensified, until she simultaneously swelled with longing and ached with profound emptiness.

Chase sensed it was time.

As he abandoned his play to kiss his way back up to her neck, her brow creased with an impatient frown. He smiled. *"Whina,"* he whispered, "Wait for me."

Shuddering with restraint, he slowly covered her body with his. He stilled for a moment, reveling in the amazing sensation of skin against skin. Her yielding breasts pillowed his chest. Her belly, warmed by the sun, seemed to melt with his. The sprinkle of dark golden hair at the union of her thighs tangled with his own black curls. He nuzzled the place beneath her ear, where her heart's fierce throbbing matched his own pulse.

Then, with a silent prayer that he wouldn't hurt this woman he loved, he eased forward and, with excruciating patience, sheathed himself inside her.

Claire sighed in sensual wonder. He felt so right within her, so perfect, as if this was always meant to be. And she felt powerful and vulnerable all at once—capable of commanding him, yet completely at his mercy. It was a heady sensation.

The mist kissed her brow, and the sunlight warmed her face. At one with Chase and with nature, she longed to stay in this magical place forever, to revel in sweet completion.

When she dared to open her eyes and gaze up at him, what she beheld in his face aroused her even more. His eyes were squeezed shut in an impassioned mixture of pleasure and pain. His lips were compressed into a single line, and a determined furrow marked his brow.

And then, almost as if he felt her gaze, he slowly opened his eyes.

They burned with a dark fire that took her breath away. Yet, as he continued to stare down at her, a softness flickered within that fire. Held within his lust was adoration. He cared for her.

"Dinch'at?" he said. "Are you hurt?"

She shook her head and smiled, and then wrapped her legs around his hips, drawing him closer in welcome. She felt her heart melting as his love surrounded her like a downy quilt.

Chase exhaled in relief. The warmth of Claire's body enveloping him was exquisite. And there was something more. He felt as if he'd come home, as if he'd completed a circle. This was his path. This was his destiny.

Even the elements had come together to bless this union— the moist air surrounding them, the rocky earth beneath them, the sun's fire warming them, the refreshing water misting their joined bodies.

There was no doubt. This was meant to be. He was where he belonged.

Claire squirmed beneath him, eager to begin the dance. He

feared he wouldn't last long. The sensation, not just of their bodies, but of their spirits connected, overwhelmed him.

He carefully withdrew from her, and then entered again, and she made a soft moan of pleasure. Again and again he eased into her welcoming warmth, trying to be as gentle as possible. Though he yearned to careen toward release and thrust forward in a triumphant finish, he bit back the urge.

An instant before he lost the battle over his desires, she thankfully found her relief. She pressed against him, squeezing him with her thighs, and it was as if she squeezed the very seed from him. His hips pounded in tandem with his heart. Brilliant light arced through his vision like sparks from an anvil, and his essence pumped from him like a crucible overflowing.

Afterward, he couldn't speak. There were no words, not even in the Hupa tongue, to describe the singular union he felt. Instead, he silently cradled the wondrous woman who'd brought him such rapture, cupping her cheek, stroking her hair, kissing her shoulder, shielding her from the outside world with his body.

Claire felt as if she were floating on a cloud, conveyed across the heavens on wings of angels. Never had she felt such tranquility. Never had she felt so spent. Never had she loved so fiercely or so well.

She squeezed his hands again. As surely as their bodies were entwined, their spirits were joined. The bond between them was unbreakable now. The circle they'd made was infinite. Their union was complete.

Gradually, her breathing lengthened and the world came back to her. She heard the rumbling thunder and whispering rush of the water. The pool winked at her with a hundred daylight stars. She smelled the moss and damp earth along the banks of the pool. A sparrow chirped in the branches above, and a faint breath of wind rustled the young leaves. A single wisp of cloud drifted across the brilliant blue sky while the stark rock baked in the spring sun.

But all the small miracles of nature couldn't match the joy she felt in Chase's arms. And when she felt him stir inside her again, she answered eagerly.

All day long, they reveled—making love, splashing in the pool, sitting in the sun, making love again. As mad as it seemed, she grew accustomed to being naked with him. It felt like they were Adam and Eve in the Garden of Eden. And with each passing moment, she felt stronger in her love for Chase, surer of their destiny together.

It was only when the sun dipped below the trees and she shivered in the darkening shade that she realized how late it had become. She supposed it didn't matter. She was in no hurry to leave. In fact, she wasn't even sure where they would go. But she didn't care, as long as she could be with Chase.

"Are you cold?" he murmured, wrapping his shirt around her and brushing the hair back from her brow.

"A little."

"Hungry?"

"Famished."

"Hmm. I saw a tasty-looking water snake around here earlier."

She grimaced, and he chuckled.

His jeans weren't quite dry, but he slipped into them anyway. "I'll build a fire."

"There's a good spot across the stream where we can camp for the night," she told him. "I'll take you there."

She took his hand—so strong and perfect in hers—and led him across the creek to the far bank. They hiked up the hillside until they emerged in a small, flat clearing among the pines.

Much later, after the sun had gone down, they dined on baked camas bulb cakes, scrambled quail eggs with pine nuts, and miner's lettuce. Claire thought she'd never had such a happy feast.

The moon rose, and the firelight licked at their faces as they held hands, gazing into the orange flames.

"Do you think the circle has been completed now?" she ventured.

One corner of his mouth curved up. "Many times over."

In feigned shock, she gave his shoulder a chiding punch, then murmured, "I think your grandmother must be happy."

"Her spirit will find its way home now."

Claire stared down at their joined hands. "And what about us? Will we find our way home?"

He was silent for so long that she began to worry that he might not answer her or that, if he did, it would be with something she didn't want to hear.

At last he spoke. "We've found our way to each other. For now, that's enough."

She nodded and leaned against him.

They made tender love one last time under the stars before the embers died. In the sweet aftermath, as they snuggled together on a lush bed of grass, he folded his arms around her.

"*Niwhdin,* Claire Parker," he whispered in her ear.

"What does that mean?"

"I love you."

Her already throbbing heart swelled, and she let out a sigh of contentment. "*Niwhdin,* Chase Wolf," she told him. "Forever."

Forever. The future might be unclear. The way forward might be full of challenges. Where they would go…what they would do…she couldn't be certain. But with Chase by her side, Claire knew she could face whatever hardships came and that, very soon, their story would have the perfect happily ever after.

She couldn't have been more wrong.

CHAPTER 18

Samuel Parker had always been an early riser, not so much because ranch work required it, but because he liked looking at the world before it fully awoke. He'd forgotten how pretty the ridge was in springtime. The air was chill, the trees were quiet, and the flighty sky changed colors like a woman making up her mind about what to wear.

Silently hiking up the ridge now by the gray-pink light the dawn had decided upon, he paused and turned to look out over the canyon. From his high vantage point at the brink of the pool, the distant forest on the opposite ridge, crowded with pine and fir, looked hazy blue. Fine morning mist settled over the lush basin below, painting the meadow like milk glazing a bowl.

The last time he'd come to this place, Margaret had been alive and their daughter had been a little girl. How had so much time passed? Claire was a young woman now. He only prayed she'd live to be an *old* woman.

Ahead of him, Frank waited impatiently. He wouldn't call out—stealth was their strategy now—but Samuel could tell by the eager glint in his eyes that they were close to their quarry.

The muddy tracks leading from the waterfall were recent. Frank waved two fingers, beckoning Samuel to follow him through the pines while the sun began to illuminate the forest in tiny patches.

They hiked uphill from the pool, passing through a thicket of deerbrush to emerge in a clearing guarded by pines. Through the dipping branches of the largest tree, among the ubiquitous red-brown of dust and rock and mulch, Samuel spied a patch of grass and something blue. At first, he didn't know what he was seeing—maybe a lost saddle blanket or a discarded cloth sack. It partially covered some pale mound, and whatever lay underneath was as tangled and blanched as the roots of a fresh-fallen tree. He squinted his eyes, then widened them as the sun suddenly cast a damning finger of light on a lock of golden hair.

He staggered, and the rifle dropped from his fingers. His gut sank as if a mule had kicked him, stealing his breath, battering his heart.

His little girl. His little girl lay there. As still as death. As still as her mother when...

Frank hissed out an oath, breaking into his thoughts. To Samuel's immense relief, the shape beneath the blanket stirred at the sound.

That relief yanked Samuel's lungs back where they belonged, but his belly was still as churned up as butter, and he clenched his trembling jaw to hold back tears of gratitude.

Then he spied the second head, one topped with hair as black as midnight. He froze, first with astonishment, then with horror, then with rage. And while he was circling that corral of emotions, he let Frank get away from him.

Not afflicted by a father's paralysis, Frank had no qualms about taking matters into his own hands.

"You godforsaken son of a bitch!" Frank snarled.

The familiar voice jolted Claire to wide-eyed awareness. She gasped, and in that one breath, realized where she was, how she was dressed, or rather *not* dressed, whose arm cradled her with casual intimacy, and who stood not a dozen feet beyond her approaching fiancé, quivering with fury.

Chase's arm was violently wrenched from around her waist, jerking aside the shirt covering her as well, which left her naked. She shrieked and caught a fleeting look of lurid hunger and rage in Frank's gaze.

He raised his rifle now, aiming it with unflinching malice at Chase, helpless on his back beside her. In another moment, he'd fire.

"No!" she cried. "No, Frank! Don't!"

There was a depraved gleam in Frank's gaze, and his lips pulled back in a sneer as he cocked the hammer of the gun.

"No!" she screamed.

She reached out toward Chase to protect him. But when she would have thrown herself over him to intercept the bullet, Chase thrust out a hand and pushed her roughly away. His mouth was grim, his eyes dark and inscrutable.

The rebuke hurt her heart more than her body. For a moment, she lay there, stunned. Frank would shoot him now. Frank would shoot and kill Chase Wolf.

"Let him up, Frank," her father growled, trudging forward.

Samuel was quaking with suppressed anger, but, to Claire's relief, his eyes had none of the bloodlust that transfixed Frank. He shrugged off his canvas coat and draped it over her.

"Let him up, I said." He knocked Frank's rifle barrel aside with his own.

Claire bit her lip. Frank's enthusiasm was thwarted for only a moment before the barbarous glimmer returned to his eyes.

221

"You gonna scalp him first?" he asked.

"No!" Claire choked on her words. "Please, Father, no. This is all a misunderstanding. Just let me explain. It's not what you..."

Her father's glare, injured but stern, silenced her.

"You. Get up," he told Chase, raising his rifle.

Chase hesitated, staring intently at her father, as if he peered into the man's soul. Then he slowly came to his feet.

Chase towered over them, and his muscular chest and shoulders gave him more breadth than either of the men, even Frank with his padded coat. Claire was sure Chase could have bested them with his bare hands, were it not for their guns.

Frank shifted uneasily, as if his prize livestock were in danger of getting away. "Of course, we don't want to do anything that might offend Miss Claire's sensibilities. Maybe you should take her off a ways into the woods until I—"

"No, Frank," her father said, weighing Chase's measure with his gaze. "There isn't going to be any scalping."

"But, sir, look what he did to her hair." The childish disappointment on Frank's face sickened Claire.

"Bring me a rope."

Claire's heart plummeted. Her father wasn't going to scalp Chase. He was going to hang him.

"Yes, sir," Frank replied.

"No, Father! You don't understand. None of this was his idea. It was my fault. I was the one—"

"We'll discuss the particulars another time," he muttered between his teeth, refusing to look at her.

She knew what he left unsaid. They wouldn't speak of it here, in public. Where her father was concerned, it was a subject to keep behind closed doors, away from society's ears. He wouldn't want to discuss it until they were safely alone within the walls of Parker House and probably not even then.

But Claire was fed up with propriety and keeping a stiff upper lip and staying silent about things that needed airing.

"There won't be another time, Father, and you know it." She was shaking like a leaf. She wasn't used to standing up to her father, and she had to steel herself against his glare of disapproval. "You're making a mistake, and I won't be silenced. This is not what it looks like. It's not his fault. I...I ran away with him, and then I coerced—"

"No," Chase broke in. "That's not true at all, Claire, and you know it. I won't let you lie for me. I stole you, pure and simple."

"Turn around," her father said, taking the rope from Frank.

Claire's heart slammed against her ribs. This couldn't be happening. She wouldn't let it. She cast about, looking for something, anything, she might use as a weapon. She might not be as brave or brawny as Buckskin Bill, but she was desperate, and that counted for something.

Her glance landed on a long stick, a sharp rock, a pine cone. And then she realized that Chase still had his knife in his belt. Why hadn't he used it?

Rather than waste valuable time wondering, she reached across and drew the knife from its sheath herself.

Chase made a grab for her arm and missed. In that split-second, she managed to get the blade up to Frank's throat. Frank's eyes and hands went wide, and a heady thrill of power went through her as she forced him back from Chase and her father.

"Let him go, Father!" she cried.

Her father paused with the rope.

Frank narrowed his eyes at her in disbelief and disgust. "Are you defending him? The no-count Injun who stole you?" He dropped his hands and might have knocked aside her blade, but she pressed her advantage, nicking his neck, which made him squeak in surprise.

"Claire, put down the blade." It was Chase, not her father, who said it.

"I will not. I won't stand by while my father hangs the man I love."

"What?" Frank was noticeably shocked. "The man you...*I'm* the man you love."

Claire gave a guilty gulp, but she didn't move the knife. "I'm sorry, Frank. I should have told you sooner. You've been a...a good friend. But I never loved you, not the way a woman is supposed to love her husband."

"What are you saying, Claire? Are you leaving me?" he whined. "For this savage?" His dismay quickly turned to a panicked anger. "Well, I think your father might have something to say about that."

Claire's father cleared his throat, but that was all.

"Claire," Chase said again, "put away the knife before someone gets hurt."

Claire shook her head. She wasn't about to give up her leverage, not with Chase's life at risk.

"Mr. Parker?" Frank prodded. "Are you going to stand for this?"

"I really don't have much choice, Frank," he replied. "She *has* got a knife at your throat."

"Lay down your rifle, Father," she said, "and that noose."

"Noose?" He frowned in consternation, but he complied, tossing the rope and rifle onto the leaves.

Claire was proud of herself. She was beginning to feel like a regular Dashing Dick. All she had to do now was confiscate the guns, and she and Chase could make a clean getaway.

Like a perfect sidekick that needed no prompting, Chase swept up the discarded rifle and swung the barrel around toward Frank.

"Go ahead and back away, Claire. I've got him."

For a moment, she hesitated. Chase's mouth was grim, his

eyes icy, his jaw hard. He looked like the villain who'd kidnapped her days before.

He wouldn't shoot Frank outright, would he? And her father...Chase had spoken of vengeance against her father. Surely he didn't intend to kill them both in cold blood. The man she'd made love to last night didn't seem capable of such violence. But the man who'd snatched her from her home and dragged her across the countryside did.

"Don't...hurt him," Claire said, realizing the inanity of her words even as she said them. After all, *she* was the one holding Frank at knifepoint.

"Not unless he gives me a reason," Chase promised, though she feared one more sneer might be enough of a reason.

She supposed she'd just have to trust Yoema's grandson. She backed away, lowering the knife.

Keeping the gun trained on Frank, Chase commanded, "On your belly."

"What?" Frank replied with a nervous bark of a laugh.

"You heard me."

"Now hold on a goddam minute. I'm not going to let a goddam Injun—"

"On your belly!" Chase snarled. "And stop cursing in front of the lady."

Frank hesitated a moment too long, and Chase cocked the gun.

Claire gasped. "For the love of god, Frank, do as he says."

Frank reluctantly complied, though he managed a final threat as he stretched out on the dusty leaves. "You're a dead man."

Claire could see that Frank was so full of hate, it was deafening him to reason. Indeed, it was probably for the best that Chase had ordered him to the ground, because Frank seemed as volatile as rigged dynamite.

Whatever hopes Claire had had that somehow she and

Chase could return to her father's ranch and live in peace were shattered. She'd been a fool to think that was ever a possibility. Exposing Chase to Paradise society would be like bringing a wild wolf into a pack of yapping terriers.

Chase *did* look like his spirit animal now—intense, calculating, and dangerous. In Claire's eagerness to make a daring escape with Chase the lover, she'd forgotten he was also Chase the avenger. Quiet rage simmered in his dark eyes.

She wasn't afraid of him, not really. She knew he wouldn't harm her. He'd told her he had no quarrel with her, that she couldn't be held accountable for the sins of her father. But she knew he still blamed her father for what had happened to Yoema, to his family.

How stupidly naïve she'd been to imagine the past could be so easily repaired, that everything would end as neatly as her dime novels.

"Give me the knife, Claire," Chase bit out, "and that rope."

A startling image of Frank being scalped and hanged popped into her mind. She bit her lip and shook her head.

Chase's frown relaxed, and he told her, "It's not a noose. I just want to tie him up so we don't have to keep a rifle trained on him."

She released her breath and nodded. Of course. But if it wasn't a noose, maybe her father hadn't meant to hang Chase after all. She backed away from Frank and handed the knife to Chase. "I can cover you while you tie him up," she offered, holding her hands out for the gun.

Chase looked dubious. He probably figured she didn't know how to handle a rifle. But she did. She was deadly when it came to tin cans.

"All right," he said, carefully transferring the rifle to her. "Just don't get trigger-happy."

While Claire kept Frank in her sights, Chase cut the rope in half.

"Hands behind your back," he ordered.

"I won't forget this," Frank threatened as Chase tied his wrists together and then joined his ankles to bind them as well.

Her father watched the proceedings with mild interest. "So how did you do it?" he asked Chase. "Was she in your room at the saloon that day? Under the bed maybe? Or trussed up somewhere?"

Chase scowled, tightening the rope between Frank's wrists and ankles. "I don't know what you're talking about."

Frank sneered and jerked at his bonds. "See, Mr. Parker? I knew we shouldn't have trusted him."

Chase didn't understand what game they were playing. He was sure he'd never seen the two white men before. But then whites often twisted words and events to suit their purposes. Sometimes they even created history to salve their guilty consciences.

He finished off the knot, and Frank squirmed in impotent rage. It was probably a good thing the man was hogtied and helpless, since he looked like he'd love to beat the hell out of a half-breed like him. And if Frank so much as lifted a finger, he was pretty sure Claire would plug him full of lead.

How could Claire have considered marrying this man? He might be handsome by white standards, with his fair hair and light eyes and pale skin. And by the quality of his clothing, which was less worn and more ornate than Parker's, he might be wealthy. But though he wore a gentleman's garments, he was no gentleman. A streak of evil tainted him like poison leaching into a spring.

Chase stood, and Claire lowered the rifle. Then he turned to Samuel Parker with the second piece of rope. "I'd rather not have to tie you up. Can we talk like reasonable men?"

Though Parker's scowl was black, he answered, "Speak your piece."

Chase retrieved his shirt, hunkered down, and gestured to the rancher to have a seat. The man smoothed his mustache, eyed his discarded rifle, decided it was too far away to make a play for it, and then lowered himself onto a nearby rock with a sigh. Claire wrapped her father's coat around her and sat in the leaves.

Chase had thought long and hard on the matter of revenge, even before Samuel Parker had sneaked into his camp. He'd considered what price he'd extract from the rancher that could possibly equal what had been done to his family. And he'd at last decided how Parker's debt could be repaid.

First, he intended to take the man's daughter from him. Of course, it would be with her permission, and she'd be free to visit him whenever she liked. But he was going to take her home with him to Hupa and make her his woman.

Second, before he did that, he intended to force Parker to tell his daughter the truth. She should know what kind of man her father truly was.

"No matter what Claire says," Chase began, slipping on his shirt, "it's true, I stole her."

Claire protested. "But you didn't—"

He stopped her with an upraised palm. "I took her against her will. I admit that. But I didn't intend to steal her. I meant to steal you."

"Me? Why?"

Chase looked with unflinching accusation into the man's eyes. He'd been thinking about this confrontation for days—facing the demon, exacting his revenge. He wanted Samuel Parker to feel every bit of the Konkows' pain, to pay for every soul that had suffered and died on the march.

Finally, he chewed out the bitter words. "For Nome Cult. For what you did to my people."

Claire narrowed her eyes at her father. Chase's words had startled him. He looked as if he'd suddenly aged ten years.

Was there something to the claims after all? *Had* her father split up Chase's family and allowed Konkow people to be marched off? Had he kept Yoema as a slave?

"You're making a mistake," her father said.

Frank jerked his head toward Chase. "Looks like the Infantry made a mistake. They forgot to put a bullet in this one."

"Frank!" Claire scolded.

But what troubled her was not so much Frank's venom as the fact that he too seemed to know about the march. Was she the only one in Paradise who'd never heard of Nome Cult?

Then Chase must be right. Her father *had* kept it hidden from her. And she could think of only one reason for that.

"Is it true?" she breathed, staring aghast at her father, who had turned pale and was staring off into the woods, as if his mind had traveled to a long time ago. "Is it?"

Frank spit into the leaves. "If you ask me, they should have killed them all when they had the chance. It's what my daddy always said. If you don't cut the head off the snake—"

"Stop it!" Claire shot to her feet with fists of blind fury. "You don't know what you're saying! That's Yoe-, my spirit mother you're talking about!"

"Your what?" Frank said with a chuckle.

Claire was so angry, she had to resist the urge to give Frank a solid kick in the teeth. Instead, she picked up his rifle and took aim at the back of his head.

"Claire!" Chase shouted in alarm.

Claire ignored him. "You apologize."

"Claire?" Frank squeaked. "Sweetheart?"

"You heard me. Tell. Him. You're. Sorry."

"Look, honey," Frank said, nervously licking his lips, "it doesn't matter what this savage did to you. Your hair will grow out, and I can look past your indiscretion. We can still get married."

"My indiscretion? What do you mean?"

"Well, it's just that you might have gotten some peculiar notions into your head, reading those rags of yours and being raised by that Injun woman—"

She jabbed him in the back with the barrel of the rifle. He yelped.

Chase tensed his jaw. He didn't know how good Claire was with a gun, but if he was reading her right, she wasn't far from shooting her foul-mouthed fiancé. He had to do something to stop her. The last thing he needed was for Claire to get blood on her hands.

To Chase's chagrin, her father spoke up. "No need to waste a bullet, Claire. You've got him hogtied already."

Claire's nostrils were still flaring with anger, but she nodded and slowly lowered the rifle.

Whether Parker had spoken out of concern for his daughter or his partner, Chase didn't know. But he was glad to have the situation defused.

"Besides," the rancher admitted, his shoulders drooping, "this fellow is probably right. I should have come clean with you about the march a long time ago. I guess you're old enough to know now."

Claire looked suddenly bewildered, like a lost child, and Chase felt a pang of regret. Maybe he shouldn't have brought it up. He didn't want to upset Claire. Then again, how could he bring her home to his parents without her knowing the truth about what had happened to his family?

Parker stared down at his folded hands for a long while before he began, reminding Chase of the elder storytellers of Hupa. When he finally started speaking, there was a distant sound to his voice, as if he were not only relating, but reliving the events.

"It was 1863," he said. "You were six years old. Things were never exactly peaceful between the settlers and the natives. But in '63 the situation grew worse. The Hickok and Lewis children were killed by Indians—vengeance killings, they said—and even though five Indians were hanged at Helltown for it, people were shaken up and wanted the natives gone, all of them. So they called out the Infantry to round them up." He paused, as if the words were stuck in his throat and he had to force them out. "Your mother was ailing. This news didn't help any. She always liked the Indians. They were good to her. They were also some of my best hands." He glanced meaningfully at Chase and then lowered his eyes to stare at the ground. "She asked me not to let the Infantry take them away. She begged me to hide the Indians. So I did. As many as I could. Then she started growing very ill, and all I could think about was her." He swallowed and looked off into the trees, but Chase could glimpse raw grief in the man's eyes. "I'm afraid I wasn't as vigilant as I should have been. Some of my hands were rooted out and taken. And there wasn't a thing I could do about it. The Infantry was shooting the ones who didn't surrender. My neighbors would have turned me in as a traitor if they'd known I was harboring Indians in the barn."

Chase was stunned. This was a possibility he'd never considered—that Parker had tried to help his people.

He glanced at Claire, whose brow was furrowed in dismay. No wonder her father had kept the march a secret from her. His little girl was about to lose her mother, and he didn't want to make things worse than they already were.

"Shortly after," Parker confirmed, his voice catching, "your mother passed."

Claire nodded and bowed her head. "What happened to the Indians?"

"They were marched off to a reservation called Nome Cult," he told her. "Not all of them made it. Some were too old to make the journey. Some were too young. Some managed to escape and returned to the ranch. But those who got caught were killed."

There was a long silence, and then Claire asked, "What about Yoema?"

Her father gave a single sad chuckle. "She showed up at the door after your mother was gone and wouldn't take no for an answer. She said a vision had told her she was to be mother to a little white dove. That was you." He sighed. "I had the ranch, a herd of cattle, a bunch of fugitives for ranch hands, and a little girl I didn't know how to take care of. So I let her stay."

Despite the grudge Chase had been carrying for days now, he couldn't keep holding it. As much as he wanted to hang on to his hatred and to repay someone for the injustice his people had suffered, he knew now that Samuel Parker was no villain. The rancher had been as sympathetic as he could be, given the circumstances. He'd been an ally of the Konkow, not their enemy.

But Chase still had one important question.

"Why did no one tell her family? We thought she was dead."

Parker perked up at that. "You're Yoema's kin?"

"Yep."

"The truth is she rarely spoke of her family," Parker said. "She thought it was bad luck to speak of those who were gone. She said her place was with Claire now. But once I knew she was dying, I sent off a letter to Nome Cult in case any of her kinfolk were alive. I expect that's why you're here?"

Claire explained. "Chase is her grandson."

The old man studied him for a moment. "I can see that— family resemblance. Well, son, you should know we did the best we could for her. She had a good doctor. And Claire fetched her all the Indian remedies she could get her hands on. I expect it was just her time."

Chase nodded, but it felt like someone had rearranged all the furniture in his brain, and he couldn't go anywhere without bumping his shins. The picture of his grandmother's life was completely different than he'd imagined, and it would take some time to adjust to this new portrait of Samuel Parker as hero, not slaveholder.

"I told you he was a good man," Claire said.

"You did," he agreed.

Samuel Parker cleared his throat and stuffed his feelings back into his gut where they belonged. He felt better having told Claire the truth, but there was no need to dwell on the past. The past was filled with pain.

"So what do we do now?" he asked the young half-breed with the rifle and Yoema's eyes.

From the ground, Frank muttered, "Well, now that you two have smoked the peace pipe, how about untying me?"

The man freed Frank, but he held onto his gun, which was probably wise. It couldn't be easy for Frank to accept a broken engagement, and nothing would give a man an itchy trigger finger like having his replacement in range.

Of course, Yoema's grandson wasn't really Frank's replacement. There was no way Samuel would let his daughter marry a half-breed. And at the first opportunity, Samuel would let Frank know that.

It was really too bad. The half-breed was admittedly forthright and brave, trustworthy and protective. He'd been resourceful enough to keep Claire's belly full and make the rabbit fur boots she was wearing. Samuel was impressed by his even demeanor and his levelheaded handling of a tough situation. He'd seen honor and wisdom in the man's actions. And Claire was obviously all cow-eyed over the handsome youth.

But that was only because she fancied those silly books that painted Indians as dashing and romantic figures. Once the reality of marriage to a native hit her, once she understood how she'd be shunned from decent society, she'd see the folly of her ways.

Samuel had learned that harsh lesson when he'd brought Yoema into his household. His neighbors had wagged their tongues, speculating that she was sharing his bed. Some folks accused him of being an Indian sympathizer. A few buyers started getting their stock from other ranchers. For Claire, it would be even worse. He'd never let her subject herself to such rejection.

Besides, Samuel had groomed Frank to take over the ranch. Nobody could buy and sell cattle like Frank. He'd be a good provider for Claire. Maybe he was a little rough around the edges and didn't quite understand Claire's affection for dime novels and wild Indians, but the young man could learn to curb his tongue to keep her happy.

And Claire would learn to love Frank. Once he gave her babies, once she had little ones to look after, her harebrained notions of running off with an Indian would fade away.

The wedding would have to be rushed, of course. Though it soured his stomach to think of such things, it appeared that Claire had been intimate with the man, and if she was already with child...

He hoped not, because it would be glaringly obvious that the child wasn't the offspring of blond-haired, blue-eyed Frank. And if word got back to the town about Claire's...activities...she'd be branded a fallen woman. He couldn't let that happen. But that was a problem he'd have to deal with when the time came.

"I buried your grandmother in a pretty spot on my property," he said to the half-breed. "I'm sure you'll want to pay your respects." It was a statement, not a question. He needed to convince Claire to come home before she tried something rash like running off with the savage.

Fortunately, the young man agreed. And thankfully, they wouldn't be arriving in Paradise before dark, because they made an odd-looking group as they hiked across the canyon and up the ridge to Dogtown. The last thing he needed was a bunch of nosy neighbors questioning Claire's state of dress and wondering about her strange companion.

"You can bunk in the barn tonight," he offered. "I'll show you Yoema's grave tomorrow." And then, he added silently, I'll send you on your way.

CHAPTER 19

Chase had always intended to go back to Paradise. He had to pick up his brother. But he had a bad feeling now about returning.

It had been too easy. Frank and Parker had been too quick to forgive and forget. Claire's fiancé, initially upset, had been soothed by something Parker said to him privately. And Parker hadn't said a word about the shocking state in which he'd found his daughter. There was too much unspoken. Something ugly was bubbling under that silence, something that might erupt when they got back to the safety of the Parker Ranch.

Chase didn't trust either of them. He supposed it was because his tribe had taught him not to put faith in white men. They broke treaties and used trickery to get what they wanted. If bribery didn't work, they used wiles, and if wiles didn't work, they used force.

He wasn't sure what to expect. But he sure as hell wasn't going to get caught with his eyes shut and his trousers down...again.

Parker didn't say much at all until midday, when he offered to share his jerky and biscuits. Frank, in what was obviously a competition for Claire's affections, casually took off his coat and unbuttoned his shirt, displaying a lily-white belly he might have been wiser to hide. Chase kept his mouth shut, realizing he could say nothing to make the situation less uncomfortable.

The sun gradually crossed the naked blue sky, shifting the shadows of the pines and leaving a vague orange glow at the horizon as it sank. It was late evening by the time they reached Paradise, when most of the townsfolk were either tucked in at home or bellying up to the bar of one of the local saloons.

Unfortunately, as they trudged down the main street, they spied the last man any of them wanted to see. A man with a silver star pinned to his jacket was pacing in agitation along the boardwalk in front of the Parlor.

He spotted them instantly.

"There you are, you cheatin' son of a gun!"

The men exchanged glances. Who was the sheriff talking to?

He hopped down from the boardwalk and came forward at an eager clip.

"It's all right, boys," he said, drawing his forty-five. "I'll take it from here."

Chase clamped his jaw. The sheriff was coming for *him*.

"Now hold on a minute, Campbell," Parker said, raising his palms. "What's this all about?"

The sheriff nodded at Chase. "This two-bit half-breed stole my poker winnin's is what."

Frank wasted no time, chiming in. "I told you he was no good, Mr. Parker. See, Claire? He's a gambler. You don't want to be getting tangled up with—"

"That's enough, Frank," Parker interjected.

Chase knew that the rancher didn't like spectacles. The last thing he wanted was for the town sheriff to know that his daughter had been "tangled up" with a half-breed.

Campbell waved his revolver. "So if you fellas will stand aside..."

"Sheriff Campbell," Claire said, resting a palm on the man's forearm. "There must be some mistake. This man can't have stolen your winnings. He's been with me."

"With us," Parker corrected. "He's been with us, up in Dogtown."

Campbell nodded. "So that's why I haven't been able to find him. He must have skedaddled right after he took my cash."

"That makes sense, sir," Frank volunteered. "He probably hid it somewhere and then hightailed it into the hills."

"Father, you know that can't be true. He—"

"Hush," Parker snarled as a well-dressed man came out of the Parlor. After he'd gone, Parker said, "I think you've got the wrong man, Campbell."

"Oh, I've got the right man." He pointed the gun at Chase's belly. "I could never forget the face of the half-breed who cost me my fortune and lost me my Maggie Ellen."

"Maggie Ellen?" Claire asked.

"She left me. Said she had no use for a man who was up to his eyes in gamblin' debt."

Chase furrowed his brow.

His brother.

Campbell was confusing him with his brother.

Drew must have beaten the man at poker. Drew never cheated, but he usually won, and some didn't take kindly to being beaten, even when it was fair and square.

He looked past the sheriff. The Parlor was the last place he'd seen Drew. Was he still there, or had he smelled trouble and left?

"Father?" Claire asked.

Two more men drifted out of the establishment, and Parker tensed. Once they moved out of earshot, he intervened, looking Chase in the eye. "You don't seem like the cheating type. You got anything to say in your defense?"

Chase clenched his jaw. The last thing he wanted was to be at the mercy of an armed white man with a grudge. But he had to protect Drew. They'd always watched out for each other.

"Nope," he said, handing the rifle to Parker.

Claire gasped.

"I told you!" Frank crowed, right before Claire turned and slapped the smug smile right off of his face.

Everyone blinked in surprise.

But Parker didn't believe Chase was guilty. Chase could see it in the narrowing of the man's eyes. "What will you do with him?" he asked the sheriff.

"Lock him up."

"That all?"

"Well, he may have an accident on the way to the jail," Campbell confided with a chuckle to Frank, whose cheek now bore the red imprint of Claire's hand.

Parker stabbed a finger in front of the sheriff's face. "You listen good, and you tell the jailer, too. If there's one mark on him tomorrow morning, you'll have to answer to me."

Campbell compressed his lips. He clearly didn't like to take orders from civilians. But Chase could see that Parker was like a *miningxa't'enk*—a chief—full of power, and the sheriff was forced to back down.

"Fine." He put away his revolver and whipped out a pair of handcuffs.

"No!" Claire cried.

"Don't make a spectacle, Claire," Parker growled.

"It's all right, *whililyo'*," Chase told her, using the endearment no one else would understand.

"I'll be back first thing in the morning," Parker promised, "and we'll straighten this all out." To Campbell, he repeated, "First thing."

The sheriff clapped the handcuffs around Chase's wrists, and Chase gave Claire what he hoped was a reassuring nod.

"Well, I guess every man has the right to a speedy trial," Frank groused. He purposely bumped Chase as he passed him, muttering, "And this'll be the speediest trial you ever saw."

Watching Sheriff Campbell lead Chase off in handcuffs was almost unbearable for Claire. What she really wanted to do was bowl the sheriff over, confiscate his forty-five and his prisoner, and head for the hills with Chase.

And then Chase looked back at her. Not the way Frank looked at her with fondness and a hint of knowing bemusement. Not the way her father looked at her with stern pride. Not even the way Yoema had looked at her, beaming with motherly adoration. No, his eyes called to something inside of her, quickening her heart, stealing her breath, igniting her senses. They penetrated her very soul with love and loyalty and honor, as if in his gaze alone he communicated to her a lifetime of devotion.

Her father said something to her, but she didn't hear, didn't move until he grasped her by the shoulder and turned her toward him. It took every ounce of strength for her to put one foot in front of the other. An invisible cord seemed to bind her to Chase Wolf now, and every step that separated them strained that cord like the sinew of a drawn bow, increasing its tension.

All the way to the ranch, she was haunted by doubt.

Had Chase won money off of the sheriff? Had he cheated at cards? She didn't want to believe it. But she didn't know what he'd been up to before coming to kidnap her. If he possessed stolen winnings, he certainly didn't have them with him.

Maybe that was why he'd gone with the sheriff willingly. Maybe he foolishly thought he'd be exonerated when they didn't find the stash.

They were at the gates of the Parker Ranch when Frank spat, "I have half a mind to go back and plug that Injun bastard full of lead."

"Frank!" she scolded.

Frank's body was wound tight as a clock spring, his mouth was working, and his fisted knuckles were white with strain. He looked like he wanted to hit something...badly.

"Won't do any good to get worked up about it," her father said.

The tension hissed from Frank like a hot poker plunged into cold water, and he vented his ire by taking off his hat to whack it against his thigh a couple of times before ramming it back on his head.

"He's got to pay for what he's done," Frank muttered.

"He'll get a fair trial." Her father shook his head. "You can't go around shooting unarmed men. I won't have any rumors of cowardice bandied about regarding the man my daughter's to wed."

Claire's breath caught. The man she was to wed? Did he mean Frank? But she'd broken off the engagement. She'd said so in her letter. He must have seen it. "Father, my note... Didn't you read... I need to talk to you about—"

"Nothing to talk about," he declared. His gaze, focused on the path ahead, was as hard and unbending as cold steel.

And then Claire realized why she should never have returned.

Nothing had changed. Her father still expected her to conform to his wishes, to move back into the house, to marry Frank, and to forget all about Yoema...and her grandson. Just as when her mother had died, he wanted to carry on as if nothing had happened.

She wouldn't do it. She wouldn't marry Frank. She wouldn't stay at the Parker Ranch. And she sure as hell wasn't going to forget about Chase Wolf.

As they passed through the gates and along the drive toward the big white house that now looked like a prison to Claire, she vowed that the next time she left, it would be forever.

Her father had promised Chase a fair trial, but she knew better. She knew the people of this town. For the most part, they were good folk, decent folk. But there was no way a brooding half-breed who'd crossed the town sheriff was going to get a fair trial.

Somehow, some way, she had to rescue Chase Wolf. That look he'd given her as he'd been led away had altered something inside her forever. It was the gaze of a man who loved her beyond reason, beyond life, beyond time. She would never again be the same Claire—Samuel Parker's daughter, Frank Sullivan's fiancée, the daydreaming little girl who hid dime novels under her bed. She felt changed, the way Oleli, Coyote, shifted shapes in Yoema's stories.

But until an opportunity for rescue arose, she'd pretend nothing was wrong. Part of that meant biting her tongue when her father suggested ways she might hide her shorn hair from the gossips. Part of it meant enduring an awkward goodnight kiss from Frank, who obviously felt it was his right, now that she'd given that—and more—to another man. And part of it meant putting up with the delay of having a maid attend to her—drawing her a bath, combing her tangled hair, and dressing her in her nightclothes.

Her father must have had the servants clean her room while she was missing. Her scissors and shorn hair were gone, and her things were unpacked and put away. That was all right. She'd do fine without baggage.

And this time she wouldn't bother leaving a note. It

wouldn't be necessary. Frank and her father would know where she'd gone.

Once in bed, she lay awake for what seemed hours, waiting for the sound of her father's pacing in the study below stairs to cease.

Finally, she heard the squeak of his footfall on the steps, and then, at the soft chiming of the mantel clock, the door of his bedroom clicked shut. After a moment, she slipped quietly from her bed to sit cross-legged on the floor, setting her oil lamp beside her. The match hissed and flared when she lit the wick, and she hoped no one saw the glow from her window as she dragged the stack of dog-eared novels from under the bed and began perusing the pages.

There had to be an answer here, somewhere among the bold escapades and wild adventures in these books. Somewhere there had to be an account of a jailbreak.

But by the time the clock below had chimed two more quarter hours, all she'd turned up was a story about a pack of Red-Skin savages who had massacred a whole town of decent folk to spring their chief out of jail. Of course, the savages were subsequently hunted down and shot by the avenging hero, one by one.

She swallowed hard and ran weary fingers through her hair. Even the authors of the dime novels had no solution for her. It wasn't surprising, not really. After all, in most of the stories, Indians were savages. They belonged behind bars. No one in their right mind would try to free them.

She slumped against the bed in defeat, rubbing her eyes, letting the most recent Beadle issue slide from her lap onto the rug. There had to be an answer. There *had* to.

Yoema had taught her long ago to believe in the will of the Creator. Everything happened for a purpose. You were like an oak leaf in the stream, she had said. If you fought against the stream, you would go nowhere, but if you let go, if you trusted the current, it would take you where you belonged. Yoema believed that was why she had been sent to be Claire's mother, that the Creator intended it.

Surely it was the will of the Creator that she and Chase Wolf live together. Why else would Yoema have talked so emphatically about the return of the Two-Sons? Why else would Chase have come to steal her away, and so soon after Yoema's death? Why else would she have fallen in love with him so completely, so deeply, that she had given him the gift of her innocence? And why else would she feel a pain akin to heartache now that he was parted from her?

They were meant to be together. She knew it. This was what Yoema meant by the mending of the broken circle. If only she could find the way...

Her gaze drifted down to the book sprawling on the floor and caught on a phrase in the midst of a spate of rustic dialogue.

"'Ef I ain't mistaken, that big b'ar left b'hind twin cubs...'" she read softly.

Twin. Chase had a twin. Yoema had said the Two-Sons would return—both of them.

His brother had come with him. He'd told her so. In fact, he must be in town right now.

Claire bit her lip. Of course! Chase had mentioned his brother was a gambler. It wasn't Chase who had taken the sheriff's gold. It was Drew. It all made sense.

If she could find his brother, she could straighten everything out. Once she found Drew and explained Chase's situation, she was sure he'd help her.

She flipped the book closed so quickly that the flame of the lamp flickered, in unison with the hopeful fluttering of her heart.

It took her little more than a minute to slip into her brown day dress and her sturdiest boots. She didn't bother with all the buttons—there wasn't time—just snagged her shawl from the wardrobe and wrapped it around her to cover the gaps.

If she hadn't been so desperate, if her mind hadn't been reeling with intrepid plots and brash scheming, she might have been more careful in her dress. After all, she was meeting a stranger, a stranger whom she had to convince of three things: that she knew his brother, that she *loved* his brother, and that getting his brother out of jail in the middle of the night so that she could run away with him was worth his getting out of bed and risking his life.

She hardly spared a glance of farewell to the room where she'd been born and raised, the room she was leaving forever. There was nothing here of value to the new Claire Parker, nothing she needed for her escape except the clothes on her back...and her favorite dime novel, which she snatched up and tucked into her bodice. But she knew that once she freed Chase Wolf, love would sustain her.

She crept down the stairs, confident that her father wouldn't hear her. After all, he'd slept through her kidnapping before.

She let herself out the window, over the same sill where she'd once scrabbled for purchase from Chase's abduction, and found herself wishing she'd never resisted.

The moon seemed to smile from the west as she stole along the drive toward the road to Paradise, and she wondered if it encouraged or mocked her, for she was about to embark on an escapade so audacious that neither Beadle nor Starr would have thought it fit to publish.

The last thing Drew Hawk expected to come through the door at midnight as he flattened himself against the papered wall of his room at the Parlor—his eyes narrowed to slits and a makeshift weapon in his grip—was a straw-haired waif who hadn't even bothered knocking.

Wondering where his trusty Colt forty-five had gone, he had to satisfy himself with brandishing a fireplace poker as she stepped into his room.

Her gasp could have awakened the dead. With his free hand, he hauled her all the way in by the scruff of her neck, then checked down the hall to make sure nobody had heard her, most especially the dark-haired beauty who had become as addicting as whiskey to him of late. Satisfied, he leaned back against the door, closing it with a quiet click, blocking out the lamplight from the hallway.

He turned the woman toward the moonlight filtering in through the curtains. She wasn't one of the regular girls.

"Who are you, and what do you want?" he murmured, unwilling to lower the poker until he got some answers.

The woman hesitated, and Drew got the idea she was thinking up a good lie.

"Don't tell me," he drawled. "You're Campbell's woman, and you've come to get back that cash I won off of him. Ma'am, I won that lot fair and square, and if Campbell has a bone to pick with me, he knows where I'm stayin'. Don't you go stickin' your pretty little nose into it, or it's likely to get busted."

Her eyes widened, and he lowered the poker, grimacing at his choice of words. Normally he was far more charming. Then again, normally he wasn't forced to make polite conversation in the dead of night. And, he thought, frowning irritably, normally he didn't spend his nights so...unsatisfied. Damn that coffee-eyed, chocolate-haired, cherry-lipped confection he'd fallen for—she'd be the death of him yet.

"Claire...Claire Parker."

Her reply startled him from his mental ramblings. "Hmm?"

"My name is Claire Parker."

Something about that name sounded familiar, but he couldn't place it.

"And I'm not Campbell's woman," she added.

"Oh."

"I'm...I'm..."

"Yeah?" Ordinarily, he could coax honey from a bee, but tonight he had no patience. "Look, ma'am, I'm in no mood for—"

"I'm Chase Wolf's woman," she blurted. "At least—"

"What?" he boomed, forgetting where they were and what time of night it was.

"That is, I was. We...he..."

"Now just hold your horses," Drew told her, groping the night table for matches. He'd get to the bottom of this, but to do it, he needed to see the woman's face, so he could tell when she was lying. He found a match, struck it, and lit the wick of the room's lamp. A split second later, he remembered he was wearing nothing but his drawers.

Her second gasp, however, had nothing to do with his lack of clothing.

"You look so..." she choked, her big green eyes moist, "...so much like him."

"Naw, Chase is the pretty one." The line was a jest between the two brothers. He'd said it so many times that he did so now out of habit.

Most people giggled at the joke. But the forlorn woman looked like she'd succumb to tears any minute. And he couldn't have that. If there was anything Drew couldn't handle, it was a woman's tears.

Against his better judgment, he set the poker beside the hearth and draped a comforting arm around the woman's shoulders. Instead of helping, it made her begin shaking with soft weeping.

"Oh, there, there, ma'am," he said, patting her back, letting her sniffle against his chest. "Don't you go workin' yourself up into a tizzy now." Her tears melted his common sense like whiskey dissolving a lemon drop. It wasn't long before he was saying things he shouldn't, making pledges he wasn't sure he could keep. "Don't you worry. We'll sort this all out."

She turned her hopeful face up toward him. She was sort of pretty, in a pale, delicate way, like a dogwood flower. "We will?"

"You bet." He had no idea what he was promising, but he'd promise a woman just about anything to get her to smile.

"Then you'll break into the jail?"

That woke him right up. "Whoa!" The explosion was less potent this time, but he knew if he kept making outbursts like that, he'd wake up the whole town. "What?" he hissed, grasping her by the shoulders.

Her face was frozen in an expression of hope mingled with fear, and, like a bolt from the blue, he finally remembered where he'd heard her name before. Samuel Parker. The rancher. He'd been looking for his little girl.

He perused her once from head to toe. Claire Parker might be little, but she was no girl. Her shawl had slipped askew, and he could see the slight curve of her bosom where she'd skipped the buttons on her dress.

Hell. He smelled trouble. For both of them.

She shouldn't be here. Not with a stranger. Not with a half-breed. And especially not with a gambler who had just won a haul of cash off of a local lawman.

"Look," he said, pressing her down until she perched on the edge of his bed. "We're gonna sit here, and you're gonna tell me everything, beginnin' to end."

It took a quarter of an hour, but she did, and try as he might to spot the holes in her story, there weren't any, aside from the careful omission of what sort of mischief she and his brother had been caught at by her father. And that was pretty obvious. As unlikely as it seemed, his brother had fallen for the woman he'd kidnapped for revenge. And gotten himself into a nasty predicament for it.

Now he knew why their father had insisted the brothers travel together. He'd thought it was so Chase could keep him out of trouble. Never had he considered it would be the other way around.

Of course, he'd have to help his brother escape. He wouldn't let Chase take a bullet for him. Besides, he wasn't about to trust the justice system of this town, not when its lawmen got so drunk they couldn't tell a pair of Kings from a pair of Jacks. He'd have to bust Chase out of jail—now, tonight—before Campbell had a chance to try him. It was risky as hell, but what choice did he have?

He retrieved his trousers from the bed and stepped into them, then yanked his shirt from the bedpost.

"Then you'll help?" the lady asked breathlessly.

"Course I'll help," he said, flashing her a reassuring smile.

He trusted it wouldn't take too long. He wanted to be back before dawn. After all, there was a beautiful woman waiting for him here, and he didn't want her filling up her dance card with anyone else.

After he was dressed, he absently reached for his gun belt and suddenly remembered where his Colt was. He'd left it in her room.

He didn't dare go for it. Even if she didn't shoot him with it when he walked into her room, he'd have to explain where he was going and what he was doing and why he was in the company of a sweet little blonde in the middle of the night.

He sighed and threw on his duster. He hoped he could manage without the Colt.

CHAPTER 20

Claire's heart raced. She felt lightheaded and elated, as if she'd drunk too much Madeira, as they wordlessly crossed the dusty road. She'd done it. She'd found Chase's brother. And he was going to help her.

It hadn't been easy finding him. She'd asked at all the hotels. It finally occurred to her to look for him at the Parlor.

It had offended her sensibilities to set foot in such an establishment. It had further offended her when the woman who ran the place gave her a thorough looking-over as if she were applying for a position there.

Once Claire explained that she had to speak to Drew Hawk about an urgent *family* matter, the woman glanced down at her belly and shook her head. Muttering something about a gambler's true colors, she led her up the stairs and pointed out Drew's room.

To be honest, Claire had been surprised he was alone. Chase had painted Drew as a philanderer, a wild firebrand as handy with the ladies as he was with a weapon. His facility with a fireplace poker she'd quickly discovered, but she wasn't sure about his charm, which was why she'd needed to turn on the tears a bit to convince him to help her.

Now that she had a notorious gunslinger by her side, all they had to do was figure out how to get inside the jailhouse.

"I'm sure there's just one guard," Claire volunteered. "You could probably get him with a single shot, right?"

He stopped in his tracks. "What?"

"I mean," she amended, "if the light's good and…and…"

He looked at her with a mixture of wonder and disgust, then walked on.

She followed, tugging on his arm to halt him again. "Chase told me you were a dead-eye."

He narrowed his eyes and drawled, "You been readin' dime novels, ma'am?"

Her cheeks flamed like a Christmas hearth. "Dime no-…wh-…bu—"

"I'm not gonna shoot anyone."

He stalked off without her, muttering something else she couldn't make out. Too mortified for words, she scurried silently after him.

"You wait here," he said when they got close to the back of the block building. He pointed to a blind of manzanitas.

She crouched beside the brush and watched him. He moved with the grace of a cat for all his size, slipping close to the edge of the wall and circling the structure. She waited for several minutes while he stole around the front of the building. Finally he crept back to where she waited.

She tried to hide her disappointment. She'd half expected him to bring Chase with him.

"There's one door, no windows," he whispered. "There's a horse tethered outside. I could hear the guard inside, playin' solitaire."

Claire frowned. She wondered how he knew it was solitaire he was playing.

251

He shrugged, guessing her question. "Rhythm of the cards."

"So you'll have to break down the door?"

He actually winced. "No."

"Then how will you..."

He rubbed his palm thoughtfully over his jaw. "We'll need a little time. And a distraction."

He grew silent for a long while after that, and she bit her lip in frustration. Finally she could stand it no more.

"But he's just on the other side of that wall," she whispered, fighting to keep the irritation from her voice. "Can't you just charge in, shoot the guard, fire a couple of times at the lock until it busts open, steal the guard's horse, and ride off into the night?"

She wished she hadn't said anything. He gave her such a look of amusement that she blushed all over again.

"And was that Dashing Dick who did that or Buckskin Bill?"

Humiliated, she verbally lashed out at him. "Chase would do it for *you*."

He grew instantly somber. "No. Even my bull-necked brother would use his brains, not his brawn." He scratched at his cheek. "What's he wearin'? Is he dressed anything like me?"

She shook her head. Chase was wearing blue jeans and a blue shirt. Drew sported a fancy white shirt and brown trousers.

"All right then," Drew said with a sigh. "Here's what we're gonna do."

After he told her his plan, Claire decided Drew was a good brother after all. He was noble, brave, and selfless. And if his crazy scheme worked, she would owe Drew much more than she could ever repay.

While Claire stood guard, Drew shuffled out of his

clothing. When he'd stripped down to his drawers, he asked her, "There. How do I look?"

She turned cautiously. "Good," she said with a nervous nod. "You look good."

One corner of his mouth curled up, reminding her painfully of Chase. "You know, most ladies say that with a little more enthusiasm." He winked at her. "You remember what you're supposed to do?"

She nodded, swallowing hard.

He gave her arm a squeeze. "Tell Chase I'm headin' south." Just before he slipped away, he winked. "And don't you go shootin' anybody, Calamity."

Claire's heart raced like a runaway train while she waited.

Everything seemed to go according to plans. She heard the jailer's horse snorting and whinnying under Drew's pestering, drawing the jailer from his game of solitaire. She held her breath as a widening swath of light indicated the jailer had opened the door to see what was up. Drew's plan was to hesitate long enough to let the man see his face.

"What in the holy hell?"

Then Drew took off like a streak. Only then did Claire realize the gunslinger was unarmed.

Muttering another curse, the jailer drew his gun and scrambled after him on foot, leaving the door wide open.

Trembling, Claire counted slowly to five. Then she ran into the jailhouse.

All night, Chase had been tossing and turning on the jail cot. He couldn't quiet the raging thoughts inside his head.

He had to protect his brother. Those charges against him were false. He knew Drew. Drew would never cheat at cards. He didn't have to.

But what if Drew couldn't be found? What if Chase had to

defend himself against the charges? He didn't have Drew's charm or his silver tongue. By morning, Chase could very well find himself with a rope around his neck.

Yet how could he die? Chase didn't feel like his journey was finished. He was meant to mend Yoema's broken circle. What sense would it make for him to pass from this world before wedding Yoema's spirit daughter, before healing the past, and without leaving children to bring honor to his ancestors?

He sat up on the cot, bowed his head over his knees, and closed his eyes, praying to Yiman-tiwinyay for a vision. But the only thing he saw were visions of Claire...her face luminous with adoration, her eyes dancing with laughter as he caught the trout, her naked tears at her grief over Yoema, the softness of her smile by the firelight, the ecstasy in her gaze when he entered her and they became one.

He pressed the heels of his hands against his eyes, trying to erase the bittersweet images, but he couldn't. It was as if the joining of their bodies had also welded their spirits together. And now, separating from her was impossible to imagine, like removing the copper from bronze.

While he sat in thought, the horse outside began to snort uneasily. He stiffened. The sound of flicking cards from the next room ceased. Chase heard the scrape of the jailer's chair across the wood floor, then footsteps toward the front door. Everything happened in a rush after that. The jailhouse door creaked open, and, with a curse, the jailer raced out of the building. Chase got to his feet, peering through the iron bars for a glimpse at what had caused the disturbance.

The last face he expected to see was the one that had haunted him for the good part of the night, the one that still kept him from sleep.

She rushed in like a sweet spring breeze, flushed and breathless, and the sight of her—as wrong as it was, as impossible as it was—melted his heart. His fingers tightened around the bars of his cell.

"Oh, Chase," she sighed. On her lips, his name sounded like a welcome wind in the pines.

For a moment, he only stared at her, doubting his eyes, doubting his sanity. How could she be here, now? How was it possible? She was so beautiful. He wanted to stay in this moment forever, to gaze into her limpid eyes, to graze her pale cheek with his breath, to drink in her womanly perfume.

"Claire, what are you doing here?"

"I've come to rescue you," she gushed. Her face shone with joy as she hurried over and closed her fingers around his.

"But how?" he asked, lapping his thumbs over hers. "If anyone sees you..."

She shook her head. "Drew has taken care of that. He—"

"Drew!"

She nodded.

"Drew is with you?"

"Yes." Her face fell a bit. "Well, no, not now. He's distracting the jailer so you can escape."

"Distracting him how?"

"He's pretending to be you, leading him on a merry chase."

"Damn! Where?"

"He said he was heading south."

Chase nodded. Drew was like Oleli, Coyote, stealing fire from the Creator. Everywhere he went, a blazing torch followed him, igniting the forest around him. Once Drew was involved, everything would become a spectacle. He wondered if it already had.

"He said something else." Claire wrinkled her brow, not understanding the message she was passing on. "He said to tell you to strip down to your drawers. And then he said he was planning to play the two-spirit game."

Chase scowled. The two-spirit game. They hadn't played

that since they were boys. It was a foolish trick, one invented by Drew. And now that Chase was grown and saw how it made a mockery of the spirit world, he didn't approve of it. On the other hand, if it helped them to escape...

"Hurry," she urged. "We've got to get you out of here."

She was right. He swiftly undressed. Whatever happened later, for now he had to get out of the cell. He was of no help whatsoever trapped in this cage. He had to find his brother before Drew got himself into serious trouble.

Meanwhile, Claire scanned the wall, searching for the key to the cell. It wasn't on the hook. She rummaged through the jailer's desk. She found all sorts of official-looking papers, a length of twine, a half-dozen cigars, handcuffs, a nearly empty flask of whiskey, a nail, even a pack of well-worn naughty playing cards. But no key.

Claire felt like screaming. She dug her nails into the wood of the desk. What would she tell Chase? That she couldn't get him out of jail after all? That his brother was out there somewhere, running for his life from a man who thought he was a fugitive?

Behind her, Chase already knew. "The jailer wears the key around his neck."

She wrung her hands. "Then what do we..." Her breath caught as she faced him. Dressed in just his drawers, he looked more like his brother than before. Only a discerning eye—or someone like Claire, who'd spent hours memorizing every muscle—would be able to tell the difference between them. "You really do look alike."

"Nope, Drew is the pretty one," he said with a smirk, reaching through the bars to pick up the padlock and turning it over in his hand.

If only they'd had a gun, she thought, they might be able to shoot it open. She was sure she'd read something about that in one of her dime novels.

"Do you have anything long and pointed, like a porcupine quill?"

Her mind retraced the objects she'd just seen. "A nail?"

"Maybe."

She yanked the desk drawer out so hard that it spilled half its contents onto the chair. She scrabbled through the wreckage, found the nail and handed it to him. He stuck the sharp end of it into the lock and started wiggling it slowly.

She cocked her head. "Where did you learn that?"

"My brother." He frowned, adding, "It's not something I'm proud of."

Claire didn't care. She'd be grateful for anything, criminal or not, that set him free. If only it didn't take so long, she thought, her heart racing as he carefully twirled and jiggled the nail.

"We can take the jailer's horse," she told him breathlessly. "It's just outside."

The only indication he heard her was the tensing of his jaw as he worked the lock.

She licked her lips. "Unless you think we'd be better off tracking him on foot."

At his continued silence, the back of her neck began to prickle with foreboding.

"Or we can take turns riding, and—"

"You're not coming with me."

For a moment she couldn't speak. What was he saying? She hadn't come just to set him free. She meant to run away with him. Perhaps he misunderstood. She forced a brittle laugh. "Of course I'm coming with you. I love you, and you love me. I'll follow you wherever—"

The lock clicked, springing open.

Panic blew through her like a rogue north wind. "Chase?"

He slipped the lock from the bars and swung the jail door wide.

"Chase!"

He shouldered past her to rummage through the jailer's possessions.

When he didn't reply, her panic turned to anger. "Chase Wolf, don't you dare think of leaving without me."

"I have to go after my brother." Once he found what he wanted, he returned. "It's too dangerous for you."

"I'm not afraid," she said, stepping close to rest her palms on his bare chest, over his heart. She gave him a shaky, seductive smile, lifting one hand to coil a lock of his hair around her finger. "Besides, we're joined now, like you said. We're like a circle, with no beginning and no end. You can't keep me from—"

Her words were swallowed up by his kiss. His mouth branded her, claimed her with a ferocity he'd never shown before. One hand tangled in the back of her hair, tipping her face up, and he bore her backward until she was pressed up against the bars of the cell. His breath came fast and desperate, his kisses bruising in their intensity, and she melted like candle wax under his fiery touch.

Then his mouth softened, his caress lightened. His fingers drifted forward, beneath her ear. His lips parted from hers, and his thumb brushed her cheek.

His eyes shone—dark and mysterious—like a well so deep she couldn't see the bottom.

"*Niwhdin*," he whispered. "I love you. Remember this. No matter what happens, I will love you forever, *whililyo*, wife of my spirit."

His words of devotion should have comforted her, but the subtle shift in his eyes chilled her to the bone. She felt something cold close about her wrist, then heard it snap shut.

She gasped. No. He couldn't have.

But the guilt of his betrayal was written on his face.

Her heart plunged to the bottom of her stomach. By the time she recovered from the shock, caught her breath, and found the courage to look down at the twin circles of the handcuffs—one around the bar of the jail cell, one around her wrist—he had already fled into the night.

CHAPTER 21

C hase chucked the nail into the bushes and headed south after his brother.

Leaving Claire had been so hard, harder than he'd anticipated. Her mouth tasted like spring, fresh and flowery and as sweet as young grass. Her skin—soft and scented from her bath—aroused his spirit, his body, his heart. And her eyes, like those of a young fawn, were so trusting.

But he knew he had to do this alone. This time the whole town would probably be hunting them, and he refused to drag Claire into another dangerous escape across the countryside.

As far as the brothers, luck was almost always on Drew's side, but evading capture and escaping with their lives was going to take more than luck. Even Drew's two-spirit game couldn't assure their safety.

And if luck turned on them, Chase figured at least he'd be comforted by the knowledge he'd kept his beloved Claire safe.

In time, she'd understand. In time, she'd forgive him for his treachery. And eventually, her heart would mend.

But for now, he must purge her from his thoughts. His brother needed his help, and Claire was a distraction he couldn't afford. So, like leaching the bitterness from acorns, he washed her beautiful image from his mind. He forced his thoughts to Drew Hawk.

He didn't take the horse. Stealing a white woman, breaking out of jail, and shackling a lady to the bars of a cell were severe enough offenses. He didn't want to add a second horse theft to his growing list of crimes. Besides, he could travel more stealthily on foot.

So, guided by his instincts and starlight, he set out due south on a quest to save his brash brother.

At first Claire was too stunned by Chase's betrayal to move. Then she was hurt and heartbroken. Then she became spitting mad.

After all the time they'd spent together, all the perils they'd faced, Chase thought she couldn't handle chasing after Drew. It was an insufferable insult.

She might not be intrepid Maude Berland, but she wasn't exactly a lily-livered shrinking violet. She'd done battle with a skunk. She'd held Frank at gunpoint. Hell, she'd even gone into a brothel to fetch his brother. He could hardly claim she was a mewling female, afraid to soil her kid gloves.

She rattled the shackle around her wrist, pulling and tugging violently at it, wondering if she could break the metal or squeeze her hand through the cuff.

But after several minutes, all she achieved was a raw, red wrist and an even more strained temper.

She didn't even have a gun to try to shoot off the lock, though she wondered if it was worth the risk. What if she missed and shot herself in the hand?

She growled in frustration. Then she sank into a pathetic

puddle of brown skirts, rasping the handcuff all the way down the iron bar of the cell.

While she was mulling over her limited options, she heard someone moving outside—rapid footsteps kicking up leaves and growing closer.

Was it Chase? Had he changed his mind and come back for her? Was it the jailer, returning from a fruitless hunt? Or was it someone else?

She quickly rose to her feet just as the intruder burst into the jail.

It wasn't Chase.

And it wasn't the jailer.

It was a woman.

She was quite beautiful. Her hair was long and coal black, part of it swept up into a messy knot atop her head. She had a beauty spot to one side of her full, rosy lips. And her dark eyes were full of fire. With a swish of scarlet skirts, she swirled with breathless haste through the doorway like a whirlwind on a mission and leveled a Colt forty-five at Claire.

"Where is he?" she demanded in a slight foreign accent. "I know he came here."

"Who?"

The woman ignored her question, instead giving Claire a pointed perusal from head to toe, sizing her up. "Are you his wife?" she bit out.

Claire frowned. "Whose wife? And will you please put down that—"

"Drew's." She gave the "r" in Drew a light flick of her tongue. Claire wondered who she was. She'd never seen her in Paradise before.

"Drew's? No!"

The woman pursed her generous lips. "His, what-you-call-it, financier?"

"Fiancée? No. Who are you?"

262

She ignored the question. "But you came to the jail with Drew, yes?"

"Yes, but—"

"What have you done with him?"

"Nothing. I haven't... Will you please put down that gun?" She showed the woman her cuffed hand. "I can't do you any harm. Who are you anyway?"

She lowered the revolver and lifted her chin, saying proudly, "I am Drew Hawk's lady."

Claire returned the woman's perusal. Her velvet gown was low-cut and tight-fitting, and the vivid scarlet hue was one no modest gentlewoman would wear. Yet she seemed to wear the dress with dignity, as if exposing a good portion of her bosom was perfectly acceptable. She must be one of the fallen women from the Parlor. Claire couldn't help but wonder just how long she'd been Drew Hawk's lady. A couple of hours?

"What's your name?" Claire asked.

"Catalina Isabella Anna Maria Borghese d'Agostino."

Claire blinked. That was a mouthful. What was that? Italian?

"Santo cielo!" Catalina abruptly exclaimed, glaring at the floor. "Those are Drew's clothings! What are you doing with them?" She took two steps forward, raised the revolver again, and narrowed her eyes like daggers. "What have you done with him, you...bad lady?"

Bad lady? That was certainly the pot calling the kettle black.

"Nothing!" she said. "And stop calling me names."

The woman's eyes flashed in threat. "If you've done anything to him..."

"Absolutely not."

"Then why do you have his clothings?"

The truth was too difficult to explain. "He...forgot them."

"You are a liar."

"Don't call me—"

She shook her head. "Drew would not forget his clothings."

"He was in a hurry."

"A hurry?"

"He was running away."

Catalina made a tiny gasp, and the revolver faltered in her grip. "Running away?" She gulped. "What means this—running away?"

Claire narrowed her gaze at Catalina, beginning to understand. The woman wasn't just a lady of the evening looking for her patron. She was in love with Drew.

"He wasn't running away from *you*," she clarified.

Catalina tried unsuccessfully to hide her relief. "Of course not," she said, lowering the forty-five. "He would be a fool to do so." She nodded to the cuff around Claire's wrist, and her brow creased as she moved forward in concern. "Who did that to you? Not Drew?"

"No."

Catalina looked her in the eye. "You cannot get free?"

Claire swallowed. It was a mistake to let an opponent know you were helpless. Any good gunslinger knew that.

But something in Catalina's eyes made Claire trust her. In fact, she suddenly realized the woman might prove to be an ally. After all, they were in similar predicaments. They both wanted to find the Two-Sons.

"No, I can't," she admitted. "But maybe you can help me. Maybe we can help each other."

Catalina hesitated. "Why should I help you? You took Drew away from me."

"I did not...that is...it was his idea to..." Claire sighed. This *was* her fault. "All right, I did talk him into coming. But I didn't think there would be trouble. I only wanted him to help Chase."

"Chase. His brother?"

"Yes. I'm Chase's woman," she said, though she wondered if that was still true. "My name is Claire." She would have offered her hand, but it was cuffed to the prison bars. "Claire Parker."

"Claire Parker." She gave Claire another swift perusal, arching a brow. "The rancher's...little girl?"

"Yes." Claire wondered how she knew that. But there was no time for chitchat. The men could be halfway down the canyon by now. "Do you think you can get me out of these?"

Catalina rushed forward without hesitation to examine the shackles, sucking in a sharp breath when she saw Claire's wrist. "You are hurt."

"It's nothing." It wasn't nothing. It stung like the dickens. But that was the least of her worries.

She had to get the cuffs off. She'd already tried squeezing out of them. Picking the lock wasn't an option. The nail was nowhere to be found. And the only thing worse than shooting off your hand was having someone else shoot it off. At any rate, the Italian lady didn't seem like she could be trusted with that revolver.

"We need something long and sharp," Catalina said.

She stared at the woman, nonplussed. Did everyone but Claire know how to pick a lock?

Before she could explain that there wasn't anything else long and sharp in the jailer's office, Catalina slipped a hairpin from her bun, which brought the black curls tumbling down over her shoulders.

While Catalina worked on the lock, Claire filled her in on the whole story—Chase kidnapping her, the trek through the canyon, falling in love, and their unfortunate discovery.

Catalina was not so forthcoming about her own history, but Claire suspected such a woman's narrative was not for the faint of heart.

It took several minutes and a lot of what Claire guessed was Italian cussing. But finally the lock clicked open, and Claire was free.

Claire gave Catalina a spontaneous hug of triumph. Then Catalina retrieved the revolver, and the two women hurried off to rescue their half-breed heroes.

Drew felt naked without his forty-five. He'd have gladly traded his drawers for his Colt. This wasn't the first time his poker skills had been called into question, and he'd found a six-shooter went a long way toward convincing sore losers that they'd been beaten fair and square.

He wondered what was taking Chase so long. He sure hoped Calamity hadn't gotten the instructions mixed up. Luckily, the jailer still hadn't spotted him hiding in the manzanitas, but the man must have sensed his quarry was near, because he wasn't in any hurry to leave the spot.

"I know you're here somewheres," the jailer called. "I don't know how you got outta my jail, but you're sure as shoot goin' back in."

The man had a revolver—a Remington, from what he could make out, which wasn't quite as accurate as a Colt. But a bullet was a bullet. From the way he was holding the thing, he hadn't fired it much, which could be good. Drew didn't know how many extra rounds the man had, but he'd only be able to get off six shots before he needed to reload.

He wondered how trigger-happy the man was.

Slowly, Drew picked up a fallen pine cone and, when the jailer had his back turned, lobbed it across the clearing.

The man whipped around at the sound and fired, blasting a couple of leaves off of a manzanita.

That answered his question.

Maybe it would be best to empty the man's weapon before Chase arrived. Besides, the gunfire would help his brother locate him.

Drew picked up a rock and hurled it in the opposite direction.

Again, the jailer whirled and got off a shot. It zinged off a tree trunk.

A few seconds later, he tossed out another rock, and the man let a bullet fly.

Drew grinned. This was going to be child's play.

Chase heard gunfire. He grimaced. Was that Drew's weapon or the jailer's?

He didn't care for guns. They were a white man's weapon. He preferred a well-made bow and arrows. But at the moment, he would have given anything for a good rifle.

He heard another shot and headed toward the sound, picking up his pace. He might be unarmed, but if the jailer had so much as parted his brother's hair with a bullet, he'd tear the man limb from limb with his bare hands.

At the third shot, he cast caution aside and went barreling through the brush.

The fourth shot whizzed past his shoulder.

By the meager moonlight, he spied the jailer in the middle of the clearing ahead. His revolver was pointed at Chase.

"Come outta there!" the man shouted.

Chase froze. He didn't think the man could see him in the shadows. But he was aiming at him, and he might get lucky with his next shot.

"Get outta there before I plug you full o' lead!"

The man took aim with his revolver, and suddenly Chase heard a familiar eerie moan floating through the trees.

The jailer whirled, trying to find the source of the sound.

Just then Drew streaked past at the far edge of the clearing, long enough for the jailer to catch a glimpse of him before firing off his next shot.

Chase shook his head. They'd never played the two-spirit game with live ammunition before. This was crazy.

But he couldn't abandon his brother. So he played his part, making an identical moan and showing his face just long enough for the jailer to see him before he tore off through the trees.

The last bullet followed close behind him as he ran.

While the man was frantically reloading, Drew moaned again and limped past at the south side of the clearing. Immediately afterward, Chase echoed him at the north side.

The jailer yelped in surprise.

Drew rustled the bushes, his head seeming to float above them, then ducked down.

Chase followed in a perfect imitation from the opposite side.

When the jailer started whimpering and fumbling with his bullets, Chase had to admit that two-spirit *was* a pretty good ruse.

This time, Drew slipped behind the jailer, close enough for the man to feel the breeze of his passing. When the man spun in surprise, turning his back, Chase ran close behind him, brushing his vest with the tips of his fingers.

The poor jailer didn't know which way to look.

Drew lurched straight toward him this time, which made the man scramble backward with a shriek.

The jailer turned to flee, only to find himself face to face with Chase.

Skidding to a halt and dropping his gun in panic, the man bolted sideways and hightailed it out of the clearing as if he were being pursued by a ghost...which was exactly the idea of the two-spirit game.

Chase couldn't help but chuckle after the jailer was safely gone. "Never fails."

Drew came out of the bushes. He had a tired smile, but then he'd been busy dodging bullets for the last several minutes. "Remember the last time we played that?"

Chase nodded. "It was for those two young Yurok girls who were visiting."

Drew sniffed. "Sure scared them."

Chase shook his head. "Scared them enough to earn us a whipping from their father."

"He should have been grateful," Drew said with a lazy wink. "One of those girls was tryin' to get me to share her blanket."

Chase laughed and wrapped a companionable arm around his brother's shoulder. Drew was dripping with sweat. He must have been running pretty hard.

"Go on now. Git." Drew pulled away and gestured roughly down the trail. "I don't think the jailer's gonna make trouble. Go grab your girl and skedaddle."

His girl. He liked the sound of that.

"What do you think of her?" he asked Drew.

"Who? Calamity?" Drew wiped his brow with the back of one shaky forearm.

Chase narrowed his eyes in concern. Drew looked awfully pale. "Are you all right?"

Drew smirked. "Sure. Right as rain." He took one staggering step. "I just..." Then his eyes rolled back in his head, and he suddenly went limp.

Chase lunged forward, catching his brother in his arms and lowering him carefully to the ground. What he saw made his heart stop.

Drew had been shot. He was bleeding from his side.

"No, no, no, no, no," he murmured in anxious denial, crouching beside Drew and examining the wound. He couldn't

269

tell how bad it was, but the bullet had struck him below the ribs, and there was a hell of a lot of blood.

"Lin-miwhxiy!" he bit out.

Why had his brother insisted on playing this foolish game? Damn Drew! He was always flirting with danger and risking his life.

And where was his forty-five? He never went anywhere without it. This was a bad omen.

Chase had to get help. As risky as it was, he had to go back to Paradise. He had to find a doctor.

But first he had to keep Drew from bleeding to death.

The sharp crack of a gunshot made Claire and Catalina freeze in their tracks, though not for long.

"Hurry!" Claire told Catalina, whose full skirts kept snagging on the manzanitas.

They increased their speed, pausing again when they heard a second shot.

"This way!" Catalina said, heading toward the noise.

Claire's heart was pumping hard now, not only from the run, but from fear. Catalina had Drew's revolver, which meant neither of the brothers had a weapon. So the shots had to be coming from the jailer's gun.

What if Chase had been shot? What if the jailer had killed him?

The third shot sounded closer and deadlier. But Claire tried to take courage in the probability that if Chase were dead, the jailer wouldn't still be firing.

That didn't stop the sharp jab of her heart against her ribs when she heard the fourth shot.

Claire caught Catalina's arm and nodded at the Colt. "Have you ever fired one of those?"

"No," Catalina admitted. "But if Drew is in danger—"

"Give it to me."

The fifth and sixth shots rang out, very loud this time, and Catalina handed her the revolver.

"That's six," Claire whispered to Catalina. "He's out of bullets. Now's our chance."

They crept forward. Claire had a fierce grip on the gun, but her hand was trembling. Unlike Catalina, she'd fired a forty-five before. She'd plugged many a tin can full of lead. But she'd never shot a man. She hoped she had the courage to do it, if it came to that.

"Wait!" Catalina said under her breath.

Something was thrashing toward them through the underbrush. Catalina grabbed Claire's arm and pulled her out of the way just in time.

The jailer still bumped her arm as he passed, squeaking in surprise.

"Spooks!" he cried as he barreled by, his eyes as wide as saucers. "There's spooks in the woods!"

And then he disappeared as fast as a runaway horse.

Claire lowered the gun and looked at Catalina. "What do you suppose that was all a—"

"Drew." Catalina had a faraway look in her eyes, as though she'd seen something Claire could not.

Then she abruptly pushed past Claire and hurtled along the path the jailer had come.

Claire tried to keep up, but Catalina was so intent on where she was going—whipping aside branches and ducking under trees—that when she stopped all at once, Claire collided with her.

Catalina spit out a long string of Italian words. Claire didn't know what they meant, but there was no mistaking the woman's rage.

"You!" Catalina bellowed.

Claire peered around Catalina. To her immense relief, not

a dozen feet away was Chase, alive and, by all appearances, unharmed. But he was hunkering down beside his brother, looking up at Catalina in surprise.

"What did you do?" Catalina cried, rushing forward at Chase. "What did you do to my Drew?"

Before Chase could answer or even blink, the woman plowed her fist into his nose. He fell off of his haunches and went sprawling in the leaves.

Claire gasped and leveled the forty-five at Catalina. "Get away from him!"

But Catalina only had eyes for Drew. He was lying on the ground, silent, and a thin trail of blood was streaming from his chest.

Claire lowered the gun in quaking hands.

Chase was already recovering from the punch. He gave his head a shake and levered up onto his elbows.

"Chase didn't do this," Claire told Catalina, as sure of that as she was sure of her own name. "Chase wouldn't hurt him."

"Oh, Drew," Catalina wailed, sinking down to take Drew's hand, holding it to her breast. "Do not leave me, *mio caro*. Do not leave me. You promised, Drew."

Drew stirred slightly, and he murmured, "Cat?"

"You promised. Remember? You promised to buy me tonight."

Claire blushed, certain she shouldn't be hearing such things.

"Sure," Drew croaked, trying to get up.

Chase rushed to his side. "Don't try to move," he told Drew, grimacing as fresh blood seeped from the wound. Then he gave Catalina a quick perusal. "Your petticoats, quick." He wiggled his fingers in demand. "Give me your petticoats."

"What!" Catalina's eyes widened as she looked ready to give him a second punch.

"To stop the bleeding," he explained.

She hesitated only an instant before she stood and began pulling out yards and yards of petticoats from beneath her scarlet dress.

Chase immediately began to apply them to Drew's wound, and Claire came to help.

Together, they managed to stanch the flow of blood and bind his wound. Then Chase hefted his brother up in his arms, and they began the tense hike back to Paradise.

CHAPTER 22

Samuel slugged back the last swallow of his morning coffee and chewed up the grounds.

He didn't trust the sheriff. The man liked to shoot off his mouth more than he liked to shoot his gun. So Samuel figured he'd best get into town early to nip the gossip in the bud and make sure people didn't start asking questions about the man the sheriff had arrested.

He also felt he owed it to Claire to make sure Yoema's grandson wasn't unjustly accused. While Samuel might want to see the half-breed behind bars for taking off with his daughter, he was pretty sure he wasn't a cheat at cards. Samuel had seen enough of the young man to know that if Chase Wolf was going to shoot you, it wouldn't be in the back. Campbell drank a bit, so maybe he'd mixed him up with someone else.

Claire hadn't come downstairs yet, but Samuel had given the maids instructions not to disturb her. She'd been through an ordeal, and she probably needed the extra rest. Besides, he was sure once she found out where he was headed, she'd insist on tagging along, and the town jail was no place for a lady.

So he rode into Paradise quietly just as the sun started peeking over his shoulder.

It looked like the sheriff had beat him to the jail. There were two horses secured outside—Campbell's and the jailer's. Samuel dismounted, tied up his own horse, and pushed open the jail door.

"And you're *sure* you weren't drinkin' last night?" the sheriff was asking the jailer.

"Not a drop," the jailer said.

"Maybe he bought you off then," the sheriff suggested, "offered you half the winnin's if you let him out?"

"What? No!"

Samuel glanced toward the jail cell. The door stood open. Except for a pile of clothing, it was empty. He ground his teeth. Had the jailer taken Chase out and had "an accident" after all?

"Where is he?" Samuel barked.

"That's what I'm tryin' to find out," the sheriff said.

"I'm tellin' you, Sheriff," the jailer whined, "he turned into a ghost and floated off into the woods."

That was the worst fabrication Samuel had ever heard. "What?"

"There's no such thing as ghosts," the sheriff said.

"That's what *I* thought," the jailer said. "But I saw it with my own eyes. He was movin' as fast as lightnin'—whoosh, whoosh—in front of me, behind me, right past me. And moanin'?" He imitated the sound—a high-pitched, warbling sound like a loon. "I emptied my Remington into him, but he kept circlin' and circlin'."

"Dammit!" The sheriff smacked the desk with the flat of his palm. "I don't know what you did or what you thought you saw, but I'm holdin' you personally responsible for gettin' my winnin's—and my woman—back."

The jailer sank onto his chair and rested his head in his hands. "Aww, consarn it, Sheriff. How am I supposed to catch a ghost?"

He knew the jailer hadn't seen a ghost, but Samuel could tell he *believed* he'd seen a ghost. Maybe the half-breed had slipped some jimsonweed or something into the jailer's coffee and gotten him to unlock the cell. The rest might have been a figment of the jailer's drug-addled imagination.

The question was where had Chase Wolf gone if he *had* escaped? Samuel half hoped he'd headed for the hills and was gone for good. But if the man cared for Claire like Samuel was afraid he did, odds were he was sticking around. And if he was still in Paradise, Samuel had to contain the situation before it got out of hand and ruined Claire's reputation.

He stroked his mustache. Where could the half-breed be? He couldn't have many friends in Paradise. But the one he trusted, the one who'd covered for him before, was the proprietress of the Parlor. As much as it grated on Samuel's sensibilities to set foot in such an establishment again, it was worth a try.

"The half-breed?" The madam seemed amused by Samuel's discomfort. "You sure you don't want to avail yourself of one of my girls? They seem a mite more your style." He frowned, and she motioned up the stairs. "Sure. Same room as before." Then she eyed his rifle. "But I don't want any trouble, you understand?"

"Yes, ma'am," Samuel said, adding in a murmur, "not if I can help it." He thanked the woman and proceeded upstairs.

He didn't bother knocking. If Chase *had* drugged the jailer and broken out of jail, he didn't exactly deserve fair warning. Instead, Samuel cocked his rifle and shoved open the door, closing it behind him with his elbow.

There was a flurry of scarlet skirts, a tumble of black curls, and the flash of dark eyes as a woman leaped from the bed to confront him.

"Who are you?" she demanded, her hands on her hips, oblivious to the rifle pointed at her. "And what do you want?"

He'd gotten the wrong room. The woman was clearly a lady of the evening. She was bold and beautiful. She had an exotic accent. And her vivid dress was cut sinfully low.

"Pardon me, ma'am," he said sheepishly, lowering the rifle. "I'm looking for—"

"Who is it, Cat?" he heard from the bed.

Samuel frowned and looked past the woman.

Chase Wolf was lying in the bed with his eyes closed. He looked horrible—pale and sweaty. His shirt was missing, and a bandage was wrapped around his ribs.

For one instant, Samuel felt concern. Had the jailer lied? Had he given the half-breed a beating after all?

And then he remembered the prostitute.

He was suddenly very glad he hadn't brought Claire. It would have broken her heart to know how quickly Chase had replaced her—and with what quality of woman.

"Well, I see you're showing your true colors, Mr. Wolf," Samuel grumbled. "I can't say I'm surprised. But I *am* disappointed. You could have at least waited till you left town to take up with..." He couldn't say the words. Instead, he gave the woman a disparaging glare...

Which she returned in equal measure, biting out, "How dare you! Can you not see he's hurt?"

"Cat," the half-breed called weakly from the bed, "who are you talkin' to?"

With a woeful little cry, she picked up her skirts and rushed to his side. "Don't worry, *caro mio*. I will make him go away."

Just how she was going to do that, Samuel never learned,

because at that moment he heard a familiar voice in the hallway, and the door swung open behind him.

"Here you go," Claire announced, balancing the big breakfast tray in one hand as she nudged the door open. "Eggs, bacon, beans, and cof-..." She stopped in her tracks when she saw him. "Father!"

"Claire?"

Claire's thoughts churned madly as her father's face turned first white, then gray, then red.

"How nice to see you," she improvised, handing the tray off to Catalina.

"What is the meaning of this?" he bit out, his face almost purple.

She could feel her cheeks growing hot as she gently closed the door, stalling for time. "I woke early this morning, and I didn't want to disturb you, so I..."

"You came to town, to this..." he began in a loud voice, then suppressed it in a low growl, "this...den of iniquity?"

"Here?" She clasped her hands. "Well... I..." Then she straightened. "Wait. What are *you* doing here, Father?"

Catalina chimed in with a smug smile and an arched brow. "Yes, what are *you* doing here?"

To Claire's chagrin, he didn't even bat an eye, but said pointedly, "Looking for an escaped prisoner."

His gaze slid to the man lying in the bed, and Claire realized her father thought that Drew was Chase. Of course, she realized. He didn't know Chase had a twin.

Suddenly, every dime novel plot she'd ever read raced through her brain, and she began inventing a story to rival the best that Beadle had to offer.

With a conspiratorial glance at Catalina, she rushed to Drew's side and took his hand. "I'm sorry, Father. The truth is I helped him escape."

Her father was frowning.

"You see, I know he's innocent. I'm sure of it," she said. "How could he have taken that money? He was with me." She ran her fingers through Drew's hair, ignoring Catalina's narrowed eyes. "I couldn't bear to think of him locked in that jail cell for one more minute." She leaned over to kiss his brow, and Catalina made an odd strangled sound that turned into a cough.

"You expect me to believe *you* broke him out of jail?" her father asked.

Claire gulped. "I had some...help." She glanced at Catalina, whose lips were compressed into a thin line.

Her father sighed, shook his head, and muttered an oath that made Claire's eyes widen.

"Nobody saw us," she assured him, certain that was his primary concern.

"The jailer claims he saw a ghost," he said.

"A ghost?" Claire gave a nervous chuckle.

Her father shook his head again. "So what did you do?" He was looking at Catalina. "Slip jimsonweed into his coffee?"

"Yes!" Claire said. "That's exactly what we did." That *would* have been a good idea. Claire wondered if her father had experience with jailbreaks.

He nodded toward Drew. "So what's wrong with him?"

"He was shot in the escape."

"Is he going to live?"

Catalina's brow crumpled. "Of course he's going to live. How can you say such a thing?" To Claire's consternation, Catalina rushed to the opposite side of the bed and lovingly took Drew's hand. "*Va tutto bene.*"

Her father's frown deepened with disapproval.

"Father, this is Chase's...sister...from Hupa." Claire hoped her father couldn't tell what language Catalina was speaking.

He pursed his lips. "His sister? Is that what she told you?" He raked Catalina's scanty attire with scornful eyes.

"I think you need to come home with me right now, Claire."

Claire had to think of a plan—quickly. At the moment, Chase was sleeping off a very long night down the hall in Catalina's room. But if she didn't get her father out of the Parlor soon, Chase might show up and ruin her story. Fortunately, she had a bargaining chip. She knew her father would like nothing better than to sweep the whole affair under the rug.

"I'll make you a bargain, Father."

"A bargain? I hardly think you're in a position to—"

"I'll come with you willingly, and I won't make a fuss, if you promise not to tell the sheriff he's here."

Her father pretended to stew about it, but Claire wasn't fooled. She was sure he never intended to say a word to anyone about Chase's whereabouts. He'd just as soon forget Chase Wolf existed. The less people knew, the better.

Still, he groused. "You really think you can trust folks at the Parlor to keep quiet about it?" He cast a sideways glance at Catalina.

Claire shrugged. "I would imagine they're pretty good at keeping secrets."

He blew out another annoyed breath and then addressed Catalina. "Is there a back way out of here?"

She nodded.

Claire reluctantly crooked her hand around her father's elbow, giving Catalina one last important message. "Please take care of...Chase...for me."

Catalina nodded again, sending Claire a silent assurance with her eyes. And then Claire left the Parlor with her father by the back door, waiting out of sight until he brought the horse around.

What he talked about on the way home was insignificant—something about cattle he was looking to buy, a shed that needed repairs, the upcoming spring dance. All

Claire could think about was how soon she could get back to Chase.

When Chase awoke in Catalina's room with Claire nowhere in sight, he wrapped the sheet around him and burst out of the door, eliciting a chorus of appreciative chuckles from the ladies loitering in the hallway.

Ignoring them, he brushed past to Drew's room and knocked softly on the door.

The woman answered. She was even more striking in the daylight with her dark hair and ruby lips, but she looked haggard, as if she hadn't slept a wink. Her dress drooped off of one shoulder, her eyes were rimmed with red, and her hair hung down her back like a tangle of black ribbons.

"How is he?" Chase asked.

She let him in, looking up at him with hopeful eyes. "He will get better, no?"

Chase approached the bed. Drew looked pale. His eyes were sunken and gray. The doctor had been able to retrieve the bullet last night, and it hadn't done too much internal damage. But the laudanum he'd given Drew for the pain was keeping him foggy. Chase wished his grandmother were alive to use her native medicine.

"He *will* get better?" the woman asked again, her brows furrowed.

"Yep. Sure," he said, hoping he was right. "Has the doc been by yet?"

She shook her head.

He pulled the covers up over Drew's chest. "Where's Claire?"

"She left."

His breath caught. "Left. What do you mean?"

"Her father came. He was looking for you. She made him believe that Drew was you."

281

"And?"

"She promised to go home with him if he would not tell the sheriff you were here."

Chase didn't like the idea of her going back to the ranch. But he had to admit it was a clever ploy. It would buy them some time. With any luck, Drew would be up and around in a few days, and they could slip out of Paradise unnoticed. No one would ever know there were two half-breeds in town. No one would know they were twins. Until then, they'd have to lie low.

The hardest part for him would be missing Claire. Until he'd been shut off from her in that jail cell, he hadn't realized how much he'd grown used to her company. Now, being without her was like being without part of his heart.

He looked at his brother, lying wounded in a whore's bed, and wondered if Drew would ever know what it was like to be truly in love, to care for a woman so deeply that you didn't think you could survive without her.

He glanced up at the lady on the other side of the bed. She was worrying her lip with her teeth. She didn't seem like one of those saloon girls who pretended to be sweet on a fellow for a few extra dollars. She seemed genuinely concerned for Drew.

He felt sorry for her. She didn't know it, but his brother had a habit of leaving ladies in the dust. It wasn't that Drew was cruel. He was just restless. Chase doubted he'd ever settle down with one woman.

The lady dipped her lacy handkerchief in the basin of water on the nightstand and used it to wipe Drew's forehead. Drew was damned lucky to have a woman care for him like that. It was too bad he didn't know it. But at least while he was unconscious he couldn't break her heart.

On the other hand, it would be a shame if the woman missed out on several days' wages for no good reason. So as much as he hated awkward conversations with strange women, he thought he should break the news to her as best he could.

"Listen, ma'am. I don't know what my brother told you, but he's not the marrying kind of man. I'm sure he paid you well for your services and probably enjoyed them too. But if you're looking for him to put a ring on your finger, I don't think that's going to happen. I'm sorry to have to break it to you this way, but..."

He trailed off as her laughter filled the room.

"Is that what you think?" she said. She waggled her fingers at him, one of which sported a gold band. "I already have his ring on my finger." She clucked her tongue. "For a twin, you do not know your brother very well."

Chase didn't appreciate her amusement at his expense. He also didn't believe that ring had come from his brother. "And you *do?* You've known him all of, what, three days?"

She shrugged. "I can tell which brother is which," she pointed out.

That was true. She'd known instantly that it was Drew who'd gotten shot last night, which was remarkable. Some of their own tribe couldn't tell the twins apart.

Still, that didn't mean Drew could tell *her* from all the other whores he'd bedded.

"Look, ma'am, I just don't want you to waste your time on my brother when you've got paying customers waiting."

"It is not a waste of time. I have no customers. I belong to Drew."

Chase scoffed. He wondered if Drew knew that. Something must have gotten lost in translation. She wasn't even Drew's type.

"What I'm trying to say, ma'am, is that my brother is a love-them-and-leave them kind of man."

She wrinkled her brow in confusion.

"A rolling stone?" he tried.

She looked even more baffled.

"A tumbleweed? One that doesn't put down roots?"

She shook her head, not comprehending.

He sighed. "My brother is the kind of man who will give a woman a kiss and then vanish into the night."

"Oh," she said, understanding at last. "That he does. But he always comes back in the morning."

Chase's shoulders drooped. The woman was hopeless. He supposed she'd have to hear it from his brother's lips then. It would probably break her heart. He just hoped, for Drew's sake, she wouldn't have a six-shooter in her hand when he told her.

CHAPTER 23

Claire had managed to avoid her former fiancé for the last three days. But this morning, her father had announced he'd be spending the night at a neighbor's ranch, leaving her in Frank's care. She nearly groaned aloud at his transparent attempt to rekindle the romance between her and Frank.

He doubtless imagined Claire would forget all about Chase Wolf once Frank came a-courting. He probably expected that the whole episode with her running away, her kidnapping, the jailbreak, and the incident at the Parlor would fade into oblivion, like an insignificant bump in the road.

He couldn't have been more wrong.

She'd decided before she'd ever met Chase that she couldn't marry Frank. It wasn't fair to either of them. She didn't love Frank. She'd only gone along with the engagement because it had pleased her father. And at that time, she would have done anything for his approval.

But things had changed. She deserved better. Frank

GLYNNIS CAMPBELL

deserved better. And she didn't really care if her father approved or not.

Furthermore, no amount of persuasion by Frank in the way of flowers and bonbons and the picnic he'd put together this afternoon was going to change her mind or her heart.

She was bound to Chase Wolf now—body, mind, and spirit. They belonged together. Whether it was destiny, God's will, or the will of Chase's Creator, there was a bond between them that was unbreakable.

Somehow her father had forgotten about that kind of bond. He'd known it once with her mother. It was a bond that survived hardship and pain and loss. It was a bond that stretched beyond the grave.

"Chicken, Claire?"

Claire looked up blankly at Frank. He was sitting across from her on the gingham square, in the dappled shade of an oak tree, holding up a golden fried drumstick in a napkin.

She had no appetite, but she didn't want to get into another discussion with Frank about how she could use a little more meat on her bones. So she took the drumstick.

He dug through the contents of the wicker basket the cook had put together.

"Biscuits, sweet butter, coleslaw, pickles, peach cobbler," he recited. "Here's a flask of apple jack for me," he said with a wink, "and lemonade for you."

She nibbled on the end of the drumstick and watched Frank as he began laying out the feast. He wasn't a bad catch. He had curly gold hair that shone in the sunlight, bright blue eyes, and a ready smile. He was trim and fit, dressed well, minded his manners for the most part, and knew how to do the two-step.

He would make someone a suitable husband.

Just not Claire.

She gazed at the bouquet of daisies he'd bought her, tied

286

up with a yellow ribbon by a shopkeeper, and couldn't help but think about the rabbit fur slippers Chase had made for her.

She glanced at the box of candy Frank had bought for her at the general store and remembered the honey Chase had harvested from the hive with his bare hands.

She couldn't blame Frank. He was doing the best he could. And Claire was sure that any other woman would be grateful for his efforts.

But he wasn't Chase Wolf. He didn't arouse her senses. He didn't quicken her heart. He didn't stir her soul.

"You know, Claire, I've been thinkin'," Frank said as he slathered butter on a biscuit. "It doesn't seem to me there's any reason to put off our nuptials any longer. It's spring, after all, a perfect time for—"

"Our nup—"

"Ah-ah-ah," he interrupted, shoving the buttered biscuit in her mouth. "Don't you worry about a thing. I've got everything handled. Your father's given his approval. We can do it this Sunday after church." He leaned forward to confide, "I've even taken the liberty of havin' a weddin' dress made over for you, and—"

"Wait!" Claire said, finally managing to swallow the bite of biscuit before she choked on it.

"No reason to wait," Frank countered. "On the contrary. The sooner we wed, the sooner we can get all this foolishness behind us."

"Foolishn—"

"Your father's practically given me the ranch," he said cheerfully, though she now detected a note of desperation in his voice. "So we'll have plenty to live on."

"But—"

He pressed a cup of lemonade to her lips to silence her. "And we can get a family started right away."

She pushed the cup aside. "But I don't want a fa—"

"Well, maybe you should have thought of that before you slept with that Injun, Claire," he snarled, splashing lemonade on his shirt.

Claire flinched, taken aback by his vicious remark.

"Come on, now, be reasonable," he said more evenly. She wondered if he was talking to himself or to her.

"Frank..."

"You know it's the right thing to do, Claire," he said, dabbing at his stained shirt with a napkin.

"Frank..."

"It's what your father would want."

"Frank..."

"It's meant to be, Claire," he said, flinging the napkin down like a challenge.

"I don't love you, Frank, and I never will." There. She'd said it. He'd forced her hand, and she'd had to tell him straight out.

"Dammit, Claire, that doesn't matter!" he blurted. "You're mine! You belong to me!"

Fear streaked up Claire's spine like lightning. She suddenly realized she was alone with Frank on a remote hilltop. If she called for help, no one would hear her.

He must have seen the worry in her eyes, because he tempered his tone. "I'm sorry, Claire. I just can't think straight when I...I care about you so much."

He reached out and took her hand. She fought the urge to snatch it back in disgust.

He spoke softly. "There's no reason to play innocent with me. I know what you did with that Injun."

Claire swallowed as his fingers closed tighter around her hand.

"But I'm still willin' to take you as my wife," he said, giving her a sheepish smile. "And there's not many men who'd say that."

She tried to extricate her hand gracefully, but he held it fast. *"You* may be willing, but *I'm* n—"

He lunged at her, planting his lips on hers before she could finish, grinding his mouth against hers and poking his tongue forcefully between her teeth. She tried to squirm away, but he held her still, grabbing the back of her head.

Shocked and appalled, she pushed and pummeled at his shoulder with her free hand, but he stuck to her like a fly on molasses.

Finally, she resorted to biting his lip, wincing at she tasted his blood.

He instantly released her, swearing and pressing his fingers to his bleeding mouth. But even that didn't deter him.

"The savage taught you to play rough, eh?" he said, licking at his injured lip. "Well, all right. We can play r—"

Before he could grab her again, Claire hauled back and punched him in the nose as hard as she could, knocking him flat. Then, cradling her bruised knuckles and without a backward glance, she scrambled to her feet and tore across the hillside, back toward the ranch.

"You'll see!" he yelled after her. "Nobody else will take you, Claire! Nobody wants damaged goods!"

That was fine with Claire. She didn't want "nobody." She wanted Chase Wolf.

Frank blinked back tears of pain as he nursed his stinging nose and watched Claire go.

She'd be back. Sooner or later, she'd come crawling back to him on her hands and knees, begging him to marry her. What he'd said was true. No man wanted to plant his seed where another man had plowed.

On the other hand, he didn't have the luxury of time. He couldn't wait for Claire to decide that he was right, that she had no other prospects. That Injun might have put a papoose in her already. Mr. Parker was a stickler for respectability, so Frank had to act quickly.

He'd tried it the easy way. He'd tried to win Claire's heart—bringing her flowers, buying her candy, taking her on a spring picnic.

That hadn't worked. She was still mooning over that confounded Wolf character. And, curse it all, instead of dangling at the end of a hangman's noose like he was supposed to, the Injun had managed to escape jail and was still at large somewhere.

It was troubling.

Frank wanted that ranch. He'd worked hard for it, spending months shadowing Samuel Parker—riding from sunup to sundown, working with the stock, learning the ropes, studying the business. And he'd invested a lot of hours courting Claire—escorting her to the town dances, buying her gewgaws, taking her to the fair. He wasn't about to give up everything just because some half-breed savage got Claire's knickers in a twist.

So if she couldn't be reasonable, if he couldn't win her over with candy and flowers, Frank guessed he'd have to go about things the hard way.

Chase had had just about enough of the two lovebirds at the Parlor. He'd never seen his brother let a woman make such a helpless fool of him. After three days, he was sure Drew was perfectly capable of feeding himself. Yet there he sat, letting that woman spoon feed him like he was a baby. It was sickening.

"Chase," Drew called from the bed.

"What?" he grunted.

Drew laughed. "See that, darlin'? My brother is sufferin' from what we call the green monster."

"Green monster?" Catalina asked.

"Envy," he told her.

Chase gave him a withering glare.

Drew explained to her. "I've got my woman by my side, lookin' out for me...feedin' me...kissin' me." He stopped to indulge in the last vice, at which point Chase rolled his eyes. "But poor Chase, he doesn't have his woman with him. He's lonesome."

"Quit it, Drew," Chase growled.

"And irksome."

"Drew."

"And irritable."

"Enough."

Catalina clucked her tongue in mock pity. "Maybe I should ask Anne or Emily to keep him company tonight."

Chase gave her a scathing glare. "No, thank you."

Her mouth twitched with laughter.

Drew chuckled once, then sobered and said, "Go see her."

Chase had been thinking about it all day. The trouble with the sheriff had been ironed out. Drew might not be turning cartwheels, but he was on the mend. Two rooms at the Parlor were costing a fortune. And frankly, Chase was getting pretty annoyed by his brother's overt displays of affection for Catalina.

Still, he wasn't sure what to expect. Three days ago, he would have jumped at the chance to see Claire. But now three days felt like a lifetime. She might have changed her mind. She might have realized how comfortable that big house was after all and decided she couldn't give it up. She might have figured that their little adventure together had been just a lark. She might have reconsidered marrying Frank, who was clearly her father's choice. Chase didn't know what she was thinking. And not knowing was easier than finding out something bad.

"Yes!" Catalina chimed in with far too much enthusiasm.

"You must go to her. Wait until night, go through the window, and steal her again." She turned to Drew. "It is so romantic, this story."

Drew grinned and caught her by the chin. "Almost as romantic as ours."

They giggled and kissed, and Chase growled in disgust. He couldn't take much more. Holed up in this bawdy house, he was getting cabin fever.

He had to get out, one way or another. Tonight. And then he had to decide whether he had the guts to face Claire.

After her altercation with Frank, Claire fled all the way back to the ranch, marched straight up to her room, and locked the door. Her knuckles still throbbed from the wallop she'd given him. But she didn't regret that punch, because he'd deserved it.

He'd been a cad. He'd tried to pressure her into a hasty marriage, planning it behind her back. He'd even gone so far as to pick out her wedding dress. How could he imagine she was so desperate that she'd wed him without caring a fig for him?

She flounced down on her bed and pressed the heels of her hands to her eyes. She wished she'd never agreed to come back to the ranch. She should have realized her father would see it as an opportunity to force Frank on her.

She wondered what her father would say if he knew just how pushy Frank had become. What if she hadn't clouted the oaf? Would he have pressed his advantage? Would he have had his way with her?

She feared that Frank believed what he said, that Claire belonged to him. He figured that since she'd allowed Chase certain liberties, she should do the same for him. He also believed that now her reputation was sullied, nobody else would want her.

But Claire didn't care what anyone else thought, as long as *Chase* wanted her.

She uncovered her eyes and stared up at the ceiling.

She *hoped* Chase still wanted her. It had been three days. His brother must have recovered from his wound by now. But she'd heard no news. And a niggling fear at the back of her brain told her that maybe Chase had changed his mind about her.

What if he'd decided she was too much baggage? What if he'd fallen out of love with her? What if he'd already left town?

She rested her fingers lightly on her stomach, which was churning with worry. Then she moved her hand lower.

Frank did have one point. She might already be carrying Chase's baby. If that was so, her father would make her give up the infant if she didn't marry. He'd never let her raise a child out of wedlock.

But she wouldn't marry Frank, no matter how desperate she was. She'd run away first.

If only she knew what Chase was thinking... If she could see his face, speak to him, feel his reassuring arms around her...

It was late afternoon when the maid brought her a tray. On it was a glass of apple cider, a square of fresh-baked gingerbread, and an envelope addressed simply FOR CLAIRE.

"Where did this letter come from?"

The maid shrugged. "It was left on the doorstep, Miss."

Claire turned the envelope over in her hands. She half expected a letter of apology from Frank. But it wasn't in Frank's precise handwriting. It was in plain block letters.

Could it be a message from Chase?

Her pulse quickened. Was it good news or bad?

She hesitated, afraid of what she might find inside.

Then, taking a deep breath, she tore open the envelope.

My sweet Claire – I cannot bear to be away from you one more day. If you still care for me, meet me in the barn tonight after dark. I will wait for you there. With all my heart, I hope you will come.

The words brought a teary smile to her face. Chase hadn't forgotten her after all. He still loved her. And he was coming for her. She *was* going to get her happy ending.

"I'll dine in my room," she told the maid. She didn't want to have to confront Frank at supper tonight...or ever again.

It seemed like an eternity before the sun began to dip behind the hills. Claire was too nervous to eat the Hangtown fry and gooseberry pie the maid brought for supper. She changed into three different bonnets before she decided to forgo a bonnet altogether. Inside her bodice, she tucked the only thing she wanted to take with her—her copy of *THE TRAIL HUNTERS OR MONOWANO THE SHAWNEE SPY*. At sunset, she started pacing, as antsy as Jesse James planning to rob the noon train.

Finally night fell. The ranch was quiet. Claire waited till the help went to bed and then padded across the parlor and stole out of the house. Across the yard, she could see the barn door was slightly ajar.

She crept along the paddock fence, then eased the door open a few inches more, and slipped into the cool, shadowy barn.

"Chase?" she whispered, squinting into the dark.

One of the horses whickered softly and stamped a hoof.

"Chase, are you there?"

All she heard was the rustle of straw and the quiet jangle of harnesses.

Maybe she was early.

She moved farther into the barn, enjoying the peace and the sweet smell of hay. Feeling her way, she found the ladder leading up to the hayloft. A sly smile touched her lips. She wondered what it would be like to make love up there.

Then she heard the door close. She turned. "Chase?"

A match flared to life, blinding her for an instant before a kerosene lantern cast a pool of light on the straw-covered floor. Then her breath caught.

"Goodness, Claire!" Frank said with sarcastic surprise. "Were you expectin' someone else?"

CHAPTER 24

Claire gulped. How could she have been so stupid? That damned letter hadn't been signed. Frank must have written it after all. And she'd walked right into his trap.

Frank shook his head, half amused, half disappointed. "And here I was hopin' you'd changed your mind."

Claire bit her lip. Frank was wearing his Sunday best, and he'd come in with a shotgun and a preacher.

"What are you doing, Frank?"

"Ever heard of a shotgun wedding, Claire?"

Claire blinked. He couldn't be serious. Shotgun weddings were for men who got women pregnant, to persuade them to take responsibility for their offspring. In fact, Chase had told her all about the shotgun wedding the miners had arranged between his own parents.

Frank patted the stock of his shotgun. "Now I'm hopin' you're not gonna make me use this. But I will if I have to."

She glanced in disbelief at the preacher, who was busy thumbing through his Bible.

"Oh, he's a real preacher," Frank assured her, "but he's just passin' through, so he's not gonna concern himself too much about the letter of the law. As long as you're of age and not my sister, he doesn't much care, ain't that right?"

The preacher nodded.

Claire's mind was whirling. She was not going to marry Frank, come hell, high water, or the barrel of a shotgun. But until she could come up with a novel-worthy plan of escape, she'd have to try to reason with him.

"Frank, you know my father will never stand for this. When he finds out what you've—"

"Now, Claire, we both know he isn't gonna give you his blessing to marry an Injun."

Her mouth opened, but no words came out, because she knew he was right.

"And he sure as hell isn't gonna let you whelp a half-breed's bastard."

He was right about that, too. She closed her mouth and clenched her jaw.

"In fact," he said, "I'm pretty sure he's gonna be glad I solved this problem…quietly."

She couldn't argue with that either. Her father would be grateful to have the whole business forgotten. Rage and frustration made her tremble.

"Now I know this isn't the fairy tale wedding you had planned," he said, "but, darn it, Claire, you're the one who got yourself into this mess."

She ground her teeth. She was damned well going to find a way out of it.

He gave her an irritating smile of pity. "Trust me. It'll all be for the best. Think of it this way, Claire. Gettin' married is like geldin' cattle. Sure, it smarts a bit, but the quicker you do it, the quicker it'll be over." He handed the lantern to the preacher and held out a hand toward Claire. "Shall we?"

Gelding cattle? Was that what he thought of marriage? Claire thought she'd like to geld *Frank* right about now. But she was completely defenseless. She didn't have a gun. She couldn't reach a pitchfork. She didn't dare so much as throw a punch while Frank had that shotgun tucked under his arm.

Then she realized there might be a weapon she could use.

She returned his invitation with a cold stare...at first. Then, feigning resignation, she sighed, picked up her skirts, and trudged toward him, hanging her head.

"There, that ain't so bad, is it?" he said when she was standing beside him, overlooking the fact that she'd refused to take his arm. Then he frowned down at her bodice and, with a smirk of disapproval, withdrew her dime novel and tossed it onto the barn floor.

She gave a tiny gasp, but resisted the urge to smack him for his trespass. Instead, she meekly lowered her eyes to the kerosene lantern that dangled from the preacher's fingers.

"Go ahead," Frank told the preacher. "We're ready."

As Frank straightened his collar and the preacher fumbled open his Bible with his free hand, Claire took advantage of their moment of inattention. Lifting her skirt, she kicked out suddenly and forcefully with her boot, punting the lantern right out of the preacher's grip.

The lamp sailed through the air, hit the wall, and shattered. Fire exploded through the broken glass. Kerosene splashed and spilled everywhere. Hungry flames erupted instantly to lap up the fuel as it spread over the dry straw scattered on the barn floor.

Frank grabbed her roughly by the arm. "Are you crazy?"

He tried stomping out the flames, but for every spark he subdued, two more took its place. Faster than Claire thought possible, the fire grew out of control, licking at the walls of the barn and gobbling up the pile of fodder beside the horse stalls.

The preacher wasted no time. He turned tail and ran out of the barn as if the fires of hell were coming for him.

Claire would have followed him, but Frank had a death grip on her, and he still had the shotgun in his other hand.

The horses smelled the smoke and started to panic. Their eyes rolled, and they began to squeal, tossing their heads and jerking at their harnesses.

"Shit!" Frank finally let go of her and prodded her forward with the barrel of the shotgun. "Help me untether the horses. We've got to get them out of here."

There were eight horses. By the time they freed the last one, Claire's eyes and throat were burning from the acrid smoke, and her face was beaded with sweat from the heat of the fire. Coughing, she staggered toward the door where the last horse had just made its escape.

But Frank stood there with the shotgun, blocking her exit. His face was lit up from beneath by the madly flickering flames. Still, that wasn't what made him look like the devil. It was the queer, speculative expression in his eyes that, despite the intense heat, chilled her to the bone.

"You know, you've been nothin' but trouble, Claire, for me *and* your father. I was tryin' to make things easy—nice and neat. Keep the old man happy, marry his daughter, take over the ranch when he kicked the bucket. But you..."

Claire coughed and cast an uneasy glance around the barn, which was fast filling with smoke. Surely Frank could scold her outside. "Frank, we've got to get out of here."

"Do we?"

She gulped. What the hell did that mean? "Yes! Right now. We have to alert the hands and fight the fire." God, she hoped the men were already on their way. She didn't like the strange light in Frank's gaze. Mustering her courage, she ignored his gun and strode toward the doorway. "Come on, Frank. We have to get—"

The butt of the shotgun struck her hard in the temple. The dull thud reverberated against her skull. Her first feeling was shock. Then pain rushed in with deadly force, and she collapsed like a puppet with all its strings cut. Lying in the straw on her side, stunned and unable to move, she tried to speak. All that came out was a weak moan.

Frank hunkered down beside her with the shotgun across his knees, but she couldn't even lift her eyes to look at his face.

"It didn't have to be this way, Claire. You could have been a respectable rancher's wife. But you've got a wild streak in you. And sometimes when an animal can't be broken, it has to be put down. The way I see it, this ranch and me, we're meant to be together. I figure your father's gonna give her to me, Claire, whether you're alive or not. In fact, now that I've been thinkin' it over, it might save me a whole lot of trouble, you bein' out of the way. I'll tell Mr. Parker I did everything I could to save his little girl. The fire just got out of hand." He sniffed. "You made your bed, Claire. Now you can lie—"

A rope seemed to drop out of the sky in that instant, encircling Frank. Claire blinked, unable to tell if what she saw was real or a figment of her rapidly fading brain. The last image she saw was the sole of Frank's boot as he was jerked backward through the thickening smoke.

Chase had decided that Yoema must be taking her time getting to the spirit world.

He'd finally been able to steal a breath of fresh air— sauntering along the darkened streets of Paradise, inhaling the crisp scent of pine, peering up at the star-salted sky— when his grandmother suddenly intruded upon his thoughts. Just when he'd almost convinced himself that Claire wouldn't want to see him, the bossy old woman barged into his brain, ordering him to go to the Parker Ranch at once.

He sighed, knowing he'd have to face Claire sooner or later and find out the truth, even if it broke his heart. He might as well get it over with. Besides, he got the feeling if he didn't do what Yoema told him, the old woman would pester him all night long.

So he headed toward the ranch, following the same path he'd taken just over a week ago when he'd first met Claire. Had it only been that long? It seemed like he'd known her all his life.

As he turned the bend, a man came running toward him. Chase stopped, and the man scrambled to a halt, squeaking in surprise. Chase saw that he was a preacher. He had a white collar, and he was clinging to a Bible.

"You all right?" Chase asked.

"Yes...mm-hmm...fine," the preacher said, clearly winded. By the way he was licking his lips and looking over his shoulder, Chase was pretty sure the preacher was breaking that commandment, Thou Shalt Not Lie.

But Chase let the man pass and hurried onward. A preacher fleeing in fear from the Parker Ranch couldn't be a good thing.

Sure enough, by the time he bolted through the ranch gates, he could see a *bad* thing—an orange glow coming from inside the barn.

There was only one thing that caused that kind of light.

Fire.

He started loping down the drive.

It must have just started. The ranch hands were only beginning to emerge from their quarters. It looked like the horses had at least gotten out. Chase wondered if the fleeing preacher had something to do with the blaze. He'd heard of fire-and-brimstone sermons, but...

He frowned. Where was Claire? And where was her father?

Maybe they were asleep in the house. He hoped so. They'd be safe there. The ranch house sat a good distance from the barn.

Chase grabbed a bucket and was about to add his muscle to the firefighting efforts when Yoema's spirit yelled sharply in his ear.

Help. She was calling for help.

Chase frowned. His gaze was drawn to the barn. Beyond the silhouettes of scurrying ranch hands and the horses milling in the drive, orange-tinted smoke puffed out through the barn doorway.

As if shoved forward by the hand of Yoema, Chase dropped the bucket and moved forward through the men and horses, toward the entrance of the barn.

Near the open door, a wave of heat blasted him, and he raised his hands in front of his face, blinking against the acrid smoke. Then, as he stood in the doorway, squinting through the haze, he could make out the figure of Frank. Frank was squatting with his shotgun across his lap, beside what appeared to be a body.

Chase thought Frank must be crazy. An inferno blazed around him, yet Frank sat there talking, as if he had all the time in the world.

Chase was about to shout at him to get out of the barn when he heard Frank say Claire's name.

Chase glanced at the body, at the fold of brown skirts, and he felt his blood turn to ice.

He didn't think.

He couldn't speak.

He seized the horse nearest him, grabbed a lasso off the barn door, and knotted it around the horse's neck. Then, with deadly aim, he dropped the looped end over Frank, yanked it tight, and gave the nervous horse's rump a slap.

Nature did the rest.

Chase entered the fiery barn, covering his mouth and nose with his shirt. His eyes watered as he hoarsely called her name. "Claire!"

She didn't answer.

"Claire!"

He dropped to the ground. She looked so white, so frail, so still. His heart clenched in despair as he crawled to her on his belly, praying to his god, his father's god, his mother's god, that she wasn't dead.

And then her fingers moved, just the smallest bit, so slightly that it might have been a trick of the heat.

But it was enough to give him hope and strength. Surging forward, he grabbed her forearm and dragged her toward him.

The flames were lapping at her skirts, and he beat them back, leaving only a charred edge. Then he took her limp body in his arms and carried her out of hell.

The sweet, cool night air riffled her hair as he laid her out gently on the ground, safely away from the barn. He could hear the ranch hands shouting orders. Someone went after the runaway horse. Someone else started pumping buckets of water. Two sobbing maids rushed over to Claire, wringing their hands.

Claire wasn't moving. Chase wasn't sure she was even breathing. His heart stabbed painfully between his ribs as he brushed her cinder-filled hair back from her brow and bent close to see if he could feel her breath on his cheek.

"Ride into town and get the doc!" he yelled to no one in particular.

Tears stung his eyes as he clasped her hand, willing her to live.

If it had been any other horse, Frank knew he'd be a dead

man. But Sadie was an old gray mare. So after dragging Frank half a mile down the road—scraping him along the rocky ground, bruising his bones, shredding his best suit and a good portion of his skin—she tuckered out and slowed to an amble.

He was lucky. He could have broken several bones or lost a limb. A mile would have killed him.

Still, he wasn't a pretty sight. He was sure of that. He was trembling in pain and shock. He could hardly put his battered lips together to whistle for Sadie to stop. Two of his fingers were bent at impossible angles. Blood dripped into his eyes, soaked his sleeves, and streamed down his bare legs. He felt like he'd gone nine rounds with a prizefighter, and he realized he wasn't even feeling the full extent of the damage yet.

With his thankfully numb fingers, he managed to loosen the lasso and free himself. Holding onto the end of the rope to keep Sadie close, he pushed himself up to a sitting position.

What the hell had happened? All he could remember was that he'd been talking to Claire one moment, and he was being dragged by a runaway horse the next.

No, he remembered something else. He'd seen a man's snarling face just as Sadie took off running.

The Injun had done this to him.

But where had he come from? How had he known Claire was in the barn?

A wave of nausea roiled inside him, and he spat out blood, along with a broken tooth, as an even worse thought crossed his mind.

What if Claire wasn't dead? What if the half-breed had saved her?

It would ruin Frank. He'd lose everything. Claire would tell her father what he'd done, and Frank's life would be over.

He couldn't let that happen. He couldn't take the fall for this. It wasn't fair.

His head started throbbing, and he let it hang between his knees while he considered his options.

Then he realized the answer had been right in front of him.

The Injun.

Wasn't it awfully convenient that the Injun had just happened to be at the ranch when the fire started? Maybe he'd come to take his revenge after all. At least Frank thought he could make her father believe that. Hell, the way Frank looked, he could even convince Mr. Parker that he'd grappled with the bastard, fighting for Claire's life.

He just had to get to the rancher before anyone else did. If Frank played his cards right, it wouldn't matter if Claire lived or died. He'd plant seeds of doubt in the rancher's mind, pin the blame on the Injun, and the rest would take care of itself. After all, who was Mr. Parker going to believe—the villain who'd kidnapped his daughter or the man who intended to marry her?

Despite the sharp pain in his ribs as he hauled himself up by the rope and leaned against Sadie's flank, his eyes were narrowed to gleeful slits. That Injun was about to discover he'd come to the wrong place at the wrong time.

Riding the horse bareback was a whole new kind of torture for Frank, even at a slow trot. He grimaced in agony, feeling his bones grind and rearrange themselves every time Sadie moved.

By the time he reached the ranch where Mr. Parker was staying, Frank was so worn out, he practically fell off the horse. Still he managed to hobble up the steps and banged hard on the door.

"Mr. Parker! Mr. Parker, you've got to come quick!"

The flames climbed higher on the roof of the barn, sending

smoke billowing into the night sky. The buckets of water were no match for the roaring beast that was feeding on the dry tinder. So the firefighting efforts were instead centered on preventing the fire from spreading to the other outbuildings.

Chase cradled Claire's wilting body in his arms. Her mouth was open, and he could see she was breathing now. But it seemed like every breath was a struggle as air rasped in and out of her damaged throat. With his thumb, he tenderly wiped away the ash that had settled on her face. He murmured words of comfort and prayers in his own tongue. But he wasn't sure she could even hear him.

He narrowed his eyes at the blazing barn as its charred skeleton wavered in the heat. How had all this come to pass? Had Frank truly meant to kill Claire? Why? And where was her father?

It didn't matter. None of it did. All he cared about was keeping Claire alive.

He asked one of the maids to fetch him a bucket of water. Then he tore his shirt into pieces, soaking them. He used the drenched cloth to dribble water between Claire's scorched lips and placed a wet rag against her reddened eyelids, hoping to take away some of the sting of the burns.

In the distance, he heard a horse approaching at a gallop. But he was too preoccupied to pay it much mind, until it slid to a halt in front of him, and Samuel Parker slipped from the saddle.

"Get away from her!" he bellowed, aiming his rifle at Chase. "Get your filthy hands off of her!"

The maids cowered in fright.

Chase knew better than to stand in the way of a father protecting his daughter. He raised his palms to show Parker he intended no harm, and then rose cautiously to his feet.

Parker stood not three feet away, frothing at the mouth,

ready to shoot Chase. But once he laid eyes on his daughter—wan and weak and barely breathing—his fury melted into despair.

"Claire," he said, his voice cracking as he lowered the rifle.

"The doc's on his way," Chase assured him.

Parker sent him a scathing glare. "So's the sheriff."

Chase wasn't sure what to make of that glare. Surely Parker didn't believe Chase had anything to do with hurting Claire.

He handed a dripping rag to the rancher. "I think the water does her good." Then he hunkered down a few paces away.

Parker snapped up the rag, then crouched beside his daughter and began dabbing at her forehead with the shirt. He was silent for a long while, though his mouth was working as he fought back his emotions. Finally he asked, "Why? What kind of an animal would want to hurt Claire?"

Chase was about to tell him.

But at that moment, skidding up on the back of a gasping, frothy horse was an apparition too bloody and beaten to recognize. As the horse wheezed in exhaustion, the man astride shouted with broken, breathless fury. "He said...if he couldn't have her...nobody could!"

Frank. That horrific mess was Frank. He was shaking a bloody finger at Chase.

"It was the Injun!" Frank said, garbling the words through missing teeth, "The Injun lured Claire into the barn...then set it on fire!"

Chase was too surprised to deny the charge. "What?"

Parker ground his teeth and glared at Chase. "Claire is all I have left," he bit out, his voice breaking. "If I lose her, Wolf, I swear I'll string you up myself."

Chase scowled in disbelief. He felt like the world had turned upside down. "You don't think I—"

Frank sneered, "He said he'd get revenge." Then he

lowered his head and sobbed, "It looks like he got it. She's dead."

"No, she's not!" Parker roared, as if the force of his words alone would keep Claire alive.

"But," Frank said, "she may be soon."

Was that hope in Frank's voice? Chase shook his head. He couldn't credit what he was hearing. He turned to Parker. "You don't think I... Hell, I wouldn't hurt a hair on Claire's head. I'm the one who pulled her *out* of the fire."

Just then, Claire coughed softly, garnering their attention.

"Claire?" Parker placed a trembling hand on her shoulder.

She coughed again and tried to open her eyes.

Chase's throat ached with emotion. "It's all right, Claire."

He had to resist the urge to weep in relief as he cradled her head.

She was alive.

Claire was alive.

"Keep your eyes closed," he told her. "It won't hurt so much." He'd learned that from spending time in the heavy smoke of the sweat lodge. "I'm here now. And your father's here. You're going to be all right."

Parker was staring at him with mistrust. Chase couldn't tell what he was thinking, but he didn't much care. He was more concerned about Claire. He took back the wet rag and placed it gently over her eyes.

"That should feel better."

She was trying to say something to him. Her lips were moving. But the effort was hard to watch.

Her father bent close. "What is it, Claire?"

She whispered in his ear, and he nodded.

"Frank," he confirmed. "She's asking for Frank."

She coughed again, and this time she clenched her fist in her father's sleeve.

Only Chase knew the truth. "She's not asking for Frank," he

murmured. "She's naming him. *He* did this." He whispered to Claire. "Didn't he?"

She nodded weakly.

Parker's jaw tensed. "You're sure, Claire?" he asked. "Frank hurt you?"

She nodded again.

Parker's knuckles turned white where he gripped the rifle, and his voice came out on a strangled whisper. "Frank?"

Parker looked ready to spring on Frank with every ounce of his rage. Chase knew, given half a chance, the rancher would shoot the murderous bastard on the spot.

But Chase also knew the upstanding Mr. Parker would never be able to live with himself if he shot Frank in cold blood, no matter how much the son of a bitch deserved it. So he placed a restraining hand on Parker's arm and said softly, "You said the sheriff's coming?"

Parker met his eyes. In that moment, a look of understanding passed between them. Justice would prevail. They would have their vengeance. Frank would pay for what he'd done. And it would be by honorable means. Parker nodded.

"Mr. Parker," Frank called out in feigned concern. "Is she gonna be all right?"

Chase, barely able to contain his own fury, bit out, "What's the matter, Frank? Are you afraid she might tell everyone the truth?"

Chase didn't think it possible, but beneath the bloody wreckage of his face, Frank blanched.

But Frank was spared having to reply when the barn suddenly creaked and squealed, wavering in the intense heat. Warning shouts went out among the firefighters. The flaming walls shifted as the roof gradually skewed sideways. Then, with an awful groan, like an injured beast succumbing to its wounds, the barn collapsed and crashed to the ground. Sparks shot out, lighting up the field like stars.

Claire flinched and gave a little cry, and Chase was beside her in an instant, clasping her hand. "I'm here, Claire. I'll protect you."

Parker grabbed Chase's arm, and for a moment Chase thought he was going to pull him away. But when he looked up, Parker gave him a stiff-lipped nod of thanks.

In the midst of the chaos of ranch hands calming the horses, workers stomping out sparks, and maids pumping pails of water to dump over the smoking coals, two more riders came galloping up the drive.

Within moments, Parker had spoken to the sheriff, who wasted no time in wresting Frank off the horse and putting him in handcuffs, while someone led the poor old nag to a watering trough.

"Claire," Chase breathed, rubbing his thumb gently over the back of her hand, "it's all right now. You're going to be all right. The doctor is here." Then he bent closer, adding, "So is Yoema."

CHAPTER 25

Claire squirmed as Catalina pinned a violet spray of lupins across the top of the long white veil covering her short hair. She hadn't been fussed over so much since the occasion of her twelfth birthday, when Yoema had spent hours weaving her hair into impossible braids.

"Be still," Catalina scolded, arranging the sheer folds of the veil so that it draped gracefully down Claire's back.

If it were up to Claire, of course, she would have simply moved into her new husband's household without ceremony, as was the tradition of the local natives.

But she was already bucking convention by marrying a half-breed. She figured the least she could do was to have a decent traditional wedding, the kind that would allow her father to maintain his respectability in town.

Of course, there were some town folk who refused to come to the ceremony, claiming it was a disgrace to marry a savage and a travesty to be wed in a barn. But it was her father who finally admitted that it was a fool who would try to please everyone. Besides, he said he could think of no better way to christen the pristine new barn his neighbors had helped him build than to have a wedding in it.

"Ah, better." Catalina cocked her head, examining her handiwork, looking stunning in her own pale peach gown with ivory trim. "The pins, they are not biting you?"

Claire smiled. Catalina's English was improving, but it wasn't perfect. "No, they're not biting me."

Over the last several weeks, Claire had grown quite close to Catalina, who had insisted they have a double wedding. Catalina claimed it was because she wanted a public occasion to prove her skills as a dressmaker. Consequently, she had designed and sewn lavish gowns for Claire, herself, and a half dozen of the most fashionable ladies in Paradise. But Claire suspected her insistence on the double wedding had more to do with sewing up her relationship with Drew before he had a chance to change his mind.

"So. Do you like?" Catalina asked, turning her around to face the beveled mirror.

Claire was pleasantly surprised by her appearance. Claire was accustomed to wearing drab, conservative hues—black, brown, blue. Catalina had originally wanted to make the gowns in the white that Queen Victoria had made popular, but Claire had argued that white was highly impractical in a town full of red dirt. So they had settled on pastels. The pale lavender of Claire's gown brought out the light in her eyes. A narrow, cream-colored ruffle trimmed the edges of the flounces, the bottoms of the sleeves, and the high-buttoned neckline.

"It's perfect," she breathed.

Catalina grinned and touched up the crown of bright orange poppies that anchored the veil covering her own thick, dark hair. "I think we will be beautiful flowers today."

Claire agreed, thinking it was clever how Catalina had chosen fabric that matched the color of the local wildflowers.

Then she turned sideways in the mirror and couldn't help but giggle. "Are you *sure* this looks right?"

"Oh, *si, si.* It is the latest fashion."

Claire had seen bustles before, but this one seemed enormous, with yards of draped fabric that made her backside feel like a big waterfall.

While she was wondering how Chase would find his way under all the petticoats and ruffles, Catalina went to the window.

"Come, come, quickly." She beckoned Claire with a wave. "Come see our beautiful men."

Claire didn't need to be asked twice. She joined Catalina and peered down at the drive, where guests were already arriving. Chase and Drew were walking together, and Claire had never seen a more handsome pair. Catalina had chosen matching suits for them in two different colors—one the color of the evening sky and one the color of coffee—and their appearance was causing quite a stir among the ladies, who had begun whispering behind their gloves.

Claire couldn't blame them. One handsome half-breed was enough to take a woman's breath away. But two...

The twins were devilishly good-looking. But they were so much more than that. They had their grandmother's strong heart, her good will, her sweet spirit.

Claire's eyes filled with moisture as she recalled how Chase had risked his life to pull her from the fire. In the days afterward, he'd watched over her while she was recovering. He'd broken the news to her that Frank had been tried fairly and hanged. Then he'd told her that he would never love anyone the way he loved her, and he'd promised to protect her for the rest of her days.

Chase Wolf, she decided, was a better hero than Buckskin Bill, Dashing Dick, and Kit Carson combined.

She dabbed at her eyes and sniffed back her silly tears. It was her wedding day, after all. She didn't want to walk down the aisle with bleary, red eyes.

Catalina leaned close and confided, "I think the ladies cannot decide which man is the most beautiful."

Claire managed a smile. "Well, we both know it's..." She looked closer at the brothers, furrowing her brow. "Wait. Didn't you say Drew was going to wear blue and Chase would be in brown?"

"Yes." Then Catalina frowned down at them and then began clucking her tongue. "Those tricksters."

Claire's eyes widened in amazement. "They did not."

"They did."

"And they didn't think we'd notice?"

They stopped to watch as Claire's father walked up the drive to meet the brothers and shook their hands.

Claire wondered, "Do you think my father can tell?"

Catalina shook her head.

Claire arched a brow.

Catalina arched a brow.

The Two-Sons were going to be very sorry they'd tried to fool their brides.

The whole switching suits idea had been Drew's, of course. Chase hadn't wanted to take the risk that he might somehow accidentally wind up marrying Drew's bride-to-be. He liked Catalina well enough, now that he knew her better. But Chase adored Claire, and the possibility that Claire might mistake Drew for him gnawed at his insides.

Drew, however, was a gambler by nature. And last night in the saloon, when the jailer they'd fooled with the two-spirit game had insisted their brides couldn't tell them apart either, Drew had told him to put his money where his mouth was. A wager had been made, and somehow, Drew had charmed Chase into going along with the crazy scheme.

It honestly amazed Chase that the two brothers could fool anyone. To his mind, they were as different as night and day. So when, after they'd switched clothes, Samuel Parker came up and clapped Drew on the back, calling him son, Chase was taken aback and a bit annoyed.

"Before the wedding, I have something I'd like to show you boys," Parker said.

They followed him behind the ranch house, across a field of grass and wildflowers, and over a small rolling knoll. On the far side was a solitary oak with sprawling branches, and at the base of the tree, a small chunk of irregular granite was sunk into the earth. It bore the inscription:

HERE RESTS BELOVED YOEMA
GRANDMOTHER OF CHASE WOLF AND DREW HAWK
SPIRIT MOTHER OF CLAIRE PARKER

The headstone was perfect. The brothers thanked him and agreed their grandmother would have been pleased.

But for Chase, it meant even more. The circle that had been broken when his people were exiled from this place was now fixed, as if it had been melted down and re-forged into a new, stronger metal. After today, after he and Claire shared the vows of marriage, that bond would become unbreakable. And since he'd made peace with his enemies and repaired the ugly past, now his grandmother would find her way home along the spirit path.

If Claire's father felt uneasy walking up the aisle beside Catalina, he was polite enough not to let on. Catalina had had no one to give her away, and though Claire knew her father still secretly suspected the Italian lady was a soiled dove, he did the gentlemanly thing and offered to do the honors.

Nonetheless, Claire was glad he didn't know that several of Catalina's wedding guests were indeed ladies of the evening, well disguised by the modest and well-tailored gowns Catalina had made for them for this special occasion.

At a nod from her father, the fiddler began playing the wedding march, and the three of them glided arm-in-arm between the makeshift pews full of guests.

The sweet fragrance of fresh-cut lumber from the mill filled the barn. The new design featured six shuttered windows that were currently thrown open, allowing the morning sunshine to light up and warm the interior.

As they proceeded up the aisle, envious sighs and gasps of awe sounded from all around them. Claire knew it was all for Catalina's lovely dress designs. Catalina smiled and gave Claire a wink, probably imagining the flood of dress orders that would come in over the next few weeks.

At the end of the barn stood the preacher and the two brothers, whose positions were reversed from what they should be. Drew stood waiting for Claire. Chase waited for Catalina. Claire wasn't sure what game the brothers were playing, but she gave Catalina a smile and a subtle lift of her brow. They'd decided to proceed as if nothing were wrong.

Claire nearly laughed aloud at the disgruntled expressions on the men's faces as Catalina reached for Chase's hand and Claire tucked her hand into Drew's elbow. Of course, the preacher, her father, and none of the guests knew what was going on, so nothing seemed amiss to them.

"Dearly beloved, we are gathered together here..." the preacher began.

Chase cleared his throat.

Claire bit back a smile.

"...in the sight of God..."

Drew coughed.

Catalina slid her sly gaze over to Claire, whose lips were clamped together.

"...and in the face of this congregation..."

Drew started fidgeting.

Chase's smoldering gaze could have burned a hole in the preacher's Bible.

Catalina looked highly amused.

Claire fought back a giggle.

"...to join together this man and this woman..." The preacher paused, unsure of the protocol, and then nodded toward Catalina. "And *this* man and this woman..."

Drew clenched and unclenched his fists.

Chase looked ready to kill something.

Finally, Claire could hold back no more. She burst out laughing, which startled the preacher, as well as the congregation.

"A moment, please," Catalina said to the preacher.

Then, to the relief of their prospective grooms and the surprise of the congregation, Catalina and Claire traded partners.

The preacher found his place in the matrimonial speech, and the grooms straightened with smug pride. Claire and Catalina exchanged one last wicked conspiratorial grin before they happily took the arms of their intended husbands and spoke the vows that would bind them together as long as they both should live.

At the reception afterward, of course, there was much made of the deception. All the womenfolk wanted to know how they could tell the difference between their husbands. The men were less vocal, probably wondering how they would use such a thing to their advantage. And the jailer seemed particularly unhappy, especially when he was obliged to pay some sort of debt to Drew over the matter.

Her father was troubled by the fact he hadn't been able to

tell them apart. "It seems I've been a poor judge of character all around lately," he said as he poured a dipperful of lemonade into Claire's glass.

She knew he was talking about Frank. "It wasn't your fault, Father. Frank had me fooled, too."

He shook his head and said softly, "If I'd lost you..."

"I know."

He poured his own lemonade and then just stared down at it. She could see him holding back tears. "I wish your mother were here to see you. She'd be proud of you, Claire."

Claire nodded. It wasn't easy for her father to say such a thing, and it meant a lot to her.

He added, "And I wish...I wish Yoema were here to see you."

Claire's throat closed. Her father might not have publicly condoned her relationship with the native woman, but at least he was recognizing it. "Me, too."

Reining in his tears with a hard sniff, he took a thoughtful sip of lemonade and looked out over the milling guests until he found Chase. "He's a good man."

She followed his gaze. "He is."

"I knew it when we were tracking him—by how he was treating Thunder, the way he saw to your comfort, made sure you had food and water. A man like that will be a good provider. In fact," he said, taking another sip, "I've been thinking it over. It seems like he might be a good man to handle the ranch."

"The ranch?"

"Of course, he'd need months of training. You can't learn cattle overnight. There are a lot of responsibilities that go with—"

With a grateful cry, Claire wrapped her arms around him, ignoring the fact that hugging in public wasn't at all proper.

He didn't seem to mind too much. He sputtered a bit, and

then she heard him chuckling. "I guess I won't have to teach him how to rope a bride."

She let him go and gave him a respectful peck on the cheek. Then she went to seek out her expert bride-roper. She wouldn't tell Chase the good news just yet. She wasn't sure how he'd feel about becoming a rancher. He seemed awfully happy with his blacksmith's shop. Besides, before they made any kind of decision about the future, she wanted to meet his family in Hupa.

She found Chase at the far side of the barn, surrounded by a bevy of adoring ladies. For a moment, Claire just stood back and stared at him, and her eyes grew soft with affection.

Yoema's grandson, Chase Wolf—as handsome as Monowano, as brave as Davy Crockett, as clever as Kit Carson, as decent as Daniel Boone—was her hero. Just as soon as she could pry him away from his cooing admirers, it appeared the two of them would be riding into the sunset and living happily ever after.

Epilog

From across the desk, Samuel Parker studied his new ranch boss, taking the measure of the man with a narrowed gaze. Two days had passed since the big wedding, and Samuel was eager to start using the barn for its intended purpose. He might as well start training Frank's replacement to find out if he had the mettle for the job.

"It's going to be hard work and long hours," Samuel warned him.

"I know."

"You've worked with horses before?"

"A bit."

Samuel stroked his mustache. "It's not a job where you can just waltz in and start barking out orders. You've got to start at the bottom, get in the muck, earn the respect of the ranch hands."

"Understood."

"And you have to get to know the other ranchers in the county. They can be your best friends or your worst enemies."

"Yes, sir."

Samuel sat back in his chair with his arms crossed, considering the enterprising young half-breed. Had he chosen the right man for the job?

"You a drinking man?" he asked.

"No, sir, not on the job."

"That's good. And you can read and write?"

"Yes."

"What about accounts? You any good with numbers?"

Samuel thought he saw the ghost of a smile cross the man's face. "I'm very good with numbers."

Samuel nodded. Then he leaned forward and gave him a stern scowl. "I won't lie to you. It's a lot of responsibility."

"I can handle it."

Samuel wondered. He wondered what else he should ask. "Can you handle a gun?"

He shrugged. "Sure."

"Not saying you'll need to," he explained, "but sometimes varmints get after the calves. You think you can handle that?"

"Varmints?"

"Coyotes, mountain lions, snakes...thieves." Samuel saw the frown that crossed the man's brow. "You ever shot a man?"

"Never needed to."

Samuel liked that answer, and he honestly couldn't think of anything else to ask. He pushed up from the desk. "Well, then, let's go for a ride. I'll show you the lay of the land."

He had a good feeling about the half-breed, even if things hadn't worked out quite as Samuel had planned. He'd just have to see if the young man had any aptitude with cattle.

On the other hand, Samuel thought, maybe he should have hired the man's *wife* instead. That wild Italian woman already seemed to know how to lead things around by the nose.

Chase huddled beside Claire next to the campfire. Every now and then, a spark would pop out of the fire and float up, as if trying to join the bright stars in the sky.

Claire had refused to stay in a hotel, even though there were plenty of decent places on the road between Paradise and Hupa. She'd claimed that since it was her honeymoon, she should choose her lodgings, and he should concede to her wishes.

He was only too happy to oblige. After all, sleeping under the stars was what they'd done since he met her.

But he'd drawn the line at eating roots and mushrooms. He took his knife and poked at the thick Parker Ranch steak that was roasting over the glowing coals.

Claire licked her lips.

"It's going to be a while," he warned.

With a stick, Claire lifted the lid of the Dutch oven, peeking at the simmering stew of potatoes, onions, and carrots.

"So what do you eat in Hupa?" she asked.

He prodded the coals with a branch and said grimly, "Pine needle soup and boiled slugs."

She laughed and punched his shoulder. "I don't think your mother eats boiled slugs."

"They're her favorite."

She laughed again, then grimaced. "If she truly eats boiled slugs, I'll give them a try."

He laughed at her pained expression, and then, taking pity on her, told her the truth. "We eat a lot of roasted salmon. Deer meat stew, blackberries, acorn bread."

She smiled on a sigh and wrapped her arms around her knees. "I hope your parents like me."

"They will love you, *whililyo.*"

"What about your sisters?"

He furrowed his brow. "My sisters may be a problem."

"Why?"

"I'll instruct them not to annoy you. But they can be troublesome. They'll probably make a nuisance of themselves—following you everywhere, chattering constantly, pestering you to tell them about your ranch house."

"Sisters," Claire said dreamily.

She actually seemed to *like* the idea that his sisters might look up to her.

Chase was beginning to think she was going to enjoy Hupa after all. He was glad. He'd been worried she would look down on his humble village, his cedar plank house, his modest blacksmith shop, that she would take one look at his large, noisy, overbearing family and flee back to civilized Paradise.

He would have to return with her if she did. He didn't think he could live without Claire. But it would be so difficult to leave his home, his family, his shop, the only world he'd ever known.

Still, that was what he was asking Claire to do.

He stared into the fire. "Do you think I should have taken your father's offer?"

"To run the ranch? No."

"No?"

"Sitting behind a desk, settling accounts, buying and selling cattle, managing ranch hands...it would break your spirit."

He shrugged. "It would give you a good life."

She leaned against his shoulder. "I *have* a good life, just because you're in it."

He kissed the top of her head. Claire always knew the right thing to say.

"Besides," she added, "it's exactly what your brother needs to make him grow up and settle down."

Chase chuckled. "What do you think Catalina said to make him decide to take the job?"

"Oh, I *know* what she said."

"You do? What?"

"I'm going to have your baby."

Chase's head popped up. "What?"

"Catalina's expecting," Claire cooed, grinning with glee. "Isn't it wonderful? You're going to be an uncle."

For a moment, Chase could only stare at her in amazement. His brother—a father? It was hard to imagine. What would Drew teach the child first—gambling or gunslinging? Still, Chase had to admit that his new title had a good sound to it. "Uncle Chase."

Claire bit her lip. She was dying to tell Chase her own good news—that in about seven months he was going to be more than just an uncle.

Then she reconsidered. Tomorrow they'd arrive in Hupa. She would see his village. She would meet his family. They'd probably sleep in one of the plank houses he'd told her about...sharing the quarters with members of his tribe and maybe even a few dogs. She might not be alone with Chase for days.

So while the stew gently simmered and the steak slowly roasted over the fire, she ran a fingertip over his luscious, massive shoulder and arched a speculative brow. "You know, Chase, this is our last night alone for a long time."

He may not have moved a muscle, but she saw the gleam enter his eyes.

She let her fingers climb across his collar bone and up the side of his neck. "And supper won't be ready for a while."

The corner of his lip curved up.

She delved her fingers into his thick mane of silky black hair. "Maybe we should be thinking about starting a family of our own."

"You think so?"

She could tell by his smoky gaze that he wholeheartedly

agreed. She let her fingers drift over to his chin and brought his face close to hers. "Mm-hmm."

Then she closed her eyes and kissed him. His mouth was warm and welcoming, and when he clasped the back of her head to deepen the kiss, she let out a blissful sigh.

She opened her mouth, enjoying the way their tongues danced together. Her hands explored him, weaving through his hair, caressing his ears, grazing his jaw.

And then he settled his hands around her waist and lifted her onto his lap, facing him.

She gasped inside his mouth as she felt the hard evidence of his lust beneath her. He made a soft groan of pleasure as he clasped her hips and moved up against her. Her cheeks flushed, and her heart beat faster as heat flooded between her thighs.

Still kissing him, she unfastened his shirt, button by button. And then her fingers encountered paper. She broke from the kiss and peered inside his shirt. "What..."

He smiled sheepishly. "That was supposed to be a wedding gift."

Her eyes widened as she pulled out her battered, smoky, waterlogged copy of *THE TRAIL HUNTERS OR MONOWANO THE SHAWNEE SPY*. Where had he found it? She'd lost it in the fire and thought she'd never see it again. "How did you..."

"I found it outside the barn the night of the fire. I was going to give it to you when we got to Hupa."

"You were?" She hugged the beloved book to her breast.

He clucked his tongue. "It was supposed to be a surprise. And if you hadn't been in such a hurry to take off my clothes—"

She gasped. "Really? Well, I wouldn't have been in such a hurry if you hadn't started poking me with your...your big...what's-it..."

He grinned. *"Whedze."*

"Whedze."

"And my big *whedze* would not be poking you right now if you hadn't kissed me like that."

"Like what?" she teased, tossing aside the dime novel, which would never be as exciting as her adventures with Chase Wolf.

He grinned like his spirit animal. "Like this."

THE END

THANK YOU FOR
READING MY BOOK!

Did you enjoy it? If so, I hope you'll post a review to let others know! There's no greater gift you can give an author than spreading your love of her books.

It's truly a pleasure and a privilege to be able to share my stories with you. Knowing that my words have made you laugh, sigh, or touched a secret place in your heart is what keeps the wind beneath my wings. I hope you enjoyed our brief journey together, and may ALL of your adventures have happy endings!

If you'd like to keep in touch, feel free to sign up for my monthly e-newsletter at www.glynnis.net, and you'll be the first to find out about my new releases, special discounts, prizes, promotions, and more!

If you want to keep up with my daily escapades:
Friend me at facebook.com/GlynnisCampbell
Like my Page at bit.ly/GlynnisCampbellFBPage
Follow me at twitter.com/GlynnisCampbell
And if you're a super fan, join facebook.com/GCReadersClan

Excerpt from

NATIVE HAWK

CALIFORNIA LEGENDS BOOK 3

D rew Hawk knew he wasn't playing with a full deck when he agreed to that offer. Nobody north of San Francisco paid a whore twenty dollars. And nobody but a shriveled old man paid a whore just to look at her.

Hell, he couldn't even believe he was frequenting a brothel when all he really needed was a place to stay for the night. But what had made him raise the stakes so high? He was behaving like a greenhorn gambler, wagering big money on a blind hand.

No, not quite blind. Even the quick glimpse he'd caught of the lady from downstairs told him she was something special. Her black hair shone like satin. Her close-fitting dress revealed sleek curves that would fit as perfectly in his hand as those of his Colt forty-five. And her bare feet were more seductive than the collective cleavage of all the saloon girls at the Winsome Saloon.

Once he heard the exotic sound of her voice from behind the door—deliciously throaty and foreign—he was sold.

Besides, he knew women. She was toying with him. He'd agreed to her terms—no "making the sex," no removing all her "clothings." But he was sure that was all part of some cat-and-mouse game of seduction. Everyone knew a man wanted most what he couldn't have. Playing hard to get was a surefire way to goose up the price. Hell, the madam was probably in on it.

Besides, it was a safe bet that Drew Hawk could get any woman out of her knickers with a single come-hither look. One provocative whisper, and he'd have her eating out of the palm of his hand.

"It's all settled then," the madam agreed. She turned to him with a pretty convincing poker face, considering he'd just offered her ten times the going rate for a shady lady in Paradise. "Give me the twenty dollars, and she's all yours till mornin'. I'll throw in the whiskey for free."

"Much obliged." He had a stash of money in his knapsack, so he rummaged in it and dug out the right silver. For a split-second, he wondered if he'd been too hasty. After all, he'd only caught a fleeting glimpse of the shady lady. What if she had the face of a mule?

But then he supposed he was a gambling man. He dropped the coins into the madam's palm.

The instant the madam opened the door wide, he felt like he'd been dealt a royal flush. The breath deserted his lungs. All he could do was gape. The lady could have demanded *fifty* dollars. It would still be a bargain.

She was as pretty as a bisque doll. Enticing ebony ringlets caressed her cheeks and cascaded over her shoulders. Her skin had a lovely glow, warm and vibrant. Her lips were rosy, her chin had an adorable cleft, and a tiny, kissable mole resided beside her mouth. Her eyes were wide and wild, like dark honey.

She gave a tiny gasp. She was fully clad in her underclothes. But she still clutched one defensive arm across her bosom and splayed her other hand in front of her nether parts as if shielding them from his view. For a sporting lady, she was pretty good at playing innocent.

When he finally found his voice, he gave her a slight nod. "Howdy, ma'am."

She gulped in response.

"May I come in?" he asked.

Why he was being so hesitant, he didn't know. Maybe he was just dumbstruck by her beauty. But he'd paid his twenty dollars. The room and the lady in it were his for the night.

"Catalina!" the madam scolded. "Let the gentleman in."

She blinked, as if suddenly waking up, and backed away from the door. She fidgeted with her garments as he entered the room. He dropped his knapsack against the wall.

"I'll be right back with the whiskey," the madam said.

Then there was a drawn-out, awkward silence while they waited for the madam to return.

After a moment, the lady attempted to strike a casual pose, resting one hip against the dresser. But she knocked over a few small bottles on the marble top. She turned away to right them, glancing up at him in the mirror.

It wasn't his fault that his gaze dropped to her lovely backside. But in her reflection, her brows drew together in disapproval.

He looked away with a sniff, whacking his hat against his thigh a few times. Then he tossed it toward the coat rack beside the door...and missed.

Shit. He never missed. What was wrong with him? He retrieved his hat and hung it on the peg.

Finally, he broke the silence. "My name is Drew, Drew Hawk."

"Mr. Hawk." She gave her head a quick nod.

A smile tugged at his mouth. Mr. Hawk? That was awfully formal for someone who planned to share a bed with him. "Call me Drew."

"Drew."

He liked the way she said it, with a little flick of her tongue over the "r."

She turned to face him then, but another long quiet ensued. Her eyes flitted over the furniture in the room, anywhere but on him.

Damn, she was beautiful. She had a figure like an hourglass, curved in all the right places. It made his loins ache just to look at her.

He cleared his throat. "Your name is...Catalina?"

She nodded, then volunteered, "Catalina Alfredo Romanesca di Lasso Ferragamo—"

The madam swept in with a bottle of whiskey and two glasses, interrupting her mid-name. "Here you go."

To his surprise, Catalina...Etcetera...rushed forward to seize the whiskey. Apparently, she was eager to start her night of drunken revelry...minus the revelry.

She poured herself a finger of whiskey and slugged back half of it at once. Then she gasped and began coughing.

"Whoa, little lady," he said.

The madam slipped out then, closing the door behind her, probably so the coughing wouldn't wake up the whole place.

He wasn't sure if Catalina's wheezing gasp that followed was from the burn of the whiskey or the fact that there was now a closed door between her and the madam. But she looked genuinely worried.

He started toward her, intending to clap her on the back a few times to make sure she wasn't choking. Her eyes wide, she backed up against the dresser.

He furrowed his brow. He'd thought the woman was playing coy. But now he wasn't so sure. Was she actually scared of him?

He'd seen his brother Chase get this reaction out of women before. His growling bear of a twin could frighten women just by walking into the room.

But Drew was nothing like Chase. Drew was a friendly

fellow. With a wink and a smile, he could charm the stockings off a schoolmarm.

Of course, he wasn't exactly smiling at the moment. And she wasn't exactly a schoolmarm. Maybe he wasn't smiling because he was still in shock that he'd paid twenty dollars to spend the night with a lady who said she didn't want to have relations with him, even more shocked that he still felt like he'd gotten a pretty good deal.

But he'd paid for a body to warm his bed. He couldn't get a good night's rest while the woman lying next to him was shivering with fear...or choking on whiskey. He'd have to convince her he didn't mean her any harm. He might be ruthless when it came to gambling, but when it came to matters of the heart, he was as gentle as a kitten.

"There's no cause to be scared o' me."

"Scared?" She straightened. "I am not scared." Then she angled her head to look at him uncertainly, arching a fine brow. "Should I be?"

Drew could think of several reasons a woman should be afraid to be in a room alone with a stranger. But he didn't need to tell her the risks of her own profession.

"Not o' me," he told her. "I've never raised a hand to a woman in my life." Then an ugly thought crossed his mind. "You ain't nervous 'cause I'm a half-breed, are you?"

"A what?"

"A half-breed."

"What is this—half-breed?"

If she didn't already know, he wasn't much inclined to tell her. But something about that tiny furrow between her brows told him he should tell her the truth.

"I'm half white and half Indian," he admitted. "My father's a Konkow."

"Konkow," she echoed.

He liked the way she said it. He liked the way she said

333

everything, even "half-breed." Her voice had an intoxicating rough edge to it, as well as a fascinating accent.

"You don't mind, do you?" he asked.

She shrugged, puzzled. "You did not decide how you were born."

"Right." He liked that answer. "So where are you from, Miss Catalina?"

"*Italia.* Italy."

He reached behind her for the whiskey and his glass, and she stiffened. He decided she was the most skittish hooker he'd ever seen.

The soiled doves he'd met were experts at seduction and usually in a hurry to ply their wares. In fact, he suspected most times they didn't get as much pleasure out of it as the men did and just wanted to get it over with.

But this one didn't seem in a hurry to do anything.

Not that he'd let that put him off. It just made seducing her more of a challenge.

He poured himself a shot, swirled it around the glass, and then tossed it back.

She followed suit, but wound up gasping and choking again.

"You all right, ma'am?"

She nodded, but her face was red and her eyes were watering.

"You ever drink whiskey before?"

She closed her eyes and shook her head.

He grinned. What on earth had made her order a whole bottle, he didn't know...unless...

His grin faded. "Wait a minute. You ever done...*this* before?"

"This?"

"Slept with a man?"

"Of course," she choked out, almost too insistently. "Yes,

yes. Many times. Many, many times."

The lady couldn't bluff worth a damn.

It was obvious now she wasn't playing an innocent. She *was* an innocent. In fact, if he had to bet, judging by how jumpy she was, he'd say she had no experience whatsoever.

"Many, *many* times?" He narrowed one eye at her. "So you know what to expect?"

"What to expect?" She poured herself another shot of whiskey. Her hands were shaky, but she managed a smile. "Not too much—what you call it—snoring, I hope."

"Snorin'?"

"Back home, my brothers snored," she said with forced humor, holding the whiskey glass in both hands and staring down into the golden liquid. "Sometimes they kept me awake all night."

Drew frowned. Her brothers? He reached out to take the glass from her. "Have you ever slept with a man *here*, in The Parlor?"

She bit her lip and looked up at him with soulful brown eyes. "To be honest, Mr. Hawk, you are my first."

Damn. He was afraid of that.

"Before now, I am the housekeeper," she told him, pouring whiskey into the second glass. Then she raised it in a toast. "But do not worry. Tonight, I am The Lady of the Evening."

She said it as if it were a noble title.

He gave her a rueful smile. Something had definitely gotten lost in translation. Clinking his glass to hers, he shook his head and tossed back the whiskey.

She contemplated her glass, considering whether she should try another gulp.

If the lady weren't so adorable and it weren't so late, Drew would have marched straight down to the madam, given her a sound scolding for trying to pass off a virgin as a whore, and gotten his money back.

Catalina was obviously new to this country. He wondered if she even knew she was working in a house of ill repute.

She was lucky it was Drew and not some two-bit drunk who'd paid for her tonight. At least Drew had some respect. Though the raging bear in his trousers would be very disappointed, he'd do the gallant thing and leave her alone.

But it was late. He didn't have anywhere else to stay. His brother was off on some wild goose chase, and god only knew where he intended to sleep. Drew had already paid handsomely for the room. It would have been a waste of a good feather bed if he left now.

Maybe if he drank half the bottle of whiskey, he could forget about the pretty little untouchable lady who'd be sharing that feather bed with him tonight.

ABOUT THE AUTHOR

I'm a *USA Today* bestselling author of swashbuckling action-adventure historical romances, mostly set in Scotland, with over a dozen award-winning books published in six languages.

But before my role as a medieval matchmaker, I sang in *The Pinups,* an all-girl band on CBS Records, and provided voices for the MTV animated series *The Maxx,* Blizzard's *Diablo* and *Starcraft* video games, and *Star Wars* audiobooks.

I'm the wife of a rock star (if you want to know which one, contact me) and the mother of two young adults. I do my best writing on cruise ships, in Scottish castles, on my husband's tour bus, and at home in my sunny southern California garden.

I love transporting readers to a place where the bold heroes have endearing flaws, the women are stronger than they look, the land is lush and untamed, and chivalry is alive and well!

I'm always delighted to hear from my readers, so please feel free to email me at glynnis@glynnis.net. And if you're a super-fan who would like to join my inner circle, sign up at http://www.facebook.com/GCReadersClan, where you'll get glimpses behind the scenes, sneak peeks of works-in-progress, and extra special surprises.

9 781634 800891